THE FINAL FRONTIER

"The new diaspora," Khukov said. "That is the Dream."

"The colonization of the galaxy," I repeated, feeling Khukov's Dream take hold. "You really believe the challenges can be met?"

"I am prepared to supervise the scientific challenge," he said. *"If* we can only unify the planets—"

"Who could do that?" I asked, realizing his thrust.

"Who indeed—but the Tyrant of Space?"

BIO OF A SPACE TYRANT

VOL. 1: REFUGEE

VOL. 2: MERCENARY

VOL. 3: POLITICIAN

VOL. 4: EXECUTIVE

. . . AND NOW, THE COLOSSAL SAGA CONTINUES!

VOL. 5: STATESMAN

"The fertile imagination of Mr. Anthony seems to know no bounds."

Science Fiction Review

BIO OF A SPACE TYRANT
VOLUME 5: STATESMAN

PIERS ANTHONY

AVON
PUBLISHERS OF BARD, CAMELOT, DISCUS AND FLARE BOOKS

BIO OF A SPACE TYRANT VOLUME 5: STATESMAN is an original publication of Avon Books. This work has never before appeared in book form. This work is a novel. Any similarity to actual persons or events is purely coincidental.

AVON BOOKS
A division of
The Hearst Corporation
1790 Broadway
New York, New York 10019

First Avon Printing: December 1986

AVON TRADEMARK REG. U.S. PAT. OFF. AND IN OTHER COUNTRIES, MARCA REGISTRADA, HECHO EN U.S.A.

Printed in the U.S.A.

K-R 10 9 8 7 6 5 4 3 2 1

CONTENTS

STATESMAN

EDITORIAL PROLOG

The Space Tyrant, as he came to be known, had risen from the status of a helpless Hispanic refugee to dominance of the planet Jupiter. One might have supposed that his career would have ended when he was deposed by his wife and exiled, but that was not the case. Hope Hubris referred to himself as a statesman: one who had lost power. But in truth his power abated only temporarily, and eventually became greater than ever before.

As usual, his narrative of events and feelings understates the solid political and economic groundwork he did, and perhaps dwells too much on his emotional life. He was a far more competent and hard-nosed executive than he pretends, and chance did not affect him as much as he allows it to seem. Not only did he fashion the program that was to put mankind into the galaxy—what he terms the Dream—he fostered the substantial bettering of the human condition throughout the Solar System, benefiting the downtrodden and abused folk as much as the leaders. I believe it is fair to say that at the end the Tyrant was almost universally respected and loved, and every day the monument to him erected in the Province of Laya, Saturn, is visited by throngs of people from all over the System. That monument is impressive, consisting of a statue of a giant man whose right hand rests upon a model of the Solar System and whose left strokes a saber-tooth tiger, his gaze outward toward the galaxy, while a woman who resembles him watches from behind. That says it all.

But in the end nothing could avail against the terminal physical malady that Hope Hubris had, though for years its nature was concealed from the public. Perhaps his knowledge of that malady contributed to the abrupt and some say insane manner of his death.

Herewith, the final volume of the biopsy of the Space Tyrant, my father.

HMH

Chapter 1

PIRATE

We might as well have been children again, though I was sixty and my sister Spirit was fifty-seven. We faced the presentation screen and gawked at the magnificence of Planet Saturn. The rings were spectacular. Of course the image was enhanced by false-color, making it more dramatic, but still it was a wonder. All the colors of the spectrum seemed to be there in the great splay of the rings, and in the roughly spherical body of the planet itself. "Beautiful!" I breathed. "Jupiter's rings hardly compare!"

Spirit murmured agreement. "But nevertheless a sterner environment than we knew on Jupiter," she reminded me. "Their residential band has about eight and a half bars pressure, and their winds are up to quadruple Jupiter's—almost five hundred meters a second."

"A thousand miles an hour," I agreed, making a rough translation in my head. In my time on Jupiter I had become accustomed to the archaic Saxon measurements, inefficient as they were. Of course such velocities were not directly experienced, because the city-bubbles floated in the wind currents. Survival would be impossible if relative wind velocity of that strength were felt; storms whose winds were only a tenth as strong had been called hurricanes back on ancient Earth, and had wreaked enormous damage. The pressure bothered me more; as a former native of space, I tended to feel claustrophobic in pressure higher than one bar, the normal atmospheric level we lived in. It had been six bars on Jupiter, and would be higher on Saturn even though the planet was smaller, because the residential band was deeper in the atmosphere.

We were on our way to Saturn because we had been exiled from Jupiter, and the ringed planet seemed to be the best prospect of those that had expressed interest in taking us. I had just one personal acquaintance at Saturn—but that one was Chairman Khukov, the highest political figure there. He had achieved his dominance at about the time I became the Tyrant of Jupiter, and we had worked tacitly together to buttress each other's power and defuse interplanetary tension. I did not really like Khukov, but I trusted him.

"Ship ahoy," the ship's intercom announced. "Passengers to quarters."

I exchanged a glance with Spirit. We were in deep space between planets; our trip had not been announced, because the new government of Jupiter wished us no ill but wanted us out of the public eye. We cooperated because my wife Megan headed that new government, and I bore *her* no ill will. She had done what she felt she had to do, and I cannot say she was mistaken. The Tyrancy had accomplished a lot of good, but had also become increasingly arbitrary about the uses of power. Power does seem to corrupt the conscience, much as alcohol corrupts judgment; from the vantage of my abrupt loss of power I was able to see how far I had been straying. But because I was who I was, I was a target, which was another reason for the secrecy of this transportation. Was the other ship merely a passing merchant, or was it something else?

We retreated quickly to our quarters, obeying the authority of this ship. This was a Saturn vessel, of the escort class, displacing (as the usage still had it) about two thousand tons. She should be fast, capable of about three gees acceleration, but only lightly armed. It was her purpose to transport us swiftly and quietly to Saturn; she would be in trouble if attacked. We snapped into our acceleration harnesses.

"Ship under attack," the intercom voice said, as if responding to my thought. "Secure—"

The voice was cut off by the impact of a strike. The ship shook, and the power blinked. We were not under acceleration at the moment; the normal course is to achieve cruising velocity, then coast to the destination, conserving fuel. The vessel was spinning to provide half gee in that interim.

"Better take evasive action," Spirit muttered. She and I had been career officers in space for twelve to fifteen years; that was three decades past, but the reflexes are never lost.

The ship did not. It drifted along on its original course, not cutting in the drive.

We got out of our harnesses, acting as one. Obviously the ship's captain was a noncombatant, uncertain what to do in battle. That would get us killed promptly enough. He didn't realize that the first thing to do was to put the ship under acceleration, regardless of its course.

We burst into the control chamber. "Get it moving!" I barked in Russian.

"But the damage report is not yet in," the pilot protested. He was young, obviously inexperienced: the kind normally used on what is called a milk run, a routine mission. "The captain has not—"

I reached down and took his laser pistol from his body. I gave it to Spirit. "Get out of that seat," I said. I didn't have time to educate him in battle procedure.

"But you are passengers!" he said. "Not even of Saturn—" Then he turned his head and spied the laser bearing on his right eye. He got out of the seat.

I jumped into it. The ship's controls were unfamiliar in detail, but I understood the principle well enough. In a moment I had the drive started.

Meanwhile, Spirit was marching the pilot out of the chamber. I knew where she was headed. I spoke into the intercom. "Captain, I am assuming temporary command of this vessel," I said in Russian. "Acknowledge, and relay the directive to your crew."

"This is impossible!" the captain sputtered.

"Captain, we don't have time for debate. I am taking evasive action, but very soon the pirate will reorient and tag us with another shell. We have to fight effectively, and for that I require your implicit cooperation." I guided the craft on a random course, getting the hang of the controls in the process. This was a good little ship, I realized, capable of more acceleration than I had judged. I verified that she had not suffered any critical damage; she was responding perfectly. We had been lucky, so far.

"This is piracy right here!" he huffed. "I will not—"

"Captain, do you know who I am?" I cut in.

"No, they did not inform—"

"I am the Tyrant of Jupiter, deposed."

He made a gasp of surprise. Then Spirit's voice came: "Chamber secured, sir. Orders?"

I had of course been distracting the inexperienced captain while Spirit made her way to his office. Now she had her pistol on him. She could not speak Russian, but the weapon was surely persuasive enough.

"Captain," I repeated. "I am assuming command. I do this because of the need to save this ship from destruction by the pirate, and will return control to you when the crisis abates. Acknowledge."

This time there was a laser pointed at his eye. "Acknowledged," the captain said.

"Direct your crew."

He obeyed, ordering the crew to obey my orders. I had taken over the ship illegally, but the authority was mine for the duration.

"Observation," I said, addressing the officer I knew would be present. "What is the nature of the enemy?"

"Destroyer-class vessel, sir," he answered promptly. "Now showing pirate colors."

That meant that the attempt to communicate with the ship had resulted in a skull-and-crossbones picture on the screen, the universal signal of piracy. The fact that it was of the destroyer class told me all I needed to know about its capabilities, which was why the observation officer had not said more. He was obviously experienced, perhaps retired to this ship after long service.

"Armament," I said. "What are our resources?"

"Five cases stungas grenades, sir," he said. "Hand weapons, laser."

It was my turn to be stunned. *Hand* weapons? What of the space cannon?"

"Dismantled, sir, in favor of the drive. This is not a combat vessel."

Obviously not! "Propulsion," I said. "What is our maximum acceleration?"

"Five point two gee, sir."

"Five point . . . !" I exclaimed. The fastest ship in my fleet in the old days had been the destroyer *The Discovered Check,* upgraded to a capacity of 4.5 gee. This little escort ship supposedly could leave that ship rapidly behind. Perhaps they had figured to outrun any trouble along the way.

But no ship could outrun shells or drones, let alone lasers. The pirate had gotten too close, and now it was way too late to flee. But we couldn't fight either—not with hand grenades.

"Spirit," I said.

"Have to try chicken," she said in Spanish. If any of the Saturn personnel knew that language, they might still miss the implication. That was the intent. If they caught on, there would be a counterrevolution aboard ship.

Chicken. When two foolish kids got into transport bubbles and headed straight for each other. Collision course— and the first to swerve was "chicken." The game had been played in one form or another for centuries, and had accounted for its share of injuries and deaths.

I nodded. The pirate was matching our velocity, or trying to, so as to have a steady target for another shot. It had made no effort to communicate; there had been no demand for surrender. It simply intended to hole us; then its personnel would board in space suits and take the spoils. It was the way of the more vicious pirates, and it was evident that they had not been rousted out of this region of space. But they were bold indeed to tackle a marked Saturn ship; that would bring a fleet out here to extirpate every pirate ship.

I oriented the ship, then jammed up the drive. Suddenly we were accelerating, in the relative framework of the two moving ships, toward the pirate.

It took a moment for the pirate to realize what was happening, for this was completely unexpected. It was like a wounded rabbit charging the pursuing hound.

The pirate reacted by firing another shell at us. That was an error; we now presented a minimal target, end-on, and were accelerating; there was little space or time for this. The pirate had to move in a hurry, or be rammed. That would likely destroy both ships.

Now our own crewmen were catching on. "Suicide!" someone screamed in Russian on the intercom.

"It is chicken," I said in Russian. "But we have less to lose than they do."

"All will die!" the voice cried.

"Armament," I said.

"Sir," the experienced officer replied immediately.

"Can you launch the lifeboat by remote control?"

"Yes, sir."

"In the manner of a torpedo?"

Now he caught on to my new ploy. "The window is very narrow, sir."

"The lifeboat!" another voice exclaimed. "Without that, we die!"

"Silence," the captain snapped. He had evidently come to terms with his demotion and was enforcing discipline under the new order.

"Watch the pirate," I said to the armament officer. "Judge the direction he moves. Assume he will accelerate at his maximum. Plot the course to intercept that escape path. I will proceed straight, accelerating at three gee till launch."

"Understood, sir."

We closed rapidly as I brought the gee up to three. That tripled the weight of every person on the ship; even in acceleration harness, that isn't comfortable. But if this ship was built to do five gee, the personnel had to have been trained for it. *I* was the weak link here; I wasn't sure I could handle more than three gee at my age and condition, at least not for long.

The pirate ship moved out of the way. It was indeed chicken. It had double our mass and at least double our personnel, and it could destroy us in any ordinary encounter. Thus it had much more to lose than we did. I had never doubted it would avoid the collision; the only question was when it would start its maneuver. Because it had foolishly tried to shoot us down first, it had lost valuable time; now it had no chance to reorient. That meant that its path was predictable. If that Saturnian officer was worth his salt—

We closed. The pirate was in motion, but barely in time.

Our lifeboat launched. Then we shot past the pirate's tail section—and the lifeboat rammed it.

We watched it in the screen as I cut our acceleration. Vapor shot out of the pirate's side. She had been holed by our missile. A cheer went up on the intercom.

I rotated our ship in place and resumed thrust. This had the effect of decelerating us, relative to the other ship. There was no rush now; I held it at one gee. "Captain," I said.

"Sir."

"My mission has been accomplished. I am returning command to you." And I knew that Spirit was putting away the laser pistol.

"Thank you, Tyrant," he said, with only a trace of irony.

"But if I may make a suggestion, sir?" I continued.

"Speak."

"We should take the pirate's lifeboat—and perhaps make an investigation of the ship to determine its identity. The men might wish to salvage artifacts also."

He hesitated. Military vessels were not supposed to take spoils, but the temptation could be great in a situation like this. "Tyrant," he said after a moment. "There will be an investigation into your actions, of course. But I believe they will establish the validity of your position. In the interim, would you accede to commanding the investigation party?"

So that any spoils taken would be my responsibility, not his. He was canny enough! He knew that no Saturn court-martial would convict the Tyrant of Jupiter—not when Saturn had invited that Tyrant to accept sanctuary there. I was sure that the entire Saturn Navy knew the political situation; this ship simply had not been advised that it was the one with the Tyrant actually aboard. Perhaps its crew did *not* know about the Tyrant's change of status, after all. In fact, this entire episode would probably be hushed up, and that would do the captain more good than harm.

"I shall be pleased to do that," I said graciously.

In fact, it might be best if my temporary assumption of authority were not advertised. It could not be concealed from the authorities, of course, but they would probably be willing to bury it if I was.

I relinquished the pilot's seat to the regular pilot and set about organizing the boarding party. We had to don suits, as there would be no pressure in the holed ship. Spirit joined me. "Like old times," she murmured in Spanish.

She was right, and I discovered that I relished the feeling. I had been thirty when I left the Jupiter Navy, just half my present age, and this activity gave me the semblance of my youth. Of course I knew it was illusion, but a person can at times appreciate illusion as much as reality. Consider, for example, the feelie helmets, which facilitate all manner of vicarious experience ranging from interplanetary travel to explicit sexual encounters. I have on occasion received great satisfaction from the helmet, and now I had satisfaction from the action occurring here in space. Danger near, Spirit beside me—I wished I could kiss her, but of course that was not feasible in our suits.

We exited the lock, and a crew of ten SatNavs came with us. Among them was the armament officer, whose competence in the clutch had given us our victory. I had learned in passing that a significant portion of the crew had been rendered temporarily unfit for duty by the intensity of our brief action; this was the first combat they had experienced. That amazed me: that Saturn should provide so inadequately for such an important mission.

Or was I overrating myself? I was no longer the Tyrant; I was an exile. So perhaps this was, after all, a routine mission.

It made sense, but was a comedown. The past decade of power had perhaps spoiled me. However, I knew that I needed to adapt to the new reality. I was now a nonentity.

We used our weak suit jets to cross to the derelict. Our lifeboat had punched a hole amidships, then evidently had been thrown clear. The aim had been perfect. Now the pirate vessel rotated slowly, leaking a faint residual trace of gas, like a planet stripped, by some calamity, of most of its atmosphere.

We used the air lock for entry, rather than the jagged hole in the hull; there was no sense in risking our suits.

The interior was ugly, of course; abrupt depressurization is rough on equipment as well as on personnel, and it was evident that this ship had not been prepared for it. I marveled at that; perhaps the Saturn vessel had never had battle experience, but how could a pirate be naive about the dangers of action in space? Many items had not been properly secured; they would have moved about during free-fall, and of course had become missiles during depressurization.

We found the first body. It was a man of Mongoloid origin, his blood-spattered eyeballs bulging from their sockets, his tongue swelling from the open mouth. Two of our party turned away; it is no fun to retch in a space suit.

"Hold him," I told Spirit. She caught the man's feet, anchoring him so that he would not float away while I searched him. I checked his body for identification, and found it. I glanced at it quickly, then passed it to Spirit without comment.

She glanced and nodded. Then she put it in a utility pocket of her suit. We went on.

What we did not tell the others was that the identification showed the pirate crewman to be a citizen of the Middle Kingdom. That was what Jupiter citizens called South Saturn, historically derived from the ancient China of Earth.

There was no pirate treasure; this was a utilitarian ship. Yet it had attacked us in the manner of a pirate, though a strangely inept one. A serious pirate would have been properly prepared for the engagement and would never have given us the chance to fight back, even in the unusual manner we had done. Something was very strange here.

We checked the arsenal and found it well equipped. But our own ship was not set up for such armament. In short, there were very few spoils to be taken. The crewmen were not interested in robbing the gruesome bodies of the dead. So we set up a marker-beacon so that the ship could be spotted for salvage, and returned to our own.

Back in our own vessel, passengers again, I got private with Spirit. "Why would the Middle Kingdom seek to assassinate me?" I asked in Spanish, just in case we were being monitored. "I'm out of power now, and when I was Tyrant I treated that nation fairly. I would say relations were good, as these things go."

"How did they know we were aboard this ship?" she asked in return. "When even the crew didn't?"

"Would Khukov have told them?"

"Unlikely."

"Unless he wanted us killed, not traceable to him." I pondered that. "He is certainly capable of such an act. But I know him. He would not do it to me. He knows he can trust me, and therefore you."

"I agree. Therefore it probably isn't the Middle Kingdom."

I pursed my lips. "A frame! We were intended to identify the personnel!"

"Except that we would have been unable to do so if they had blasted us in space."

"The USR fleet would have done so, though," I said. "That was a suicide mission, staffed by incompetents."

"Like ours," she said.

That made me pause. "No, not incompetents, I think. They must have had to reach pretty deep to find a crew that did not know I had been deposed and exiled and was being shipped to Saturn. With a phenomenally fast ship. This one must have been used as a courier ship to key territories, very fast and private, always avoiding combat and slipping by, outrunning pursuit. It could have returned from a three-month mission and been sent immediately on this one. Who would expect a noncombatant ship for this mission?"

She nodded agreement. "Everyone seems incompetent at first blood. Once the situation was plain, the captain accepted your authority, and that armament officer is a good one."

"So we are left only with the mysteries of who is the real assassin, and how the ship spotted us."

"I don't like such mysteries," she said.

"Neither do I. Yet it is like old times."

She smiled. "Like old times."

I put my arm around her, and she melted into me. Those old times had been horrible, but not without their redemptions.

Chapter 2

DREAM

Our approach to Saturn was not direct. Saturn is not a single political entity; like Jupiter, it has several major and minor nations. We were going to the Union of Saturnine Republics, which occupied virtually all of the Northern Hemisphere. The Southern Hemisphere was dominated by the People's Republic of the Middle Kingdom, and the rings and moons were all under other control. Thus we avoided these and went to the USR's major artifical ring station, where Spirit and I had been once before, when I was Governor of the Jupiter state of Sunshine. From there we transferred to a ferry to the great port city of Vostok, and thence to a flight to the capital, Scow. Or rather, in the native rendition, Skva; no need to Saxonize it here.

I'm sure that Chairman Khukov was a busy man, but he made time for us. Within an hour of our arrival we found ourselves in his private suite, seated in comfort. He had aged visibly, with what hair remaining to him turning off-gray, and he had put on weight—but what does one expect of my generation? His appearance was not the basis of his office. We conversed in English, for Spirit did not speak Russian and Khukov's knowledge of Spanish was never advertised. His talent was like mine: He read people, and therefore could manage them. This was what had brought each of us to power. We trusted each other because each of us understood the other in a way no other person could. Differences of language or culture or politics became insignificant in the face of this fundamental understanding.

"The pirate attack," Khukov said, coming right to the point. His mind evidently remained sharp. I had first met

14

him when I was the Jupiter ambassador to Ganymede and he was the military liaison there; we had taught each other our native languages. "I'm sure you know it was no doing of mine."

"The personnel had Middle Kingdom identification," I said.

"So my personnel inform me. But though relations between the USR and the Middle Kingdom are not perfect, those folk are not that clumsy. They would not carry such identification."

"So we assumed," I agreed. "But who, then? I presume you did not advertise our presence aboard the ship."

"It was what you would term an inside job. I have lost the services of a trusted secretary."

"I know how that can be," I murmured, thinking of Shelia, my woman of the wheelchair who had sacrificed her life for me. Her death had tipped me into a siege of madness leading in due course to my ouster as Tyrant.

"No one was to know of your presence," Khukov said. "We used our fastest small ship, though the gees were restricted in deference to your age. To all others it was a routine courier voyage. The crew itself—"

"Was unprepared for combat," I finished. "I preempted control on an emergency basis; no onus should attach to the captain."

"None does; I recognized your touch the moment the news reached me. He will not suffer. But the episode is an embarrassment to me, and heads have rolled."

"You know the origin and motivation of the attack?"

"The nomenklatura."

Spirit and I looked blank.

Khukov smiled. "Brace yourselves for a small lecture on Saturnine internal politics, for this is relevant to your interest. You know that we are theoretically a classless society, unlike you of the decadent capitalistic planets. But we have classes, and of these the most privileged is the nomenklatura, the bureaucratic stratum of the Party. Those in all the key positions of the Party, the military, and the secret police belong to this hereditary class. *I* belong. They pass themselves off as mere civil servants, but they are the true rulers. Our society is stultified, because the nomenklatura wants no change; it wants only perpetuation of its own power. This is your enemy—and mine."

"But you said you belonged to it," I reminded him.

"To belong physically is not necessarily to agree with its precepts," he said. "I could not have achieved my present position without the support of the nomenklatura. But once I gained the position, my horizon expanded, and then that of the nomenklatura became too narrow for me. I sought to reform our system, to eradicate corruption, to make of Saturn a truly superior power." He shook his head. "The task was more difficult than I had suspected."

"Infinitely," I agreed ruefully.

"But I believe I could have done it—indeed, could do it yet—if it were not for the entrenched opposition of the nomenklatura. But I cannot do with it what I could with rebellious peasants. I would be removed from power if I tried."

"I understand," I said with a smile. As he knew, I had just been removed from power myself.

"I could not even demilitarize space, as I promised you I would," he said. "I intended to, but when I tried. . ."

That sobered me. As Tyrant, I had steadily reduced the Jupiter military initiative, using the monetary savings to bolster other aspects of the society. I had done this with the assurance that Khukov was doing likewise. Of course no early reductions had been apparent in either budget, because existing commitments had had to be met, but no new initiatives had been sought.

"Have no retroactive concern," Khukov told me. "We did not seek to attack Jupiter. I had no desire for war, and the nomenklatura desires victory, not combat. In that we are in accord. But the waste of resources for weapons which do not work, that profit only those who construct them . . ." He shook his head.

"Yet how could this lead to an attempt to assassinate a deposed foreign leader?" Spirit asked.

"Two possibilities," Khukov said. "One I hope is the true one; the other I hope is not. The first is that it is not to the nomenklatura's interest to have too much peace in the System. With a pacifist in power at Jupiter, and the Middle Kingdom minding its own business, what need is there for new weapons contracts? So if some animosity could be stirred up by the assassination of a not-too-important personage of the one by the other, the USR would certainly have to keep alert and strong, and military graft would not be questioned."

"The secrecy of the mission was such that news of the assassination might never be released," I said.

"Indeed. The second possibility is that the nomenklatura sees the Tyrant of Jupiter as a direct threat to its interests, so acted to eliminate that threat immediately."

This perplexed me. "How could I be a threat? My power is gone."

"Your power may be restored."

I shook my head. "It is my wife who has deposed me. I will not oppose her."

"Restored *here,*" he said. "It is in my mind to make you my hatchet man, as your idiom puts it."

"I have had enough of the exercise of power," I demurred.

"I think not. No man ever has enough of that. But I am not suggesting the abuse of it. I am suggesting that you can do one necessary thing for me that I cannot do for myself. Because you are the Tyrant, known to my people and to the rest of the Solar System as the great benefactor of your planet, they would support you in a way they would nŏt me."

"I am not going to try to usurp your power!" I protested.

"That is why I can use you for this. I know that you are the one person who *could* challenge me, who *won't.* I cannot trust any member of the nomenklatura similarly. Thus you become the ideal person to implement the Dream."

"You want me to eradicate the nomenklatura for you?" I asked, dismayed.

"That is merely the first step. We cannot accomplish anything until that power is broken. But what use to break it, if it is only replaced by new corruption, and the festering animosities of the System continue to be aggravated? It is the whole of mankind that needs renovation, not just one little part of it."

I knew by my reading of him that Khukov was getting into something of supreme importance to him. I had had experience with a dream before, and it had taken me to prominence in the Jupiter Navy, and thence to the Tyrancy itself. "What is your dream?"

"The unification of the species in harmony," he said.

"An excellent dream," I agreed wryly. "But difficult to implement."

He waggled a finger at me. "A dream without substance is worthless. I have a mechanism, if it can be implemented. Do you remember how the society of ancient Earth was ready to explode, to destroy itself by internecine warfare, until the onset of the gee-shield?"

"That gave man the Solar System," I agreed. "The pent-up energies were released positively by the expansion into the new frontier, rather than turning destructively upon themselves."

"And now that frontier has been conquered, and the energies are turning destructive again, exactly as before," he continued. "But with a new frontier—"

"To divert man's destructive energies—" I said, beginning to visualize the dream.

"And provide man a common challenge," Spirit added. "But what could that frontier be?"

Khukov made an expansive gesture. "What else? The galaxy."

"But the gee-shield can hardly do that," I said. "Gravity is not much of a problem in interstellar space, so shielding it doesn't make much difference. For that kind of travel, we need sustained thrust that could take us up toward light speed, and even CT drive isn't enough. Even so, it would take a decade or so just to reach the nearest star—where there might not be anything worthwhile for colonization anyway. It's not enough just to get there; there have to be resources to exploit. Just the problem of growing new bubbles to house increasing population—that requires planets like Jupiter and Saturn. The answer always comes out the same: There is no solution in interstellar space."

"Ah, but there *is,*" he insisted. "If we can find those suitable stars for energy, and suitable planets for material resources, and get to them. Five, six new systems to start, more when required. We know they exist; our problem is locating them. Reaching them."

"Confirming them," Spirit said. "To make the enormous investment and risk of decades-long travel to them worthwhile."

"But a light-speed drive would make this feasible," he said, "Go, explore, return, report—within our lifetimes, late as our lives are getting. Discovering the galaxy."

"A light-speed drive is a fantasy," I said. "A relativistic impossibility. Only radiation does it."

"Just suppose, Tyrant, that there were a breakthrough of this nature. A mechanism to convert a physical object to the equivalent of light, without destroying it. And to restore it to solidity on demand. What then?"

I toyed with the notion, intrigued. "Convert atoms to photons? Surely these would travel light-fashion, instantly outward, a complex wave. Virtually massless—what happens to the mass of the original?"

"It converts to energy, the energy of light-speed travel. And back to mass at the other end."

"If a spaceship could be changed to light, travel as a beam, then be solidified at the far reflector—but are we conjecturing living creatures too, or merely inanimate shipment?"

"Living things. Human beings, Complete city-bubbles, perhaps. Largely self-contained units."

"Even so, four years to Alpha Centauri, and more to others—a city would not be self-supporting that long."

"But if the city becomes light, time within it becomes infinite, and for the passengers, nonexistent. They could travel four years, and to them it would be not even a moment, no time at all. It would feel like instant matter-transmission. No supplies used, no energy expended, merely a new star beyond."

"Suspended animation," I said. "That might make it feasible, indeed." I sighed. "But since there is no such device . . ."

Khukov smiled. "Ah, but there may be. I had a report

three years ago, which I disbelieved, but I was intrigued, so I examined it. Now tests are commencing, and we shall shortly know whether this is a drug dream or reality. If reality—"

"Then it would be worthwhile to seek the political breakthrough," I finished. "To get our entire species organized for the great new frontier. For it would have to be done on a System-wide basis, as it was done on an Earth-wide basis before. The new diaspora of mankind."

"The new diaspora," he echoed. "That is the dream."

"But to unify mankind for an effort like this—that would be as great a political challenge as a scientific one," I said. "Each planet would want to dominate it, and there would be war to establish proprietary rights to the best prospects for colonization."

"There was not such war before," he reminded me.

"When Earth colonized the Solar System," I agreed. "But then the need was desperate and the leadership inspired. No nation gave up its share of the pie. Thus the political and economic and military situation of Earth was reestablished in the System—with all its problems. We have been flirting with the same disaster as before, on a larger scale."

"But the same solution offers," he persisted. "Except that the galaxy is vast beyond the aspiration of man to fill. It would take a hundred thousand years merely to cross it, and much longer to colonize it. I think we would not soon again see a crisis of confinement."

"The colonization of the galaxy," I repeated, feeling Khukov's Dream take hold. "You really believe the challenges can be met?"

"I am prepared to supervise the scientific challenge," he said. "I believe it can be met, if there is cooperation by the other planets. First we must develop a large-scale demonstration project, to prove that it works, and to establish its feasibility in a fashion that all men will believe. That will cost some hundreds of billions of rubles, and I think Saturn could not do it alone. That places it in the camp of the political challenge. If we can unify the planets—"

"Who could do that?" I asked, realizing his thrust.

"Who but the Tyrant of Space?"

"But I have lost my base of power!" I protested.

"Have you? If you snapped your fingers, would the Jupiter Navy not hasten to do your bidding?"

Because Admiral Emerald Mondy, my former military wife, owed her position to me, and in the past decade had consolidated it quite thoroughly. "But I would not ask—"

"And the Jupiter industrial base—would it not support you too?" he persisted. "And the common folk of the planet?"

He was of course correct. All the basic elements of Jupiter power were mine to call on. But I had accepted the termination of the Tyrancy because my current wife, Megan Hubris, required it. I trusted her judgment more than I trusted my own, and preferred to see to the orderly transition of power during my life rather than risk the chaos that might follow my death as Tyrant. "Still—"

"And your wife—would she not support the Dream?"

I knew she would. "Yet—"

"With agreement and support from Jupiter and Saturn, proper management should bring the other planets in line," he said. "It is an opportunity that exists only now—because only while I am in power here will Saturn support a thrust it does not dominate, and only while the Tyrant lives will Jupiter do the same. Now is the time politically as well as scientifically, and if we do not act at this juncture, our species may destroy itself before such a chance again occurs."

"But the nomenklatura will oppose this," I said, returning to his earlier consideration. "So you propose to use me to eliminate their power, for the sake of the dream."

"Exactly. I cannot oppose them directly—indeed, they would have eliminated me by now if I did not control the Spetsnaz and the secret police—but I cannot commit sufficient resources to the Dream while their power remains. But you may be able to accomplish this."

Those were dread units indeed that he mentioned. Spetsnaz was the USR's ruthless terrorist strike force, an army in itself, whose mission was to paralyze a potential enemy through selective assassinations and bombings before overt hostilities commenced. Had it seemed that I, as Tyrant, intended to make war against the USR, the first thing I would have had to do was to guard against a Spetsnaz mission. As for the secret police—indeed, the man who controlled that had the very nerve center of power on this planet. But these were Khukov's mainstays, not mine. "How? I cannot simply go into the Saturn society and start firing personnel!"

"I will put you in charge of our farm program," he said. "You will be directed to quadruple the harvest in two years."

"Two years! That would be a revolution!"

He smiled. "Yes, I suspect it would require heroic measures—such as the prompt elimination of anyone who interfered with it in any way. We know who will interfere."

I nodded. Khukov and I both knew well the applications of power. I would be a hatchet man indeed. But with my sister to organize it, I could certainly make progress.

I looked at Spirit. She nodded; she was ready for this.

I extended my hand to Khukov.

Another thing occurred at this time, a minor episode really, but it touched me. It was a letter from my daughter, Hopie Megan Hubris. She was now in her mid-twenties, but to me she was always my little girl of nine or ten, or of fifteen. She was with the Department of Education of Jupiter, and from time to time she published papers on this subject, yet I always perceived a little-girl quality in what she wrote to me.

Dear Daddy,

I was so concerned when we got the news about your ship being attacked in space, though the excitement was all over by the time I knew. Don't scare me like that! You aren't a Navy officer anymore, you know.

Megan is setting up the new government here. You know, most of the people you put in are remaining, at least until senators and representatives can be elected. There was a lot of grumbling about things when you were in power, but already there's grumbling about how much better things were in the "old days" of the Tyrancy. I just thought you'd like to know.

Take care of yourself, Daddy. I miss you already.

And I missed her! I showed the letter to Spirit, and she nodded. "A daughter's a daughter, for all of her life," she murmured. How true!

Chapter 3

WOMAN

Saturn, as the local saying went, was not colonized in a day, and my farm reform program was not instituted any faster. Spirit and I had to get down to some homework, nominally on the Saturn farm program, but also on the nomenklatura. We had grown accustomed to having comprehensive staffs to assist us, and we were not young; in addition, Spirit did not speak Russian. Texts were available in English but not in Spanish, to our regret.

The upshot was that we got a secretary. She was approved by Khukov's staff, which meant we could depend on her, but I trusted my own reading more. She was Saturnian, but of occidental descent; the USR is really more of a Western nation than is generally thought. She surely had a Saturnian name, but employed a code name, as was standard practice in this line of work, so we knew her simply as Tasha.

Tasha spoke several of the dialects of the Union, including that of the Kranian Saturn Republic where the most productive farming was; she would be a help there, for I knew only the standard Russian. She was a competent typist and computer operator. She knew most of the great cities intimately, from Skva to Kov, and understood the complex bureaucratic mechanisms of residence within them and travel between them. She was also young and attractive and intelligent and even-tempered. In short, the ideal secretary.

Of course she reported everything we did to her superiors; that was a matter of course on Saturn. It would have been suspicious if it were not so. No personnel were cleared for service of this nature who were not primarily agents of the government. Since I had nothing to hide from Khukov, this didn't bother me.

What did bother me, as we spent weeks reviewing the statistics and personnel of the farm bureau and the Kranian SR, was Tasha's sex appeal. At first she was chill and formal and beautiful, but as time passed she relaxed and unbound her fair hair and became warm and informal and luscious. I was sixty, but by no means immune to female presence. As her blouses became more sheer and her skirts shorter and her attitude more accommodating, I reacted exactly as any man would. Tasha was letting it be known, in the quiet arena of body signaling, that she found me interesting.

Certainly I found her interesting. The increasingly supple curvature of her bosom and the firmness of her lengthening thighs were stripping years from my age. I knew that if I wanted a woman for sexual purpose, all I had to do was requisition one; Tasha herself would put in an order and the pool would provide whatever description of girl I desired. But I was never keen on anonymous flesh, and less so as I aged; I preferred to have a larger relationship.

So in due course, when Spirit was away on related business, I took Tasha to a private chamber and kissed her. She accommodated me so expertly in this, too, that I knew that it was considered to be part of her job description. I was reminded of the ancient Saxon joke about a secretary not being considered a permanent fixture until screwed on the desk. As with many jokes, there was truth in it; Tasha was evidently prepared to be permanent. I was sure she was making it her business to learn as much about me as possible, and to report it, but I do have a certain way with women and like to think that she would have been similarly amenable if not required to be. I drew out the seat of the couch, converting it to a serviceable bed; even the furniture was accommodating.

She let me undress her, for she knew too that the typical occidental man likes to believe he is in charge. Her body was exactly as her clothing had suggested: perfect in detail. It was evident that Saturnian notions of beauty aligned with those of Jupiter. She was full and soft without being extreme.

I stripped as she lay on the bed, discovering myself to be too eager for the culmination to resort to any subtleties of approach. I took down my trousers and undershorts, but was overcome by desire before getting to my shirt. I approached her, and she lay supine, smiling and spreading and lifting her legs. I dived for her, and those legs circled my torso and locked behind me while her hands came up to grip my collar on either side.

In retrospect I consider myself to be a fool. I had had experience with the martial arts, including judo, and I well knew the nature of the Osae-waza, or art of holding, and the Shime-waza, or art of strangleholds. But I was overcome by lust, and so missed the signals. I plunged for her genital region, and got inside—and her wrists twisted and locked against my throat, cutting off my breath. It was the reverse cross lock, lightly but firmly applied.

"Finish your business, lover," she murmured, drawing my face down toward hers. As she did, the strangle tightened, as was its nature. Her right hand gripped my collar on my right side, and her left on my left, so that her wrists crossed, and the closer she brought my neck to her, the more firmly those crossed wrists dug in. "It is your last."

I tried to break free, but that is almost impossible when such a hold is properly applied. I couldn't twist out, because her legs held me in place, and I couldn't pull back, because the leverage was hers. Even my intimate connection to her body facilitated that lock; my loin could not rotate. What a position!

"Kiss me," she said, drawing me lower. Instead I reached for her face, for my own hands were free. In a desperate situation like this, I was prepared to strike or gouge; anything to make her grip on my throat break. But immediately her hold tightened, and I grew faint. She had had a choke on me, which cut off my air, but it can take some time for that to deprive a person of consciousness. The tightening put pressure against the buried carotid arteries, cutting off the supply of blood to my brain, and that could put me out in five seconds. My hands fluttered helplessly.

She eased up, and the blood and a little air returned. There was no question: she knew the potential of this lock, and was toying with me. She could render me unconscious or dead at any time, despite my experience in combat.

"Finish it, lover," she repeated, nudging my ribs with her thighs. "I would not wish you to die unfulfilled."

Some finish! I remembered the notorious historical woman of a death camp who had taken lovers from the condemned, then had their skins fashioned into lampshades. Such romance loses its appeal quite rapidly.

But what could I do? If I did not make some show of obliging her, she would simply kill me immediately. So I used what very limited freedom remained to my body, and I thrust, finding little pleasure in it despite the original delight of the connection, and thrust again, going through the motions. I was really stalling for time, yet I could not see what use I would have for a few more minutes. Spirit would not return for another hour, at least, and no one else would intrude on our privacy. Tasha had plenty of time to play with me before she dispatched me.

"You can do better than that, Tyrant," she said. "What would all your prior conquests think, if you had plumbed them no more efficiently than this? Move it!"

Brother! She was like a cat with a mouse, first trapping or crippling it, then playing with it, having no intent to let it survive. But how could even the smartest of mice survive that game?

Then I had a notion. I had lived a good deal longer than she had, and had had advanced training in specialized combat techniques. It had been decades since I had practiced them, but I had not forgotten. There had been one line of nerve attack that had at one time fascinated me. A choke can take minutes for full effect, and a strangle seconds, as I explained, but the right pressure on the right nerve can be instantaneous. Furthermore, a nerve attack is more versatile than a neck lock, because it can be applied to any part of the body, and does not require that body to be anchored in place. If Tasha was ignorant of this system of techniques—

I increased the vigor of my thrusting, obliging my captor, who evidently got her satisfaction from forcing a climax in the victim she was about to kill. No doubt her own climax would be set off, not by mine, but by her perception of my body stiffening in the rigor of termination. Some people are like that.

Meanwhile, I slid my hands around behind me. She might have been aware of this, but unconcerned; her legs were far stronger than my arms, and I could not force them apart that way. Perhaps, again catlike, she relished the futility of my attempt. I took hold of her left ankle with my left hand and her right with my right. Then I slid my left hand onto her right ankle, though this was a difficult stretch, and held it in place. My achievement of this grip was facilitated by the slight leeway she was giving me to enable me to thrust into her.

Now I had her right foot precisely placed. This was important, for I could not see it, and the nerve I required was not readily accessible. I stroked that foot with the fingers of my right hand, searching out the precise spot.

"Forget it, lover," she said disdainfully. "I am not ticklish." And she tightened the lock momentarily, warning me to keep to my proper business.

Then I lifted my right hand and brought it down hard, striking her foot. I was going for a particular bone that would in turn impact on the key nerve. This was at best a difficult trick, and my present circumstance was far from the best.

But it worked. Her foot stiffened as the pain lanced through it. Involuntarily she drew it away, breaking the lock her legs had on my body. Ready for this, I whipped my left hand about and forward and down to her inner thigh as I withdrew from my prior thrust, giving myself some room. I jammed my thumb into another nerve there.

Tasha gave a truncated scream of amazement and discomfort, for suddenly her entire leg was numb. Now she could not hold me, and I withdrew and scrambled with my legs, pushing my body into a forward somersault. Her hands had to let go, lest her wrists be broken.

Even as I rolled across her face, I twisted, catching her head. I found my place again and dug into the nerves of her neck, half stunning her. She was helpless, unable to make her own body respond.

Then I had the respite to reconsider. I had known this woman for three weeks, and had read her many times. Nothing had suggested that she was capable of such an attack. How could I have been mistaken? Was my talent going bad, or was there something else?

I realized that I had to question her, and not politely. But torturing women has never been my notion of fun. How could I get her to tell me what she was surely conditioned never to reveal?

Well, she evidently had a hankering for terminal sex. Perhaps I could reverse this.

I assumed the original sexual position, setting her hands loosely against my throat, clinging to my collar. But I had pressed the nerves in her shoulders, and now her arms lacked volition; she could not throttle me. I set her legs about me as before; their hold too was ineffective. We had the form but not the substance of her reverse cross lock.

I thrust into her, as before. "I am about to climax," I said. "What will you do then?"

Dazed by my succession of nerve blocks, she responded, "I will strangle you to death."

"Why?"

"Because you represent a threat to the system."

"What system?"

"The established order of Saturn." This was working well; she believed I was about to die, so her resistance to imparting information was relaxed. Perhaps she even wanted to reveal it, as part of her expiation.

"The nomenklatura?" I asked.

"Yes."

"How did they get an assassin past the screening process?"

"They have many moles."

A mole. A person who performed some routine office for an indefinite period, then abruptly surfaced as a spy or agent at a critical occasion. Such a person could be conditioned not even to know she was a mole, until the correct circumstance triggered the transformation. That explained how Tasha had eluded my discovery. I read a person's attitude and intent; I could not read what the person did not know.

Tasha had been conditioned to manifest as an assassin when I, or perhaps any man, entered her body sexually. Obviously she had been well trained for this. I had left my shirt on, giving her the opportunity to use the cross lock; had I been entirely naked, that would not have worked, but she would have used some other technique. There are many ways to kill a naked man bare-handed. Perhaps I was fortunate that she had chosen this one, so that I had had the chance to remember my counter to it.

So I had foiled the nomenklatura plot. But was that enough? If they could get a mole through Khukov's defenses once, they could surely do so again—and next time it might be a man equipped to kill without warning, with a single strike. I remained vulnerable.

Unless I found a way to deceive this enemy about the prospects of my demise. Tasha had not been on any fixed schedule; she had manifested as an increasingly attractive and willing sexual partner, but no one could know how long it would be before I took advantage of that. It might have been days, or weeks (as was the case), or months. Probably the nomenklatura didn't care; they were assured that eventually I would get around to it, and then I would be dead. Thus they had no need to imperil their position by any other attempts against me; they had their sleeper placed.

What I needed to do was keep Tasha, who was, after all, an excellent secretary, but not attempt any further sex with her. In that manner she should serve as my protection from my enemies.

But I didn't want her mole-self forever lurking, waiting to assassinate me. Could I recondition her? I was not expert in this science, but I could try. Perhaps if she believed, in her assassin guise, that she already had killed me, then she would not be inclined to try again.

So I played it through. I continued my motions, working up to my sexual climax, which despite my narrow escape was not really difficult. Tasha remained an infernally attractive woman, after all, and aspects of this en-

gagement were reminiscent of the manner I raped
Roulette, half my life ago. What a woman Rue had been!
Still was, for my taste, though she was now nearing fifty.
The thought of her enhanced my performance, and in due
course I erupted in creditable fashion.

"Now I shall do it," Tasha said, smiling grimly. She
tightened her lock.

Her effort was not sufficient, but I made up for it with
my performance. I gagged and held my breath, trying to
make my face go mottled, and in due course collapsed. I
came down on her luscious torso, my face separated from
hers only by her grip.

Tasha lifted her head to touch my lips with hers. We
kissed, in our fashion, though I remained carefully unresponsive, playing dead.

But I knew I wasn't fooling her. Dazed she might be,
but she could still tell the living from the dead.

She rolled me off her, then got up, went to the bathroom, dressed, and put her hair and makeup back in order. She left the room without speaking again.

I got up and followed much the same routine. Soon I
returned to the main office, where Tasha had resumed
work.

I hesitated, then approached her. "How's it going?" I
asked.

She flashed her décolletage at me. "We're making progress, Tyrant. We'll be ready for a field trip in perhaps
three days."

I read her as she talked. She was the normal secretary,
with no killer instinct. She surely had no memory of her
attempt on my life. Once the sexual encounter was over,
she had reverted to her innocent state. And to her effort
to seduce me. It was as though the past half hour had not
happened.

What disturbed me was that, though I had just had my
sexual satisfaction of her, her manner and appearance
still turned me on. Of course I knew better than to ever
get intimate with her again—not unless I first tied her
down! But if she could tempt me even slightly, immediately after my satiation and my close escape from assassination, she would surely tempt me more as time passed.

I would be wanting this woman, despite the danger. Perhaps even *because of* the danger, because there is a special challenge to possess the woman who is emphatically not a casual plaything. At my age, it seemed to be more natural to flirt with the inevitable extinction, as if by averting it I could deny its inevitability.

I could not afford to take that risk. Yet I did not want to expose Tasha's nature, thus clearing the way for some new threat. What should I do?

I had another inspiration. The solution lay not with Tasha, who was what she was, but with me. I needed to arrange to eliminate any future temptation I might feel for her body.

We worked on the research until Spirit returned. She knew immediately that something had happened; my sister does not read people the way I do, but she knows me as well as anyone ever has. She made no comment, but when the day concluded and Tasha departed for her apartment, Spirit looked inquiringly at me.

"I accepted her seduction, and she tried to kill me," I said simply. "She's a mole—an assassin mole."

"And you don't want to eliminate her?" she inquired with raised eyebrow.

I explained my thinking on that matter. "But it's dangerous," I concluded. "She still tempts me."

"You always were a fool about women," Spirit said. "Fortunately, they always were bigger fools about you."

"Not this one. If I touch her again I may not survive it."

"Put a pacifier on her," she suggested.

I smiled. Of course that wasn't serious. A pacifier makes a person lose volition, and it can indeed be used for rape, but that never appealed to me any more than rape itself did. What I wanted was of course impossible: Tasha's willing, nonmalicious acceptance of my advances.

"So what do I do?" I asked, somewhat plaintively.

"You get another woman."

"Another woman might well be another mole," I pointed out.

"Not if the source differs. You can get a guaranteed

safe woman, with all the qualities you require." She seemed amused.

"What source?" I asked, perplexed.

"Your wife, of course."

"Megan?" I asked, appalled.

"She knows your tastes, I suspect."

I realized that she was serious. It would be presumptuous to suggest that my sister resents any part of my life-style, including my romantic affairs, but perhaps she suffers a certain impatience on occasion. I'm sure she regrets my breakup with Megan, as I do myself.

I pondered, then decided to call her bluff. "Then send Megan a message from me: 'Send me a woman.' "

Spirit smiled enigmatically. "I shall."

And she did.

Chapter 4

FARM

We traveled—Spirit and Tasha and I, and our security personnel—to the Saturnine Republic of Kraine, and to the bubble city of Dessa within it. This was south from Skva, but the phenomenal differentiation in wind velocity made that direction largely meaningless. Dessa circled the planet significantly faster than did Skva, so while its geographic location was south, its actual position could be around at the far side of the planet. This was part of the rigor of Saturnian society that we had not experienced on Jupiter. It made intercity travel more complicated than elsewhere, and tended to set apart the different bands, resulting in greater isolation of subcultures. Saturn, far more than Jupiter, was a conglomeration of peoples, as its overall designation indicated: the Union of Saturnine Republics.

We used an airplane provided by the government; apparently we counted as Party officials, and as such did not mingle with the common herd. Certainly that was safer, considering the two assassination attempts that had been made against me. I glanced covertly at Tasha, still amazed that she should change character so thoroughly, becoming a sadistic killer before reverting to her pleasant innocence. Again I felt that dangerous attraction; I wanted to possess this woman again, perhaps because I knew she was truly forbidden.

We navigated the currents and homed in on Dessa. It was on the so-called Black Sea, which was a band of turbulence generated by the shear between winds of radically differing velocities. It was possible to navigate the sea, but not to live in it, for the irregular storms that manifested would have severely shaken any city-bubble.

Actually, our preliminary research suggested that the political turmoil of this region was just as severe as the geographic violence.

We landed and in due course were ensconced in an office complex very like the one we had left in Scow. Dessa was not the largest city in Kraine, or even the third largest, but it did have most of a million residents and was important as a port. During System War One it had been occupied by five or six conflicting forces in succession; in System War Two it had suffered a quarter million casualties by massacre or deportation. Yet there was no sign of those past ravages now; it was a busy and seemingly prosperous city.

Within a day I had my interview with the Party official in charge here. I was sure he would never have agreed to see me if I hadn't come with the highest recommendation; as it was, he was unable to refuse, lest he be summarily removed from office. At this point I no longer remember his name, and in any event it's not important; I will simply call him Comrade Ivan, and re-create the essence of our conversation as accurately as is feasible.

Ivan was the ranking person in Kraine, and could have resided in the capital city, but preferred this port city. He curtly presented the statistics of trade and output, showing how things had improved recently and how quotas were being fulfilled. It looked good enough on the surface—but I had done my homework. "This fifty million tons of wheat," I inquired. "Is this export or import?"

He frowned. "Import," he said somewhat reluctantly. "We are the chief port city for this region, and do much business with other planets."

"But shouldn't the USR be a net exporter of grain?" I asked.

He harrumphed. "Well, in the majority of years it is, and of course Kraine itself has generated a surplus. But we got a very good price—"

"A surplus for the USR as a whole?"

"For Kraine. We supply grain to other—"

"Because Kraine is the major harvest region of this planet," I said. "Why, then, are you importing grain on such a scale?"

"There have been adverse conditions recently," he admitted. "But our five-year plan—"

"Is running calamitously below expectation," I said. "The fact is, Ivan, your administration is a disaster."

"Not mine!" he cried. "I do not make policy! I only follow directives. I am doing as well as is possible in my circumstance."

My reading of him confirmed his belief in this. He was basically a good man, a Party appointee but not stupid. He had to defend the status quo, because he would be removed if he did not, but he was really not to blame for its shortcomings. This was why I had selected him for my first approach, though he was not the ranking official of the Party structure, merely of this region.

"Ivan, I have been assigned the task of doubling the wheat harvest in two years," I said.

He choked, trying not to laugh. "Best of fortune, Comrade Tyrant!" he wheezed.

"I do not intend to rely on fortune, Comrade. I intend to deliver."

He shook his head. "The legends of the Tyrant of Jupiter are great indeed! But this is not Jupiter. There are elements here that will foil any attempt to—"

"What elements?" I asked sharply.

He became nervous. "Merely factors that—"

"Listen, Ivan, I am not any secret agent of the Party attempting to trap you into an unpatriotic utterance. I am the Tyrant, acting under direct authority of Chairman Khukov. I rank you, and I mean to have your complete cooperation. Do you need time to verify this?"

"No, Comrade Tyrant," he said grimly.

"Then tell me directly what you deem to be the prime causes of the underperformance of this region with regard to farming. I will not condemn you for those."

He grimaced. "Tyrant, you can have me removed from office now, but after you depart, there will be other influences. You put me in a very difficult position."

I had encountered this sort of thing when tackling the Pirates of the Belt. Those who supported me did not dare to do so openly, because they would be killed after I left. I had handled that by eradicating the enemy pirates.

"I will protect you from those other influences," I said.

"This is impossible, Comrade! They—"

"Such as the nomenklatura. When I depart this region, none will remain in power."

Ivan was shaken. "You can do that?"

"That is what I came to do."

He stared at me. "The harvest—is only a ruse?"

"I intend to do that too. The two go together."

He shook his head again. "If any other person said that, I would deem him insane!"

"Do you remember Big Iron of Jupiter?" I had destroyed the power of the iron cartels by executing all their executives. I do not look back on that episode with particular pride; it was a function of my madness following the death of my closest secretary, Shelia. But it was a useful reference for those who doubted the resolve of the Tyrant.

He gulped. "I remember."

"I will protect you," I repeated.

And so Ivan told me what I needed to know: the names of all those Party officials who stood foursquare against progress and efficiency. This confirmed the list I had worked out in the course of our research, and fleshed it out. These men had to go.

"But I must act at the proper time," I said. "Do not repeat this dialogue to anyone in the interim."

"Comrade Tyrant, you may be certain I will not!" he agreed.

He also told me of the rampant inefficiency and lack of motivation among the workers. "They could do better work if they wanted to," he said. "But they have no desire. They sneak as much of the harvest as they can to the black market, and seem to take perverse pride in wasting much of the rest."

"Why should this be?" I asked, as if I had no idea.

"I think it is historical," he said. "Kraine has always wanted to be independent but has constantly been besieged by foreign powers. It never asked to be part of the Saturnine Union; it had no choice. After System War One, when the Uranians battled the Bolsheviks, Kraine declared its independence. But the foreign armies overwhelmed it, and after three years of war in Krainian territory there was massive famine. Five million Kranian people may have starved. After that came the forced collectivization; thousands of peasants were killed resisting it, and millions lost their holdings. Is it any wonder their sons still smolder under this yoke? They have only enmity toward the power that disenfranchised them."

I nodded. "In Jupiter we have free enterprise."

"We had it here, once. But today all must work for the benefit of the state—except the nomenklatura, who work only for themselves."

"And who therefore are the most dedicated to their cause," I agreed. "But suppose I restored free enterprise to Kraine?"

"This is Saturn, not Jupiter!" he repeated. "The entire philosophy differs."

"I am not sure the philosophy counts as heavily as the reality. Suppose we called it progressive socialism. Could you administer such a program?"

Ivan spread his hands. "I would try."

I went out to a collective farm bubble and talked with the supervisors and the peasants. I could see that they lacked motivation.

I spent two weeks going from city to city and from farm to farm, meeting the people, talking with them, not so much to gain new information as to establish my presence, so that they would believe me when I addressed them by holo. The Tyrant of Jupiter was here in Kraine, deposed and exiled from his own planet, but determined to improve the harvest here. I knew the word was circulating throughout the region. They knew of, and generally respected, what I had done on Jupiter, and they understood that there had been no war with Saturn in that period. Could the Tyrant do anything for them? So by the time I was ready to make my mass address, they were ready to listen.

Then I spoke. First I clarified my mission: to double the harvest. "Chairman Khukov has given me complete authority to do what is necessary to accomplish this. I believe that the workers of Kraine are capable of it; all you need is fair administration, and reason to do your best. I will give you fair administration—but first it is necessary

to clean out the bad element. I hereby declare the entire
political hierarchy of Kraine to be abolished, its members
placed in protective custody until they are able to arrange
their departure from this republic."

The feedback monitors showed a sea of blank faces.
They could hardly grasp what I was saying; they wondered if it were a joke. Then the military personnel I had
arranged to alert swung into action. Every member of the
nomenklatura in the entire region of Kraine was politely
apprehended. The cameras showed the complete astonishment of these officials; they had had no warning.

Ivan himself was arrested and brought to me. He alone
had known of this. On camera, I asked him: "Comrade
Ivan, do you understand that your power has been dissolved, and that of all in your administration?"

"Preposterous!" he spluttered.

"Take him away," I said.

The men escorted him away. This was part of my promise to him: He had cooperated fully, and now I was protecting him by making an example of him. None of the
nomenklatura would seek revenge against him, because
he was obviously as much a victim as they. But he would
be reassigned to an equivalent post elsewhere, where he
would administer a similar brand of progressive socialism, as would others of the deposed staff, as warranted. I
had all their names, thanks to Ivan's information. The
majority would be less kindly treated; they would be in-
corporated into the working force at low levels and barred
from administrative positions. This was the first abrupt
step in the disenfranchisement of the most powerful class
in the Union of Saturnine Republics. I was commencing
the hatchet job for Khukov.

"Now we shall establish the good element," I continued, as if this audacious and amazing act were routine.
"Each collective farm bubble will hold an election to
choose representatives to come to me in the next few days.
From these I will choose new administrators. Their job
will be to facilitate production by any reasonable means,
and to distribute the rewards for success." I smiled, seeing
more blank faces on the monitors. "We are instituting
what I term progressive socialism. I do not question the

validity of your political or economic system; I am merely amending it slightly. There will now be direct material rewards for every bubble that improves its performance over that of the past season: special privileges and higher pay for every worker in it. The bubble that improves the most will receive additional rewards. And the region that shows the most sustained improvement over the coming years will have the first choice of the Dream."

Then I told them of the Dream of galactic colonization. "The technology has not yet been properly tested," I cautioned them. "But Chairman Khukov is working on it, and in two years there will be a practical test. If this is successful, he will proceed to the major project—and if Kraine has contributed significantly to this by providing the rich harvests needed to support such an effort, Kraine will have the chance to colonize a complete new planet elsewhere in the galaxy, and the leading bubble will have the first choice of location on that planet."

I continued, clarifying it for them, but that was the essence. They might not believe me immediately, but what I said was to be confirmed by Chairman Khukov, and then the belief would come. The broadcast was limited to Kraine, but of course the news would leak out, and then the rest of Saturn, and indeed the rest of the Solar System, would quicken with interest.

Of course this is simplified; the neglect and mismanagement of centuries is not reversed by a single speech. My address was mostly a statement of intent. What counted was the follow-through, and Spirit handled that. As always, I was the figurehead, she the reality. She had long experience in Jupiter government, and before that in the Jupiter Navy, organizing chains of command and implementing effective programs. We had already formed a nucleus of solidly committed personnel to operate the new system. The new people sent by the collective farms would come first to me for screening; that was my talent, and while I do not disparage it, I have always been aware that superior personnel are only part of the total picture. I would weed out the unfit, and the fit would be organized and trained to run the program.

There was also the matter of prices and taxes. Prices

had been kept artificially low, for the benefit of the con-
sumers but that had made it uneconomical for those independent farmers who remained. Taxes on these were
high, helping to complete the disincentive. I had made a
forceful case to Ivan, and to Khukov, and gained their
reluctant acquiescence: a freer market, without artificial
pricing, and nominal rather than punitive taxation. We
wanted to make it pay to farm.

We expected to take a loss the first season, as the re-
organization was accomplished. We hoped to regain the
prior level of production the next season, completing the
year on an even keel. Here there were two seasons in a
year. We can get three at Jupiter, and more in the inner
planets, but Saturn is so much farther out than Jupiter
that the light from the sun is only about one quarter as
intense, or something like a hundredth the intensity of
the light at Earth's distance; I misremember the exact
figure. This means that the light-focusing lenses have to
be relatively enormous, and even so the season is shorter.
Saturn, in just about every significant respect, is a more
formidable planet to live with than is Jupiter. Perhaps
that is just as well, for it helps prevent its regressive political system from dominating humanity.

But we were surprised. We were not imposing masked
free enterprise on a population that rejected it; rather, we
were restoring it to a population that had always desired
it. The peasants were eager for greater self-determination
and for the rewards of their own efforts, and once they
understood that my changes were serious, and that the
dread secret police had been instructed to ferret out the
remnants of the restrictive order and not to bother the
enterprising peasants, they got into it with a will. There
must have been an appalling level of cheating at all levels, because the first season showed a fifteen percent improvement in the harvest, and the second season jumped
another thirty-five percent, with every sign of further im-
provements to come. We did indeed double the harvest in
two years—a feat I really hadn't expected to accomplish.
Our real objective, remember, had been to eliminate the
nomenklatura; the harvest had been mostly the pretext.
Perhaps I should have been less cynical about my own

words; the citizens of Kraine evidently took them seriously, and made that aspect of the Dream come true. Kraine was never my homeland, but in retrospect I feel as though it could have been, and I would not mind retiring there.

Dear Daddy,

You have some nerve, asking Megan for a woman! I mean, of course you always have women, everybody knows that, but you don't have to rub Mother's nose in it, do you? Oh, well, you are what you are, and this is just to let you know she's doing it. I told her she should send you a wench from the Navy Tail, someone with about thirty years' experience and warts on her bottom, but she just smiled and said she thought she could do better than that. I thought you had a sexy Saturnine secretary, anyway; don't tell me you don't know what to do with her!

Oh, well, I suppose I'm just out of sorts because Megan stepped down, and the special elections are done, and now we have a representative democracy again and it's so darned dull. Not like all that activity in Saturn! You fired all the bosses in Kraine? It's a wonder you didn't get assassinated on the spot! Oh, that's not funny, I shouldn't joke about it. But do try to stay out of trouble, Daddy; I'd hate it if anything should happen to you, even if you can't keep your hands off all those women.

Robertico sends his love. He says he wants to grow up to be just like you. That shows all the sense *he* has!

Chapter 5

SMILO

But we did not remain in Kraine. Once we had set the reforms in motion and assigned the top personnel, we left it to them to follow through. This might seem careless, but the fact is that once I have selected competent and honest personnel, and once Spirit has organized a system for them, very little further attention is required. A competently managed hierarchical system can take care of itself. In fact, even an incompetent bureaucracy can hang on tenaciously, as the nomenklatura showed, or the prior "good-old-boy" network I had rousted from Jupiter. We went on to the industrial sector, which was almost as fouled up as the farm sector. Saturn had raw resources that rivaled those of Jupiter, but squandered them through inefficiency and corruption. Having shown how to realign the farm, we now had to do the same for the shop.

We hit the research tapes again. Theoretically the capacity of the mind does not diminish with age, but I felt my years here as I wrestled with metric equivalents I had not used since my youth. The metric system is superior to the hodgepodge used in Jupiter, but one remains most comfortable with what one is most familiar with. We reviewed the dossiers on the top personnel, looking not so much at the nomenklatura, whom we knew had to be removed, but at the ranking technicians and engineers, who knew their fields but could not make policy. This promised to be a tougher challenge than the farm had been.

We traveled a lot, for key elements of industry were spread across the planet, and a number were in orbit in space. Saturn had an excellent ferrous base, with many iron mines in the turbulent atmosphere of the Ural current, and iron-processing plants in that vicinity. Unlike Jupiter, Saturn was self-sufficient in this vital resource, but managed it so poorly that it was on the verge of becoming a net importer. That caused Khukov to grind his teeth, as I could readily understand. The situation was similar with the nonferrous metals; a great deal of gold was processed, and this was vital for the purchase of supplies such as wheat, but the gold mines were mostly in the inhospitable Siberian bands, where few people settled voluntarily. We would try to motivate these workers as we had the farmers, but our chance of success was smaller.

Actually, this assignment was a compliment. Khukov had said he would handle the scientific matters if I handled the political ones, but with the evident success of Kraine, he decided that the two should not be separated. He concentrated on holding his power, and provided me the maximum support. This might seem like a strange arrangement, but Khukov and I understood each other. I was becoming very like his executive officer—and of course Spirit was mine.

Meanwhile, there were other problems. One of them was Tasha: I still wanted her. My message to Megan had been acknowledged, but action on that would take months, if only because of the travel time between Jupiter and Saturn, and I was not geared to wait that long. As I explained, I have always preferred known women to unknown ones; when I was in the Jupiter Navy I got myself qualified for a female roommate at my earliest opportunity, so as not to be dependent on the anonymous Tail. I maintained continuing relationships with my Navy wives long after our sexual contact had abated. Perhaps it is a function of my talent: I learn to know women well, and I *need* to know them well. I say it as shouldn't: Women are more than sexual objects.

I worked with Tasha every day, and she was a good secretary and a good woman. She didn't know she was a mole. She continued to flash her anatomy at me in off moments, never realizing that her buried alternate personality made a mockery of such inclination. How I wished I could oblige her, without invoking the assassin!

But I knew I could not. Therefore my fascination with her was idiocy—yet it remained.

"What am I to do?" I asked Spirit privately. "I desire that woman, and have no acceptable alternative. I do not want to rape her, yet if I approach her normally . . ."

Spirit sighed. "Then you will have to get into bondage. Tell her it's a game. Maybe she will go along."

"Bondage," I repeated, exploring the implications. "Maybe it would work."

"Oh, it will work, if you're careful. But you may not enjoy it."

"That is a risk I'll have to take. But I want you on hand, in case—"

"I understand." Indeed she did.

So, when Spirit was nominally out but actually nearby, I approached Tasha again. "I desire you," I told her directly.

"And I desire you, Tyrant," she replied. "I thought you would never notice."

"But my tastes are perhaps not what you would consider normal. I have hesitated, for that reason. I would not want to cause you distress."

"Oh? How would that be?"

"It is a matter of fantasy," I explained. "I have in my days possessed many women, but each is unique to herself. I must be with a given woman the way I see her—and I see you as a ravished captive princess."

"That does not sound bad," she protested.

"But the princess is bound. She is helpless to resist her captor, however much she might wish to."

"But I would not resist you, Tyrant! I think you are still more of a man than those young ones."

I enjoy such flattery, however insincere—but actually she was not insincere. It was part of her job description to try to seduce me, but she had indeed come to appreciate my qualities.

"Then you would not object to—?"

She held out her two hands. "Bind me," she said.

I took her at her word. I put her hands up behind her head and tied them so that she could not free them. Then I stripped her as well as I could—some apparel simply hung up near her head and had to be left—and put her on the bed. I tied her two feet to the posts, so that her legs were apart. "Can you break free of that?" I inquired.

She struggled briefly. "No. The cord hurts when I try."

"Then the monster shall have at you, wench!" I exclaimed, tearing off my own clothing. Indeed, this business had excited me; perhaps I had more of a taste for bondage than I had suspected. But I think it was mostly that she was a lovely young woman whom I did desire, and she was now exposed quite effectively. Any attractive woman, laid out like that, would turn on any normal man; bondage did not have to be an aspect of it. At least, so I prefer to believe.

I got on her and into her—and abruptly her personality changed. I was watching for it this time, fascinated by this as much as by the sex itself. She tried to reach for my neck, but could not, and tried to bring up her knees, but could not. "What's this?" she spat.

"This is known as consenting sex," I replied, thrusting deeply.

"I'm tied!" she exclaimed indignantly. Evidently she had no memory of the activities of her normal self.

"Why, so you are," I agreed, changing my position enough to nuzzle her right breast.

Her torso bucked. The breast slammed into my face, but of course a weapon like that could do no harm. "I'm glad to have you responding so well," I said, licking her nipple.

She made a sound like an attacking pig, an ugly squeal, and wrenched her nether section violently about. This had the effect of hastening my climax. "Thank you!" I gasped amidst it.

She snapped at my face, but, alert for this, I held my head away and completed my enjoyment of her body.

"I'll kill you!" she hissed.

"With kindness, perhaps," I said, pausing to savor her breast one last time. Then I dismounted. "Thank you for a unique experience."

She spat at me, literally, but even that missed.

The irony was that I really had enjoyed it, more than I felt comfortable with. I do not like to think that there

is any significant sadistic component to my enjoyment of
a woman's body, but perhaps there is. At any rate, I had
possessed Tasha again, in the only way I safely could.

I cleaned up and dressed, uncertain when it was safe
to untie her. But when she saw me clothed, her nature
changed; I could read it immediately. "Aren't you going
to do it?" she asked.

I doubted that I was capable of doing it again at this
time, to my regret; age had slowed my performance more
than my desire. But before I released her, I experimented.
I sat beside her on the bed and ran my hands over her
body, savoring its charms. I kissed her bosom. She did not
change; apparently only penetration itself invoked her demon identity. That was good to know; it should be safe to
kiss her in the future, and to indulge myself in other ways
with her, so long as I avoided that particular action. I
would have to verify that, in due course.

"I think I am older than I believed," I said regretfully.
"You are beautiful, but perhaps another day?"

She shrugged as well as she could in her bonds. "I am
disappointed, of course. But I understand."

Certainly I hoped that was untrue! I wondered what
she would conclude when she cleaned up and discovered
that more had occurred than she remembered. Probably
that, too, would be blotted out of her consciousness, as it
had been before.

"Perhaps if I tied you instead?" she suggested.

"Not while I live!" I said, smiling, as I untied her. For
surely I would not survive the experience. Why, then, did
that, too, tempt me?

This project entailed a lot of traveling. We rode the
Trans-Berian Railroad from Skva to Vostok, stopping at
the industrial cities along the way, surveying a situation
that was an ongoing disaster. Spirit developed a competent staff of Saturnians I had interviewed and cleared;
many of them spoke English, but she labored to learn
Russian so as not to have to depend on translators for
sensitive or complex arrangements. Tasha was increasingly useful to her, serving as a language teacher, and I
was glad we had elected to keep her. I think, in her nor-

mal state, Tasha was even developing some enthusiasm for the job we were doing; it was clear that we were instituting reforms whose time was long overdue.

I have described our general approach in the Kraine episode, so will bypass the details of our subsequent campaigns. What stand out in my memory are the personal events. But they do relate to the larger mission, so perhaps they are not irrelevant. As with the programs on Jupiter, they tended to assume lives of their own after we initiated them, and my direct participation became unnecessary.

We had skunked the nomenklatura in Kraine, but the power of that class was by no means broken, or even seriously compromised. The nomens had seen me as a threat and had tried to assassinate me twice: in space as I approached Saturn, and through my secretary Tasha. My action in Kraine had, in a manner, been my counterstrike. Now they understood my power and realized that I was much more of a threat than they had supposed. What had been an incidental effort to eliminate me now became more determined. I was fortunate that they did not control the more effective mechanisms of Saturnian policy, such as the Spetsnaz; otherwise I would have been in far more direct peril.

They still could not be obvious, because any direct opposition to Khukov's directives—which included the whole of my own efforts—could result in their elimination as a subversive element. Thus there were no direct laser-shots taken at me, or bombs planted in my luggage. But the subtle approach turned out to be just about as deadly, and for a time we were in doubt about survival.

The first occurred near the bubble-city of Lovsk, in the heart of the iron region. I had taken a bubble car to drive out to one of the steelworks, with a reliable driver. Spirit was busy with the paperwork; I was really on a spot factfinding mission for her.

The currents can be rough around the mountains. The Urals are not the fiercest obstructions on Saturn, despite the deep metals churned up there; the ranges near the swift equator are far worse. But they were quite enough for me in the tiny car! I had to fight to avoid becoming motion-sick. My driver, evidently acclimatized to this, navigated the throes of the highway with a certain grim enjoyment, almost as if waiting for me to demonstrate my inferiority by grabbing for the barf bag. Give me a nice, straightforward battle in space, any day!

Then the driver frowned, glancing at his instruments. "Pressure rising," he muttered in Russian.

I felt a claustrophobic chill. "Routine?"

"*Nyet.*"

He hit the Mayday button, and our distress signal was broadcast. The Saturn bubbles were sturdy, for the ambient pressure was over eight bars, or eight times Earth-normal. But that sturdiness went for nothing if there was a leak.

Now I felt the increase, or imagined I did. "Can we make it to shelter in time?"

"Have to," he grunted. But he did not look at all certain.

"Pinhole leak?" I asked.

He nodded a grim affirmative. That was about all it could be, to account for the slow increase. Bubblene was tough stuff, about as tough as existed, but sometimes it was flawed, and a leak could develop. Once started, the leak would inevitably increase. The increase could become explosive—or more properly, implosive. Then we would be crushed by the horrendous external pressure.

"Must plug it," I said.

"Can't hold out eight bars!" he muttered fatalistically.

I suppose he was a typical Saturnine, resigned to the outrages of fortune. I was not. "Can if we spot the leak in time," I said.

I cast about for a mechanism. Here the driver helped. "Got a pipe," he said.

"A what?"

He brought it out. "Bacco. Smoke it sometimes."

Oh—one of the containers of pseudo tobacco. Some folk still used the stuff, igniting it and sucking in the vapors through a tube below the container. This habit had once been quite widespread, but the deleterious effects it had on the human body caused it to be outlawed several centuries ago. Today the only remnant of it was the harmless imitation. But this had one immediate advantage, in this crisis: It generated a minute quantity of smoke.

He filled and lit his pipe, puffed on it, and held it before him. A curl of smoke wafted up from it.

He moved it slowly about, the smoke following. The process was infuriatingly slow, in the fractional gee used to make the car float, but this was all we had.

When he held the pipe low, we got a deviation. "Draft," he said.

"You trace it down; I'll get a tool!" I said. I cast about for something suitable. If this had been space, there would have been a repair kit with hull patches. But this was not space, and no ordinary hull patch could withstand eight bars.

"Toolkit in back," the man said as he oriented on the slight draft.

I scrambled back and found it. It was a shoemaker's outfit, with a hammer and stapler and awl. Evidently the folk here were strong on hand trades, as perhaps they had to be to make up for the interminable delays and inordinate expense of necessary articles. But this car was no shoe!

"Found it," the driver said. He was down on the floor now, and the pipe smoke was swirling violently. There was a leak, all right.

If only I had something to plug it! But shoe cement would never hold, and I couldn't hammer in a staple.

Then I perceived the obvious. The awl! It was a slender rod of metal, almost needle-thin, with a rounded plastic ball on the end. That was exactly what I needed!

I grabbed it and joined the driver on the floor. Now I could hear it: the faint hiss of atmosphere pressuring in. Eight bars outside, one bar inside; it would keep coming until the pressure equalized. But an awl, normally used to punch holes in leather, could put a lot of pressure on a small point. More than eight bars' worth.

I set the point, then pressed it into the tiny hole. If this worked, we would have it plugged; if instead it aggravated the leak, we would be dead that much sooner.

It worked. The leak stopped. I had, as it were, my finger in the dike.

"Drive on," I said, with affected casualness.

He hastened to oblige.

We made it to the steelworks. Then I was able to relax, my hands shaking. It was a little thing I had done, but if it hadn't worked my life would have been forfeit.

The personnel of the steelworks inspected the bubble, using their equipment. The leak appeared to be artificial: a tiny hole drilled to intersect a natural flaw, so that the stress of travel could cause the flaw to give way and amplify the leak. Had I not plugged it, the aggravation of the leak could have eliminated the traces of the tampering. My death would have been judged to be an accident, an act of fate.

I proceeded with the tour of inspection, asking questions, making notes, interviewing personnel. But my mind was distracted by the event of the leak: It had been another effort to assassinate me. I don't think a person ever becomes completely inured to such efforts.

A few days later, without warning, I suffered stomach cramps. "Poison!" I exclaimed, then wondered if I was being paranoid. It was probably only a bout of indigestion.

But Tasha insisted on rushing me to the hospital, and I was too sick to protest. The doctor checked me, ran a quick test, and nodded. "Contaminated yeast," he said. "Medication will nullify it."

"This happens often?" I asked.

"The spores mutate, in the uncontrolled conditions of the atmosphere; our quality control is not as apt as Jupiter's," he said. Saturn, of course, was using the supplementary yeast-farming system I had helped develop on Jupiter, in which the spores were cultivated in the atmosphere itself and harvested as convenient. This had solved Jupiter's food problem, and presumably would solve Saturn's, once the special problems of its environment were dealt with. Obviously those problems had not yet yielded!

I took the initial dose of medication at the hospital and was given supplementary pills of another kind to take at regular intervals. It seemed that the contamination was active, and tough, as it had to be to survive the radical exterior environment, so that an extended period of medication was necessary to make certain it was expunged from the human system. Fortunately the Saturn medical establishment was competent; I should be in no further trouble.

Except that I did have further trouble. My cramps returned worse than ever after I started on the refill prescription. I was promptly back at the hospital for treatment.

"What's this?" the doctor demanded, appalled. "This is not the prescription!"

He had it analyzed, and it turned out to be concentrated contamination of exactly the kind I had suffered from before.

The pills had been exchanged for more poison. It turned out that the pharmacy was not at fault; its product had been eliminated, and the poison substituted, somewhere between the filling of the prescription and its delivery to me. Conditions were crowded; a number of people could have had access to the collected prescriptions in the interim. The culprit could not be identified.

But we knew. The nomenklatura had struck again. Like a nebulous ghost, it had waited and watched, and found a way to make another attempt on me that would, if successful, seem like a mere flare-up of the original malady. Inadequate medication would be blamed. But thanks to the promptness of Tasha's reaction, and the competence of the doctor, that had been foiled. There was nothing inadequate about the socialized medicine of Saturn!

Nevertheless, I had had a bad double dose of an extremely ornery contaminant, and harm had been done. It was, the doctor warned, too early to be sure of the full extent of it, but certainly I had suffered some liver and kidney damage. Since the liver could regenerate, and the kidneys had enormous overcapacity, I was probably all right, but he urged me to report back regularly for retesting. I, however, was developing an aversion to hospitals and intended to ignore this advice. And so I did. In retrospect I see this as one of the major follies of my life.

I suppose I thought the Tyrant was indestructible. Nature has her way of educating idiots like me.

We remained on guard, but already there had been too many close calls. We had to abolish the nomenklatura before it abolished us! But we had to proceed in proper order, or all would be for nothing.

So we proceeded, warily. We were assembling a comprehensive list of personnel to be eliminated, and a similar list of those to be promoted. Under competent and motivated management, Saturn's industry would improve; I was sure of that. But it had a long way to go, for aside from the military complex, it was in an abysmal state. I wished we could import a few thousand technical supervisors from Jupiter.

One problem was theft, and another was sabotage. Much of this might be because of disaffected workers. Proper motivation should help, but until we could set our program in motion, key installations had to be protected. But even the police were not to be completely trusted; some crimes were evidently committed despite the knowledge of the guards. How could we eliminate this complication?

In Jupiter we would have gone to technology, setting up laser perimeters that would detect and foil any unauthorized intrusions. But Saturn lacked that kind of technology in the civilian sector. We needed something considerably more primitive, but just as effective.

"Animals," Spirit said.

As it happened, Saturn had been doing research on animals. In Sibirsk there was a massive project dedicated to the reconstitution of primitive species. We were sure this would not be altruistic; there was bound to be some militaristic motive. So we inquired, and in due course managed to cut through the bureaucratic resistance and arrange an inspection.

We visited. The complex was in its own bubble, separate from the city and restricted; even the local residents hardly knew what went on there.

It turned out that they meant the appellation "primitive" literally. They were using gene-splicing techniques to breed back extinct species, some of which were prime prospects for guard duty.

They had, it seemed, made progress toward the recovery of Earth's Pleistocene mammals. *Equus*, the ancestral horse, had a range within this bubble; Spirit, with a woman's fascination with horses, wanted to see that. I wanted to see *Amphicyon*, the huge ancestral dog. It was an irony that contemporary horses and dogs were rare today, because of the wasteful expense of maintaining them in space, but the more primitive variants were being bred in the name of research and defense.

We had the tour. The interior of the bubble was like a monstrous zoo, with many layers of exhibits and many more of laboratories and storage facilities. The outer levels had vast fields planted with special high-gee-tolerant grasses and shrubs, to be grown and harvested for the grazers. The ceilings were huge day-glow panels, emulating the course of natural sunlight, cloud, and night.

"But I thought the stress was on guard animals," I said innocently. "Surely hay-eaters aren't—?"

The guide smiled. "Some of the grazers are quite competent guards," he said. "There are aggressive horned species that can stand up to almost any predator, such as *Bison crassiocornis*. But it is true they are not the best guard animals, because of their need for constant grazing, and their manure. Our herbivores are grown mainly as prey for the carnivores."

"Oh," I said, disgruntled. Of course the true predators would need food, and if they were to be truly lean and vicious, they had to hunt it for themselves. Survival of the fittest: never a pretty business.

We went to the upper levels, where the gee reduced toward Earth-norm. We did indeed see the primitive horses, right back to *Merychippes* and *Mesohippus*, the dog-sized, three-toed version of the Oligocene epoch. It was strange to see such a horselike creature so small.

And we saw the canines I had come for. There was *Canis dirus*, a primitive wolf, and of course *Amphicyon*, the primitive dog that surely was the wolf's match. There was the Eocene's *Mesonyx*, perhaps the earliest canine, though the line can be hard to draw. "How are they for guard duty?" I inquired.

"There are some problems," the guide confessed. "The primitives are less intelligent than the moderns, and their pack instincts less developed, which means that they are slower to accept the principle of mastery. The truth is, the modern breeds remain the best guards."

"But you don't breed superior modern canines?" I asked.

"We breed only the types specified," he said.

I exchanged a glance with Spirit. Here too, the no-menklatura dominated, seeing to it that no project become too efficient in the pursuit of its objective. That would shortly change.

We continued to the upper reaches, where gee was less. Here there were enormous and high chambers, reaching to the center of the bubble. These were for the flying creatures.

We gaped, for there in the air was an impossibly monstrous bird, reminiscent of the fabled roc. *"Teratornis,"* the guide said. "The largest flying bird ever to exist. It has a wingspan of twelve feet. But it is a carrion-eater, not a hunter, and cannot operate in confined quarters; it remains a novelty."

"Flying bird," Spirit said. "There were larger land-bound birds?"

"Oh, certainly." The guide showed us to a closed-off chamber, where a bird taller than a man stood. *"Diatryma,* seven feet tall when he stands up straight, a ferocious predator on small mammals." We looked at the massively muscled legs and the huge claws and monstrous beak, and agreed that small mammals would have been in trouble, and perhaps some larger ones. "But the birds, as a general rule, aren't smart," the guide continued. "They can be trained only marginally—and again, the modern ones are superior to the primitives."

We started down, to the far sides of levels we had ascended before. We saw the huge Miocene pig *Dinohyus,* as tall as a man and almost as massive as a hippopotamus, the largest of land-dwelling swine. "Now, pigs," I said. "They are relatively intelligent, aren't they? And with tusks—"

"They may be our best prospect," the guide agreed. "The appropriate breeds can be tamed and housebroken, yet remain effective fighters. Of course, again—"

"The moderns are better than the ancients," I concluded. We certainly knew the direction to encourage future research.

We came to the section devoted to the felines. "In many respects, the cats are our most effective present product," the guide said. "They are unmatched as individual predators, on a pound-for-pound basis, and their natural preference for lurking and pouncing enables them to surprise intruders that would avoid running dogs." He smiled faintly, for the term "running dogs" remained a popular disparagement in Saturnine circles. "However, they have a tendency to revert to wild behavior, and that can be awkward for the proprietors as well as the intruders."

I nodded. Even small cats could be wild, and large ones could be savage. The felines were more independent than the canines, a quality I respected, but an organized society had diminishing use for independence. The Saturn philosophy found it easier to embrace the somewhat slavish, lick-master's-hand attitude of the dogs than the bug-me-and-I'll-scratch one of cats.

"Don't you have ways to differentiate the friends from the enemies?" Spirit asked. "A cat doesn't have to be friendly, if it knows whom to obey and whom to attack."

"We are working with smell," the guide said. "The cats tend to go into a killing frenzy when they detect certain odors, while other smells tend to pacify them." He stopped at a box mounted on the wall and opened it. "Here, for example, is the pacification odor. We keep it strategically placed, in case of emergency. Unfortunately, it has an unpredictable effect on some felines, and of course intruders could use it also. So we prefer to seek other mechanisms." He handed me a sample tube. "You can test this on one of the caged animals, if you wish."

I took the tube. "Let's complete the formal tour first."

"However, we do have some prospects with the weasels

and ferrets," the guide said, showing the way to the next complex of chambers.

Suddenly an alarm sounded. The guide glanced nervously about. "That means an emergency," he said. "An animal must have escaped. We had better get to a safety chamber. There's one in the ferret complex."

But before we could get there, the chamber door behind us burst open and a monster appeared. It was catlike, but larger than any tiger, with two six-inch fangs.

"*Smilodon!*" the guide cried in horror. "That one was due to be destroyed!"

Indeed, it was the dread saber-toothed tiger—right in the hall with us. It paused, recovering its balance, orienting on us. It growled with a certain anticipation.

We were too far from the exit to reach it before the horrendous cat could catch us. Someone was bound to become its prey. It was clear that a single stab with those fangs could kill a man.

"This chamber is empty," the guard whispered, grasping the handle of a door behind us. "We can shut it in the hall—"

He opened the door, and we scrambled through: Spirit, the guide, Tasha, and me. But before the guide could secure the door, the tiger smashed into it. The guide was knocked aside, stunned. Tasha screamed.

Spirit's laser pistol was in her hand, bearing on the tiger. "Don't fire," I protested. "We have the pacifier!"

Spirit held her fire. This was a combat situation, and she and I were versed in combat. We never acted carelessly when lives were at stake.

I opened the tube and quickly smeared its foam on me. Now I was protected. I had no weapon, but hoped I needed none.

I approached the tiger, trying to put myself between him and the other three people. "Take it easy, Smilodon," I said, extending my odor-covered hand.

The tiger sniffed. Then he sneezed. Then he growled.

"He's reacting wrongly," the guide exclaimed. "He's one of the exceptions! It's maddening him!"

Evidently so! But it was too late for me to unsmear myself. I backed away—and the tiger strode forward. He opened his mouth, and his jaws gaped to almost a full right-angle aperture. Those tusks now pointed right at me!

I knew I could not escape this beast; the cat seemed to weigh close to a thousand pounds, and was hugely muscled, with stout yet sharp claws. The supreme predator! How on Earth had it ever come to be extinct? Perhaps it had consumed all its prey and had none left!

I knew I was in extreme peril, but I didn't want to kill that animal. I had never seen such a superb example of survival fitness, and that appealed to me on a special level. But if the tiger sprang, Spirit's laser would catch it before it landed; she would not let me be killed, and her aim had always been perfect. I had to find some other way to pacify this creature.

The odd thing was, I thought I understood him. I felt almost an empathy with the tiger, who had broken from his cage or confinement before being killed in the name of a failed experiment. I was the Tyrant, another type of failed experiment. Lord of the jungle, lord of a planet, deposed—what was the essential distinction? Smilodon was alive beyond his time, and so was I.

I focused my talent, trying to comprehend the reality of this superb creature, not merely the illusion. Did the tiger really want prey—or did he want freedom?

He wanted, I decided, neither. He wanted acceptance. That would encompass freedom. This was not his world, and he understood that; he could not survive alone, here. The only place he could hunt naturally was in a bubble chamber, when some frightened animal was loosed to him. A stupid tiger might settle for that, but not a smart one.

A smart tiger—that was what made this one adverse. He rebelled against the confinement of plastic walls, but also against that of tailored odors. He knew that the smell was not the essence. Since his brain was wired into smell far more than was a man's, that was a considerable revelation, but he had accomplished it.

"Tiger, tiger," I breathed. "I know you. I respect you. Come to me as friend, not as prey." My words were not what counted; rather it was the sound of my voice, and the motion of my body. I had no remaining fear of this creature, and not because of Spirit's laser; I understood Tyrants of any stripe. My talent was working, causing me to react in subtle ways that few other people comprehended, returning encouraging signals to the tiger.

The Smilodon was perplexed, discovering in me something unanticipated. I continued to respond to his reactions, reinforcing those I deemed desirable, dissipating those I did not approve. It was the same way I interacted with human beings, that enabled me to judge them and trust them. It was more difficult with this animal, because I was not attuned to animals, especially not prehistoric tigers, but the principle was the same. I could come to know a person well enough in just a few minutes to account for a certainty that others might require years to master. That was why I always interviewed the key personnel of a new enterprise, and why my enterprises always worked well. So now I was relating to this magnificent animal in the same way, and if I were successful I would have a rather special friend.

The tiger stood and watched me, his ire turning to curiosity and then to interest. Slowly I approached him, doing what I supposed could be called a kind of dance, though there was no set footwork or body motion to it. It was all response and counterresponse, body signal built on signal, hint and suggestion and agreement. The tiger could have bashed me to the ground with one swipe of his massive paw, or chomped me before Spirit's laser could be effective, but the developing understanding that I offered prevented him from doing so. It was as though he had spent his lifetime among those who spoke an incomprehensible foreign language, and abruptly had discovered someone who spoke his own, however haltingly. Naturally he listened!

I cannot properly describe all that passed between us, for that was in archaic tiger signals, while this is in contemporary English, with much of the dialogue translated from Russian. The language of animals relates far more to odor and nuance of body expression than to sound, and our written languages are but renditions of sound. But in essence I reassured the tiger that, though I was a puny man, I had some notion what it was like to be a powerful tiger, and understood his condition. Further, I could intercede with my kind for a measured freedom for him, and respectful treatment. These are poor approximations of concepts that are not complex, merely different from human notions.

The essence was that the tiger came to accept me as his representative among my kind, and I accepted him as my representative among his kind. There were not many of his kind at the moment, but that was not important; the understanding was valid. And so, by certain definitions, we were tame.

I gave him a hug, and he licked the side of my head with his rasp of a tongue. We turned to face the others. "My friend will be coming with me," I said.

The three just stared. My words evidently weren't registering.

"You," I said to the guide. "Go get in touch with your supervisor. Tell him that the Tyrant is assuming responsibility for the rogue Smilodon. He may not be the ideal guard for others, but he will do for me."

Somewhat numbly, the guide departed.

"Now, if the two of you will approach, singly, slowly, I will introduce you," I said. "It is better that he realize that you are friends of mine, because he is not really tame."

Spirit, knowing that I was serious, approached. "Hello, Smilo," she said. I realized that she had named him. The tiger sniffed her, twitched his whiskers, and turned away.

"He recognizes you now," I said.

Spirit retreated, and Tasha came forward. She looked as if she were about to faint. "Be at ease, Tasha," I said. "Smilo only attacks strangers."

She nerved herself and stood for the tiger's sniff. He growled, deep inside, and she jumped. "Yes, I know," I murmured to him, my hand on his shoulder reassuringly. "But she is bound."

Tasha turned a frightened, perplexed gaze on me. "Why—?"

"You are a mole, programmed to kill me when I try to make love to you," I told her. "Smilo smells that trap."

In her fear of the tiger, she did not question my statement. "Why did you not have me killed?"

"Tigers have their uses," I said. "So do moles."

Indeed it was so.

Chapter 6

FORTA

Actually, there were complications. Smilo had to be housebroken. That meant setting up a suitable toilet facility for him, which consisted of a monstrous box of kitty litter that had to be changed after each use. It meant setting up heavy curtains for him to stretch his claws on. And a place for him to sleep, close by me. He spent a lot of time sleeping, or at least resting; his huge muscles were capable of phenomenal feats of strength, but not of endurance. He couldn't settle down on my bed; he had the mass of a small horse. But he was happy to snooze under it, after we set up a high enough mattress for me. We had to wash him fairly frequently, lest the feline smell become too strong; but soon enough we became acclimatized to it. He learned to like sponge baths. He wouldn't touch cat food; he had to hunt for his supper. That meant returning him to the experimental complex, which was equipped with an appropriate hunting range. Certain zoos also had facilities, and some industrial complexes. Since the most likely marauders of state facilities were human, Smilo and his cousins were trained to hunt human beings. Because Saturn did not pussyfoot around with enemies of the state, any such marauders caught were left to the predators to consume; it was believed that this had a salutary effect on potential criminals. I daresay it did.

Smilo knew me, and was able to accept those others I spoke for, especially when he had fed recently and wasn't hungry anyway. He would not attack a friend. But we were uncertain of his capacity for friendship in larger numbers, and preferred to keep the exposure low. So my circle of personal acquaintances was restricted, and that really was not such an inconvenience. As the Tyrant of

Jupiter I had been isolated for security reasons, and these remained valid; I was comfortable with a small circle. Spirit and Tasha were it, for now, and the assigned guards; we let Smilo get to know three of them, so that they could take eight-hour shifts continuously, and I believe they came to consider it a privilege to share the duty with Smilo. If any strangers approached, the tiger would rise and growl, and consent to be pacified if the known guard indicated that the intruder was to be tolerated. Once a supervisor made an inspection, and the guard arranged to forget to give Smilo the toleration signal; the three guards had quite a laugh about that when things were private again.

Yes, on the whole Smilo was a worthwhile addition to our group. He never quite accepted Tasha, but I demurred when she offered to resign. "If you did that, those who sent you would know of the discovery of their ploy," I said. "They might then send another assassin. I prefer to remain with the known danger. Also, I suspect that they would not be pleased with you."

She considered that, and paled. She decided to stay. "But what—what if you lose discretion and—?"

"Remember the game of bondage?" I asked. "I gave you to understand that I was not up to the completion. The truth is that I had the completion, but that was erased from your memory when you reverted to your normal state."

She was appalled. "But if what you say is true, you ran a horrible risk!"

"True. That is why I propose no further affair with you."

She mulled it over. "How was I?"

I remembered the illicit excitement of virtually raping a bound woman. "You were wonderful—but that is not the way I prefer to know you."

"Can't I be deprogrammed? I wish—"

"I wish too," I said. "But I think only those who programmed you can deprogram you, and I doubt they would."

She sighed. "You know I want you."

"And I want you. But it is forbidden. I must take another woman."

"Was it this way in your time on Jupiter, when you went from woman to woman?"

I hadn't seen it in precisely that way, but this was not the occasion to quibble. "They learned to live with it," I said.

Halfway satisfied, she returned to her work.

Meanwhile, the effort to renovate USR industry proceeded. We made wholesale replacements in the supervisory personnel of the key departments, eliminating the nomenklatura and promoting the most competent underlings, so that normal operation hardly missed a step. Then we introduced the free-enterprise incentives, in the name of progressive socialism, and reworked the basic organization. The most efficient and reliable workers got bonuses, and the best managers got promotions, and product pride was stressed throughout. The quantity and quality of output improved, slowly at first, then with greater authority. Like a giant and heavy-laden locomotive, the industrial machine gained velocity. In the name of the Dream, it accelerated.

There were strenuous protests, of course. To these Khukov spread his hands and shrugged and said, in effect, "What can I do? I promised to let the Tyrant have his way if he delivered, and he is delivering."

"But it is not good communism!" they insisted.

"Well, the Tyrant is not a good Communist," he pointed out. True words!

Again, I don't want to oversimplify. We spent many months on this effort, and Spirit developed a formidable apparatus of implementation, and there were almost daily minor crises. Some aspects of industry suffered erosion, and some were disasters, but overall there was a net gain, and this gain was increasing with the passage of time. The Saturn esprit de corps was firming. More raw iron was being processed, more large bubbles were being harvested, more and better machines were coming off the assembly lines. Perhaps more important, the common man was coming to support the new order, as his pay nudged upward and his taxes nudged down and more goods appeared on the shelves at lower prices. Progress was only token at first, but the common comrade was quick to appreciate its nature. The Tyrant was gaining support in proportion to the economic improvement, as is usual in such cases throughout the System. Common folk care little for ideology in their secret hearts; they care for their own comfort and security.

Of course the nomenklatura was now desperate. My progress and Khukov's seeming powerlessness were wiping out this class. It was obvious that I had to be eliminated soon, or the nomenklatura would be out of power. Yet still, any too-obvious attempt on my life would backfire (that term dates from the ancient days of internal-combustion engines; it means a counterproductive effort) against the perpetrator. Thus the number of "accidental" incidents multiplied, and it became evident that Saturn was no safe place for me to be, for now.

Khukov had come to a similar conclusion. "I think it is time for you to become an interplanetary emissary," he said. "I will arrange it. Meanwhile, take a vacation."

"A vacation?"

"Drop out of sight. Go to Beria."

This was his way of advising us that things were becoming quite difficult in the mainstream of the Communist paradise. It had become a full-time job for him to protect me and hang on to his own power while the repercussions of the changes we wrought occurred. Here, the opposition tended to express itself with lasers rather than with votes, and a number of cities were under martial law. He had said he would back me, and he was doing so, but at the cost of the erosion of his power. In time, as the full fruits of the reforms were harvested, his position would strengthen, but right now it required much courage and conviction to hold the line. I had no stronger confirmation of Khukov's belief in the Dream, and in his belief in my own commitment to it, than this; I was reaping much of the credit among the common folk for the reforms, but it was his dedication that made them possible.

We went to Beria. If life was hard elsewhere in the

USR, it was arduous here. We settled in Dvik, at the northern extreme, and the dread cold seemed to reach right through the bubble wall and into our bones.

Of course we had paperwork to keep us busy, but I was soon climbing the walls, figuratively. I found myself looking at Tasha and wondering what was wrong with bondage. But I knew there were only so many chances I could take before something went wrong.

Then Forta arrived. She was the woman that my wife Megan sent; it seemed that during these months Megan had searched her out and arranged for her to travel to Saturn. Such things are not arranged instantly; there are clearances to be obtained and private affairs to be concluded, and of course the voyage between planets takes several months. Thus about six months had passed since my message to Megan, and this was her response.

I knew my wife, and my wife knew me. Our separation, more than a decade before, had been a philosophical necessity without bad feeling. I would have remained with her until death, had that been possible, and she knew it; she also knew that all other women were lesser substitutes, the bread and water of my desire when I could no longer possess the cake and cream. There was no jealousy in Megan, only understanding and tolerance. I trusted her to know exactly what I meant when I asked her for a woman. As far as I was concerned, this arrival was just in time.

Her name was Fortuna Foundling. If that sounds stupid—well, so does Hope Hubris, when you consider it. What, after all, is in a name? It is the person who counts. Khukov was later to dub her "the muddy diamond" with no disrespect intended; he appreciated her value immediately. A good deal faster than I did, actually.

I was on tenterhooks as the complicated process of Saturn travel and security clearance brought her slowly to me in Dvik. Was she beautiful? Intelligent? Affectionate? An athlete in the boudoir? Knowledgeable in System events? What kind of woman would my wife send me? I had never before asked her for a favor of this nature.

At length the bus-bubble arrived at the Dvik station. The passengers straggled out. Most were tired workers, glumly back from meager vacations in the more pleasant bubbles to the south. The last to debouch was, by her clothing, from Jupiter. She must be the one.

I don't want to be unkind, but there is not any really polite way to describe my disappointment. This woman was tall and trim and evidently of mixed blood; there seemed to be touches of Mongol and Saxon and Negroid derivation in her. Her dark hair was bound back into a bun, and her face was shadowed by a feminine hat that might have been six or seven centuries out of date. She wore a suit that was almost military in its stern cut, though of no service with which I was conversant. She appeared to be in her mid-thirties. She was definitely no showgirl.

She glanced about, then spied me. She strode toward me, extending her hand. "Worry?" she inquired in English. "Forta Foundling."

She was the one, all right; no one in Saturn knew my old nickname. Well, no doubt the secret police did, but it was not the sort of appellation they would think to use.

I took the hand. It was as callused as that of a physical laborer. I looked up and saw her face clearly for the first time. It was a shock.

Forta's face was so badly scarred as to make it hideous. It looked as if she had put her head in the blast of an accelerating spaceship. Patterns of scars matted her forehead and cheeks, and the eyebrows were lost in the ruin. Her ears hardly showed; perhaps they had been cut off. Her mouth seemed to be little more than a slit amidst the tortured tissue.

"Childhood accident," she said matter-of-factly, evidently used to the very kind of stunned reaction I was evincing.

I found myself tongue-tied in the manner of a teenager. I could not see Megan as practicing either a joke or any kind of obscure vengeance on me; neither type of behavior was her way. But virtually all of my women had been beautiful, herself included; she knew my taste in that regard. How could she have done this? There had to be a rationale.

Spirit stepped in. "I am his sister. We have a place for you. Let's get your baggage."

"This is all," Forta said, hefting her single suitcase.

We went to our rented car. I drove while Spirit and Forta talked. Spirit arranged this, knowing that I needed a pretext to keep to myself.

"We have been very busy," Spirit said. "We have been reorganizing Saturn industry, and that entails a great deal of research. My brother interviews the personnel, and I see to much of the implementation. Are you trained in this area?"

"I regret I am not," Forta said. "I do, however, have secretarial skills."

"We already have a secretary," Spirit said. "We really had not thought of you in that capacity."

"Naturally not," Forta said, evidently smiling. I was not looking at her; I kept my eyes scrupulously on the netted channel ahead. The mystery of this woman was growing, and it was not a mystery I was enjoying.

"Are you trained in diplomacy?" Spirit inquired.

"By no means."

Even Spirit was somewhat at a loss. But she rallied. "Perhaps if you would fill us in on your background . . . ?"

"Gladly. I was found on Mercury thirty-two years ago, during one of the civil-rights altercations there. My parents may have been killed by the authorities of South Mercury, or merely driven out and prevented from returning. It is possible that I was left for dead, because of the injury done my face. I was picked up by a relief mission and taken to the Amnesty Interplanetary office in Toria. I understand they tried to investigate my background, but of course things are difficult for those of mixed race in that part of the System, and they had no success. So I was christened Fortuna Foundling, being fortunate merely to have survived as a foundling."

"Apartheid," Spirit murmured. "I understand that torture is employed in that region. But why a baby should be subjected to—"

"There is no proof of torture," Forta said. "It could have been a mining accident. The conditions in Mercury's sunside diamond mines—"

"What was a baby doing in a sunside mine?" Spirit asked, an edge to her voice. She had seen a lot, and was toughened to it, but she was shaken by the obvious suffering Forta had experienced.

"Those of mixed race in that region must earn whatever type of living they can," Forta said. "The wages of two would barely support a family, and it is possible I had only a mother. She may have had to take me to the mine, lacking any way to care for me separately."

"And if a Saxon mine-boss discovered you—he could have poured acid on your face, and left you, just to spite your mother for bringing you," Spirit said. "Then fired your mother and driven her away."

"That is the conjecture," Forta agreed. "But I must say that I was well cared for by AI. My face healed, but of course they lacked the funds for plastic surgery. I have spent my life with AI; when I became adult I joined as one of their agents. That has been the story of my life, until this point."

"I wonder if there has been a misunderstanding," Spirit said. "We are not engaged in the investigation of human rights, here. We are on assignment for Chairman Khukov of the Union of Saturnine Republics, being in exile from Jupiter. I should not think that you would care to be connected to this enterprise."

"I did not come as an AI representative," Forta said. "I came as a woman."

"You are not on assignment?"

Forta laughed. "Naturally not! Megan would not assign anyone to duty of this nature. I volunteered."

Still I stared straight ahead. Spirit was guarded. "You volunteered—for what?"

"To be your brother's mistress."

There was a silence. Spirit knew my tastes, and knew that I simply was not turned on by this woman. Under what illusion had Forta made this major decision?

"I have had experience," Forta said after a moment. "I am competent. And I very much admire the Tyrant. I consider it a privilege to serve in this capacity."

It was time for me to tackle my own problem. "How well do you know me?" I asked.

"About as well as any person not of your family or prior staff knows you," Forta said. "I have made a study."

"Then perhaps you know that I do not have relations with strangers," I said.

"True. And you seldom have relations with unpretty women." Aware of my reticence, she continued: "I intend to be the exception."

"I am sure you are a well-meaning person," I said cautiously. "But—" I was unable to voice the thought.

"I think that once you come to know me, you will appreciate my qualities," she said. "If you care to read me, you will see that I am confident of your eventual satisfaction."

"Show me your power," I murmured under my breath, in the old Navy idiom, with irony.

"Read me," she repeated firmly. It was definitely a challenge.

I realized that it would be better to settle things now than to let them drag on. Spirit took over control of the car, and I spun my seat around to face Forta, who sat in back. I read her, using my talent.

The first thing I picked up was, indeed, her complete confidence. This woman believed in herself. This belief did not seem to be based on ignorance; she had had experience in many disciplines, and had verified the accuracy of her perceptions. She knew herself to have significant liabilities, but also knew that these had been compensated for to the extent that they had become net assets. She approached me not as a stranger but as a long-familiar subject, and regarded my conquest as a matter of convenience rather than challenge. She had suffered formidable privation, not merely that of the face, and survived with increasing strength. Indeed, that strength of character, forged in a very hard school, surrounded her as if she wore a suit of medieval armor; yet she was not resisting my probe, she was facilitating it. I had known hard women, and talented women, and combinations of the two, but none harder or more talented than this one, except my sister.

My sister—who also had a scarred face and hands. Spirit, as a child of twelve, had saved me from death at the hands of pirates by taking hold of a rocket-propulsion unit and firing it inside the bubble boat. She had wiped out the pirates, but had burned her hands and face, for the thing was no toy. Today she wore gloves in public to conceal the scars and the little finger she had lost in another aspect of that encounter, and could pass for a weather-beaten man when she showed her face but not her body. She had never had restorative surgery because she wore her marks with pride.

Forta was of this nature. She resembled my sister, though her scars were far more apparent. Evidently Megan had seen this in her, and believed that I would be pleased. Yet I did not care to take a woman like my sister as a mistress, and not merely because of the appearance or the implied sense of kinship. I preferred softer flesh for love, even when it was resisting me, as was the case with Tasha. I preferred a yielding, accommodating attitude, rather than a hard and challenging one. In short, I did not regard an Amazon as a suitable love object.

Then something strange happened. The face of the person before me blurred and changed, and so did the body. The contours rounded, the expression changed, and the body signals flowed into a different pattern. I had never observed this type of change in a person before; normally the unconscious signals that I read are fixed, varying only in intensity as the mood shifts. This one was becoming a different person, somewhat as Tasha did when her mole manifested.

Then I peceived the presence of Helse, the girl I had known when I was fifteen and she sixteen. The first of my two great loves. She had initiated me into sex and romance and set her stamp forever upon me. She had died, but lived on in my awareness, coming to me when I most needed her. I knew that I still faced the body of Forta, but it was Helse who faced me. Helse could assume the body of whatever woman I was with, and give me the joy of herself through that body. *Helse, my love!*

Then the signals changed again, and Helse faded. For a moment there was the confusion of mixed signals, like that of a palette whose colors have flowed into each other inartistically. Then they formed into a new presence.

Now it was Megan who met my gaze. Megan, my second great love, and my wife of more than a quarter century. She was older than I, and physically frail in her age, but her indomitable sense of decency and fair play shone through, and I still loved her. Had the separation not come upon us, I would never have touched another woman, as I have explained here, and this she knew. Technically, I was guilty of adultery, many times over, but she understood: I would return to her the moment I could. In that sense, each lesser woman was a complement to Megan: my effort to gain some partial share of her through sublimation. *Megan, my love!*

Finally that presence, too, faded, and I resumed my awareness of the original: Forta Foundling, whom Megan had sent. And of myself: my mouth had fallen open, and my eyes were glazing. For I knew that this had not been any idle vision of my own; I had not gone into any trance state or alternate awareness. I had experienced both often enough to know them when I chose to. I had been reading Forta—*and the signals had changed.* She had become each of my loves in turn—without speaking a word.

I spun my chair again, facing the front of the car, breaking the contact. Dazed, I stared into the atmosphere of Saturn as the bubble coursed along the netted channel, one of a line of such bubbles. Spirit glanced curiously at me, as if to inquire whether Forta had shown me her power.

Indeed, she had done so.

Chapter 7

RISING SUN

Forta was what I must term a signal chameleon: She could emulate the facial and body signals of other people. Her talent was, in a fashion, akin to mine: she could generate the signals I could read. Thus she could emulate, in a rather subtle but fundamental manner, those people she had studied—and she had studied my two loves. Megan she had obviously examined firsthand; Helse she must have derived from scattered references. In retrospect, I concluded that her rendition of Megan had been superior to that of Helse, and that made sense. After all, how could anyone except me know Helse's signals, except in the sense that they were common to Hispanic girls of that age?

This helped explain why Megan had sent her. Forta could be all things to all men, in a fashion, and she could to an extent represent Megan for me. Except for the matter of her face. But even to this there was an answer.

When Forta unpacked, it turned out that her suitcase contained not a wide variety of clothing but a most versatile array of costumes and masks. These were not crude plastic masks; they were contour-clinging, lifelike things that could readily be mistaken for living flesh when animated by her expressions. In fact Forta was an accomplished mime: she could don mask and costume and mimic her chosen character so cleverly that the resemblance was startling. At my behest, she donned her Megan set, as she called it, and in a moment it was as though my wife entered the chamber. The mask-face, the hair-wig, the walk, the gestures, the subtle body signals—I was shaken despite my comprehension of the device. She was so very like Megan that I longed to embrace her.

Then she spoke—and with Megan's voice, complete with the nuances that I had thought only I appreciated. "Why, Hope—it is so good to see you again," she said, and extended her arms to me, in exactly the way Megan had done when our marriage was active.

I knew better, but I couldn't help myself. I stepped forward and took her in my arms. I kissed her—and did not even feel the mask. It seemed like a living face, despite my knowledge. Yet this was not my wife, but another woman acting her part. I knew that Forta could and would take that part as far as I cared to have it go, right through the sexual aspect, and would emulate Megan even in that. This was my closest possible approach to my wife, and it was offered with my wife's collaboration.

But that was not, I discovered, what I desired. If I could not have Megan herself, I did not want any imitation. I broke the contact and turned away, my emotions churning.

Forta understood. She returned to her chamber, and in a moment reappeared as herself. "Or any other form you prefer," she said simply.

Spirit had been present. She shook her head. "If I had not seen it . . ." she said.

I preferred to mull the matter over in my subconscious for a while. "We have a job to do on Saturn," I said. "How can you facilitate that?"

"I can serve in a secretarial capacity when required," she said. "I realize that you already have a secretary, but perhaps Spirit could use me. I can also emulate either of you, should you require doubles for safety."

"To become a target for assassination, in lieu of one of us?" I asked, appalled. "We would not ask that of you!"

"But I would do it at need," she said. "I can also serve as a courier, and as translator."

"You know other languages?" I asked, interested.

"Not exactly. I have translation apparatus that facilitates the limited ability I have in that regard."

"That I would like to see," I said.

She demonstrated. She had a pocket multitongue language computer, with capsules for the individual languages. An earplug enabled her to hear the ongoing translation in Afrikaans, her native language and the one she thought in. It developed that she had been using the translator for English, though she did speak that language, because it was easier for her to hear words in her own language, then translate her reply, than to deal completely in English.

"¿Español?" I inquired.

She smiled, checked through her file, brought out the Spanish capsule, and inserted it in the machine. "Sí," she said.

"But if you do not know it, how can you speak it?" I asked.

"I have a prompt," she explained. This was a plug in her other ear, that fed her the words she subvocalized. The unit had a receptor at her neck, so that she could in effect speak without being heard by others, and so her Afrikaans word for "yes" produced the prompt of the Spanish "sí." She understood phonetics, and knew the basic sounds of many languages, so that she could speak remarkably well despite the adaptation. I would have thought she was a slightly slow Hispanic, had I not known. It was amazing how she could do this ongoing translation, with only slight pauses in her speech, ordinarily unnoticed in dialogue. This was a formidable skill.

"You can do this in Russian too?" Spirit asked.

Forta demonstrated the Russian capsule. I was impressed; she did speak with an accent, but intelligibly. She could make herself understood, and she could understand anything spoken to her in that language, provided she was prepared for it with the appropriate capsule. She had the dialects, too.

I don't want to oversimplify this. Language is more than a collection of words, and the syntax of a language may be the essence of it rather than the vocabulary. But Forta had made a study of the fundamental patterns of the major language trunks, and researched constantly to improve her skill, so that the actual words were most of what she needed to make sense of other tongues. It was an accomplishment that was on a par with her ability to do emulations.

I had occasion to meet with others who used unfamiliar

languages, even within the Saturnine Union, as I had discovered in Kraine. Yes, Forta would be useful to my work here!

The heat did not let up; the nomenklatura remained determined to eliminate me. Khukov reluctantly concluded that I could not safely remain on the planet. If I showed my face in public, one of their assassins would go for me first, then if caught would commit suicide, and the body would have no ties to the employer. If I remained in hiding, eventually they would ferret out my location, and send in a bomb. They were no longer interested in being careful; I had to be eliminated, for it was obvious that they were otherwise doomed.

"But you have proven yourself," Khukov said on the private holophone. It looked just as if he were sitting in our chamber. "The procedures you have instituted will carry through to their completion, perhaps more slowly without you, but inevitably. You can now be spared for greater things."

I smiled wryly. What could be greater than the renovation of the planetary industrial base?

But he wasn't joking. "I want you to negotiate with Rising Sun."

"With who?"

"In your terms, Titan, our greatest moon. In the Solar System, Titan is a satellite of Saturn, and this does not accord with their social perspective, any more than their ancestors considered Japan to be an island satellite of the continent of Asia. So they prefer to call themselves the Empire of the Rising Sun. It would be well for a diplomat to remember that."

"Rising Sun," I agreed. "But can the occidental Tyrant speak for the oriental aspect of Saturn?"

"In many respects, that moon is closer to your planet than to mine," he reminded me. "Remember, it was Jupiter who occupied it, after System War Two, not Saturn. Now it is an industrial giant in its own right, and we would like to establish better trade relations."

"I'm sure Titan will trade," I said. "But it sells finished

products, and your interplanetary credit is weak. What can you offer?"

He told me what the USR had to offer. I nodded. "I believe I can handle that."

"And it will keep you safely off-planet, while the disturbance here dies down," he concluded.

Thus we undertook our mission as liaison between Saturn and Titan. It promised to be an intriguing challenge.

Titan bore a certain resemblance to my planet of origin, Callisto. Khukov had termed it moon, but as he had noted, we of the satellites prefer to call them planets in their own right. Indeed, it was never more than a convention of convenience to call them moons; any such pair is actually a set of bodies in space orbiting each other. When one is larger, the perturbations of its orbit tend to be less, and so it is deemed to be the primary, but one might as readily term it the secondary mass. Certainly to us of Callisto, Jupiter seemed like a giant satellite.

Callisto was somewhat under two million kilometers out from Jupiter; Titan was somewhat over one million out from Saturn. As interplanetary distances go, that's a similar league, and it made Saturn appear larger from Titan than Jupiter did from Callisto. Callisto completed an orbit in under seventeen days; Titan in just under sixteen. Callisto had a diameter of just under five thousand kilometers; Titan just over. Their densities and masses were similarly close. They could have been sister planets, as far as I was concerned.

But there were differences. The surface temperature of Titan was fifty degrees Kelvin colder than that of Callisto, and while Callisto was airless, Titan had a substantial atmosphere; its solid surface was completely hidden from exterior view. Critics refer to that atmosphere as solid smog; the natives refer to it as the basic stuff of the origin of life. Certainly it represents a rich chemical environment from which the natives process many products, and its pressure of one bar (the same as Earth's) facilitates the operation of city-domes in the surface. It is the only planet besides Earth itself whose atmosphere is dominated by nitrogen.

Politically, it was another matter. Titan was colonized by the Japanese of Earth, and they maintained their rivalry and often enmity with huge Saturn. Because Titan's position in space is far superior for the direct launching of ships, Titan's Navy became more formidable than Saturn's. It was, as Khukov remarked, Jupiter, not Saturn, that took on that Navy during the Second System War, and reduced it to impotence, and occupied Titan itself. Thereafter, Titan was forbidden to manufacture arms, including fighting ships. Instead, she had turned her energies to commerce—and shortly became a System leader in the construction of merchant ships, and in computerized technology. It was a metamorphosis that perhaps the nominal winners of SWII had not anticipated. Titan had beaten its swords into plowshares, and was now stronger as an economic power than it had been as a military power. Jupiter itself imported so much from Titan that it had a sizable trade deficit with that planet. That is, Titan was making a lot more money than Jupiter was. Yet Jupiter was still committed by treaty to undertake the military defense of Titan. Today Titan was happy with the arrangement, but Jupiter was chafing somewhat. It was a nice irony.

Irony: which brings my thought to iron. There was Titan's problem. It had been able to mine its own iron, but its industrial base had expanded far beyond its natural resources, and it now required far more iron than it mined. Iron was of course the metal of power for the System, because it could be handled magnetically. Processed into contra-terrene iron, or CTI, it was the fuel for all major ships and all major cities and all industrial complexes. So the irony of Titan was that this source of natural iron was hungriest of all for imported iron.

This was a hunger I proposed to address on this mission.

Our party was transferred in space to a Titan—excuse me, Rising Sun—merchant vessel and conveyed to the surface of the planet. This was an interesting experience in its own right. The atmosphere was deep, and developed a brownish hue as we descended. It was not stormy, as I had half feared, but very thick; soon it obscured anything that might have been any distance. I began to feel claustrophobic, until I reminded myself that one bar was the pressure limit; there was no way that our ship would implode! Not when the internal pressure matched the external pressure.

We landed; the fractional gee, about one-sixth Earthnorm, made this feasible here. I had been so long in the atmospheres of the giants that I had lost the feel for "hard" landings. A car-bubble limousine carried us toward Kyo, the capital. This ride, too, was fascinating; Sprit and Tasha seemed as interested as I was, though Forta took it in stride. Perhaps the environment reminded her of that of Mercury. Smilo, who had submitted to the indignity of a cage for this part of the journey, snoozed.

We cruised along a highway that curved around mountains of methane ice, and beside ponds of liquid methane from which methane vapor ascended slowly back into the dark sky. Brown methane snowflakes drifted down to coat every solid surface. This just happened to be the spot in the System where the temperature was at the "triple point" of methane—where it could exist simultaneously in solid, liquid, and vapor states. I suppose that to the natives this was a matter of course, but it certainly impressed me.

Kyo loomed as a huge dome, girt by many lesser domes. I understand that the main city has more than ten million people, and the region as a population center is much greater. I was surprised to note that it was not a bubblene dome—bubblene being the material from which all floating city-bubbles are made, because it is one of the few substances tough enough to withstand the multibar pressures of the big atmospheres—but a comparatively flimsy plastic one. But again I reminded myself: With internal and external pressure nearly equal, the dome was not for pressure, but merely to contain breathable atmosphere and suitable residential temperature. Titan was fortunate indeed in this respect.

We entered the lock and were treated to another marvelous sight: the oriental splendor of the culture of Rising Sun. I saw a shrine with multileveled upward-curving roofs, diminishing in size as they ascended. I saw dwarf trees growing in a special little park. The civilians wore brightly colored sarongs or pajama-type suits, and the petite women had their hair ornately dressed. This was, indeed, the heart of the Orient!

But elsewhere the city was intensely settled, looking quite modern. Evidently the citizens of Rising Sun valued their cultural heritage but did not let it interfere with practical matters.

We were conducted to an elegant apartment complex, where we were abruptly left to our own devices. This of course was the oriental way; our hosts were not really ignoring us. They were preparing for our diplomatic encounter, without bothering us with the mundane details. We enjoyed ourselves at the heated pool-sized bath, and had a fancy multicourse banquet. Smilo, released to roam the sealed region of the suite, condescended to tear apart a realistic-looking steak. His presence, perhaps, was another reason we were being left alone.

Forta did not actually enter the bath; she remained clothed, politely aloof. But Tasha did, and her body was spectacular in the bathing suit. This of course set my private passions spinning. I had placed such hope on the arrival of Forta, but talented and useful as she surely was, she was a disappointment romantically. I had not wanted a woman who could emulate the aspects of other women I had known; I had wanted a creature in her own right. Something young and soft and sexy and not too intelligent, if the truth be known. Forta was none of these; Tasha was most of them.

But her mole-conditioning remained, and I dared not touch her, willing as she might be. Forta was the one I was supposed to touch, little as the prospect appealed. I grimaced as I sat at the rim and dangled my feet in the water.

Tasha swam up. "I will purchase handcuffs," she murmured.

"Thank you, but I do not care to be cuffed," I said.

"For me," she said. "For my hands and feet, and you will have the key."

Oh. The prospect was illicitly tempting. But I demurred. "I am supposed to be through with you," I said. "I have another woman now."

"That is why I must have you soon," she said. "Once you go with her, you will never again go with me." She turned her face to me, and I saw that it was wet in a fashion that I doubted could be attributed entirely to the water of the pool. "Oh, please Tyrant—I want you so much! Bind me, rape me, anything—only take me one more time."

I considered. The truth is, I have been known to have this effect on women, and it pleased me to know that my advancing age had not nullified this aspect of my personality. I did desire her, dangerous as she was to desire. So I did what I knew I should not have done. "Buy the cuffs," I said.

"Oh, thank you!" she exclaimed, flouncing out of the water to embrace me.

Smilo jumped up, growling, and stalked toward us. Tasha quickly disengaged, splashing back into the water. Smilo did not have the fear of water that some cats did; he could swim, but generally preferred not to get his fur wet without reason. Since Tasha was no longer bothering me, by his definition, he did not find it worthwhile to pursue her in the pool. But he settled down beside me watchfully.

I reached out to pat his lovely hide. "I'm afraid we shall have to put you in the cage, for the occasion," I said. "I trust you understand." For obviously it would be very difficult to get close enough to Tasha to make love while the tiger was on guard.

On the following day we were granted the interview with the Shogun, or principal dignitary of the planet. For showcase visits, foreigners were generally routed to the Mikado, whose duties were purely ceremonial, but the Shogun had genuine power of decision.

Of course the interview was by holo; the Shogun was too important to risk in direct personal encounters, and the mechanism of translation suffered. This way, his image appeared real, as did mine to him, and his words were automatically translated from Japanese to Spanish, so that except for some unavoidable misalignments we seemed to be speaking each other's languages.

"So good to meet you, Tyrant," he said, lifting his hand in the greeting that was accepted as equivalent to a handshake on such occasions. "I have long admired your management of Jupiter."

"Thank you, Shogun," I replied. "I tried in vain to eliminate Jupiter's balance-of-trade deficit with Titan."

"But you did give us a run for our money," he said, smiling. He glanced to the side. "What a beautiful Smilodon! Have you any of those for export?"

I hadn't thought of that. "I would give you this one, Shogun, as a gesture of amity between Saturn and Titan. But he is wild, responding only to me. However, I am sure there will be tamer ones available in due course."

"I would not put Saturn to such difficulty," he said.

I was reading him. He really did admire the tiger! "Perhaps a matched pair," I said. "Breeders."

"Breeders," he echoed, and now the longing was manifest. Titan had a long history of martial arts, now stifled by the terms of the treaty, and admired superior fighting animals.

I signaled Tasha. She nodded and went to our interplanetary phone. It was possible that we would be able to confirm the assignment of a pair of Smilodons before this interview was concluded. I knew that Saturn would not want to let them go, but would do so at my behest. We desperately needed the good graces of the Shogun.

The Shogun had been coolly formal. Now he warmed noticeably. "It seems strange to encounter you as the representative of Saturn, rather than of Jupiter," he remarked.

"I prefer to think of myself as representing the human species," I said.

He was genuinely interested. "If it is not impolite to inquire, how would that be?"

"Chairman Khukov and I share a dream. You are of course aware of the manner that increasing population and diminishing reserves of natural resources are putting pressure on our civilization."

He smiled marginally. "I am aware," he agreed, with phenomenal understatement. Titan suffered as much as any planet from these very maladies, and had done as much to accommodate them as any.

"Our dream is to alleviate these conditions by opening the final frontier to man: that of the colonization of the galaxy."

"I am interested." Indeed, I could tell that he was—and also that this news was not a surprise to him. Evidently he had arranged a relatively prompt interview with me because his informational network (it's not polite to call it spying) had notified him of the project. Now he would have the news directly and openly, and that, by the conventions of his culture, was important.

"We propose to construct a station to transmit entire spaceships, in the form of light beams, to the planets of neighboring stars," I said. "We believe the principle is sound, and are now developing the technology to make a demonstration model. But there are certain complications."

He had known, but still I saw the Dream reach out and encompass him. "A second diaspora," he breathed. "Like the one to the Solar System, but greater. To each culture, a full stellar system."

"Or complex of systems," I agreed. "Without apparent limit, for even when the galaxy is filled, there are other galaxies."

"Therefore no further need for war." As the proprietor of the only planet to have suffered the detonation of the so-called planetbuster missiles in war, he had a deep understanding of the consequences of such activity.

"No need of war," I agreed. "Saturn has no greater liking for it than does Rising Sun, and if the truth be known, Jupiter is not particularly partial to it either. The human resources squandered in war represent an abomination. How much better it would be to use those resources in the effort to colonize all space. Each planet could devote whatever share of its economy it chose to its own program of colonization, interfering with no others."

"But would not the best systems go to the first comers?" he asked. "That could cause friction."

"Chairman Khukov is handling the technical details," I said. "I am working on the social aspect. It is my hope to establish a cooperative plan of colonization similar to that which enabled the nations of Earth to spread to the System without dissension as to the manner of it."

"Carrying the ancient enmities with them," he remarked.

"The galaxy is so much larger, perhaps the ancient enmities can at last be allowed to fade."

"But the details of the galaxy are not known," he protested. "How can a fair apportioning be arranged?"

"This is one of the complications I mentioned," I said. "It is indeed a challenge to make an equitable distribution of territory without information. My preliminary notion is to assign regions as segments of a sphere centered on Earth, extending the historic geographic territories outward to space. Thus the map of historic Earth would become the map of the galaxy, with each nation entitled to whatever it finds within the cone of space defined by its outline."

"But Earth turns," he objected alertly. "The cones would be continuously fudged."

"For this purpose, the map would have to be fixed in place," I said. "Perhaps a particular time could be set—"

"And there could be war over the setting of that time," he said. "Each nation wishing to fix it at the point most advantageous for itself."

I nodded ruefully. "It seems I had not thought it out properly."

"By no means, Tyrant," he said generously. "You have the right notion, merely a problem in implementation. The stellar geography already exists; we have but to invoke it."

"It exists?" I asked blankly.

"The constellations," he said. "Occidental mythoi differ from ours, but I daresay there could be some accommodation there, as the basic map of the sky as seen from Earth or any other planet in the System is similar. Saturn would naturally be assigned what you call Ursa Major, or—"

"The Great Bear!" I exclaimed, perceiving it like a rev-

elation. "A huge constellation, as befits a large local geography."

"And Jupiter would of course take Aquila—"

"The Eagle!" I concluded. "But hardly the size of the
Bear—"

"But the Eagle is in the plane of the Milky Way, which
is the body of the galaxy," he pointed out. "A cone of
territory projected beyond that would include far more
stars, ultimately, than that projecting beyond the Bear,
which is not in the galactic plane. Thus the immediate
advantage of Saturn would be offset by the long-term advantage of Jupiter. I suspect your governments could recognize the fundamental fairness of that."

"And Draco, the Dragon, for the Middle Kingdom," I
continued. "Adjacent to the Great Bear, of course."

"Or for Rising Sun," he said. "The serpentine configuration aligns with that of historical Japan, which is also
near the Bear."

I realized that I had committed a gaffe. "Rising Sun, of
course," I agreed hastily.

He smiled. "It shall be worked out in due course; there
may be many duplications of representations."

"But the system as a whole is certainly superior to my
notion," I said. "I believe you have provided the necessary key to the peaceable apportioning of space."

"You are too kind." He was pleased. "If I may inquire,
what are the other complications of this project?"

"Resources," I said. "Saturn has raw resources, but
lacks proper industrial capacity to exploit them efficiently. This project will be phenomenally expensive, even
in the pilot stage."

"But with potentially astronomic rewards," the Shogun said.

"True. But at the moment, it is a strain on Saturn's
resources. That is why we hope to enlist the participation
of others."

"Such as Rising Sun," he said, "that just happen to
have a highly developed industrial base."

"This is true."

"In fact, you seek investors."

"That might be another way of putting it."

"What might Saturn offer, in return for such investment?" The Shogun was of course nobody's patsy.

"Raw iron," I said.

He nodded. "I believe it could be possible to deal."

Of course it was possible! There was hardly anything Titan needed more than iron, in quantity. This could solve its problem. "If Rising Sun were to be kind enough to consider providing advanced equipment, and the technicians to operate it—"

"I am not certain it would be expedient to ship such things to Saturn. Without in any way implying that Saturn would do so, I must say that there may be those who would be concerned about the borrowing of proprietary information for purposes other than intended, such as advanced computer chips—"

Saturn had a bad record in that regard, of course. Technology had been stolen similarly from Jupiter, to our great annoyance. But I had an answer. "Do you by chance remember the compromise I arranged with Ganymede, when I was ambassador there?"

"Tanamo," he said immediately.

"If Saturn should construct a base for the development of the launching site of the demonstration program on the planet of Titan, employing personnel of Rising Sun, coded similarly—"

"That is an interesting proposition," he said. The compromise of Tanamo had assigned the base to Ganymede, for its use as a port, but the personnel controlling access to the base had remained Jupiter citizens. In this manner, each party had been assured that the base would not be misused. I was suggesting that Rising Sun retain possession of the base, while Saturn contracted the access and used it for the space exploration project. This would give Rising Sun intimate participation, and her equipment and personnel would not leave the planet. It would also provide Saturn a vital base for the project, for Saturn's access to space was severely limited.

"Perhaps the matter could be presented to your governing council," I said. "I merely present Saturn's interest."

"That presentation shall be made," he said. "But I re-

gret to say that a certain distrust that has existed historically may not be abated immediately."

He was understanding the case. The antagonism between Saturn and Titan had been long and bitter. "If
there is any way to facilitate understanding and acceptance—" I said.

"Saturn may be distrusted, but our relations with Jupiter have been more amicable in recent years. If Jupiter
had an interest in this—"

"I hope in due course to enlist Jupiter's participation,"
I said. "But at the moment I am not in good repute there."

"The Tyrant remains in excellent repute here," he said.
"I confess that contact with Saturn might not have been
as amicable if a conventional representative had been
sent."

"Such as one of the nomenklatura?"

He smiled knowingly. "However, there is one whose
continued presence would serve to abate skepticism here."
He glanced meaningfully at me.

I was taken aback. "I had it in mind to meet with you,
then return—"

"To the hospitality of the nomenklatura?"

He had a point. Titan was certainly safer for me, and
there was indeed a job I could do here, facilitating the
organization of the new base. I no longer represented Jupiter, but it seemed that to the folk of this planet I remained a useful symbol. Symbols are important to all
human cultures, but perhaps more so to those of the Orient.

"I would be very pleased to accept your hospitality, if
Saturn concurs," I said. "In the interest of forwarding the
Dream."

"This may be a dream we shall be pleased to share,"
he said.

We raised our hands in the gesture of understanding.

Chapter 8

LADY OR TIGER

The limited treaty between the USR and Rising Sun was considered a diplomatic coup, though all I had done was present a proposal of mutual benefit. It was as though I had gone from Tyrant to Rising Politician, in a sense a retreat, but a comfortable one. Shipments of iron ore (that is, unprocessed material sifted from the nether regions of accessible Saturn atmosphere that was rich in iron) moved to Titan, and a base was constructed on that planet at a near-record pace, while technicians studied the details of the breakthrough process. I interviewed the Rising Sun personnel, weeding out the unfit in my fashion; Saturn retained veto power in this respect, and I was serving Saturn's interest. It was a type of thing I was good at, but since I did not speak Japanese I required Forta's assistance. She translated, using her special equipment, while I judged the technicians' reactions, and it worked well enough. Thus I was making myself useful while also serving the broader purpose of reassuring the Rising Sun public by my presence.

But the work was neither arduous nor dangerous; consequently I began to feel out of sorts. My eye turned again on Tasha, who remained as attractive as ever. I knew I shouldn't touch her, under any conditions, but that only made the temptation stronger.

One afternoon when Spirit and Forta were at the base, seeing to a complexity of its operation, Tasha forced the issue. She produced four sets of handcuffs: the old-fashioned kind, with a mechanical key. She didn't have to say a word; the moment I saw them, I knew I was going to do it.

I went to the bedroom, where Smilo was catnapping in

his chamber under my bed. "Sorry, friend," I said. "I need to confine you for a while." And I dropped the cage door to the floor, snapping it in place. He was accustomed to this; it meant that he was off duty for the duration, and could drift into a sound sleep. Animals do not necessarily mind confinement, when they trust the confiner.

Then I followed Tasha into her bedroom, which was adjacent to mine. We represented a small Saturn enclave in the Titan city nearest the developing base; no one and nothing approached it without authorization, making it safe from assassins. We were really very comfortable here, with a benign confinement similar to that I was practicing on Smilo.

Tasha stripped and stood before me. Oh, she was lovely! She stretched, and I watched her breasts lift and her abdomen thin with the motion. I couldn't help myself; I stepped in and hugged her.

"Not yet," she murmured. "Fasten me down."

She spread herself on her bed, and I locked the handcuffs on her two wrists and two ankles, and to the available anchorages at the corners of the bed. She was secure.

I was eager with the pent-up desire of weeks, but I made myself go slowly. I suppose I hoped that if I worked her up properly, she would not change to the mole. Perhaps I was merely trying to delay that change, as it was Tasha I really wanted. So I kissed her, and ran my hands across her body, and tickled her and tousled her hair and tongued her breasts, and she responded in the appropriate ways.

There was a growl from the other bedroom. Smilo had realized that something was going on, and that I was touching Tasha, and he didn't like it. I do not think it was jealousy of the attention that motivated him, as I could touch the others without bothering him; I believe he sensed the mole in Tasha, like a lurking demon, and knew her to be a threat to me. He meant well, not understanding that I was aware of this threat and had acted to nullify it. So I understood his growl but had to ignore it.

Tasha was writhing, not with pain but with pleasure. She was on the point of climax, and I had not yet proceeded to the essence. "Please . . ." she whispered.

Naturally I obliged. This had already been a longer

period with the real Tasha, in this mode, than I had enjoyed before; perhaps, knowing the futility of it, the mole would not manifest this time. I embraced her and entered her.

She changed as it happened. Her body tightened, and her teeth bared. "So you summon me again, Tyrant!" she said, her voice assuming a hissing texture. "Enjoy me while you can!"

Damn! I had hoped—but of course that had been foolish. It was entry that triggered the change. I could never truly possess Tasha, only the mole.

Her legs wrenched, first one, then the other. This enhanced my sensation. But something was odd. I glanced down—and discovered that her legs were free. The handcuffs remained, but they had ripped out of the anchorages on the bed.

Horrified, I looked at her wrists—and they too came free, the cuffs dangling. I had failed to check the security of the anchorages; now, too late, I realized that they were inadequate. Tasha may not have known this, but the mole did.

I tried to disengage, to leap off her. But her legs came up to clamp me in a painful scissors, and her arms swung to catch my head and lock it down beside hers. *"Now* finish your business, Tyrant!" she hissed in my ear, and bit it.

This time I could not get my arms back to press the nerves of her feet, or up to reach her neck. She held me secure, and her grip tightened cruelly the moment I tried to move. She had the chains of the manacles across the back of my neck, digging into it, and I was helpless.

"Scream, Tyrant!" she said into my ear. "I want to hear you suffer!" And those chains abruptly cut in hard.

It was useless, but I screamed. "Smilo!" I cried, though I knew that he was confined and could not help me. I had fashioned my own demise, oh so neatly!

Smilo roared in response. He thrashed about in his cage, trying to break out.

"How delightful!" the mole said. "The animal wants to help." She bucked her hips against me as well as she could without releasing the scissors, and clenched her internal muscles, trying to force my climax.

In my pain and desperation, I remembered something. The bars beneath my bed were secure—but the bed itself was not. It consisted of adjustable panels, and it seemed to me that these were not locked. "Smilo—up!" I cried.

There was a pause, then an answering crash. The tiger had stood, his massive body thrusting against the ceiling of his cage, and that ceiling had sprung loose. The base of my bed was designed to sustain maximum weight pressing down from above, not from below. Smilo was working his way out.

"Oh, damn!" she said, as if this were a mere inconvenience. "I'll have to finish you immediately."

She tightened the chains, drawing them down around my neck, constricting it, cutting into my flesh. But Smilo was wasting no time himself; he bounded into the room. I saw only his shadow as he landed beside us and hesitated; I realized that he didn't want to bite me.

Then he decided on his spot and did bite. His fangs plunged into the mole's shoulder and neck, on the side away from my own head. The woman jerked as those terrible weapons sought her vitality; it seemed that the tiger knew instinctively where to bite to cripple instantly. Her legs released me, and her arms slackened.

I fought my way free of her embrace. I thought she would be dead already, but realized in a moment that she wasn't; she had been paralyzed by the bite, and death would occur more slowly. It was the way of the cat, to allow for additional entertainment by the prey before final dispatch. Perhaps it was fitting that the mole be treated this way, exactly as she had tried to treat me.

Smilo stood over us, his heavy breath blasting down on my head. I realized that he was waiting for me to get clear, so he could finish the prey in his own fashion.

The woman shuddered. Then her eyes opened. "Oh, Hope," she said raggedly. "Please . . ."

It was Tasha! The mole had been banished by the terrible bite, or had perhaps deserted when she realized that her mission was lost, leaving the body and the agony to her host. "I'm sorry," I said. "The mole got free—"

"Please," she repeated. "One time . . ."

She wanted me to complete the act I had started! "But you must have medical attention!" I protested.

She only looked at me pleadingly. She was dying, and this was her dying wish.

I realized I had to do it. It was her passion for me that had brought her to this pass, and she deserved its fulfillment. It was the only chance that Tasha proper would ever have to make love to me.

I did it. I thought the twin horrors of her nearly successful attempt to assassinate me and her mauling by the tiger would turn off my own passion, but this was not the case. The moment I made the decision to proceed, the urgency was upon me, and I erupted in her with the sensation of a volcano. I kissed her amidst it, and this heightened and extended the experience, and I knew from the reactions of her body that it was just as transcendent for her.

And all the time, the tiger stood over us, breathing.

It subsided at last, and she sighed and lost consciousness, and then the horror of the situation came to me more strongly. I could not simply let Tasha die!

"Back off, Smilo," I said. "You've done your job."

Obediently, the tiger backed off. Perhaps he figured I wanted to play with the prey some more. I checked the two great stab wounds in her neck and shoulder, surprised to see that they were bleeding only modestly; evidently no artery had been punctured. I covered her with a sheet and hastened to the phone.

"Emergency medic," I snapped, and the phone, tuned to my language, obliged.

In a moment the face of a Rising Sun medic appeared. "Woman bitten by tiger," I said tersely. "Send ambulance to this address." I gave the clearance code so their unit could approach our complex.

"It is being accomplished," he said politely, holding his gaze aloft. That was when I realized that I stood naked before the phone's video pickup, my member only partially detumesced. It was obvious that more than the tiger had had at the woman! Well, it would add only a minor episode to the legend of the Tyrant of Jupiter. I cut the connection.

In a few minutes the ambulance arrived. By then I had gotten into my clothing and taken my stand by Smilo, so as to reassure him about the intruders. They worked efficiently, checking Tasha's vital signs. She was not dead, but had sunk into a coma. They performed spot medication and carried her away.

Then I cleaned up the blood-spotted bedclothes and reassembled my own burst-asunder bed as well as I could. Smilo had certainly saved my life! While I deeply regretted what had happened to Tasha, I knew it was neither the lady's fault nor the tiger's; it was mine. I had done a foolish thing, and paid for it with the near loss of my own life and perhaps that of my secretary. It was not just that I had yielded to forbidden passion; I had been careless about it. That was what bothered me most in retrospect: All I had had to do was check those anchorages to make sure they were secure. I was getting careless in my age, and I did not like that at all.

In due course Spirit and Forta returned, and I acquainted them with the events of the hour. Neither commented; evidently they hoped I had learned my lesson. I hoped so too.

Tasha, as it happened, did not die. The excellent Rising Sun medical treatment she received saved her life and her health; all that remained was two physical scars that she chose not to have removed, and perhaps a similar number of emotional scars that she chose not to forget. She resigned as my secretary and applied to Rising Sun for sanctuary as a defector, and this was granted. She cooperated fully in their investigation of the nature of her mole; they were very interested in the particular type of conditioning used, and after considerable labor they succeeded in blocking it. She then took a job as translator and office worker for one of their executives, and I'm sure she gave him much satisfaction. Certainly I was pleased to know that she had made the transition; she was a good woman, just unsuitable for association with me. Not while Smilo remained with me. Because even with her mole nullified, there would have been trouble if I had tried to

have further sexual relations with her, and surely I would
have tried if she had been constantly with me. There is,
as the ancient saying goes, no fool like an old fool.

Of course I was left out of sorts, romantically. I was in
what might be termed a sexual depression, whether the
result of age or reaction to that lady/tiger episode I am
not sure, so sought no companion of that nature. But so-
cially I felt a need, and it was difficult to meet.

Thus my attention gradually returned to Forta, who
had come to be my mistress but who had not pushed the
suit. She remained confident, as she had said, that once I
came to know her properly, I would appreciate her qualities. Indeed, this seemed to be true; she now moved into
the secretarial position Tasha had vacated, and performed excellently. She helped coach me on the language
of Japanese, using her sophisticated translation device,
so that I could communicate increasingly well with my
hosts. In fact, a great deal of my energy during this period
went into the learning of this language. I was always apt
at tongues, but seemed slower now than in the past; I
prefer to think that this was because of the difficulty of
this particular language, but am prepared to concede that
at age sixty-one or -two I was not as supple mentally as
in my youth. I have no joy of aging, but do try to accept
it with reasonable grace. In the course of working with
Forta on this, and generally, I came to understand with
increasing conviction the remarkable abilities she possessed. She was as versatile a person as I had known.

But her face—it was simply not in me to be physically
attracted to a woman who looked like that. I cursed myself as a fool—so what else is new?—but could not override
that private repulsion. As a worker she was excellent; as
an object of romance, she was a null.

Meanwhile, the base developed, and the pilot project
with it. I call it pilot, but it was nevertheless huge, a tiger
in its own right. Rising Sun was putting an enormous
amount of effort into it, assisting with the financing as
well as the personnel; I was involved in the negotiations
to give Rising Sun a larger amount of control and credit,
in proportion to its practical support. It had become a two-
planet effort, and I am glad that my presence and influ-

ence facilitated this. There was a constant flow of iron ore from Saturn to Titan, and, before long, a counterflow of Rising Sun expert technicians to Saturn, helping to modernize their facilities and production policies. The work that Spirit and I had done on Saturn was of course not complete; we had set the stage by putting the nomenklatura on the defensive, but it was the Rising Sun practical know-how that made real progress possible.

Thus, in about two years, the sample demonstration of the new technique was ready to be made. I deem it a significant event in the history of our species.

Dear Daddy,

So you got a tiger! Well, I guess it happened some time ago, but the new government put a hold on news from Saturn—they seem to be trying to heat up the cold war again, I don't know why—so I didn't learn of it until recently. But I think it's terrific! A big old Smilodon from Earth's paleontology! Just take care he doesn't bite you. I wish I could meet him!

Business is booming here, but I am uneasy, because I know they are flooding the economy with money so that things will be positive for the next election. That didn't happen during the Tyrancy. Oh, well, it's really not my business; I have enough to do just keeping up with education. There's a drive on to censor some of the texts used currently, and of course I have to oppose that. Thorley has been writing some pithy columns on the subject. It's amazing how eloquently he can arrange to call a governor an idiot without actually saying it outright.

Take care of yourself, Daddy, and watch that tiger!

Chapter 9

DEMO

It was time for the demo: the first demonstration of the process for transmission at light speed. I had discussed this with Spirit and with Forta, and come to an agreement. Then I had discussed it with Khukov, and he had demurred. "Tyrant, this project is moving well only because of you. I cannot afford to lose you."

"But if you believe in the technology—"

"I *do* believe! But the risk is too great. We can use anyone for this, and after it is successful—"

"But after the test, there is still the remainder of the System to enlist," I pointed out. "It stands to be a long, difficult task, at best, and perhaps it will fail. We have to have the resources of Uranus and Jupiter, or the effort is wasted. Only the united System can afford the expense of the major project. This will go far toward getting the attention of every planet."

"You could do it after the technique has been proved reliable," he said.

"But the point is, I must establish my faith in it at the outset. There will be no occasion as important as the first."

"But if it fails, through some trifling error—"

"It will only fail if the theory is invalid. We already know from the laboratory that it works for matter, and for small living animals and plants. The only doubt remains about human beings, in a genuine travel situation. That doubt must be totally resolved, at the outset. There can be no better way to resolve it. Then the political aspect will become possible. A technical success without the full political impact will be useless; the one is as important as the other, and we must have both."

And so, reluctantly, he agreed. The political aspect was, after all, my agreed domain, and I had the right to play it my way.

Thus it was that Spirit and Forta and Smilo and I were conveyed by shuttleship to the orbiting test ship, and given possession. It was small, intended for a crew of three and a passenger load of four, but Smilo's mass qualified him to be all four passengers. This was a public event; the newsships of all the major planets and many of the minor ones were present, and we interviewed them freely as we proceeded. I piloted the ship, enjoying the feel of her. She was named *Hope,* an honor I had not sought but did not regret. After all, she was the hope of the future of man, as we saw it.

"Yes, it is a three-light-hour test flight," I said, in answer to a query from a reporter on the screen. "From the orbit of Saturn, here, to the orbit of Uranus, cutting across to the far side at a slant to avoid the sun. We shall be transformed to light, and will then proceed at light speed in the direction the transmitter is aimed, until we are intercepted by the receiver tube at the other end. Three hours to Uranus!"

I knew the System audience would be properly impressed; that trip would ordinarily take three months, by standard travel. In fact, we would arrive there at the same time as the news of our departure did.

"But suppose the alignment is off, and you miss the receiver tube?" the reporter asked.

"Then we go to another star," I replied, smiling. It was a joke, but a grim one; that was exactly what would happen. But there would be no receiving tube deep in the galaxy, so we would travel forever.

"But the computer aligns them perfectly," Spirit put in. "If they are not aligned, the transmission will not be activated. There is no danger."

"Still, there *is* a risk," the reporter persisted.

"I wouldn't have anybody else take a risk I wouldn't take myself," I replied, and smiled bravely. Oh, they would eat this up, all across the System! As a publicity ploy, this was working perfectly.

But as we approached the transmitter station, which

most resembled a ship-sized tube in space, an alarm sounded. "Unauthorized vessel intruding!"

The newsships quickly oriented on the intruder. It turned out to be a destroyer that had masqueraded as a newsship itself; how it had gotten past the clearance procedure was a question whose answer I was sure would cause some heads to roll. It was headed for us.

A Saturn battleship guarded us. Immediately it challenged the intruder, but received no answer. Therefore it warned all other ships clear so that it could commence firing. This was a formality; it could score readily enough on the intruder without hitting any of the authorized vessels.

In response, the intruder fired a missile cluster at us. We were far enough from it so that there was plenty of time for the battleship to laser the missiles down. But then the cluster split apart, and suddenly there were thousands of decoys, mixed with a few genuine missiles. That complicated things considerably.

The battleship attacked on two fronts: It fired a barrage of missiles at the intruder, and simultaneously used its lasers to knock out the missiles heading for us. But it was difficult to tell which were real and which were the decoys, as the latter were designed to simulate the real ones for just this purpose. The battleship had to take out *all* the apparent missiles—and I knew from my own Navy experience that some of them would reach us before that happened. With luck, those that reached us would be decoys, harmless. But it was a gamble.

Then a new alarm sounded. "Sub alert! Sub alert!"

Spirit whistled. "The nomens are really after us this time!" she said. "They sneaked a sub in under cover of the missile action."

"And we know its target," I agreed. "Hang on; I'm taking evasive action."

I spoke figuratively, for we were already strapped in. But it was rough on Smilo, who didn't understand about erratic space maneuvers; his body was thrown back and forth. That couldn't be helped.

The missiles and decoys corrected course to maintain their orientation, closing the gap between us. Those were sophisticated decoys! But the real menace was the sub, which would launch a torpedo when it got the range. That would be target-seeking too, and there was no chance it would be a decoy.

Sure enough, our torpedo alarm activated. The sub could not be seen, but the torpedo could, and it was uncomfortably close.

"Got to run for it!" I said. I maxed the drive, and we took off at four gees. Hoo! That just about stopped my old heart right there! But the missiles still gained on us, and so did the torpedo.

Then the torpedo detonated; the battleship had scored on it with a laser. But we knew the sub was still there, and it would fire another torpedo when ready; this was a loser's game, for us.

"Go for the transmitter!" Spirit said. She was cool, of course, though Fortuna seemed frightened. She had reason!

Of course! I went for the transmitter, which we had been approaching anyway. Its personnel, cognizant of the situation, would be ready; they would activate it the moment we entered it.

Our torpedo alarm sounded again. This one was closer, and closing on us faster; the sub had zeroed in on us.

But the transmitter was closer yet. "This demo had better work!" I muttered as I oriented on the seemingly tiny aperture of the tube and maintained acceleration. Because if it didn't, and we were not sent out at light speed, the torpedo would take us out at its speed.

I won the race to the transmitter. Our ship plunged into the tube—and out the other side.

"Oh, no!" Spirit breathed. "They didn't transmit us!"

But in a moment I knew she was wrong. "Look at the environment!" I exclaimed. "The light ambience is only a quarter what it was. This is Uranus orbit!

"But we didn't take any three hours!" Forta protested.

"We took it; we simply weren't aware of it. There is no time at light speed, as far as we're concerned; it's like being in suspended animation."

"Of course," Forta agreed after a moment. "Silly of me to forget." In this manner she dismissed the magnitude of the accomplishment we had seen: successful light-speed travel. It had worked! Man could now travel to the stars, with no more apparent time lapse than we had experienced. We could colonize the galaxy!

Now we saw the escort ships of the Uranus nations arriving. We were definitely there!

In a moment we were in video touch with them, and I was repeating what was obvious: we had arrived in good form and, no, we had not been rendered into zombies. The mechanism was viable.

"But how is the tiger?" a reporter asked.

We checked. Smilo looked spacesick, but he was intact. "We had a little complication at the other end," I explained. "Smilo wasn't anchored, and he took a beating. But cats are tough. I'm sure he'll be available for interviews in due course."

The reporter laughed, and so did we. It was a great feeling.

But our relaxation was premature. A ship with the emblem of Helvetia was approaching. Spirit and I accepted this with equanimity, because Helvetia, colonized by the historic Switzerland, was to be our host country during our stay at Uranus.

Uranus, you see, is more fragmented than is Jupiter or Saturn. It equates to the ancient Europe, and has many languages and cultures, and a turbulent history. Because it would have been confusing to have all the political entities of Earth represented by identical names in their colonies, the colonies assumed names of their choosing, and these were generally based on long-standing cultural affiliations. On Earth of twenty-five centuries ago, the territory later to be known as Switzerland was occupied by the Helvetian people, and so this was the name selected for their colony on Uranus. They have maintained their policy of nonviolence, and their interest in technology and finance; Helvetian equipment is some of the finest in the System, and their city of Rich is perhaps the leading financial center of Uranus. (Cities tend to be abbreviated forms of their counterparts on ancient Earth, so Rich derives from Zurich appropriately.) At any rate, we felt quite comfortable about accepting the hospitality of Helvetia, though this was our first visit to Uranus.

"I smell a rat," Forta said.

I glanced at her. "You don't like Helvetia?"

"I like it well; I have been here before. But Helvetia has no ships of that class in its Navy."

"Why not?" I asked. "Historically, on Earth, the region was landbound, but there is no such thing in the System. Helvetia can have any navy it can finance—and it is a rich little nation."

"Isn't that a cruiser?" she persisted. "A ship of war?"

"She's got a point, Hope," Spirit said. "Why should a peaceful nation support a war vessel?"

"They *don't* support any warships," Forta said. "It's policy, not finance. That ship can't be theirs."

"We can verify its credentials in a moment," I said, reaching for the communications panel.

Spirit's hand intercepted mine. "If that ship is a ringer, it will blast us out of space the moment we try to verify it. Our assassins are fanatics."

"But if we don't go with it, it will realize that we know," I said. "And if we do go with it—"

"The tube," Forta said tightly. "Will it—?"

"Titan personnel operate that tube," I said. "Let's see how smart they are." I spoke casually, but we all knew that we were in trouble.

I touched the communications panel. "Glad to see you, Helvetia," I said, addressing the cruiser. "Bear with me a moment; I want to fetch something at the tube." And I cut my drive, going into free-fall, turned my ship about, and accelerated back toward the tube. Of course this meant I was still traveling the way I had been going; it would take a few minutes for our drive to reverse our course. But since the cruiser had been matching our velocity, this had the effect of making us draw away from it.

The cruiser did not reply. It simply matched our velocity again, performing a similar maneuver and accelerating to compensate for our change. It was not about to let us get away.

I goosed the drive, increasing our gee. Smilo gave a

growl, not liking this. The cruiser matched us again.
There was no longer doubt in my mind; that ship was
stalking us, determined to keep us within the range of
its weapons so that it could take us out anytime. Because a cruiser is a major ship, worth a lot of money to
someone, it was not eager to become a suicide mission;
it preferred to wait for opportunity or necessity to deal
with us, always hoping that we would finish our minor
errand and then dock with it, the four of us walking
quietly into its trap like flies into the web of a spider.
Then we would disappear, and so would the cruiser, and
the powers of Uranus would be left with a mystery, and
no Tyrant to meet with.

I guided our ship straight toward the tube. "Minor matter," I transmitted to the tube personnel. "You know what
I want."

There was a pause. Then the Rising Sun technician
came on my screen. "As you wish, Tyrant," he said politely.

We oriented on the tube and accelerated right for its
aperture. Because this was a pilot model, it wasn't trim;
it was oversized, with clumsy-seeming attachments.
Later generations would be sleek and trim, instead of
big enough to handle the proverbial barn. The pursuing
ship closed on us, perhaps becoming nervous about our
destination. If we transmitted back to Saturn—

By the time we entered the tube, the cruiser was almost on our tail. We shot through, and out the other side.
The cruiser entered right behind us, barely squeezing in—
and disappeared.

We experienced an abrupt jolt, as though a star had
just gone nova behind us. Our tail section heated and
melted, and our drive cut out. We were boosted forward,
but we were dead in space. Smilo took another bad fall.

But ships were constructed for exactly this type of acceleration. Our drive was gone, but our hull was intact
and our cabin power remained on. We had survived.

"What was that?" Forta asked. Her bun of hair had
come apart, and she looked disheveled.

"We may have been struck by a laser," I said, "or the
equivalent."

"Oh—they fired at us!" she said.

"Perhaps," Spirit agreed.

"Where are we?" Forta asked nervously.

"Right where we were," I said, checking out the equipment to ascertain whether we retained communication. "The tube did not activate, for us."

"Then where is the other ship?"

I smiled grimly. "That may be difficult to determine. You see, the tube did activate for it."

"You mean it's a light beam, on its way to Saturn?"

"It's a light beam," I agreed. Spirit caught my eye, and I said no more.

"So it was transmitted while we were not," Forta said, amazed. "But how—"

"The Rising Sun personnel understood our wish," Spirit told her. "Our wish was to be free of pursuit."

"How clever!" Forta said.

Spirit and I were veterans of the Jupiter Navy and of combat in space. We had never liked destruction and killing, but we had been hardened to it in war. It was war we were in now, as anonymous forces sought to assassinate us to prevent us from making our play to unify the planets around the galactic project. The personnel of that ship had been ordered to kill us, quietly if possible; we had had to take them out. We had done so.

The face of the Rising Sun technician came on our screen. "Are you satisfied, Tyrant?" he inquired.

"Quite," I agreed. "Shall we agree that this matter is finished?"

"Agreed, sir," the tech said.

"We appear to have suffered some damage," I continued. "Possibly from a laser attack. Please request assistance for us."

"A laser," the tech agreed. "We shall see to it, sir." He clicked out.

"Damn good personnel," Spirit murmured.

"They are highly trained, of course," Forta said.

We did not comment, but that was not what Spirit had meant. The Rising Sun tech had shown very special judgment and discipline, and our interchange had been more significant than either party cared to advertise.

You see, Rising Sun was forbidden by treaty to produce weapons of war. The light-projection project was considered to be technology of peace, but it had certain difficult philosophical aspects. If a ship was transmitted to another tube, this was a peaceful operation. But suppose a ship was transmitted—and there was no receiving tube? Or the beam of light was deflected on the way? Then there would be no reconversion, and that ship would probably never manifest in solid state again. When that happened, was the tube a weapon instead of a tool?

The Rising Sun personnel had understood me. They had let our ship pass through untransmitted. They had activated the system for the following ship, so that it became light and beamed forward at light speed. Thus it had been removed from this scene, and could no longer threaten us.

But it had entered the tube immediately after us. Our vessel had blocked its forward path. When it became light, it had struck us. Probably most of it had passed around us, but that center section that overlapped us had melted our tail. It takes a lot of light to equal the mass of any part of a ship. That part of it would never arrive at the receiving tube—if, indeed, that tube even remained in place, let alone tuned for reception. Since this had been an unplanned transmission, the Saturn tube had no reason to be activated, and no light-speed message to it could reach it before the ship did.

That ship was dead. Spirit and I knew it, and the personnel of the transmission tube knew it. Forta didn't know it, and perhaps it would be some time before the rest of the System caught on. The tube had just been used as a weapon. Did that put Rising Sun in violation of its treaty? I thought not, as its personnel were only obeying my directive, and in any event, they were only employees of the Union of Saturnine Republics, which was not bound to peace. But it could make an ugly case. So we had tacitly agreed that nothing untoward had happened. That the enemy ship had lasered us just before it transmitted, and subsequently suffered an unforeseen accident. It was a temporary conspiracy of silence.

But they certainly were good men. They were civilians, but they had acted with military judgment and dispatch and discretion. I could now appreciate why Rising Sun had been such a formidible adversary, back in the days when it was warlike.

This had been more of a demonstration than we had planned on—but a most effective one.

Chapter 10

PERSUASION

We transferred to a legitimate Helvetian vessel and were brought to the planet of Uranus in proper style. Uranus was smaller than Saturn, its diameter less than half and its mass somewhat over a seventh. Of course every other body in the immediate Solar System (that is, excluding Nemesis, which is really a companion star, rather than a satellite) is minuscule compared to Jupiter, whose mass is greater than all the rest of the System combined. Still, Uranus was a giant compared to Earth, being over fourteen times its mass. Its surface gravity was actually less than that of Earth, but its escape velocity twice Earth's. People assume that the two should vary together, but this is not so; Uranus' far greater mass brings up the escape velocity, while its lower density brings down the gee. Saturn is similar in this respect, also having a lower surface gee than Earth.

The most remarkable thing about Uranus is its orientation in space. It is tilted by close to a right angle, so that its poles are in the sun's ecliptic. It is as though the planet has fallen over, and all its rings and satellites fallen with it. This means that in the course of its eighty-four-year revolution about the sun the North and South Poles take turns pointing toward the sun, making for days and nights about forty-two years long. It also rotates backwards—they call it retrograde—so that the sun would seem to rise in the west, to a person on the equator, if it rose at all. That depends on the season, of course. The truth is that for those who live in the interior of a bubble in the atmosphere, with artificial light, it really does not make a lot of difference.

As we came in we saw the relatively calm atmosphere,

clear to an amazing depth. One would have thought that there would be terrible turbulence, considering the oddities of the planet's situation in space, but this was not the case. It reminded me of a deep ocean, for the large amount of methane provided a greenish hue. It seemed very pretty to me, as planets go. The atmosphere rotates in about twenty-four hours, making it very similar to Earth in this respect, though the planet itself is faster. Since the city-bubbles are in the atmosphere, that is what counts, for human beings.

We came down to Helvetia. Its bubbles floated slightly higher than the majority, and their wind current differed accordingly from those of the majority, so they were relatively isolated geographically. It seemed that the Helvetians liked to live in the mountains, as it were. This perhaps complicated their operations slightly, but did give them a certain independence, and that seemed to suit them.

The city-bubble that was to be our base of operations was Eva, long known as an interplanetary meeting place. I had half expected to spy the citizens going about in colorful shorts and hats, but in truth they were almost indistinguishable from residents of Saturn or Jupiter, except for their language. Helvetia had three or four official languages: French, German, Italian, and Romansch. I believe the majority spoke German, but Eva was in the French section. None of these did Spirit and me much good, our languages being Spanish and English. Fortunately many of the residents of Eva also spoke one or both of our tongues, and in any event we had Forta. She spoke German and French, and was able to translate the others with her equipment. She was the right person to have along.

I don't care to dwell on the rituals of introductions and arrangements; suffice to say that the process I dismiss here actually required months, because of the bureaucratic mechanisms and protocols entailed. Uranus was a nest of rival systems, each seemingly trying to upstage the others or to gain special advantage for itself. Most of its component nations had formed the Uranian Common Market, which meant that tariffs and other impediments to trade were lowered between members, and this seemed to have a beneficial effect on their separate fortunes, but many problems remained. I felt as if I had stepped into a nest of scorpions. All were impressed with our demonstration of the feasibility of light-speed travel; each wanted all the benefits for itself, and none wanted to pay for them. I could not address the planetary leaders in a single group, obtain their commitment to the project, and be on my way; I had to hold a private audience with each leading executive, who was noncommittal until he knew of the positions of the others. What had been intended as a one-week stay stretched out into months, with no end in sight.

I was never a phenomenally patient man, and age had not softened me. In those early days of frustration I was building up an unhealthy head of pressure. Spirit encouraged me to become a tourist, visiting the attractions, but though I am capable of appreciating such things, my ire at the waste of my time made me an inadequate tourist. I'm afraid the Eyeful Tower was wasted on me, however remarkable it may be as a structure in orbit.

One day Spirit went out on some routine matter, and I settled down with a helmet and holo chip, seeking diversion. Unfortunately, all that was readily available was the normal entertainment fare: feelie sex. This reminded me of what I was missing in that department. I preferred the real thing to a creation of the helmet, and what could I do about that? Phone for a professional girl? That had never been my way. Disgusted, I removed the helmet.

A young, buxom Hispanic woman walked in. My first reaction was alarm: This suite was supposed to be secure against intrusion. My second was amazement: This was a phenomenally attractive creature, by my definition. My third was shock: *I knew this girl!* She was Juana, my first Navy love. And my fourth was disappointment: I realized that this was Forta Foundling, doing a mime.

She was good at it, though. Obviously Spirit had coached her on it, for this was Juana as I remembered her forty years ago, before advancing age plumped her out. Not perfect, of course, for Spirit could neither have noted nor conveyed all of the special things I knew about Juana. But close enough to be quite intriguing.

I was interested in the technical aspect. Forta was tall and slender and somewhat angular, yet this creature seemed shorter and full-fleshed and rounded. I realized that some of it was Forta's genius with the signals; a thin body that sent plump signals did appear rounded. I had not before realized the extent to which this could be true. Obviously Forta had rehearsed plump signals, and applied them to this characterization. But it was more than that; a considerable amount of that flesh was genuine. How could that be?

I concluded that I had not really been looking at Forta. She had worn an angular style of clothing, perhaps projecting that quality when it wasn't really hers. Now she was projecting the opposite, in effect doubling the distance. However she did it, she was expert at the illusion.

Now I studied her face. It was a mask, of course, cleverly done but not truly alive. She had trained her hair down and around it to conceal the border, and it was flexible and thin, so that it moved with her own expression. The eyes and mouth were especially lifelike; I realized that they had to be her own, buttressed by makeup. I looked, but I could not see the line of mergence between the mask and her true features; there seemed to be none. She must have used foundation creme or something to flesh out her features where the scars would show, and contact lenses to modify her eyes. Oh, she knew her business, without doubt!

And what exactly was her business? To distract me. She had come to be my mistress, and I had ignored her. I had come to respect her abilities as a worker; she had become as good a secretary as I had ever had, with one exception. That exception—

No! I refused to let the memory of Shelia, my crippled but perfect secretary of more than twenty years, destroy my mood. Shelia had died protecting me; the devastation of that loss had brought me to the verge of madness. Perhaps a bit beyond the verge. I had recovered, perhaps at the point my wife Megan ousted me from the Tyrancy, and I preferred to remain recovered. I remembered with distaste some of the things that had seemed justified by that madness. Better to play Forta's game now, and think of Juana.

Actually, Juana had been my secretary too. We had been lovers—roommates, in the Navy fashion—until I became an officer. She had elected to remain enlisted, and therefore became off limits to me, to our mutual regret. She had been such a nice girl, lacking the drive that had brought my later wives to their pinnacles of success. It would be nice indeed to return to that world of Juana, when I was young and really not very experienced, and she, the survivor of rape, had been as young and less experienced, so that my sex with her always had to be gentle. I had at times been less than satisfied, wanting to have some more lusty fling, but in retrospect I conclude that my occasions with reluctant Juana—no, not really reluctant, merely subdued; she did what the Navy required, and tried her best to make it nice for me, and that effort of hers did indeed make it nice even if it wasn't spectacular—well, those occasions had been as good in their way as any. It is the total relationship that makes it good, not just the raw sex. The single touch of the beloved's hand is more meaningful than the most spectacular sex with a known professional.

Juana was standing before me, waiting for my thoughts to complete their course. I knew she was not, yet chose to accept her validity; Forta's effort was as worthy in its fashion as Juana's had been in hers. I raised my hand to her, accepting the presentation, and she came slowly to me, as Juana would.

I took her hand and drew her down to sit in my lap. Her bottom felt plush in the way I remembered, and her bosom was full and soft. I put my head against it, and she put her arms around me, and I felt as though I were eighteen again.

Here is the oddity: I did not take Juana to bed. I did not even undress her, or reach inside her clothing. She would have cooperated, I know, but that was not, as it turned out, my true desire. I just sat there, with her warm soft body against me, and I didn't move. I didn't speak, I didn't stroke, I didn't really do anything except remember. Perhaps I slept, without changing position, for abruptly Spirit was in the room, and I knew she had planned to be absent two hours, time enough for me to complete whatever business with Forta I was going to. But I had not completed it; I remained embraced by her, savoring the eternal moment. I had never experienced anything quite like this—not even with the original Juana. That was part of what made it so amazing. Forta had become a better Juana than the original.

Spirit merely glanced at us, and nodded, and went on to her room. I remained a further time as I was, but slowly the mood ameliorated. I realized that my legs were going to sleep; I was no longer young and robust and durable. I had to change my position and break the spell.

Finally I did so. I moved, and she got up. Neither of us had spoken during this entire session, and we did not speak now. She simply walked away from me, back to her own room, and I sat for another time, dazed by the wonder of it. Then I got up and resumed the day.

One thing I had learned: Forta was no longer to be neglected. She was now, indeed, in her fashion, my woman.

Spirit labored diligently to make the necessary connections. We had always worked this way: She did the behind-the-scenes work, while I handled the public scenes. She would produce bodies for me to interview, and I would pass on them, not because I was the superior individual but because that was my talent. I knew that during this period of inactivity on my part, Spirit was forging the elements of our campaign to bring the major nations of Uranus into the Dream. Forta, as our secretary, was kept busy doing spot research on situations and personnel.

There was an item that I remember largely by re-creation, because at the time I did not realize its significance. It serves as an example of how Spirit worked, and how she utilized whatever resources we had to accomplish our purpose. It happened somewhat like this:

"What do we have on General D?" Spirit asked Forta.

General D was our contraction of the name for the President of Gaul. He was an enormous old pear-shaped man who had come out of retirement to assume the lead-

ership of a divided nation. We considered him to be a
difficult man, set in his ways, which were no one else's,
but it was true that he had forged a kind of national unity
that had been lacking in that nation for some time. We
expected him to be our most formidable challenge, because he disliked participating in anything he could not
dominate, and he had always been a leading anti-Sat-
urnist. If we could gain his commitment, the other nations would fall into place more readily; if we could not,
we might have to write off Uranus.

"The man's impervious," Forta replied. "Once his mind
is set, neither heaven nor hell will change it. Here they
say, 'There's the right way, the wrong way, and the General's way.' That's about it."

I remembered. As the Tyrant of Jupiter, I had of course
had dealings with the nations of Uranus. The General,
nominally an ally, had as often as not been a thorn in my
side. He saw reason only on his own terms. I had mostly
worked around him, leaving him to his own devices, so
we had gotten along. But if there was one thing the General really respected it was power—and now I was coming
to him not as an absolute ruler but as an underling, a
supplicant. He would consider it a matter of honor to be
difficult.

"I seem to remember that there was one he listened
to," Spirit said.

"His daughter. But she died five years ago, and after
that he stopped caring about any opinion but his own.
There is no ameliorating personality around him now."

"His daughter," Spirit said musingly. She glanced at
me. "They to tend to wrap their fathers around their fingers."

Again I remembered: my daughter Hopie, now in her
late twenties, sometimes sweet, sometimes imperious, always my darling girl. There had been a quarter-century
media campaign to determine the identity of her mother,
for my wife Megan had been beyond bearing age when I
married her, and Hopie was adopted. Hopie resembled me
in so many important ways, from appearance to blood type
to personality, that there was no question of her lineage,
but of course I had never spoken of her parentage except

to acknowledge that she was the bastard offspring of a
married man and a single woman. It is one of the anom-
alies of our culture that it is the child of an illicit union
who is blamed, rather than the perpetrators. But from the
moment of the adoption, Hopie was licitly mine, and yes,
she did wrap me around her little finger on myriad occasions. I wished she could be with us now, but of course I
would not have her share the status of exile, so she remained on Jupiter.

"I could study her," Forta said.

Spirit nodded. "If you are willing."

"Megan knew of the Dream," Forta said. "She felt I
could help in its realization. I see no ethical problem here,
especially considering the alternative."

So Megan had learned of Khukov's Dream! Of course
secrets could not be kept, but I found this interesting.
Megan was a leading advocate of System peace, and would
do anything she could to forward it. She had understood,
of course, that when I asked for a woman, I meant one I
could take to my bed, and she was realistic enough to
accept this. After all, she knew me well indeed. But naturally she had honored my request in a manner calcu-
lated to forward her desire as well. Forta's nominal
position might be as my mistress—and I knew that it
would soon enough be actual—but her real thrust was to
facilitate peace and reduce the horrors of war and tyr-
anny. Yet how could a study of the General's dead daughter accomplish any of this?

As I said, this scene passed without making much of
an impression on me at the time, and my reconstruction
may have embellished it somewhat, but that was the essence. Its significance registered only after the denoue-
ment.

We finally got our interview with the General. One of
the complications was his refusal to utilize the holo technology. It was possible to transmit the complete image of
a person and his surroundings in three dimensions, so
that he seemed to be physically present, and this was normally employed for important meetings. I had used it
when interviewing the Shogun of Rising Sun. For one
thing, it saved the inconvenience of physical travel time;

for another, it eliminated any question of assassination, for a weapon smuggled into such an interview could not be effective against a mere image. Staff members offstage from the holo pickup cameras could signal their man, giving him necessary cues, so that he did not suffer embarrassing lapses. When the interview was over, each party could relax immediately, being right at home. The recording of the interview could be rerun as convenient by either party, questing for significant aspects after the fact. No wonder it was the most popular mechanism for such encounters; I certainly preferred it.

But the General was old-fashioned, and did not trust modernistic devices, for all that this one had existed for centuries. He believed only in face-to-face summit-type meetings, and not too many of those, and that was it. If I wanted to address him, it had to be his way. This included his language, French; he would not deign to discourse in our common language, English, though he knew it. So I went, at his convenience, and brought along my sister and secretary; this was as elaborate a party as we could muster. We duly presented ourselves at the palace in the city-bubble of Aris, Gaul.

The General in person was surprisingly affable. We had been braced for boorishness, but he was the soul of hospitality and cheer. He shook my hand, and we took seats. He certainly was physically impressive, both in magnitude and in atmosphere. He seemed every centimeter the leader. He had also done his homework; he knew why I was here and what I wanted of him, in general and in detail. But I knew as I read him that his mind was already made up, and that this was merely a formality. He was not about to render himself subservient, by his reckoning, by participating in the galactic project.

Thus there was no point in talking with him. I was here merely for show. To show that the General could summon the Tyrant like a lackey, to be informed that there was no sale. Three years ago, when I remained in power in Jupiter, he never would have tried it. The sheer arrogance of the man excited my admiration as much as my ire; one seldom gets to experience such towering certainty and folly.

Spirit caught my eye as I exchanged inconsequentials with the General via the interpreter. I gave her to understand my reading, by the slightest nod: thumbs down. I knew she had anticipated as much. She in turn made an unobtrusive signal to Forta, who stood at the edge of the room.

Forta turned around a moment, as if suffering an attack of vertigo. She was doing something to herself; was she really sick? I saw her only peripherally, as I could not take my overt attention from my host. But then she turned again, her aspect changed. She stepped toward us.

The General paused, glancing at her, startled. He got to his feet.

"My secretary," I said. The translator started to speak, but the General negated him with a curt gesture.

"Vous avez tort, père," Forta said. I saw now that she had entirely changed her hair, and she wore one of her masks, so that she resembled a young woman who would have been attractive except for her overly large nose. That nose resembled that of the General.

The General looked stricken. *"Ce n'est pas ma faute,"* he said.

She only gazed at him, shaking her head sadly.

Abruptly he addressed me directly in English: "What do you see here, Hubris?" He was severely shaken.

"Only my secretary," I said innocently. I realized now that Forta was emulating the General's dead daughter.

He shook himself and blinked. He looked again at Forta. It was as if he saw a ghost.

I glanced again at Spirit. What was the point of this charade?

"You support this man?" the General asked the ghost.

Forta nodded in a special manner. I did not know his daughter's mannerisms, but I was sure Forta did. "Why are you talking to my secretary?" I asked, as if I didn't understand.

"And if I agree?"

Forta approached him, lifted her face, and kissed his cheek. Then she walked slowly out of the room.

For a moment the General stood stunned. Then he

strode after her. Spirit and I remained where we were, letting this play itself out.

All that the General found in the other room, of course, was my secretary, Forta, who could in no way be mistaken for his daughter. Disgruntled, he returned. "You saw only your secretary?"

Spirit and I nodded together, too polite to remark on his erratic behavior.

He considered. "Gaul will support your project, Tyrant," he said abruptly.

"Your generosity and foresight are much appreciated," I said. "The greatness of Gaul will long be commemorated." We concluded the interview with the usual amenities.

In the private airplane that Helvetia had provided for our use, I braced Spirit. "What did you do?"

"Helse manifests to you on occasion," she replied. "Why not his departed daughter? She had a dream for humanity; all he needed was a reminder."

And in the face of our insistence that it was only our secretary he saw, the General had realized that his daughter was manifesting to him alone. He could deny us, but he could not deny her. So he had risen to the occasion and done what his beloved daughter wanted. Such persuasion is not to be resisted.

I thought of my own daughter, Hopie. If she had died, and later manifested to me in that manner, I would have done what she wanted, too. I respected the General not less for that, but more.

After that success, the others followed more readily. We interviewed the Kaiser of Prussia, and the Kings of Bohemia, Lithuania, and Etruria. It was a pleasure for me to visit Castile personally, because that was of course colonized by the source of the Hispanics, the peninsula of Spain on Earth. There was no trouble converting Castile to the Dream; Castile had watched my progress on Jupiter all the way to the top, and had broken relations with Jupiter when I was deposed. It was a real pleasure to be welcomed where Spanish was the natural language.

Serbia, Macedonia, Jutland, Lapland, and the others

fell into place, one by one. Each was an individual case, of course, and negotiations were at times intricate, but the understanding that the major transmission tube would be constructed here was conducive.

Spirit was of course tied up with the arrangements, and though I was busier than I had been, I still had dull times too. I had thought that age would bring me greater stability of emotion as my passions faded, but this was not the case. I was becoming more conscious of the diminishing time remaining to me in life, and I wanted to savor as much of it as I could.

Thus it was that when Juana came to me again, I was more than willing to be persuaded that she was worthwhile. I knew this was no vision, and that she was Forta doing an emulation, but I stepped right into the game, and it ceased to be a game. I opened my arms to her, and she came into them, and I swear even the scent of her was the same. The true Juana was not dead; she was in her sixties, as I was, and grandmotherly, no longer any object of manly passion. This was the Juana of age twenty, shy and nice and voluptuously endowed.

I kissed her, and her lips were soft and sweet. Her face might be a mask, but it seemed genuine to me. Surely her breasts had been enhanced, for Forta simply was not of the magnitude that Juana had been in this respect, but they seemed the same. I drew back a little and passed my hand over her bosom, and she drew back nervously—exactly the way Juana had. Weekly sexual activity had been required in the Navy, and Juana had honored that, but she had always been conscious of the rape she had suffered, and was always somewhat reticent. How had Forta learned so much?

"The lights," I said.

She smiled. "The lights," she agreed, sounding exactly as Juana had sounded.

I turned off the lights. The darkness was almost absolute, but I found her and kissed her again. Then I led her to my bed. My foot touched a furry body; Smilo was snoozing there, as usual. I reached down to pat him. "This is all right, friend," I assured him. And it was; it had only been Tasha, in her mole aspect, that had set him off, with reason. He knew Forta, whatever her guise might be, and had no objection to my contact with her.

We stood by the bed in the darkness, and I took the clothing off her body. Soon she was in bra and panties, and the bra was just as full as Juana's had been. I hardly even pondered the matter; I left the bra in place, preferring to maintain that fullness, rather than stripping it with the cloth. The panties I took down, and then I put her on the bed. She remained somewhat reticent, but offered no opposition. Juana had always depended on me to initiate the act of sex, and to bring her through it successfully; with her it had to be acquiescence, never desire. But I had always chosen to believe that within that framework, she did appreciate it; I think I could not have done it otherwise.

I did it now. As I climaxed, the mood of it overwhelmed me, and I kissed her savagely. "Juana!" I gasped.

"Hope!" she responded, and her arms hugged me close.

That did something to me. I cannot say I understand it, but it was in its fashion wonderful. I held her and I cried, silently, my tears coursing from my face across hers. We lay there for some time, intimately embraced, and though we shifted position in due course so that my weight would not be on her, we remained embraced, and I fell asleep.

When I woke, she was gone. Juana had always done that, too, preferring to clean up without disturbing me. I got up and went through my own toilet, and returned to the office section of the suite.

Forta was there, as usual, sifting through information on the computer. She was as severe and angular as ever, and when she glanced at me there was no trace of intimacy. She knew that no one could be turned on by that horribly scarred face.

"You remind me of Tasha," I said. "Inverted."

She smiled somewhat coolly and returned to her work. I retired to a book, but my mind was not on it. Forta had just become my mistress, as she had said at the outset she would. She had assumed another guise for the purpose, but it had been her body and her mind in reality. Tasha had sent me perpetual sexual signals, but turned killer when the connection was made; Forta sent me none, but was as spectacularly apt in the performance as I could imagine. Truly, it seemed I had been with Juana!

Yet if I could complete the act with a woman playing a role, why could I not do it with the woman as herself? I did not know, but knew I could not. I remained a fool, in the masculine way: Appearance was more important than reality.

Just as it had been with the General of Gaul. He had known that my secretary was not his daughter, yet the aspect of her was so compelling that, to please it, he had reversed himself. How could I call him a fool, when I understood the situation so much better than he did, and still was governed by the illusion? Forta's art of emulation had persuaded the General to do what was best for the System, and had persuaded me to accept her offering, despite my understanding.

Dear Daddy,

I must confess, that was some demonstration you did with the light drive! It wasn't broadcast on Jupiter holo for some reason, but the news got around. Turning an entire spaceship into light—just imagine! I understand that Uranus is all agog, but they are underplaying it here, saying that the reliability is uncertain and that you were lucky you weren't killed.

I wish you were back here, and not just because I am concerned for your welfare. But the present administration will never permit your return. Perhaps they will let me visit you at Uranus or somewhere; I'd like that. There is so much I could tell you!

Take good care of your tiger, Daddy. . . .

Chapter 11

TITANIA

Having done what we could on the Continent, as it was locally termed, we next tackled the islands. The most important of these were Umbriel and Titania, two moons about a quarter million and two-fifths of a million kilometers out from the residential band of the planet, respectively, and just below and just above a thousand kilometers in diameter. These were tiny, on the scale of the satellites of Jupiter, but physical size was no necessary indication of importance.

The fact is, there is a lot of area available on a solid moon. We become accustomed to the limitations of the city-bubbles in the atmospheres of the major planets, where space is always at a premium though distances between cities are vast. On an airless moon like Titania the cities still need to be enclosed by domes, but many, many domes can be set up in limited territory. They won't collide; the common anchorage makes it feasible. So an entire nation of several tens of millions of human beings resides on a moon that would fit inside the merest whorl in a major planet's atmosphere.

Titania, small as it seemed in space, had inherited the British Empire tradition. Indeed, at one time it had had major holdings all across the Solar System, including the entire planets of sparsely settled Neptune and densely settled Earth. Today the Titanian Commonwealth remained, but the political and economic power of Titania itself was much diminished and still waning. The System was simply too large to be dominated by one tiny moon! But the influence of the so-called Saxon culture remained, with English being perhaps the most prevalent second language in the System.

We landed at the monstrous city-dome of Don, situated in the channel of Tems, near the South Pole of the moon. Since the moon did not rotate on its own, one face being locked toward Uranus, there were no problems of adjustment; the near face could be treated in many respects like a flat terrain. All of the significant human habitations were on this face; the far face was left for mining and light-collection and special projects. Perhaps this was just as well, for the light lenses were monstrous, quadruple the diameter of those of Jupiter. There was no mystery about this; Uranus is almost four times as far from the sun as is Jupiter, so equivalently larger lenses are required to focus the sunlight to similar intensity. Truly is it said: If you want to know where you are in the System, look at the size of the light lenses. These ones had to gather sunlight from a region just about three hundred times as large as that to be covered by Earth-normal daylight. That left huge areas in shade.

I had, as I mentioned, become accustomed to the floating bubbles of the major planets in the course of the past thirty years. My youth had been spent on Callisto, where there were landbound domes. But there was little similarity to those domes here. Callisto was a much larger body than Titania, and used the gravity lens to focus the gravity of the planet and bring it up to Earth-norm in the cities. Thus the domes sat firmly and immobily on the surface.

These domes did not. They were mounted on firm bases, and were in the form of monstrous cylinders, spinning about their axes. They depended on centrifugal gee, exactly as did the bubbles floating in atmosphere. This was similar in principle to the domes of Jupiter military bases on moonlets or planetoids, but Don was of a completely different scale. It was one of the largest cities in the System, as populous as Jupiter's Nyork or Langel, though not as large as RedSpot City had become. Here in the ice-covered valley, it was phenomenally grand; the landscape gave it contrast.

We took the shuttle subway into the city proper, for entry was via the interior of the pedestal on which it rotated. There was so little gravity on the surface that it seemed almost like free-fall; we had to strap in to prevent sailing into the ceiling with every bump. I believe Titania's surface gee is about one-thirtieth Earth-norm, though I would have to look it up to be sure; certainly it is very slight. It becomes difficult to judge by mere physical sensation.

The subway capsule made a right-angle turn and carried us upward into the city. Then it descended, and we gained weight. Of course this was relative; we were actually facing straight up, away from the surface of the moon, but now it seemed like the horizontal.

We debouched at a station on a lower level; it was easy enough to tell by the higher gee. They were prepared for our arrival, for the section was cordoned off. I can't think why; I had Smilo on a leash. Our inprocessing was remarkably efficient, and before we knew it we had been assigned a nice cottage in the country, well up toward the Scot border. We did need a place to stay, as it was evident that formal negotiations were not going to be any more rapid here than they had been on the Continent. I knew better than to protest the glacial course of such things; I represented the interests of Saturn and Titan, and Titania's relations with either planet were not phenomenally good. Also, the fact that I had negotiated first with Gaul would not sit well here. But if I had come to Titania first, the General would have been totally intractable, and not even the ghost of his daughter would have swayed him.

We boarded a tram, which was a sealed travel-capsule that loaded itself onto a wheelbase and a set of tracks once it exited Don. It traveled swiftly northward across the frozen surface, guided by an old motorman. Smilo decided he liked this part of the journey; he prowled along the length of the tram and peered out the ports. The motorman seemed a bit nervous at first, but relaxed when it became clear that the tiger accepted him as one of the functionaries. Soon he was announcing the stations we passed.

It seemed that Titania was divided into many small counties, and at our velocity we crossed each one quickly. There was Hert and Bed and Hamp and Leic in the first hour. We saw the spinning domes of the cities of Wat and

Bed and Hamp and Leic; evidently the counties were usually but not invariably named after their leading cities. The tramway tracks divided and crossed and merged throughout, and there were many other trams on them, speeding from city to city. This was a busy world!

The landscape itself, apart from the tracks, was completely barren. With no atmosphere there was no weather, just the rock ice. It reminded me of Callisto, when my family had gone out in quest of a bootleg bubble to Jupiter, seeking a better life. We had found, instead, betrayal and misery and death, and our own kind treated us more savagely than did the barrenness of space. I had been but fifteen, then, naive about the ways of man. I had not remained so. I have wondered whether I would have been better off had I never left Callisto. Certainly I would have for the short term, because then I would not have witnessed the brutal rape of my sister Spirit or the slaughter of my father, or suffered the privations of space. But neither would I have found my first love, Helse—or lost her. My military career would never have occurred, and my political rise to the Tyrancy would not even have been a dream. I had to conclude that my life, taken as a whole, had been correctly guided, despite the early horrors of it.

"Derby," the motorman announced. I began to see what was not there, outside: the green pastures, the picket fences, the cows and the gardens of the olde England that this world emulated, and I felt nostalgia for it though I had never been there. What a joy it must have been to live on Earth, shielded by its breathable atmosphere: an entire planet habitable without suits or domes or devices of gravity and light concentration!

We passed the industrial city of Manch, where freight lines converged, and on into the county of Lanc, and a mountainous region. Here the mountains were genuine; jagged crags rose up beside the tramway. One tends to think that small worlds should have small mountains, but the diminished natural gravity enables them to be rougher in outline than the larger ones.

At last we came into Cumber, relatively sparsely settled, where we were to stay. The authorities had wanted to get Smilo well away from temptation! The tracks wound

about in an effort to avoid the rising contours, and finally
gave up and climbed, passing over the heights. I suppose
these mountains were minor compared to what could be
found elsewhere in the System, or even elsewhere on Titania, but here in our tiny capsule they were quite impressive. I saw vertical rises I would have been afraid to
climb, even in the fractional gee, and a chasm between
peaks that looked right for a glacier.

"Scafell Crag," the motorman said, announcing the site
the way he had the counties.

Then down into the valley, and on to our destination,
Carl. There we had to leave the tram and take a limo to
the cottage, which was a mini-dome east of the city. Here
I became aware of another feature of the landscape, that
had perhaps been present throughout, but missed because
of the velocity of our tram travel. There were paired cords
stretched across the terrain, each being set about a meter
above the ground, supported at intervals by T-shaped
structures. They connected to each separate dome, and
divided and crossed in much the fashion of the tramway
rails.

"Power lines?" I asked Spirit, perplexed.

"Ley lines," the limo driver said, with a private, knowing smile.

"What are they for?"

"For walking," he explained. "Use the rollers."

I had the impression that he enjoyed our perplexity, so
I dropped the subject. But I watched the lines. Occasion-
ally a set crossed the road we were on, and they did this
by rising up on ramps to either side and crossing above
the level of the traffic. I could see how a person in a suit,
walking on the low-gee surface, might use the lines as a
handhold—but why would he cling to them dangling above
the road?

The driver deposited us at the cottage. This was based
on the principle of the cities, being a disk that spun about
its axis, with entry from below. The limo entered the garage, which was a kind of air lock, and when the pressure
equalized we stepped down into the chamber. A lift conveyed us into the center of the disk above, and a ladder
led down (again it was a horizontal "down") to the resi-

dential floor. Smilo was learning to navigate these contours, but he obviously felt better once normal gee returned. The driver departed, and we were on our own.

The first thing we did was rest. Travel is wearying, and Spirit and I were no longer young. We had been in trace gee for several hours, and that tends to disrupt the normal bodily processes. So the four of us settled down for a nap, and then another nap, and the night's sleep, and in due course our systems settled down and we were ready for food and work.

We ate sparingly the next day, and Smilo was content to gnaw on a pseudosteak and use the sandbox. Forta got on the phone and ascertained that it was a local holiday, so there would be no political activity for another day. This was just as well, for it gave us more time to adjust.

Smilo was getting restive, having been in confined quarters for some time. Normally I had taken him out for a walk or run somewhere, because a big cat lives not by snoozing alone; he needs exercise in a psychological as well as physical way. Here there were no halls to use, but we had prepared for this contingency by having a space suit made up for him. We hadn't used it before, and now seemed to be the time to try it.

I unpacked the suit. These things are very light, and fit the body so comfortably that they can be worn for prolonged periods. The material stretches just enough to allow circulation of air about the body, but not enough to interfere with motion. Its insulative properties are phenomenal; hardly any heat is lost, and that's important, because the temperature of this surface was in the neighborhood of $50°K$, or considerably closer to absolute zero than to human living temperature. I'm sure the technology in a modern suit is about as sophisticated as that in a holophone, just of a different nature. There is of course oxygen-refreshing apparatus, and recondensation, and our suits were guaranteed for two hours before requiring the exchange of breathing cylinders.

"You're taking him out?" Forta asked. "Better review the ley system."

"The what?"

"I have researched it this past hour. Those ley lines are

a joke, named after the old supposed lines of ancient monuments in England, Earth. Here they are merely cords used to hold walkers down to the planet, so they don't go flying with every step. The natives do a lot of walking, as many of them don't have cars—cars tend to fly, too, unless they have somewhat adhesive tires the way the limo did—and it's easy enough to get about when you know how. They use the rollers." She went to the wall, and there hung several devices that looked like antique paint rollers. She took one down. "You hook this under the line from the right, and hold it firm, and it rolls along the line and keeps you down."

I considered that. It seemed feasible. "Why not hook in from the left?"

"This is Titania; traffic travels on the left side of the road. So you are always on the left of the line, and when you return you come in on the other side, which is still your right."

I hefted the roller. Its operation seemed simple enough. "But how is Smilo going to use this?"

"I think he has a problem."

"Well, he needs his exercise, so we'll tackle that problem," I decided. I put the suit on the tiger, noting with approval that the extremities were reinforced to be impenetrable by claws. It would be a tragedy if Smilo extended his claws to get a good grip on something, and punctured his suit and died. As it was, I suspected he would have an uncertain time.

Finally I put the helmet over his head. It was completely clear, so he could see well, and sound would be conducted by the ground, as well as a mini suit radio locked on our mutual channel. "We have to wear these to go out," I explained, hoping he would understand enough to accept it. He did know that the outside was a region completely unlike the inside.

I donned my own suit, and the two of us used the personnel exit lock, emerging from the opposite side as the garage. There was no point in having to recompress such a large amount of air as was required for a car, when we were only two.

"Now, Smilo," I cautioned him as we emerged. "Take

it easy on the leaping; I fear you could achieve escape velocity if you really tried, and that would be awkward indeed." I had no leash on him now; I would not be able to hold him down if he leaped anyway, and I wanted him to have the maximum freedom.

Smilo took a step—and drifted off the ground. Startled, he scrambled with all four feet, accomplishing nothing.

"Easy," I said, reaching out to catch him by a suited paw. I held on to the ley line that terminated here, anchoring myself, and drew him gently down. "Maybe if you hung on to the line—" I realized that I should have attached a safety line to him, similar to those used in space, though I wasn't sure how he would react to this.

He took another step, but this time did not sail. He was learning. Cats have a natural sense about motion, I think, and he was a cat. I urged him to the line, showing him how firm it was; he could hook on to it with a front paw or maybe his suited tail and stay down.

I set out, using the roller as prescribed. It worked well. Each step tried to send me up, because I hadn't learned to eliminate the automatic lifting component to my stride, but firm pressure on the roller and the line kept me down. There was a trick to using it; it would be easy to spin about the line if I got the leverage wrong. But I was mastering the trick.

I set off along the line, my roller rolling faster as I picked up speed. Smilo experimented, then achieved a kind of horizontal leap that had almost no lift. Soon enough he was outdistancing me, seeming to flow across the rock-ice. He was enjoying himself, and that was why I had risked this.

Before I knew it, we were far from the cottage. It was fun, zooming along the ley line with my roller buzzing; my vertical thrust was translated to horizontal thrust, provided I kept the angle right, because of the vectors. It might be likened to squeezing seeds between the thumb and forefinger: heavy pressure and small motion translates to fast motion in another direction. Leg and roller squeezed me forward at a velocity I could hardly have achieved, let alone maintained, in ordinary gee. Smilo seemed to have found similar leverage.

But a little went a long way. I did not want this to get out of hand. So after about twenty minutes I ducked under the paired lines and started back toward the cottage. As I did so, I happened to glimpse the road we had arrived on—and I saw the limo parked on it, behind a bluff, out of the line of sight of the cottage. Curious; had it stalled? I might have checked, but it was off the ley line, and I didn't quite trust myself to untethered navigation. The limo had a radio; it could call for help if it needed to. Probably the driver was simply taking a snooze between calls, out where no one would bother him.

Smilo seemed to have had enough too. He accompanied me back without protest. Soon enough we arrived back at the cottage, and entered the air lock. When the pressure equalized, I lifted back my helmet, then saw to Smilo's. "How was it, friend?" I inquired. "Not quite like hunting in Pleistocene Earth!"

We took the lift to the disk and rejoined the girls. "Great stuff!" I exclaimed. "Ask Smilo!"

But Smilo was already settling down under the bed, suit and all. "Hey, I have to undress you!" I called, but he ignored me. Well, if he was that comfortable in the suit, it could remain for a while. I got out of mine and joined Spirit and Forta at the table, where food awaited me.

I was warm from the exertion. The plastic chair was cool, but in a few minutes it was warm. Then it was more than warm. "What's with this furniture?" I asked. "It's as though it's heating by itself!"

Spirit was perplexed. "Mine, too, now that you mention it."

Forta's face turned grave. "And mine. Just now. I wonder—" She got off and turned to examine her chair. She put her face down and sniffed. "Oh-oh."

"Bad plastic?" I asked.

"I could be wrong," Forta said. "But I think we'd better get out of here in a hurry. Get into your suits."

"A bomb?" Spirit asked, jumping up and fetching her suit. I followed suit, in two ways.

"On Mercury they developed some ugly products for antipersonnel purposes," Forta said, scrambling into her own suit. "Not just the plastic explosive, but plastic inflammatories and plastic poison gas. Some of it is set off by a critical temperature, and is self-sustaining thereafter; some of it by a critical mass. But always bad stuff."

Indeed, the three chairs were beginning to melt and bubble, and noxious vapors were rising from them. We clapped our helmets into place, and I dived for Smilo and hauled his own helmet on. "Move, cat!" I barked.

We crammed into the lift and dropped down to the exit. My last view of the interior of the cottage was of yellowish haze suffusing the living space. Poison, surely—that would eliminate all occupants, without damaging the hardware. A very neat, quiet way to take out a roomful. Right when everyone was gathered together. Set for three chairs being used, not one or two. There might not even be any alarm. If Forta hadn't caught on, and if Smilo hadn't already been suited, some or all of us could have been killed.

"Those chairs could have been there for months," Spirit said on the suit radio. "If parties of one or two used this facility, they never would have been activated. But somehow—"

"They were for us," I agreed.

We emerged on the surface. "We can walk to the next dome," I said. "It's easy enough, with the ley line. Follow me." I set my roller in place and started out.

Smilo set out as before, with excellent control, seeming glad enough for another experience. Spirit and Forta were clumsy with their rollers, understandably.

I looked back at the cottage. It spun placidly, evincing no sign of any problem. "We should have sounded an alarm," I muttered. In my haste to get Smilo ready, I hadn't thought of that.

"I did," Forta replied. "The bobbies should be here within fifteen minutes."

"But we should still move along," Spirit said, her helmet turning as she looked about the landscape.

"You think they'll have a backup?" I asked.

"If they're serious."

"Then maybe we shouldn't be talking now," I said. For our suit radios could be picked up at some distance.

But it was already too late. A car was coming down the road, moving swiftly. It was the limo.

Spirit looked at me without speaking. I understood her question: Was that limo coming to help, in response to the alarm, or was it the assassin's backup?

Spirit touched the side of her suit. She had a laser, of course. Strict weapons-control laws kept such things out of the hands of the civilians, and the murder rate was low on Titania, but Spirit was never without hers. The bureaucrats had had to give her a special dispensation. But we couldn't fire at the limo driver without being sure—yet if we did not, and he was the enemy, we could be lost. What should we do?

It was my decision. Spirit always deferred to my authority, not because I was any better at making spot decisions than she was, but for the sake of appearances. I decided not to risk it. I made a hand signal: forward and to left and right.

They understood. We picked up speed, the two of them following me along the ley line, as the limo approached on the road. Was it able to travel off the road? Perhaps we would find out.

The limo came to the place where the road intersected the lines, near the cottage. It pulled off the road. Ice dust powdered up in a cloud as its wheels ground in. "Snow tires," I heard Spirit murmur. Those were the kind that adhered to ice as well as to the special surface of the road. The limo could indeed travel cross-country.

That seemed to answer the question of motive. A legitimate vehicle should not have been so equipped. Or should it? Not all the cottages were on developed roads; perhaps the limo was used as an emergency vehicle. So it still could be coming to help us.

We still couldn't risk it. We ran on along the line. I was leading, with Spirit second and then Forta. There was a line crossing ahead, and that was what we had to reach before the vehicle caught up to us. If the limo was friendly, it was a harmless misunderstanding that the bobbies could sort out; if not, we had a way to confuse it.

I reached the intersection—and continued straight on. Spirit reached it, slowed, and took off to the right. Forta went left. Now we were scattering, so that the limo could not attack more than one at a time. If it attacked one, the other two would know. The chances of it taking all three of us out before the bobbies arrived were slight. It would have to pick its primary target. If it wanted to help, it could pick up anyone; if not, it would come after me.

The limo zoomed up to the intersection, and our doubt was abolished. Not only did it come straight on after me, it took no trouble to avoid the other ley line. It ripped right through it, tearing it off its supports and snapping it. Spirit and Forta were sent sailing as the cord contracted and gave their rollers no support. Only my own line remained.

Then, realizing that it could neutralize me similarly, the limo swerved to intersect my line. In a moment this snapped, and I had lost my anchorage. I could proceed only slowly without it, while the limo retained full mobility.

I looked around desperately for some kind of cover. To the side was mountainous territory, the crags projecting vertically. Apparently there had been expansion and fracturing here, causing crystals to break off. The properties of ice at 50°K are not the same as when it is near its melting point; it is as hard as any rock, and can cleave like a jewel. Even in the dim natural sunlight, those crystalline faces shone. There were surely shards like daggers, deadly to my suit. But useful as weapons, too.

I headed for the crags. But I had to move horrendously slowly, to avoid sailing into the sky. I did not want to sail, for then I would have no leverage; the limo would simply drive to my projected landing point and nab me there.

The limo didn't bother. It headed straight for me, accelerating. It intended to mow me down!

I saw that there were crevices in the ice rock. I anchored the toe of my right foot in one. As the vehicle bore down on me, I waited until the latest feasible moment, then launched myself horizontally across the ground, diving for another crevice. The limo was unable to compensate at this range, and narrowly missed me. I grabbed for my new anchor-crevice, missed, bounced off the ice, and ricocheted up like a stone skipping across water.

For the moment I was helpless. But my trajectory was low, and the ground uneven. I was able to catch at another crevice as I glided down, and stopped myself. I turned to watch the limo, that had far overshot me.

It was braking, intending to turn and come at me again. There was no sign of the bobbies; probably the limo could make a dozen passes before the authorities arrived, and three or four should be sufficient to flatten me or to rip a hole in my suit.

Now I saw Smilo loping in, handling the terrain much better than I did. Cat's weren't hunters for nothing! But he would be no match for the limo, whose pressurized cab made it an armored vehicle. "Stay clear!" I cried, knowing that Smilo would recognize my voice on his suit set.

The limo turned, reoriented, and headed for me again. Smilo was coming in too, angling to intercept the vehicle. "No, Smilo!" I cried. "That's not a buffalo! Your fangs will only puncture your own suit!"

Then Smilo leaped and sailed. He collided with the limo, indeed as though it were a buffalo, coming down on its bonnet. His body was so solid, and his impact so great, that the limo was shoved off course. It careered past me, the huge cat somehow clinging to it, blinding its driver.

Luck gave me a significant break. The limo smashed into a low outcropping that ripped out a wheel and holed it. Air puffed out as it came to a halt, wrecked.

But Smilo had been riding it. The cat was hurled forward as the limo crashed, and rolled across the rock. It took some time for him to come to a stop, and when he did, there was no sign of animation. Smilo was unconscious or dead. My luck had cut both ways.

There was a stir at the limo. A lock opened, and the driver climbed out. He was suited. That was further evidence that he had come seeking trouble, for normal operations did not require suits. The limo was supposed to drive from air lock to air lock.

Now I realized that the manner it had parked nearby, but out of sight of the cottage, should have alerted me. What business did it have there? No business, it seemed, but to lurk in ambush, watching, in case the trap within the cottage was not effective.

Well, at least we were on equal footing now. The driver could not move any more efficiently afoot than I could. I could keep my distance from him until the bobbies arrived.

I was mistaken. The man walked across the land without sailing. Evidently his boots were coated with the same adhesive that kept his tires anchored. How I wished I had thought to get some of that! Yet why didn't the natives use it?

As I watched the man walk, I realized why. He was sure, but slow. The ley lines made for much faster traveling, and so the natives opted for simplicity and speed, having no need to go cross-country anyway.

But I was slow too. I tried to keep my distance, for I saw the gleam of steel in his glove: a wicked needle. Here in vacuum, a long, hard needle was as deadly as a sword, for one suit puncture was all that was required for the kill.

I cast about for one of those ice slivers I had conjectured to be here, but saw none. Either the rock did not fracture in that manner, or all such slivers had been removed, perhaps by foraging youths. There was only the bare rock and the projecting crags.

The crags. Their faces looked almost sharp enough to saw through a suit. If I grabbed my opponent and shoved him against such an edge . . .

But I realized that this was an unlikely scheme. Assuming it was the same driver who had brought us out here, the man was half my age and husky to boot; I could not reasonably hope to manhandle him. Of course I was trained in martial arts—but he would not have been given this assignment if he were not competent in combat. My best bet was to stay out of his reach, for the few remaining minutes until help came.

I made for the crags, and he made for me, but he was gaining. That spike in his hand loomed larger. If only I had a similar weapon, or even something to throw! But there was nothing.

He closed on me, and I knew I could not avoid this

confrontation. So I played it as aptly as I was able. I made as if to leap out of his reach just before his extended needle reached my suit. He lunged, hoping to catch me just before I lifted. But I did not leap; I whirled and caught his extended arm instead. I twisted it into an aikido configuration, quickly relieving him of the needle; but before I could secure it for myself, he jerked around, and it flew away, beyond our recovery.

I tried to convert to a throw, hauling him across my back. In this gee, he wouldn't go down, he would fly into the sky. But he hung on to me, and he was indeed younger and stronger than I, and reasonably versed. He executed a counterthrow, and it was effective. I sailed.

But in the struggle, he had not watched the lay of the land. I flew toward the outcropping I had been headed for, and low enough so that I did not clear it. I contorted myself around, got my feet in front, and landed against the glassy vertical face of the crag. I used this to push off toward the spot where the needle was falling.

Too late he realized what I was up to. He tromped toward the weapon, but I beat him to it and picked it up. Now I was armed and he wasn't. "Approach, idiot," I invited him.

I knew he heard me, for all suits are tuned to the common frequency. But he did not reply in words. He looked around—and saw the police vehicle coming down the road. My rescue was at hand.

I could tell by his attitude, even masked by the suit, that he had come to a decision. His hand went to a suit pocket.

Oops! If he had an illicit laser pistol—

He did. Apparently he had decided to be hung for the whole course, knowing that he couldn't get away anyway. He was going to take me out first, then perhaps turn the weapon on his own suit. He had nothing to lose now.

I scrambled in slow motion for the crag, needing to get behind it. One touch of the laser beam would finish me exactly as the needle would have! But the distance was still too great; he could fire from where he stood and tag me before I reached it. The bobbies were now crossing the rock, and would reach us shortly, but it would only take seconds for that laser to do its work.

I gazed hopelessly at the shining, mirrorlike face of the crag. I felt like a butterfly pinned to a board, and that bright surface was the board. He could hardly have had a better target!

Unless—

I gauged it as carefully as I could, as he took his stance and aimed. It wasn't right.

I hurled the needle at him. My aim was beautiful; he had to leap out of the way to avoid it. He sailed; it took him some time to come down, and that gave me a chance to improve my position. But I did not flee toward the crag; I knew he would land and reorient before I could get beyond it. I made my way sideways, placing myself directly between him and the bright cliff face. I seemed to be a better target than ever!

He landed and got himself righted. The police vehicle was now quite close. If he was going to hole me, he had to do it soon.

He fired—and I was already moving to the side, having read his intent by his body attitude. My talent was serving me despite the masking effect of his suit. The beam missed me and struck the crag behind me.

He corrected and fired again, but I was moving again, and the second shot missed. I raised an arm to wave at the bobbies, just in case they didn't realize what the situation was. "Here!" I said. "He's lasering me!"

He fired a third time, as I gambled all and leaped straight up. The laser passed between my spread legs, reflected from the glassy crystal face of the crag, and scored on my attacker. Air puffed out of his suit, and he flew up, propelled by that leak. But his flight was his doom, for he would be dead of suffocation and decompression before they could catch him.

I had done what I had tried to do: use his weapon against him. Twice the reflected beam had missed him, but the third time had been the charm. Had that not been the case, he would have picked me out of the sky without difficulty, for I could not have maneuvered there to avoid him. I had gambled and won.

But I was no longer concerned about my own health, but about Smilo's. I hurried to his body—and as I approached he lifted his head groggily. He had survived! He had been stunned, but his suit had not been holed. I more or less fell on him, hugging him as well as I could in our suits. He had saved my life again, by putting the limo out of commission. How glad I was that he had not sacrificed his life in that effort!

The rest was simple enough. Apologetic about the breach of their security, the authorities of Titania were eager to show their solidarity in the cause of peace, and supported the Dream. But they had a requirement: since they could not in conscience pledge support to a Saturn project, they pledged it to the Tyrant's project. It was necessary for me to assume the mantle of director of the galactic colonization effort. Of course I had to clear it with Chairman Khukov. "Why do you think I sent you there?" he replied somewhat laconically, four hours later when his response arrived. Even at light speed, a communication between Uranus and Saturn takes hours.

Of course he had known that the nations of Uranus would be more likely to support the former Tyrant of Jupiter than they would the present power of Saturn. I was no threat; I had no government. Thus I was a convenient focal point, a figurehead. But the project was real, and with the considerable economic and industrial potential of Uranus supporting it, it was becoming feasible.

Chapter 12

TRITON

The main project required a solid base, with standard gee, available raw materials, a pool of industrial workers, and plenty of safe space for testing. The environment of Uranus was unsuitable; it had no large moons, so that all its gee was centrifugal, and its environmental resources were being strained to maintain its industrial base. Its pool of qualified workers was large, but it seemed easier to move them to a distant site than to put the site in their vicinity. The space around the planet was filled with activity, making it awkward for testing dangerous new systems. Most Uranian nations had distant colonies that they used for such activities.

This was the key to the solution to the problem. There happened to be a quite suitable moon in the Titanian Commonwealth of Planets, and after due hassle the Uranian nations of the Common Market agreed to use this site.

Thus it was that I went with my small party to Triton, the large moon of Neptune. That is, with Spirit, Forta, and Smilo. I hoped we would not soon again be wandering the barrens in space suits.

One might have supposed that the political history of Triton would be similar to that of Neptune. That was not the case. Titania had dominated both in the prior century, but the two were pretty much isolated from each other. Triton was of similar size to the giant moons of the Jupiter system; in fact it seemed much like my planet of origin, Callisto. Of course it was much farther out from the sun, so the light lenses were close to six times the diameter of those of the Jupiter region, and it took four hours for light to reach it from the sun. This made this region less than desirable for human colonization, and both Neptune and Triton had received convicts from Uranus. That, however, was in the past, and today both regions were doing well.

Triton's surface was cold, but was not made of ice; there were rocks of conventional nature, and indeed, there was mining for that most precious of metals, iron. There was a modest atmosphere of methane, which helped hold in a little heat and made it slightly easier to maintain the city-domes. The huge size of the planet in relation to its population made the enormous light lenses feasible, and it really wasn't evident, inside the main city of Auck, that this was the System's most distant outpost of true civilization. It is true that the planet Pluto is farther out from the sun, but Pluto is actually smaller in size than Triton and has only scientific observation stations on it. But this same isolation from the main population centers of the Solar System was what made this region so well fitted for this particular project. If anything went wrong, the disaster would be less. Of course that was not the way it was presented to the residents of Triton; for them it was explained how great the benefits of this massive technological effort would be for the region.

And massive it was! The estimated cost of the main projector was approximately one trillion dollars, and there would be massive subsidiary investments, apart from the inevitable cost overruns. I knew just the man I would have wanted to supervise, but he was on Jupiter, and old, and Jupiter was the one planet from which I could not draw. My reputation as Tyrant facilitated progress elsewhere, but the controlled Jupiter press excluded all mention of me. Which was really too bad on several grounds. Not only did it deprive the citizens of Jupiter of news that would surely interest them, and exclude that planet from the thrust into the future that this project represented, it was also a lamentable step backward. Never during my Tyrancy had there been any restriction on the press or speech. But it was not my business; I was in exile.

But I was in charge here, by the unlikely collusion of the rulers of Saturn and Uranus, and I intended to do the job properly. The Dream had not originated with me, but

it had become mine in much the way of a woman, being
at first intriguing, then compelling, and finally my life. I
knew that this was my final project, and I was satisfied
that it be this. What a beautiful thing we were making:
the instrument for man's conquest of the galaxy! So I labored diligently in my fashion, interviewing personnel in-
terminably so as to have the proper infrastructure for the
purpose. Spirit was of course organizing that, with Forta
very ably assisting; Megan had sent me an extraordinarily capable woman!

I dislike going into tedious detail on routine matters
that are in any event available in the public record, so
will just say that once again we succeeded in assembling
an efficient and massive structure whose personnel were
uniformly dedicated to the Dream. Technicians of Saturn
and Rising Sun worked with those of the nations of Uranus for the common goal. Saturn was paranoid about the
militaristic capacity of Prussia, and not sanguine about
that of Gaul, and had never really appreciated the Titanian Empire, but here the effort was cooperative, and
friendships were being formed. The scientist of Saturn
who had made the theoretical breakthrough for the light
drive traveled himself to Triton to participate; I was present with Forta, assisting in translation and facilitating
the personal interaction, but there was no problem. The
scientific community did not share the political suspicion.
The leading Prussian scientist approached the Saturn scientist, pumped his hand in the occidental manner, and
exclaimed "Genius!" He referred to the nature of the
breakthrough. I knew that it was going to be all right.

As the construction proceeded and the personnel
meshed, my position became more token than legitimate;
the project could proceed without me. I remained on Triton mainly as a symbol; the planets were contributing to
the project of the Tyrant, for the benefit of mankind, not
for the aggrandizement of any individual nation or philosophy of government. That was what made it work. That
and Spirit's constant adjustments, eliminating inefficiency wherever it threatened.

I was hardly aware of the diminishing need for my participation, before Forta took up the slack. I had taken

Smilo for a stroll around the premises of the enormous
new dome that had been cultured and lifted as a bubble
from the deep atmosphere of Neptune, and set entire into
the ground of Triton. I used the leash, because the tiger
understood that this meant that no one was to be attacked, and the personnel had become accustomed to his
presence. In fact, someone had fashioned a mascot, a
model of a saber-tooth tiger, with the legend *Smile, O
Tyger.* There were posters depicting a gigantic tiger's paw
reaching for the stars. A sports organization had even
formed, termed the Tiger's League. So I enjoyed these ex-
cursions, and so did Smilo. There are worse things than
being a mascot, as both of us understood.

But when I returned to our suite this day, Spirit was
out. A woman stood awaiting me. She was dark-skinned
and had fairly short black hair, and her body was lanky.
Her face carried a somewhat challenging expression.

"Emerald," I breathed, recognizing her. Of course it
was Forta in mask and costume, but it was also my Navy
wife Emerald, as she had been at about age twenty-five.
Emerald had been something special. Of course all my
women are special, but she more so than usual. She was
a tactical genius, whose career had been stifled by Navy
prejudice against Blacks and women, until she joined me.
Then she had taken over my body and my career with
equivalent dispatch and success. I believe that physically
she was the least endowed of my women, having a rather
boyish figure, but she may have been the most effective
lover. We had separated for career reasons, not from any
personal disaffection, and indeed our careers had continued. I had in due course become the Tyrant of Jupiter,
and she the Admiral of the Jupiter Navy. I had appointed
her to that position, and she had brought the support of
the Navy to my position at the crucial moment. In a sense,
our marriage had never stopped; there was no way I would
ever act against her interests, or she against mine.

Standing there, gazing at her, I experienced an abrupt
and powerful surge of nostalgia and desire. Emerald in
the contemporary frame was about sixty-four, getting
somewhat plump, and long married to another officer, but
the Emerald of my memory was exactly this young figure.

I remembered the first time I had approached her, only to solicit her participation in my Navy project, and she had demanded sex and then agreed to be my wife. I hadn't asked her to marry me. But her intellect and determination had swept aside my hesitancy, and never to my regret. While it is true that a man normally prefers an acquiescent woman, he can also appreciate a dominating one. Women come in all types, and all are wonderful in their fashions.

"Well, get it on, Worry," she said abruptly, her voice exactly as I remembered it. Perhaps my memory was even guided by Forta's interpretation, because when I had been memory-washed, my Navy experience had been the last to return to me, and even a decade later I could encounter lapses. But she had used my private Navy nickname, Worry, too, which lent further authority to the emulation. That was from my song, "Worried Man Blues." She certainly did her homework, and I appreciate that.

She strode up to me, reached up, caught my head between her hands, hauled it down, and planted a decisive kiss on my mouth. And I swear, that was an authentic Emerald kiss. Juana had been ever reticent; Emerald was as thorough a change as could be imagined, and I was amazed again that both parts could be so aptly played by one who could have known neither at these ages.

She disengaged with equivalent abruptness, grasped my arm, and hauled me along to the bedroom. "Do I have to do everything for you?" she snapped. Abashed and delighted, I removed my clothing while she stripped hers. In moments we both were naked, and she remained exactly as I remembered her, her breasts small, her hips narrow, her body slender throughout but dynamic.

She shoved me back on the bed, then leaped atop me, forcing my knees apart with the type of expertise found in judo so that she could get in between them. Her very flesh seemed to move independently, rubbing against my belly and legs. Her breasts pressed hotly against my chest as her thighs closed about my member, bringing it urgently alive. "Bet I can polish you off within three minutes," she said challengingly as she manipulated my anatomy with the flexure of muscles I had hardly remembered existed.

"Make it three hours!" I pleaded.

"That's inefficient." She proceeded to the culmination, her hands all over my body, and sure enough, despite my best intentions, I found myself climaxing within her in just about three minutes.

I found I couldn't leave it there. I'm seldom satisfied with things exactly as they are; I need to know the causes and effects and underlying truths. So as she made to get up and leave, I held her. "You have had your will of me," I said. "Now talk to me."

"That's not the Navy way, Worry," she said. "We have a ship to run."

Which was exactly what the real Emerald would have said, in fact *had* said, more than once. Emerald had never been my creature; I had been hers. In private. In public she had always deferred to me, in the manner of all my women. Sometimes I had suspected that it was a conspiracy between them, to manage me; if so, it had been successful. It has been said of me that I was always a man for the women; there is more than one way that truth can be taken. But Emerald had needed no conspiracy to handle me. I remember when Spirit walked in on us in bed one morning and ripped off the sheet to get us up, exposing us both naked. Then the other officers, male and female, had trooped in for a staff meeting. Emerald had retaliated by spreading her legs before Spirit's husband and inquiring whether there was anything there that his wife hadn't shown him. One seldom sees a man blush like that.

"Penny for your thoughts, Hope," Emerald said, pausing. After all, today there was not a ship to run.

"Just wondering whether there *was* anything there Spirit hadn't shown him," I said.

She laughed. "No. She showed him more than I had to show." She cupped her left breast with her left hand, as if weighing it.

"Give me that!" I said, taking the breast in my own hand.

"Watch your step, Worry, or I'll have to do you again."

She was so absolutely like the original! I grabbed her and hugged her and kissed her, overwhelmed by her aptness in the role.

"Damn," she muttered as if to herself. "He's calling my bluff." She took hold of me where it counted. Sure enough, I was coming alive again. I was amazed; I had thought the days of my consecutive arousals were past. "Well, in the interest of scientific investigation . . ." she said, and proceeded to work on me again.

"It was a joke," I protested insincerely.

"Not any more," she said, taking me in. Those internal muscles of hers began to work, and she deep-kissed me simultaneously, her tongue mimicking the action below. It took much longer, this time, for indeed I was not forty years younger, but the process and the culmination were sheer delight. Indeed, my second climax seemed longer and stronger than the first, though perhaps I deceive myself in this. Subjectivity can be wonderful stuff.

Again she made to depart, but again I held her. "You bring me such memories, you're so skilled," I said. "How did you learn all this?"

"I study my trade," she said.

Evidently so! I reached to touch her mask. "I can hardly believe . . ."

She drew back. "You must play fair," she murmured.

I sighed. "I have never known a woman like you."

"Surely true," she agreed, and now she left. Soon she was back at her secretarial work, in her own guise, as if nothing had happened.

I have covered this episode in rather more detail than I might otherwise have done, because it was the last time in my life that I was able to perform consecutively. That may be a matter of no consequence to a woman, but to a man it can be significant. It seemed, in its fashion, to signal the misfortune to come.

Emerald was with me each time thereafter, just as Juana had been with me on Uranus. I seemed to be reliving my early years. I wondered how she would manage my next bride, who had been of an entirely different configuration, physically and emotionally. But I could wait for that; having Emerald with me like this seemed, in an almost tangible way, to be restoring my youth.

It was illusion. Before long I felt every decade of my age. In fact, I felt more than my age.

It was Emerald who realized. She had approached me in her fashion, which was aggressively, and stripped me, but I was slow in responding. I felt awful. "Hope, you're ill!" she exclaimed.

"Can't be," I muttered. "No diseases here."

"No *contagious* diseases," she corrected me. "Stand up, let me look at you; I've had some medic experience."

She had had more than that! Wearily, swaying, I stood naked before her. I winced as my feet took the weight; my big toes hurt.

"Your legs are swollen, your color's bad," she said. "Hope, I think you've got gout."

"Got what?"

"Inflammation of the joints, retention of waste fluids," she said. "Symptom of loss of kidney function. We saw it on Mercury, and the other inner planets. It used to be thought a rich man's disease, but conditions in some modern areas have brought it to the poor, too."

"How can I have kidney failure?" I demanded querulously.

"That I would like to know. Let me get you dressed. I'm taking you to the hospital."

"But I can't let it be known I'm sick," I protested.

She considered. "Yes, that is true. Let me get in touch with Spirit." She set me on the bed and went to the other room. I lay there in a funk.

Before I knew it, Spirit was there, and Forta was in her natural state. Such was my condition, I didn't even regret the loss of what had promised to be an exciting afternoon liaison. "I'll bring a doctor here," Spirit said. "No one must know."

Then the doctor was there. He checked me with his instruments and nodded gravely. "Dialysis," he said.

"What?" I asked stupidly.

"Your kidney function is down to less than five percent," the doctor informed me. "Acute renal failure. We can tide you over with dialysis while we work out a course of long-term treatment."

"But what is dialysis?" I asked.

"Very simply: blood cleaning. We have to arrange to do the job that your kidneys are not doing."

"We don't want the public to know the Tyrant is sick," Spirit said. "If he goes to the hospital—"

"But that's where we are equipped for this," the doctor protested. "We need to set up a loop—"

"A what?" Spirit asked. This business was new to both of us; neither Spirit nor I was equipped to handle it.

"A connection between an artery and a vein that we can use to tap into the blood supply," the doctor explained patiently. "We have to run it through the dialysis machine for several hours."

"Several hours!" Spirit exclaimed. "Why so long?"

The doctor seemed almost to sigh, but he explained. "The blood supply can be run through the machine fairly expeditiously," he said. "But that is only part of the problem. The wastes that the kidneys normally remove from the blood have built up in the tissues of the body. Thus the blood must be cleaned and recirculated so that the tissues can discharge their wastes into it, which in turn can be removed by the machine. This process cannot be hurried. The living kidneys normally operate continuously, but it is not convenient to have the machine do this. So we use it perhaps three hours at a time, every two or three days, until either kidney function is restored or a kidney transplant occurs. Now, this man must be treated promptly; those wastes are not doing his body any good."

I visualized my bloodstream as a river clogged with garbage, a veritable sewer, now that the treatment center had broken down. "I'll take the dialysis," I said with resignation.

"But the publicity—" Spirit said.

The doctor protested, but I was not just any patient; I was the Tyrant. News of my illness would spread across the System at light speed, literally, and the project would suffer, for I was its unifying symbol. In the end they had to bring the equipment and surgeon to our suite. It was necessary to give Smilo a pacification pill, for we were not sure how he would react if he saw and smelled a doctor cutting into my flesh and taking my blood.

I don't remember much of the initial surgery; they put me out with a general anesthetic. My system resists all intrusions, but requires a while to organize for any one, so I was unconscious this time. When I woke, I had the loop: plastic tubes inserted into my left arm in two places, through which my red blood circulated, passing from artery to vein via the loop.

I inquired groggily when the dialysis was going to be, because I felt awful. That was when I learned that it had already been done. They had kept me sedated for six hours, and run through the whole process.

"Then why do I feel worse than before?" I demanded, properly irritated.

"That's normal," the doctor reassured me. "Tomorrow you'll feel better."

"Normal to feel worse after treatment than before it?"

"Dialysis is rough on the system."

Evidently so. But it was done, and I could relax. I settled into a somewhat drugged slumber.

Next day, sure enough, I did feel better. More correctly, less bad. I got up to go to the bathroom, swayed dizzily, and realized that I really didn't need to go. No kidney function meant no urine.

Forta appeared. "Let me help you," she said quickly, catching my arm as I swayed.

"Send me Emerald," I said grumpily.

"You aren't in condition for that, Tyrant!" she protested.

"For sex, no. For comfort, yes."

"How about Juana, then?"

I considered. I discovered that though Juana was certainly the comforting type, I was not ready to retreat to her time. Once I started retreating, where would it end? But I certainly wasn't ready for the next, Roulette, who was as highly potent in sex appeal as any woman could be. Emerald, aggressive as she could be, could also be understanding. "I'll stand pat."

Forta shrugged. She helped me sit on the bed, then left

the room. In a moment Emerald returned. "You asked for it, sir, you got it," she said.

"Remember Mondy?" I asked.

"That's later."

"But the potential to understand, to nurture, had to exist before," I said. "He was a badly disturbed man, but you helped him. Will help him. Help me now."

"Listen, Worry, you've taken an injury. It's not fatal, and probably not permanent. A few days, and your kidneys will resume their function, and you'll be off the loop. So all you need to do is rest and plan ahead."

She made absolute sense, and I needed that. But I needed more. "Just hold me," I said.

She pushed me gently back to lie on the bed, and she lay beside me, and put her arms around me as well as was feasible, and drew my head in to the hollow of her neck, and there we lay. "You're a good woman," I said.

"You're a good man," she replied.

I drifted back to sleep, and when I woke she remained, sleeping beside me. I lifted my head, feeling better, and gazed at her face. I was tempted to remove the mask, but felt it would be somehow like abusing her. Instead I lowered my head and kissed her lips.

She woke, startled, and I laughed. "Fear not, damsel; I have not deprived you of your virtue," I said.

"You're feeling better," she stated.

"To sleep in the arms of a good woman—that's good medicine."

"So it seems," she agreed.

I felt better all day, but on the following day I began to degrade, as the wastes accumulated in my blood and tissues. I was due for another dialysis treatment, as my kidneys still had not recovered their function.

The doctor arrived with a dialysis nurse. He checked my loop. He shook his head. "Some clotting," he said.

"I see no clot," I said.

He smiled briefly. "You are thinking of external clots, which are hard knots of blood. Internal clots are long strings attaching to the irritation. When they break off and travel through the bloodstream, they can cause trouble elsewhere. That is not something we feel sanguine about." He smiled again, indicating humor. The term *sanguine* referred to blood; that was the pun.

"Where do they travel?" I inquired, morbidly interested.

"It can be anywhere. Sometimes they can exist for some time without causing harm. But if they snag in the lungs, or the brain—"

"Get rid of the clot," I said.

"We'll use heparin," he said. "That in effect thins down the blood so as to avoid clotting in the machine. It should eliminate the problem. After the treatment we'll neutralize the heparin. There should be no problem, as long as we remain on top of it."

"Stay on top of it," I agreed.

The nurse proceeded to the dialysis. This seemed to be a complicated process in detail, but she knew what she was doing. Soon my blood was coursing through the machine. I felt a little faint, but realized that this was probably psychological; the machine, the nurse assured me, used only a fraction of the amount of blood that the early models did. In any event, it would all be returned to me.

The principle of dialysis, I learned, was to run the blood through filters and osmotic solutions, so that the wastes passed out through the cellophane membrane while nutrients passed in. It was possible to feed a person through dialysis, or to medicate him, in addition to purifying his blood. The machine was not and could not be the equal of the natural kidney function, but the treatments would keep me alive and healthy until my own kidneys recovered.

This time I was conscious during the dialysis. I saw my blood flow through the tube in my arm into the machine, and the return flow to my vein. In the early days, the doctor explained, so much blood had to enter the machine for processing that the patient might lose consciousness or go into shock. But today only a relatively small amount of blood was used, only about a cup, and the treatment was so thorough that in only a few seconds that blood was back in the body, completely restored. The machines had originated as big as bureaus, but this one was only about thirty centimeters long. The blood went in one end and came out the other, refreshed. But the actual time of dialysis could not be cut, because the limitation was that of my body, not the machine. They could not pump the blood through faster than my blood vessels could handle it.

Now the doctor questioned me, trying to ascertain the source of my malady. "The kidneys don't simply shut down out of perversity," he said. "There had to have been poisoning or illness to cause this reaction. Until this point we have been concerned merely with pulling you through, but we don't want to finish without having a clear notion of cause."

I wanted to know the cause too! "I have always been healthy," I said. "The only problems I have ever had have been from injury or torture or poison."

"Those could do it," he said with a small, grim smile. "Injury in the past less likely perhaps, but—torture?"

I explained about my session as a prisoner of my political opponent, just before I became Tyrant. I had been made to feel pain by a nerve stimulator, and had been memory-washed.

The doctor shook his head. "I think not, in that case. But what of poison?"

"Food contamination, actually," I said. "Enemies in Saturn managed to feed me contaminated yeast. I suffered some liver and kidney damage—" I broke off, realizing what I had said.

The doctor nodded. He questioned me closely about the episode. "That would seem to account for it," he concluded. "I'm surprised they didn't require you to come in for regular examinations, to forestall this very occurrence."

"But that was over three years ago!" I said, not wanting to admit that they *had* required that, but that I had disobeyed. "I recovered, and have had no trouble since."

"I fear this is bad news," the doctor said. "I had assumed that this was a case of acute nephritis, but it may be chronic."

"Acute what?"

"Each of your kidneys has on the order of one million tiny units, called nephrons, that process the blood in parallel. There is more than one type of nephron, but for our purpose we may assume they are all identical. Each does a complete job of cleaning the blood it handles; this is no assembly line. Essentially, the nephron filters out the solids and processes the fluids of the blood, where the wastes are. It recovers from that fluid all the useful ingredients, and allows the rest to pass on out of the system: the urine. What affects one nephron is likely to affect them all, and when the nephron shuts down, your body has no way to eliminate its waste products. So blood urea nitrogen builds up—we call it BUN—and—"

"I understand," I said, not caring to get that technical. "So when there is trouble with the nephron, that's nephritis."

"Correct," he said. "And I am a nephrologist, a doctor specializing in these matters."

"But why is an acute case to be preferred over a chronic case? Is it milder?"

"No, the opposite is apt to be the case. Acute nephritis can take you out in days, if untreated, while you can go for years without even being aware of chronic nephritis. The acute condition can occur as the result of some temporary insult to the tissue, such as poisoning; once the poison clears, the nephrons recover, and you have no further trouble. This may have happened when you suffered the food poisoning. But sometimes the damage is limited, and the shutdown is only partial, or only a percentage of the nephrons are affected. Since the body has an enormous overcapacity, you can lose as much as ninety percent of your nephrons, and suffer no ill effects; the remaining ten percent do the whole job. But beyond that, it can get awkward. At five percent capacity, you do feel it, and below that—"

"You mean, an acute case could have knocked out ninety-five percent for a week, but a chronic case may have been working up to it for three years, and I only felt it when the critical level of damage was reached?"

"Exactly. Now, this is not a diagnosis. We shall have to do a biopsy for that. But I believe we should not delay on that."

"A biopsy?"

"We take a sample of the kidney tissue and analyze it

in the laboratory. Then we can tell the state of the nephrons."

"Better do it," I agreed. "But if this is chronic instead
of acute, does it mean there's no cure?"

"It means we'll have to schedule you for transplant,"
he said. "Your kidneys are marvels of accommodation,
but once they're gone, they're gone. Fortunately, modern
immunosuppressive techniques make kidney transplant
feasible in the vast majority of cases. Thanks to your support, Tyrant, we have a fully competent transplant facility here on Triton. We shall have you functioning
normally again, never fear."

I glanced across at Spirit, who had remained mute
throughout. It was possible that we knew something the
doctor didn't.

The nurse concluded the dialysis. Thanks to my discus-
sion with the doctor, the hours had passed without notice.
They cleaned up the equipment and put it away, and restored my loop to its normal loop configuration, and gave
me the neutralizer to the heparin employed to prevent
clotting during treatment. Smilo came up, and I stroked
his massive head. "Don't chew on that loop," I cautioned
him. I had been afraid at one point that the odor of blood
would unhinge his equilibrium, but he was a well-fed tiger, and he knew the smell of my blood and would not
attack me. Henceforth he would not be sedated during my
treatments.

But some hours later I got up to get something to eat—
my diet was temporarily severely restricted, to prevent
avoidable accumulation of wastes or fluid—and passed out
without warning. The next thing I knew, the doctor was
back. Evidently he had done something to restore me.
"What happened?" I asked.

"Heparin rebound," he said curtly.

"Say in layman's terms?"

"We give you heparin to prevent clotting," he explained. "But the blood's ability to clot is an important
survival feature; without it you would be hemophiliac,
and could suffer internal bleeding. So after the treatment
we neutralize the heparin. Unfortunately, sometimes the
neutralizer wears off before the heparin is out of the sys-

tem, so the heparin rebounds when it isn't wanted. Evidently my error; every human body is unique to itself, and I misjudged your tolerances. I shall see that it doesn't happen again."

He was a competent and honest man, and very good with explanations. I had confidence in him. Evidently I had rated the best.

In due course they did the biopsy and confirmed the diagnosis: chronic nephritis. "Actually, glomerulonephritis," the doctor said. "The glomerulus is the filter at the beginning of the nephron. Your own immune system did you in."

"How's that?" I asked, alarmed.

"Your food poisoning evidently had an infective component," he said. "That is, it came across like a disease, and your immune system fought it. You seem to have an extraordinarily effective immune system. I researched the Saturn records on your prior episode, and discovered that this particular strain was unusually harmful, and you received a double dose. You could have died; some did, from the single dose. But you recovered remarkably. Unfortunately, in some cases the body's immune system mistakes some of its own tissue for that of the harmful intrusion, and the glomerulus is especially subject to such error. So your system made antibodies against your own glomeruli, and systematically took them out. Now that process is virtually complete. Had your immune system been less vigilant—"

"I have a good immune system," I agreed glumly. "It can throw off any drug."

"Well, that is not precisely the way it operates—"

"It's the way mine works," I said. "I cannot be addicted. It helped me throw off the mem-wash rapidly enough to save my political career, too."

He did not debate the issue, but I could see he did not believe this. He departed.

"This is going to interfere with a transplant, too," Spirit said. "No way your system will tolerate a foreign kidney."

I nodded glumly. "Maybe the doctor will have an answer."

The doctor did. "Immunosuppressive therapy," he said. "Standard procedure for transplantation. We go for the closest possible tissue match, then damp down the immune response."

"Better test it first," I warned.

"Naturally."

He tested it—and my body threw off the immune suppressive drug. This didn't occur immediately, but the doctor was monitoring my response closely, and very soon realized what was happening. In addition, my body had built up an immunity to the heparin, and clotting was a problem again. They had to change to a different anticoagulant, and establish a loop on a new site. "I have never encountered this before," the doctor admitted, intrigued.

It was evident that the transplant the doctor had planned on would not be feasible; my immune response could not be permanently suppressed, other than by heroic measures that we agreed were not warranted. "But we can use a synthetic kidney. That's one grown from neutral tissue in the laboratory, that does not excite the immune response. Unfortunately, it is relatively bulky and clumsy, being three times the size of a normal one. But it will do the job."

"All the same, better test me for reaction to it," I said.

He did—and my body rejected it. "This is unique in the annals of medicine!" the doctor exclaimed, almost with admiration. "Your body really *can* reject inanimate substances!"

I was not as thrilled with this confirmation as he seemed to be. "No synthetic kidney, then."

He sobered. "I'm afraid not. However, dialysis is not merely a short-term expedient. We can set you up for CAPD—"

"For what?"

"CAPD. Continuous ambulatory peritoneal dialysis. That employs your own peritoneal membrane, so there is no problem of rejection. The fluid is put into your abdomen, and the blood filters through—"

"And my membrane would heal to cut off what it took to be leakage," I said grimly. "Can you test for that?"

He ran his tests, and confirmed my suspicion. "This is

truly amazing," he said, evidently thinking of the case history he would write on this that would make him famous. "Your body renders itself impervious to modification by such means."

"This has been quite useful in the past," I said. "But it is losing its appeal."

"Still," he said with a certain artificial cheer, "regular dialysis can be rendered almost as convenient. We can set up an AV shunt—"

"A what?"

"An arteriovenous shunt. That is, a direct connection between an artery and a vein, using no plastic loop, so there is no clotting problem. This can be tapped into for each dialysis."

"May not work," I warned him.

He tried it, and it did work—for a couple of dialyses. Then the clotting got bad, and when the surgeon checked into it, he discovered that my blood vessels were healing, and the shunt was in the process of being cut out and the normal separate artery and vein bloodflow restored. My body would not tolerate the foreign meddling.

Thus we were reduced to the loop, which even with the anticoagulants was only good for as few as three dialysis sessions before the clotting became too awkward. The clotting was because my body was laboring to heal itself, but it was dangerous, just as my immune system's attack on my own kidneys had been dangerous to my long-term health. My system was too independent for its own good.

"How long can this continue?" I asked the doctor.

"We are much more efficient at developing sites for dialysis," he said with assumed cheer. "It is unfortunate that we can not reuse a site once we have finished with it; the scar tissue and the threat of clotting prevent that. But we do far less damage than was done when this technique was new. I'd say you can continue for a decade or more, by which time there could be a breakthrough that would extend it further."

"But my illness must not be known," I said. "How long can it continue without showing?"

"You mean, on your arms? You want them free of scar

tissue? And your neck? That cuts it in half, approximately."

Half. Five years. I was sixty-four years old now; that set my limit at sixty-nine. Somehow I had thought I would live forever; now it was clear that this had been overly optimistic.

"I'll need to travel," I said. "Can I be dialyzed elsewhere in the System?"

"Why, certainly," he agreed heartily. "There are dialysis clinics on every planet."

"Without outsiders knowing?"

"That I can't say. Each planet has its own regulations."

"Can I hire your nurse to go with me, so it can be done privately?"

He smiled. "Tyrant, you don't need to go to such an extreme. We can train you for home dialysis. Designate someone on your staff, and—"

"I'll do it," Forta said immediately. "I have had some experience with field medicine; I'm sure I can handle this."

"It is not hard to learn," the doctor said. "The process has been greatly simplified since the early days. But it requires serious commitment, because one mistake can be like forgetting to seal your suit before stepping outside the dome."

"She can handle it," I said. I knew Spirit would be willing to do it, but Spirit was busy running the show; it was better to leave her free for that.

So Forta trained for dialysis, and in due course she handled the job, three times a week. She learned rapidly and well; her only bad moment in training was when the nurse slipped some dye into the works, and it looked as if the dialysis machine were leaking blood. This might seem like a cruel prank. It was cruel, but a necessary part of the training. Forta took one appalled look at the leak and launched me into the bypass mode so that my blood no longer coursed through the machine. Then, saying nothing to me, she opened the machine to check the tubing. All was in order. Unwilling to accept that, she inspected every aspect of the process closely, and finally located the source of the "leak": the vial of dye. She made a kind of growl in her throat that set Smilo's ears perking, and fished out the vial. She resumed the dialysis, and when the nurse made a "routine" check Forta acted as if nothing had happened. This might have been a mistake, because if a genuine leak went unnoticed, disaster could follow. But when the nurse discovered that the vial was gone, she knew, and Forta passed. I had been tuning in to a program on a holo, and hadn't even realized that anything had happened; I picked this up later. We learned that this was a regular part of such training. Suppose a real leak developed when there was no professional nurse available to set it right? The home dialyzer *had* to be competent, and to keep her head in the crisis.

There was of course more to my malady than this, but I believe I have covered it sufficiently. I acclimated to the regimen, and learned to cope with the postdialysis depression, which was a physiological thing, and to schedule public appearances when I knew I'd be in my best form. I was now dependent in a literal way on the machine and on Forta, but was able to cope. Between times, Emerald was with me, and yes, I could still make love, though not as frequently or as vigorously as before. Emerald was very good for this, being ready to take the active role, and I valued her support for other reasons than this. So the fact is, this period of my life was not one long depression; it was a series of brief depressions, and a constant challenge to find new and unobtrusive sites to tap into my blood supply. My legs developed an increasing pattern of scar tissue. But Forta was not one to be turned off by scar tissue, and in this devious way I found myself thankful, for the first time, that she was as she was.

Meanwhile, the galactic project grew, and it was evident that it was going to be a success. But we needed more financial and industrial support, and more raw materials. After two years on Triton, it was time for me to travel again.

Chapter 13

PHOBOS

We shipped to Mars via the projector; not only was it much faster than regular travel, it was a matter of principle. Every time the Tyrant made such a trip, the entire System took note, and gained confidence; the new process really did work. The receiver tube had been moved there in advance, of course.

Mars had been colonized by what was, loosely, the Moslem community of Old Earth, which had occupied parts of Asia, Africa, and Europe. On Earth this had been the major site for the production of oil, then an important power source. Today it was an equally major site for iron, and the leverage this provided the nations of Mars was similar. The Iron Producing Energy Cartel, or IPEC, had levered the price of iron phenomenally high, squeezing the rest of the System unmercifully. Then alternate sources of power were developed, notably solar energy, and the demand for iron decreased. Today IPEC was in disarray, with no immediate prospect of improvement. The iron nations had allowed themselves to become dependent on the huge income from their iron exports, and were having difficulty cutting back. Several of them were overproducing iron, in violation of IPEC's guidelines, and so the price continued to drift erratically down.

It was a situation that I expected to change.

We emerged from the tube at the Mars orbit and proceeded to our rendezvous with the red planet. And I received a surprise.

With each location, I had had another woman. There had been Tasha at Saturn, and Juana at Uranus, and Emerald at Neptune. I thought the most luscious of my early women, Roulette, would manifest next, and I con-

157

fess I looked forward to that. But instead I discovered
Shelia, my longtime executive secretary and later lover,
confined to a wheelchair.

It was Forta, of course; Shelia was dead. But I think I
gaped, the first time I saw her, for she was so very like
the woman I remembered, in appearance and nature, that
I was virtually overwhelmed. A wig, a mask, skin cream
to render her Saxon, and the wheelchair—oh, what a
memory she evoked!

"What are you doing here?" I asked, somewhat in-
anely.

"I have a score to settle with Big Iron," she replied.

I went into another loop of memory. Big Iron had tried
to assassinate me, but its cleverly intricate plan had been
foiled by Shelia, who had sacrificed her life for mine. In
vengeance I had destroyed Big Iron, washing its corporate
body in genuine blood. I had set up the Shelia Foundation, to minister to those injured in the legs, as Shelia
had been. I had tipped somewhat into madness, the north-
west wind governing my awareness, trying to recover her
in my fancy, but unfortunately my sanity had returned
and she was gone.

Now she was back, in a manner I could accept, and I
understood. Iron had killed her; Mars was the source of
iron. The iron magnates of Jupiter were gone; I had na-
tionalized all their assets, and that shattered egg would
never be reassembled. But Big Iron was not merely a Jupiter phenomenon; it was a System phenomenon. IPEC
had no known complicity in Shelia's death and the madness of the Tyrant, but certainly a measure of sympathy.

When the leaders of Mars saw my secretary, they would
wet their pants, perhaps not merely figuratively. All the
buried guilt of their association and cooperation with Big
Iron of Jupiter would surge forth, and the veritable fear
of Allah would besiege them in the form of the Tyrant.
The executives of iron were as tough as their product, but
they would feel the acid of uncertainty now. That was
good.

"But I think not at first," I said, as I pondered this.
"Timing . . ."

"Timing," Shelia agreed, smiling.

I couldn't help myself. I went to her, flung my arms about her and her chair, and kissed her waiting lips.

I had become somewhat accustomed to Forta's powers of emulation, but each new demonstration impressed me again. The signals were there; in total darkness and without the wheelchair I would have known that those lips were Shelia's. She was all soft and subdued and accepting in exactly the way I had known, and even the wholesome faint body odor of her was the same. The chair and the clothing were merely props for the less perceptive observers to note.

I lifted my head and gazed at her. The mask was so realistic as to be almost impossible to spot, and the way my eyes were tearing I could not have detected it anyway. What a woman!

"Oh, Hope," she said with resignation. "You've gotten your face smeared." And she lifted a handkerchief to wipe off the lipstick.

I buried my face in the warm hollow of her neck and cried. She held me, patting my back reassuringly. In due course she cleaned me up again, though her own face was smeared, her hair mussed.

Then she wheeled herself to her room, leaving me. I found a chair and sat in a daze until Forta returned.

"I think we had best take care of the dialysis," she said in businesslike fashion. "It's a little early, but Spirit is setting up the first appointments for tomorrow, and you need to be in top shape then."

"True." I wondered how much of her impact on me was her talent, and how much was my developing weakness because of the wastes that had accumulated in my tissues. It is claimed that a person on dialysis can live a completely normal life, apart from the treatments, but this is an exaggeration; the awareness of one's dependence on the machine and the dialysis nurse never wholly departs, and the necessary cycling of one's life is not normal for one who never had to exert such discipline before. With me, also, there was the matter of repeated minor surgery for the emplacement of new loops. This was having a slowly destructive effect on the vessels of my legs. I wondered whether I would in time have to retire to a

wheelchair. But, thinking of Shelia, I did not find that a
horror. I only ever truly loved two women, but others came
close, and I think Shelia was the closest, in her unassum-
ing way.

As Forta proceeded through the dialysis, Smilo came to
nap beside me, as had become his habit, and I stroked his
great head. He did not purr; evidently that was not a trait
of his breed. But he might as well have. I reflected on the
manner that I always found myself surrounded by completely loyal and talented people, whatever my situation.
It was true that it was my talent to recognize people for
what they were, and to attract and hold the best. Still, it
was not entirely my own doing; those people had come to
me not because I summoned them but because they recognized my need and generously served it. Shelia was an
example; we had hired her young and handicapped, perhaps doing her a favor. But as her extreme competence
manifested, she could have obtained a lucrative job anywhere else. She had remained because of loyalty, and I
think I had loved her, in my limited fashion, for a decade
before I took her as a mistress—if, indeed, that is not a
denigration of the relationship she offered. Then she had
given her life for me. . . .

I blinked, returning my attention to Forta as she
worked. She had used her talent to become Shelia for a
time, and this had been wholly real to me despite my
knowledge of the situation. Now she was herself, angular
and scarred and efficient. I remained amazed that a single
woman could manifest in such different ways. Surely Forta was the most remarkable woman I had encountered,
perhaps not even excluding those I loved. Yet much as I
respected her nature and competence, I had no desire to
embrace her in the fashion I had Shelia. I was foolish, of
course; I was allowing the outer aspect to determine my
inner feeling. I marveled at this attitude of mine almost
as much as at her ability. The psychiatrists are wrong: to
understand a thing is not the same as dealing with it.
Forta's aspect was no mystery to me, but still it dominated my reaction to her.

When the dialysis was complete, I rested. One might
wonder at this, as I had been relaxed throughout the

treatment, waiting for the blood to circulate and be cleansed. But there is wear on the system, and rest and sleep was the best course following treatment. I wasn't hungry; my diet was restricted anyway, and it was easiest to include nourishment in the dialysis itself. I tended to get thirsty, but could not drink, because my body had no feasible way to eliminate the surplus fluid. So I could drink immediately before a dialysis, knowing that the treatment would take care of it, but not after.

All this meant that I tended to be out of sorts after treatment. Not truly depressed, despite the way I tend to think of it, because the dialysis also restored my system to equilibrium, and depression often is organic in origin. But unsatisfied. This time I lay on my bed, wishing that things were other than they were, resenting my incapacitating ailment. I had always been healthy and well coordinated; I did not like being old and limited.

Then the wheelchair rolled into the room. Suddenly my world brightened. I put out my hand, and she took it and held it to her bosom, and with a sigh of sheer contentment I slept.

Mars has about half the diameter of Earth, and about a tenth its mass. All the inner planets are tiny compared to the major outer planets, of course; Earth is less than a tenth the diameter of Jupiter, and Mercury is just about the same size as my body of origin, Callisto, technically a moon of Jupiter. Of course the inner planets have greater densities and masses than the outer moons, but it does provide perspective.

The economic and social impact of the inner planets is not minor, however. Their nearness to the sun gives them a phenomenal advantage in light energy, and they are rich in accessible minerals. This was of course what gave Mars its leverage: its minable iron. I have mentioned how the planet overplayed its hand, so to speak, and had fallen upon relatively hard times, but iron remains one of the most valuable resources of the System, and Mars remains its prime source.

Geographically, Mars is largely barren. Huge expanses of the surface are rocky desert, and though it has atmosphere, all human residence is within domes. For a long time it was thought that Mars had little water, but it turned out that there was a reasonable amount, and the cities really have not been in want on that score. There are periodic and phenomenal dust storms, that the domes weather without concern. Sand dunes form and dissipate, and wind-sculpted patterns called yardangs are common. The largest volcano in the System is here: Olympus Mons, twenty-six kilometers tall.

Politically, the planet is violent. Its very name suggests war, and the reality conforms. It was colonized by the Moslem community of Earth, and the terrain demarked as seemed appropriate to those several nations. Each definition of "appropriate" was unique to the nation who made it, and warfare was chronic from the outset. But in a very general way, the colonists from mountainous Iran and Turkey took over the densely cratered elevations of southern Mars, while those from the regions closer to Earth sea level took the vast volcanic plains of Mars. Iron is mined throughout, though with the greatest facility in the Rabian region of Mars.

The source of greatest conflict has been Phobos, the larger of Mars' two tiny moons. Phobos has no iron, and is smaller than many fragments of the Belt. But it was settled by the folk of Israel, and the Moslem effort to eradicate the Jews was hardly abated by the shift of venue. Phobos could hardly have survived without the strong support of Jupiter, and the nations of Mars have tried incessantly to use the leverage of their iron to erode this support, without notable success. Phobos, weak on territory and physical resources, was strong on human resources, and alertly maintained its political influence on Jupiter. It had perhaps the finest intelligence (i.e., spy network) in the System, and its position in low orbit about the planet, barely six thousand kilometers above the surface, enabled it to watch virtually the entire planet closely and constantly. Still, survival remained chancy, and Phobos' economy was in chronic disarray.

I knew before I started that I could not get what I wanted from Mars without finding some sort of solution to the Phobos question. But what solution could there be

to a problem that had existed for centuries, intractable to
all other efforts? It was a Gordian knot, and it was generally conceded that only a fool would attempt to solve it.

Still, the Dream motivated me, and my time in life was
now measured, so I was ready to play that fool.

The surface gravity of Mars was just over a third Earth-
norm, and the escape velocity not much more, so our small
ship was able to land directly on the planet. I went first
to Rabia, as this was the richest of the nations. We settled
in the port near the capitol, Yadh, and accepted a ride on
an elegant coach to the city proper.

Yadh was a beautiful city. It had been revamped when
the price of iron was high, and Rabia had been among the
richest nations of the System, per capita. The landscape
outside it was red and rocky barrens, but within the dome
were exotic trees and elegantly sculptured modern buildings. It was possible to do more on a planet, particularly
one with an atmosphere and reasonably stable surface,
because larger domes could be made, and they didn't have
to rotate for gee. The shield below the city focused the
natural gravity, tripling it; that was all that was required. We caught glimpses of the veiled women of the
city going about their business; if we hadn't know it before, this would have made it clear that we were not on
Triton anymore.

We were taken to a palatial residence with the most
modern appointments. There was even an exercise garden
for Smilo, stocked with a number of rabbits. "Smilo
doesn't eat rabbits!" Spirit muttered. "They're too small."
But as it turned out, the tiger did enjoy stalking them; it
was the hunt that appealed, not the size of the prey. We
left him alone to his garden of delights.

Well, almost alone. It seemed that there were holo pick-
ups there. The Rabian representative explained this to us,
somewhat diffidently: They would like to leave these on,
so that the action could be broadcast for the edification of
local viewers. It seemed that the rabbits had been dubbed
infidels, while the tiger was the Scourge of Allah; many
people were interested in the outcome of the hunt.

I consulted with Spirit, and shrugged. We were here to

obtain the cooperation of these people with our project, and to enlist them in the Dream. If this helped . . .

In due course we had our meeting with the King himself. This was of course via holo; all of us preferred that. A translator was provided, but my secretary Forta made notes of her own, using her equipment. I say "we"; actually women were not permitted in man's business, in this society, so Spirit and Forta were excluded. They were in another chamber, but the notes were being made. Rather than render this literally, which would be tedious, let me give the essence, digesting an hour's meeting down to a few sentences.

After exchanging due formalities and pleasantries, and establishing that I spoke for the Triton Project with authority and was supported explicitly by Saturn, the States of Uranus, and the Commonwealth of Titania, and that the King spoke for IPEC, we got down to business. "We need more iron," I said. "The project is straining the resources of Saturn, which was never a major exporter of this metal. We would like to draw on the resources of Mars."

The King smiled cannily. "And what do you propose to pay for our iron?" he asked.

"We are hoping you will accept credits toward the exploration and settlement of the galaxy," I said.

"Credits!" he exclaimed, guffawing. "We require tangible present-day money, not pie in the galaxy!"

I looked about. "I presume only authorized personnel have access to this negotiation?"

"You may be sure of that, Tyrant."

"Then let me speak frankly. We need iron—a lot of it. You need money. We have none for this purpose, but we can arrange for a higher price for your iron. Enough higher to make cooperation worth your while economically on a present-day basis. This in addition to the credits toward colonization of the galaxy, which may be worth a great deal to you within the decade. As investments go, this is prime."

"You talk of magic, Tyrant," the King said cynically. "But we are fair; we listen. Wave your wand; show us how we may, as you say, have our cake and eat it too. Show us your power, Tyrant."

He was borrowing from the idiom of the Jupiter Navy. He knew, of course, what was coming; he was not ignorant, and his ministers had briefed him well. But it was necessary for him to make this challenge, and for me to meet it. This dialogue was private, but the other leaders of Mars who were tuning in on it had to be satisfied.

I showed him my power. "Your problem is that output of iron has increased while the market has diminished," I said. "While Rabia has exercised considerable restraint in the mining and marketing of iron, so as to stabilize the market, others have not. Thus the price has fallen, and will not rise until demand increases considerably or production decreases equivalently. We propose, in effect, to accomplish the latter. This can be done without controls or verifications. We expect the price of iron to triple in short order, then find its level in that range."

"Magic," the King repeated.

"The mechanism is this: All the iron exporters of Mars will contribute half their iron to the Triton Project. This will of course solve our problem of energy, and greatly facilitate the completion of the project, enabling us to commence the colonization of the stars within the decade. But the immediate effect will be to cut the iron available for the local market—that is, the Solar System—by half. That will generate an instant shortfall, and the price will rise. There will be bidding for the iron, and this will cause a further rise. Our calculation of market dynamics indicates a net tripling; I shall be happy to provide our data to your experts for confirmation. You shall thus receive fifty percent more, in gross terms, than you do today, despite the fact that you are charging for only half your output. There will be no cheating, because no nation will be permitted to sell more than the amount it contributes to the project, and that contribution will be a matter of public record, as are the sales. Those who overproduce will contribute that much more to the project. I think they will elect a certain restraint in the matter."

The King stroked his beard, considering. "I doubt that Jupiter would go for this," he said. "It is the System's major importer of Iron, and it is very sensitive to the price of that import."

"I no longer represent Jupiter," I reminded him. "I represent the interest of the project, which is backed by Saturn and Uranus, who are less dependent on Mars' iron."

"But Jupiter has ways of making its displeasure felt," he said delicately.

"So do I," I said.

He gazed at me and nodded. "Tyrant, I am interested in your proposal. But I am minded to verify your ability to oppose Jupiter. Would you accede to a small additional demonstration of your power?"

Small demonstration, my eye! Here came the kicker. "In the interests of understanding and harmony, I would accede," I said.

"Certain elements of our cartel have another concern," he said. "They feel that there is an objectionable presence among us, and wish to be free of it."

"I will not undercut Phobos," I said firmly. "I received sixty percent of the Jewish vote, male and female, when I ran for President of Jupiter, and I do not forget my friends."

He smiled placatingly. "Nor would we ask you to, Tyrant. Neither do we forget our own friends. But it seems that Phobos has taken possession of territory belonging to one of our number, and we feel it only fair that this territory be returned."

He referred to Deimos, Mars' outer satellite. In one of the Mars–Phobos wars, David had slain Goliath and taken possession of coveted territory by force: the other tiny moon. This was of course an extreme irritation to Mars.

Thus the King had thrown the Gordian knot directly into my lap. This was the true price of his cooperation: the return of Deimos to Mars' suzerainty. The issue that no other party had been able to resolve.

However, we had anticipated this, and researched it—Forta did good work!—and were prepared. The problem had not been solved before because Mars had not truly desired a solution; it preferred a war of extermination with Phobos. But now, with the promise of resumed wealth in iron, Mars would desire a solution, and we could play on that desire to untangle the knot at last. At least, we would give it our best try.

"It seems to me that something could be arranged," I said offhandedly. "When reasonable people meet to discuss a problem—" I paused, as if just thinking of something. "Normally something is offered in return for property, however that property may have been obtained. Do those of your number have any particular inducement?"

"Phobos' right to exist," he said succinctly.

I gestured, as if not understanding. "Of course every nation has a right to exist! I am sure none of us question this. I was thinking of, perhaps, trade agreements?"

"First the return of the territory; then other matters can be considered."

I pondered briefly. "Now, I do not claim to be experienced in such matters," I said mildly, and the King had to stifle a snort, for the Tyrant had an excellent track record of diplomacy, including especially that of the gunboat variety, which this was. "But it occurs to me that the other party might choose to reverse the order of those matters. Perhaps I am mistaken; certainly I can talk to it."

"Perhaps some juxtaposition of events could be arranged," the King said cautiously. He was of course yielding just that minimum necessary to make negotiations feasible without alienating the hard-liners who were monitoring this interview.

In due course we concluded it, and shook hands in the occidental manner: a token touching of the holo images, of course, but accepted as binding. The first hurdle had been passed: Mars was greedy enough for profit to consider making peace with Phobos. That was, if I can be excused some mixture of metaphor, a giant step.

We went to Phobos. This was the tiniest of satellites, an ellipsoid whose longest dimension was barely twenty-seven kilometers. The total surface area was about five hundred square miles, if I may lapse into the archaic Jupiter measurement. This meant that, almost uniquely in the System, the actual territory occupied by the colony

was smaller than that of the parent state. Israel on Earth
had had ten or fifteen times as much surface.

But there were compensations. The inhabitants of Phobos were able to use the interior as well as the surface of
the body, and had indeed tunneled it throughout. Thus
Phobos had become virtually a single city, whose parts
were separately spinning domes connected at their axes.
In fact, it was hard to tell where the natural surface of
the body was, because additional bubble cells projected
from it, spinning on their tethers like beads. Indeed, the
entire surface was alive, because of the rotation of each
unit. Phobos had made the most of its limited physical
resources.

As we approached I thought of the manner this tiny
state had held off the massed malice of the remainder of
Mars. Phobos had the will and technology and expertise,
and had used these to foil the comparatively clumsy attacks against it mounted by several planetary nations. It
was an open secret that tiny Phobos even had the planetbuster bomb, having collaborated with Mercury and the
Republic of Wan in the Saturn rings to develop and test
it. That, combined with Phobos' position above Mars, gave
it an effective threat. That was one reason that the other
nations of Mars were satisfied to negotiate for the return
of territory, rather than merely overwhelming the satellite with fleets of ships. Mars did not care to risk a planetbuster bomb that could be so readily delivered to any of
its major cities.

A tug latched on to our ship and brought it inside Phobos, to the internal spaceport. The sophistication of this
intricate docking was impressive; the Phobos personnel
knew their business. Soon we were in our new suite.

It was our fortune that we arrived at official night. That
gave Forta time to dialyze me, and Shelia time to put me
to bed. I really would have liked to have her in bed with
me, but it was too awkward to lift her from her wheelchair, and anyway, the sexual component had never been
the important part of my relationship with her. Shelia
was unable to use her legs, but this did not show; they
were not shriveled. I had made love to her a number of
times, knowing that she welcomed it, but I had always

had to do most of the doing. I preferred just to hold her hand and be with her, respecting her totally.

But Forta, too, needed her rest. "Go, sleep," I told Shelia. "Smilo will baby-sit me tonight." And so it was.

The next day I felt better, and was ready for the interview with the Phobos President in Aviv. There was no foolishness about women here; for one thing, the President was a woman. Spirit was beside me, and welcome, and Forta was present in our holo group. Nevertheless, it was I, as the Tyrant, who spoke.

"The Triton Project needs Mars iron," I said, as if this were news. "Mars may accede—provided some arrangement can be made in connection with Deimos."

"You understand," the President said, "that Salem is there. This city is holy to us, and we are reluctant to let it go."

"It is holy to Mars, too," I reminded her. "And, indeed, to the folk of a number of planets. It seems to me that joint hegemony would be appropriate."

"Tyrant, what do they offer?" she asked sharply.

"Peace."

"They have offered that before, and always reneged. How can we be expected to trust them this time?"

"They have greater incentive this time."

"They are clever," she said. "They will seek to cheat on the iron quotas."

"They will be a matter of public record."

"There are ways to avoid the public record on particular transactions."

"Not if they are administered by Phobos," I said.

She laughed. "Never would Mars agree to that!"

"It might, if the tube were based on Deimos, under your authority."

She pursed her lips. "The tube?"

"The iron must be shipped promptly to Triton," I explained. "It is best to use a light projector. Naturally we would not want that to be incompetently administered. I suspect that Phobos has the required expertise, and could be depended on to keep an accurate and public record of all shipments routed through this facility. There would be payment for this service, of course—perhaps a guaranteed share of the iron passing through. Perhaps one quarter of one percent?"

The President had evidently been caught by surprise by my offer, but her brain was like a computer. She instantly appreciated the power and prestige of such an office, and the chance to participate in the supertechnology of the light projector. The fact that Phobos was chronically desperate for iron was perhaps a secondary consideration. "One percent," she said.

"This is to be half of the entire production of Mars," I said. "Such greed does not become you."

"Half percent," she said with a grim but knowing smile.

"I believe that might be arranged," I agreed. I knew from my reading of her, as well as from the situation, that Phobos was now as eager to deal as Mars had been. The President had joked about settling in the one region of Marspace where there was no iron, but it was no joking matter. "But suzerainty—"

"I will have to consult with the Knesset, of course," she said with a tiny smile. "But I suspect that if warlike Mars is ready to make a lasting peace, fearful Phobos will not interfere. For a true and lasting peace, Phobos will make any sacrifice."

"I will obtain commitments from the parties I represent," I said, "if you will do the same for yours."

"Give me a few days," she said. We touched holo-hands.

Phobos was as good as its word, and of course I was as good as mine. The elements were in place for the demilitarization of Deimos and the establishment of a major Titan base there, Saturn concurring. The significance of the Titan connection was that the demonstration projection system had been established there, under the authority of the Tyrant, and Titan did not have the negative reputation on Phobos that Saturn did. No Jews had been historically maltreated on Titan.

But it remained necessary for the nations of Mars to ratify this multiplanet treaty, and that was by no means certain. We knew that this serious involvement of Phobos would give the radical Martian states warlike thoughts. So it was that we prepared for my concluding address

most carefully. The psychologicial aspect was as important as the substance.

Forta prepared me by doing the dialysis on the day
before; we seemed to have succeeded in keeping this aspect of my existence secret, though probably Phobos fathomed it. Shelia did join me that night in bed, and though
I was not quite up to the act of love, I sincerely appreciated her nearness and comfort. I woke refreshed in body
and mind.

Spirit had flash cards with the pertinent facts, in case
I should suffer any lapse. We would be making the address from Phobos, but it would not be appropriate to have
women participating. In deference to this, the President
of Phobos did not participate; a leading male member of
the Knesset stood in for her. This was male business, on
the surface.

The address was set up in the form of a private meeting
between the Tyrant and the King of Rabia, but it was
being broadcast throughout the environment of Mars, and
we knew that the other planets of the System would be
snooping on it. That was why certain things would not be
openly spoken. We knew that the fanatics of Mars had
threatened militaristic action if Phobos were given any
part of Mars' iron; the King was more moderate, but had
to have solid reason to overrule them, for some of those
states employed assassination as a political tool. The majority of the IPEC nations were realistic about the benefits to be reaped by this accord, but had to seem to be
against it until the extremists acceded. It was really to
those extremists that I was making my pitch.

The King came on in holo, seeming to be right in the
room with me, and I with him. The distance between Phobos and the surface of Mars is such a small fraction of the
distance that light travels in a second that the delay in
transmission of signals is really not noticeable.

I reviewed the proffered terms of the agreement, pointing out the price for Phobos' cooperation. Phobos would
free Deimos provided the Holy City remained open to all
worshipers of the three faiths involved, and that there be
peace between all Martian nations, and that Phobos administer the tube for the transmission of freight and keep

the records thereof. "There will thus be no favoritism or
distortion of records," I pointed out. "Phobos will receive
a set share of all transmissions, and all transactions will
be immediately publicized, so none of the iron exporters
will have opportunity for error." This had been an extremely uncomfortable issue with Rabia, because while it
had honored the iron-production guidelines, at great cost
to itself, others had not. It was actually an advantage to
have those records administered by a common enemy. The
private sales to consumer planets would also be put on
record, because Phobos would now have to clear those
shipments from Mars; any attempt to exceed the fifty-fifty
quota would quickly become apparent. I did not reiterate
the likely effect on the price of iron sold commercially in
the System; that was understood.

"I appreciate the clarity of your summation, Tyrant,"
the King said. "However, I regret to say that we are not
prepared to have Phobos interfere in any fashion with our
affairs. We see no reason why the tube should be set up
at Deimos; indeed, deep space might be a better—"

He broke off, for something strange was happening. A
veiled figure was entering the chamber. It was actually
in mine, but the holography made it appear with complete realism in his chamber too. The figure was in a
wheelchair.

"But the Triton Project cannot spare vital technicians
for routine projection duty," I said, paying no attention
to the figure behind me. "Phobos has the necessary personnel, so it behooves us to take advantage of them."

The King's gaze was nominally on me, but actually
fixed on the figure behind me. I knew that the gaze of all
the unseen viewers was similarly focused.

Slowly, as I talked, the figure lifted the veil clear, and
Shelia's face was revealed. The mask employed in this
case was exceptionally fine, and she had practiced diligently with it; it would be almost impossible to distin-
guish it from the real thing by visual means alone, which
was all that was available to the viewers. I knew that the
holo records of all the Mars nations would be frantically
searched for matching images of Shelia, and her motions
and actions would be studied. I knew what they would

discover: This was that woman. My innate ability to read people is superior to that of any machine I know; if the nuances of personality could deceive me, they could deceive anyone. They would verify that this woman was my former secretary Shelia.

But of course Shelia was dead, killed by Big Iron. And Big Iron was dead on Jupiter, killed by the Tyrant. What, then, could this manifestation portend? The iron magnates of Mars would be shaken. I could not see them, apart from the King, but I knew.

When the King did not answer me, I launched into a friendly reminiscence. I described my prior compatibility with the essential industry of iron on Jupiter, and the manner we had brought prices down to what we deemed to be reasonable levels. As I spoke, Shelia stared meaningfully at the King, who froze. Suddenly it seemed that he wanted to terminate this interview, but he could not; our business had not been completed, and others were watching. He might have little respect for women as a species, but he knew who Shelia was, and his own cue cards were now advising him of the confirmation of identity. He knew he was seeing a ghost. Like General D of Gaul, whose dead daughter had manifested in my presence, he was having difficulty maintaining equilibrium.

"Of course there was an unfortunate incident," I continued. "I regret I had to discipline those companies somewhat; perhaps I overreacted. But I am a Latin; my emotions can dominate my better judgment. I'm sure you understand."

The King looked doubtful; evidently he was now getting conflicting cues from the other representatives of Mars. There was no consensus, which left him in the lurch. I signaled Shelia, unobtrusively.

She wheeled forward. "Hope!" she exclaimed. "I fear they mean you ill!"

I paused in my monologue. "Is someone here?" I asked, looking about. My gaze passed right by Shelia without focus; it was as though she weren't there.

I shrugged. "I beg pardon," I said to the King. "I suffered a momentary distraction."

"Hope, they are evil people!" Shelia cried. "They mean to kill you!"

I suffered myself to be shaken, as by some unheard voice. Then a bit of the Tyrant's madness began to manifest. My eyes widened slightly and my lips thinned. "I feel a chill," I muttered.

"I am sure that some accommodation can be made," the King said quickly. Now his attention was on me.

"Don't trust them!" Shelia urged me, speaking like a paranoid conscience.

"I'm not sure," I said. Saliva appeared in the corners of my mouth, and my gaze flicked erratically about the room as if searching for something.

"You are tired, Tyrant," the King said. "Let us conclude this business expeditiously, so you may rest." If there was one thing for which the Tyrant was remembered, it was his siege of madness, which had manifested in some amusing and some devastating ways. No one could be certain in what manner or with what force this loosening cannon would strike. But they knew one thing that would set it off instantly.

"No!" Shelia cried. "They are *iron!*"

I hesitated as if distracted. The King strode across the chamber and his hand reached for mine, seeking the handshake that would seal the agreement. In the age of holo and recordings, such a signal had legal force. "It is agreed!" he said. "Peace and trade, to mutual advantage!"

I blinked, becoming aware of my situation. Automatically my hand came to join his holo-hand. "Peace and trade," I agreed.

Shelia, disgusted, wheeled her chair about and rolled out.

It was done. We terminated the meeting with the customary amenities. I knew that there would be sessions between the King and the extremists, but it would be apparent to all who studied the holotape that something strange had occurred, and that the King had elected not to risk the loss of a significant agreement that promised not only to elevate the price of iron, but to return Deimos at least nominally to Mars' suzerainty.

For there was indeed no telling what the Tyrant might do in his madness. He was capable of the most unpredictable and bizarre acts. The agreement might not be ideal, by the standards of the Mars extremists, but the possible consequences of the loss of the agreement were likely to be considerably less palatable. The members of IPEC knew that the Tyrant had no brief for iron as an industry, and that both Saturn and Uranus supported the Tyrant's project and would feel constrained to take umbrage if the Tyrant took offense at anything occurring at Mars. They would realize that even if this were an elaborate ruse, the consequences to them would be the same. And they would never be quite certain that it was a ruse. Moslem customs and beliefs differed from those of the Saxons or Hispanic cultures, and the appearance of a ghost did not have the same significance to them. But if I had looked about again, and seen and heard Shelia, all bets would have been off. The King had had to play the game. Too much was at stake to do otherwise.

Hope Hubris always had seen ghosts. Now others were seeing my ghosts too.

Chapter 14

EARTH

Earth was amazing. The planet was blue, and half covered with clouds, and so pretty that it brought tears to my eyes. All that atmosphere!

We docked at Luna, which had been colonized by the Ceylonese and was now known politically as Serendib. It was much like any other planet, airless and cratered, with its city-domes brought up to standard gee by gravity lenses. Then we took a shuttle to Earth proper, and landed at the capital of Delhi.

We stepped out into the unfettered ambient air of the planet and gazed about us in wonder. We breathed. It was hard to get used to the notion of breathing outside a ship or bubble or dome; I kept thinking that my breath would catch, because there was nothing to contain the air. I knew that Spirit and Forta were experiencing similar reactions. It just didn't seem natural to be on the surface without cover.

And there was the sun. It bore down at exactly Earth-norm intensity—without a concentrating lens. I found myself peering into the sky, trying to spot the outlines of the lens that my background believed had to be there.

We rode in an open car toward the central city, and passed a lake. We almost gaped. Here was this enormous open body of water, just lying there! A fortune in liquid, being used for decorative purpose, one of myriads on the surface of this marvelous planet.

The city was beautiful, I'm sure, with the architecture typical of its culture. But I have virtually no memory of it, only of the wonder of air and sun and open water. I was in a daze as we reached our suite. Perhaps I was overdue for dialysis, but I think it more likely that I was simply overwhelmed by the reality of the dream planet that was Earth. The rootstock of humanity had come from here, and perhaps that contributed to the awe of it. I had never been here before, but in a sense I was coming home.

I had my dialysis, and rested, and a new woman joined me. She was Hispanic, and young, and beautiful. At first her signals were uncertain, and I realized that this was because neither Forta nor Spirit had met her, and knew too little of her to make for a comprehensive emulation. But I knew her, and she firmed for me as I reacted. "Dorian Gray," I said.

That was the name I had given the woman who had shared my captivity during my memory-washing. She had been an agent, intended to subvert me, so had not given me her name. Now she was dead, and all I had to remember her was her son, Robertico, whom I had promised to take care of. I had done so; he was now about fifteen years old, and remained on Jupiter. My daughter Hopie had been his baby-sitter and effective big sister, though there was no blood relation between them.

My affair with Dorian Gray had been illicit. I have known a number of women, but always legitimately, with that exception. I don't count the Navy, of course. The Jupiter Navy had required a sexual event on a minimum of a weekly basis, and discouraged permanent romantic associations for enlisted personnel. When I became an officer, I had been able to marry, on a temporary basis, and that had been an improvement. As a civilian I had married Megan and been true to her until our separation, when I had been served by the women of my staff. But Dorian Gray had been out of turn, as it were. I had just been mem-washed, and did not know whether I would ever be free again, and she was there and supportive and she filled a temporary but overwhelming need. Though assigned to subvert me, she cooperated with me, and enabled me to recover my memory faster than my captors realized, so that I could turn their play against them and win the Jupiter election instead of throwing it away. She had paid with her life, not the first or the last woman to do so, and I had never been able to repay her service, other than by taking in her baby son.

Thus I had mixed emotions about encountering her now. But I knew it was only an emulation, and it was the way that Forta could serve me, and so I accepted it. For the first time I instructed her in the nuances of the signals of characterization, so that she could become her role more perfectly, and soon she had it down as well as my recollection could make it. I admired that talent, akin to my own in a complementary sense.

So it was that Dorian Gray lay with me, and though the postdialysis period was not my best, I did have sexual congress with her, and it was much as I remembered it. Then I had been incapacitated by loss of memory and isolation and uncertainty and torture; now I was incapacitated by the failure of my kidneys. The parallel seemed close enough.

Next day we met with the Prime Minister of Earth, who was a woman as tough and politically realistic as the one I had encountered on Phobos. There are not many women in power in the System, but those who are are as competent as any man. Natural selection plays its part, I believe. Certainly she was no-nonsense with me.

She wore a colorful toga, looking native, but she addressed me in English, so that Forta did not have to translate. The meeting was physical—that is, without holo—and private, with only the two of us. I accepted this peculiarity because I knew that the Prime Minister was no fool, and wanted privacy. There was thus no record of our conversation.

"Tyrant, Jupiter has not been the same since you departed," she informed me brusquely. I read her with surprise; she was not making a compliment, she was making a statement of opinion buttressed by fact.

"I have been out of touch with the Colossus recently," I said. "My concern is with another matter."

"We shall get to that in a moment," she said. "I thought you should be advised that, though Jupiter's government remains nominally democratic, the moment your wife stepped down the predators moved in. Bad things are happening there."

I could have protested that I was unconcerned with Jupiter politics, being in exile, but in this privacy there was no need for any such ploy. I had many roots on Jupiter, and I was aware that things were not ideal; now I could get solid information. "Who is running the show?"

"Tocsin."

I made a soundless whistle. Tocsin had been President before me, and had been completely unscrupulous. He was the one who had had me abducted and mem-washed in an attempt to make me throw away my bid for the presidency, and he had used every political device to keep me out, and had tried to have me assassinated too. All that had stopped after I became the Tyrant, and he had caused me no more trouble. But it seemed that once I had departed the scene, Tocsin had seen his chance to return to the arena, and that was bad news indeed. My wife Megan, in her integrity and generosity, had of course restored the representative system of government and stepped promptly down, but now the sharks were feeding again. "I had hoped for better," I said with deep regret.

"Of that I am aware, Tyrant," she said. "You will do what you deem it proper to do, of course. I merely want you to understand that Earth would not find it amiss if the Tyrancy were to be returned to Jupiter. When Jupiter sneezes, the entire System shudders. You were always practical and fair."

As Tyrant of Jupiter, I had tried to foster good relations with the other planets of the System, and Earth, after an initial period of doubt, had in due course recognized the Tyrancy as the legitimate government of Jupiter. Trade had improved, and Jupiter tourists had increasingly flocked to see the historic sites of Earth. But Earth, traditionally, did not interfere in the affairs of other planets, except to serve as arbiter when requested. This was an unusual statement the Prime Minister was making. "I represent Saturn now," I said cautiously. "I have stayed well clear of Jupiter, lest there be any misunderstanding."

"You represent *humanity* now," she said firmly. "Your project cannot succeed without the participation of Jupiter, and the present powers there will never accede to your interest. You must reconsider your position, Tyrant."

Shaken, I nodded. If this woman told me that Jupiter was going wrong, it was certain that it was. I realized that I had been naive to turn my back on my planet; I had thought I was honoring the exile that my wife had crafted, but I had reckoned without the sharks.

The Prime Minister turned abruptly to the subject we were supposed to be on. "Tyrant, you know that Earth will support the Triton Project. We would be glad to participate. Our need for new geography and new resources is critical. But we have little to offer."

I was surprised again. "But India expanded to govern all of Earth, after the diaspora to the System," I said. "It was the only nation to eschew the exodus. With all of Earth's territory and resources—"

She smiled grimly. "Tyrant, we had a population of a billion before the colonization of the System, and that was seven centuries ago. In addition, not all the citizens of other nations emigrated; a number elected to remain, accepting the new government of the planet. The major regions became client states, and we have tried to treat them fairly, though of course they are now Indian states, populated primarily by our people. Today Earth has a greater population and fewer resources than it had then. Our need to expand is desperate. If we could this time go to space, to colonize some totally new system or constellation of systems—" She shook her head, smiling wistfully, and I saw that the Dream had taken her. "We are at your mercy; we will pay any price we can manage, to join in that project. But we have nothing you need."

No wonder she had made this interview private! She would be deposed in short order if her constituency learned of this statement. She trusted me to be discreet, and I would not disappoint her.

But I had of course come prepared. "There is a price you can meet," I said. "But you may not wish to."

"I suspected you would have a price," she agreed. "The greatest statesmen always have teeth in their negotiations."

That was an interesting way to put it. "Saber-toothed teeth," I agreed, smiling. I intended to take Smilo for a tour of an Earthly jungle; it would be the rarest of treats for him.

"That, too." But she was not smiling.

"I have been testing the light-projection technology myself," I said. "I have not asked any other party to risk what I would not risk. But there may *be* risk."

"You have traveled freely about the System, and you seem as sharp as ever."

"I am not. I have lost my kidneys. I believe this is co-incidental, but it is true that the condition manifested after I began using projection travel, and that if it were known, there would be alarm and suspicion about the projection technology. That alarm needs to be abated before it begins."

"It surely *is* coincidence," she agreed. "But I understand. There must be no question about the safety of projection, before the System trusts its billions to it. If there were accruing physical complications in those who projected—"

"Precisely. It will be necessary to test it thoroughly, not merely for efficacy of travel, but for the subtle effects on personnel. My consultants inform me that a suitable test would consist of perhaps a hundred thousand living people, from all races and of all ages and cultures, traveling perhaps a hundred times each, back and forth across the System. This would of course be expensive in the material sense, but the greater problem is to find that number of volunteers to take such a risk. I think that if any planet were to provide the volunteers, the rest of it could be organized."

"A hundred thousand lives," she murmured. "And a formidable staff to manage the logistics of the projections, and the feeding and care of the volunteers. The records alone would require a heroic effort."

"And the services of many doctors and specialists," I agreed. "There must be no question at all of incompetence or incompleteness. The major projector at Triton should be ready by the end of the decade; by then there must be no question of safety."

"Earth has the requisite numbers and diversity," she said. "Are you saying that such a unit of personnel made available for such testing would constitute an acceptable entry for the project? That we could share in the colonization of the galaxy?"

"Yes."

She didn't even hesitate. "I shall issue a call for volunteers. It will take several months to process them and establish the initial records of age, culture, and health."

"It will take a similar period to establish the testing stations," I said. "This is apt to be pretty dull work for the volunteers; they will simply be shipping back and forth across the System, without pause for tourism."

"But those volunteers, once proved out, will be the first to be granted visas for emigration to the galaxy, if they choose," she said. "But I think it would be better, Tyrant, if you could make appearances at certain sites to present the case. You are known throughout this planet; there will be a greater diversity of volunteers if they hear it from you personally, as it were. My government is necessarily somewhat remote from portions of the globe."

"I shall be glad to," I said.

We shook hands. All of this was unofficial, but we had our understanding. Earth would join the Triton Project.

We took a genuine airplane flight to the State of China. There are airplanes at the big planets, of course, but they fly from bubble to bubble, never touching land. This craft took off from land and returned to it, a novelty to us.

Most of the Chinese had emigrated to South Saturn centuries ago, but the Prime Minister was right: many remained. The expanding population of India had taken over most of the land surface, but certain regions had been designated reservations for the original culture, and these were pretty solidly oriental. Things were peaceful; those who did not like this state of existence had emigrated.

I gave a public address at the great city of Peiping, with Forta translating, and explained the need for volunteers. "Only a few will be chosen," I cautioned them. "For those it will be a risk, for we do not know the long-term effects of repeated projection. But we must be sure that each race of man can survive projection in health, before we allow emigration to the galaxy. You have the chance to do a significant service for humanity."

They did not react significantly, and I thought they were cool to the notion. But I discovered that this was merely the polite reserve they showed to the visitor; before I departed China, more than a million volunteers had registered. Perhaps no more than thirty thousand of these would be accepted for the program; but it was a rousing vote of confidence.

We went on to Moskva of the Soviet State, which reminded me eerily of its equivalent on Saturn. Here I addressed them directly in Russian, and here they knew me. "Tyrant! Tyrant!" they cried in unison. As Tyrant of Jupiter I had first opposed Saturn by force of arms, then established a détente; but they were thinking of my current status as a representative of Saturn. It was evident that the people of Earth identified with their colonies in the System, and kept track of them, exactly as the colonies identified with their origins of Earth. I was touched, and it showed, and there was no sin in that. They knew that I would not betray the people of Saturn, or of this state. I had become a statesman, in the manner of an attorney: I was for hire, but I was loyal to my employer and the interests of that employer.

We moved on, to the city of London in the State of England, a Saxon enclave. I pondered briefly whether to take a side trip north, but was afraid I'd find ley lines and an assassin waiting. Even Smilo seemed a trifle nervous about that.

Then we flew across the Atlantic Ocean, a body of liquid so monstrous that a moon could fit in it. The three of us gaped down at it, mesmerized. I think this was the strangest of all the strange features of Earth: the hugeness of its oceans of water, so incredibly extensive that their expanse was greater than the total of the land area. Leviathans could dwell in it, storms could form on it, ships could sail on it, using cloth structures to catch the wind instead of gee-shields to block gravity, and never see land for days at a time. Waves rippled on it, stirred by the wind, always traveling but never arriving. Water—perhaps the most precious substance in the System, for the purposes of man. The stuff of life itself, normally frozen fast to the surface of some barren moon, or dissolved in the turbulent atmosphere of a planet too solid to approach without gee-shielding. Water, the magic fluid. I could have watched it forever.

We landed in the bubble, uh, city of New York in the American enclave, where I was welcomed again. Then we rented a car, so as to take a drive down the continent to the region of Florida, the analogue of Sunshine on Jupiter. We needed no driver; we had a programmed vehicle, so we could ride the Appalachian Highway and see the scenery. Smilo, too big for this vehicle, was to be put under pacification and shipped down to meet us there. He would be entertained at a zoo, where there was a compatible mini-landscape, and contemporary tigers. The proprietors were interested in whether one of his breed could or would mate with a modern tigress. I suspected that Smilo would not be bored.

Spirit, Forta, and I got into the car. Its doors closed and it started up. We watched, intrigued, as it drove itself through the city and to the nearest access to the Continental Highway. There were no stoplights of the type that history texts describe; cars shot through the intersections, programmed to avoid collisions, at a velocity that would have been disastrous for human piloting. We winced as cars passed at right angles just before and just after ours; only the master traffic controller could guarantee their courses. We were relieved when the car peeled off into the access; now we were free of the cross-traffic.

Our vehicle picked up speed and soon was traveling at better than a hundred miles an hour, in the local measurement. It climbed to the elevated ramp, and we looked out across the checkered terrain of this local continent. How green it was!

After an hour, our necks were sore from our constant turning and gazing at the wonders of the world. Now we were heading into a darkling cloud, in fact a thundercloud, and soon rain was spattering on the transparent dome. What an experience! Actual, natural rain! A jag of lightning showed ahead of us for an instant. "Oh, lovely!" Spirit breathed.

"I wonder why man ever left Earth," I inquired rhetorically. Indeed, it seemed a foolish thing, at this moment.

We came to an intersection, and the car curved west. "That's odd," Forta said. "I thought we were programmed for Florida."

"We are," Spirit said.

"Then why did we just take the turnoff to Kentucky?"

"It must be on the way," I suggested.

"It isn't."

"Verify our programmed destination," Spirit said.

Forta touched buttons. The car's little screen came to life. DATA INSUFFICIENT, it said.

"I smell a rat," I muttered.

"Stop the car," Spirit said.

Forta sat in the driver's seat and touched the MANUAL OVERRIDE button. But the car did not turn over the control. Instead the screen showed UNAUTHORIZED INPUT.

"We're captive of the vehicle," Forta said. "I hate to say this, but—"

"Nomenklatura," Spirit and I said together.

"Must have had a mole in Earth's vehicle-programming department, who slipped in a false routing," Forta agreed.

"Which means we are headed for their destination, not ours," Spirit said. "It could be a hideout to hold hostages—"

"Or a stone wall at a hundred miles an hour," I concluded. "Arranged to resemble an accident. An accident of vehicle programming."

"Which accident we blithely walked into," Spirit said grimly.

"And which we had better walk out of," I said.

We pondered ways and means, and experimented. The car remained unresponsive to our directives; we could not guide it. It was moving at a hundred miles an hour, which made any attempt to leave it suicidal. It had a radio contact with the traffic satellite for this region, so as to coordinate it with the programs of the other cars on the highway, but it refused us access to that radio.

"We could start smashing the wiring from inside," Forta suggested.

"And careen out of control and into a collision with another vehicle," Spirit said. "That may be what they want."

"They want us dead, any which way," I said.

"Perhaps we could open a panel and short out the remote control," Forta suggested. "Then we could contact the satellite, and get a corrected program."

We tried it. But as soon as we pried at the panel, a warner blazed on the screen: UNAUTHORIZED INPUT—SELF-DESTRUCT IF PARAMETER BREACHED.

"Which means we wreck if we get in," Spirit said dryly. "They aren't novices."

"They probably hired a crack unit," I said. "The equivalent of Spetsnaz. Professionals."

"We need to think of something they haven't anticipated," she said.

"If this were in space, I'd signal SOS to another ship," I said.

Spirit laughed dryly. "I am getting homesick for space."

"But maybe—" Forta said.

We looked at her. "You want to signal a ship?" I asked.

"Not a ship. A car. If there are any military vets here, or merchant marine retirees—"

"I think you just earned your day's pay," I said.

Spirit took the rear, I the front. We took down the archaic rearview mirrors that were useless for a programmed vehicle but still required by archaic regulations, and used them to flash in the sunlight that had returned after the storm passed. The domes of the other cars were transparent, like ours, or translucent, depending on the occupants' desire for privacy. That desire did not seem to be strong; we had seen a woman doing up her hair in one car, and children playing in another, and a couple making love in a third. No one seemed to care what went on in neighboring vehicles; it was the privacy of indifference. With reasonable luck, we could penetrate that isolation.

I flashed at the car directly ahead, shining my beam into its canopy. I used my hand to interrupt it. FLASH . . . FLASH . . . FLASH FLASH-FLASH-FLASH FLASH . . . FLASH . . . FLASH, in the ancient SOS pattern. I attracted the attention of a child, who faced back and stuck his tongue out

at me. I switched to the next car over, as this was a mul-
tilane highway, and tried again. This one simply rendered its canopy opaque to shut out the intrusion. I tried
a third, but its occupant was asleep. Those were all I could
reach at the moment; I would have to wait for the pattern
to shift, introducing a new car into my range.

"Got a nibble," Spirit murmured. "Teenager, maybe up
on code."

I turned around and watched. The kid jogged his
mother, who evidently was not amused; the canopy went
opaque. Another down. This was not as easy as we had
thought it would be.

How much time did we have before our guidance program brought us to its mischief? It might be hours yet—
or minutes. We could not afford to assume the former.

Then a car drew up beside us, and a man peered
through. Evidently he had heard about the way we were
harassing other cars. I wished I had a poster to write on,
so that I could display a message, but I did not. So I used
hand signals. SHIP OUT OF CONTROL, I signaled.

The man looked blank. But I saw him using his radio.
Even if he thought we were pranksters, that could help;
if a police car came to investigate—

Another car approached, drawing up behind the other.
This one had a woman in uniform.

"Navy!" Spirit breathed. "Earth coast guard by the
look; she'll know signals." And she began hand signals of
her own.

The woman returned the signals. She did know them!
Soon Spirit conveyed to her the essence of our problem.
The woman went to her radio, then returned with this
news: The program for our car was classified, and could
not be touched. The station would not revise our route.

"Because we are VIP visitors," I groaned. "They are
protecting our secrecy."

But Spirit was already following up. She signaled that
we were in trouble, and had to be rescued, regardless of
what the satellite said.

The woman was doubtful. "How can I be sure this is
not a prank?" she asked, approximately, in signals.

"We'll have to tell her," I said.

Spirit made the signals for top man and for Jupiter, and pointed to me. I faced the other vehicle as squarely as possible, and assumed my most Tyrantish expression.

The woman stared, recognizing me, but disbelieving. What was the Tyrant of Jupiter doing in a car on Earth? Evidently she had not been paying attention to recent news.

I focused on her, tuning in as well as I could through the two domes and the intervening space. As her doubt strengthened I shook my head no; as her belief returned I nodded yes. She knew the Tyrant could read people, and she realized that I was accurately reading her. It was enough.

She got on her radio and summoned help. Now at last a police car arrived. The officer evidently had a picture of the Tyrant on his screen; he peered closely at me, verifying it. He spoke into his radio, and the woman answered. Then she signaled us: "You're really in trouble?"

"Programmed for wrong destination," we agreed. "Possible assassination attempt."

She relayed that to the officer, who evidently did not understand signals. He considered, then made his decision.

"He will lose his job if this is a ruse," the woman signaled. "But he will take you out manually." I repeat, this is only approximate; signals lack the grammar of spoken language.

"No ruse!" we signaled back.

Another police car arrived. The first one drew in front of us and slowed. Our car slowed automatically to avoid contact; that was a built-in feature. But the second police car closed from the rear, preventing escape. This was no doubt the way they took out illicit drivers who refused to honor police signals. The two cars sandwiched us, and though our car tried to escape, it could not; magnetic clamps were now attached, and it was captive.

They brought us to the side, and then to a substation, where we stopped. The woman who had helped us pulled in behind. We were released. Now direct verbal communication was possible. We identified ourselves, and the screen verified us. In a moment the local chief of police came on the screen. "Tyrant, your vehicle malfunctioned, and you summoned assistance by means of hand signals to this woman?" he asked.

"True," I agreed. "Without the assistance of this woman, we would have remained captive of our program. I would appreciate it if you could ascertain what that program had in mind for us."

The chief had obtained the authority to override the classification of our program. He glanced at the readout, and whistled. "Tyrant, that program would have had you driving into a deep lake, your vehicle sealed. Then it was set to self-erase. You would have suffocated before we managed to find you, and it would have been an inexplicable accident."

"Then I think we owe this woman our lives," I said. "Can she be rewarded?"

"I did not seek reward!" the woman protested. "I didn't even know for sure that it was genuine!"

"Perhaps a paid vacation to the planet of her choice, with her family?" I asked the chief.

"If you request it, Tyrant—" the chief said.

"Put it through," I said. "I'm no longer young, but I still value my life." And I turned and gravely saluted the woman.

She almost fainted. Then, confused, she returned my salute, though this was of course backwards; in any military system, I ranked her enormously. Realizing this, she looked flustered, so I stepped up and kissed her. "Farewell, good woman," I said. She would have a story to tell her grandchildren.

Reports of this episode of the malprogrammed car were of course exaggerated. News spread about that a bomb had been aboard, and that I had broken open a window and climbed to the roof and leaped to another car, appropriating it for rescue purpose. I confess I rather liked that story, but it was of course ludicrous; I simply was in no physical condition to do such a thing. The truth, as usual, was relatively tame; I record it here merely so that the final record can be accurate.

The State of America arranged alternate transportation for us, and we arrived in Florida in good order. We stopped by the zoo to see Smilo; he was glad to see me, but it seemed he had not completed his business with the tigress, who was coming into heat, so we left him for a few more days. We spent a couple of days touring the origins of our Sunshine experience on Jupiter; it was fascinating. We even took a hop to the island of Hispaniola, which to me was Callisto, and to Haiti, where Spirit and I had figuratively been born, knowing it as Halfcal. What a strange returning! I spoke there, and the people welcomed me screamingly, knowing the affinity. I might have been born on a moon of Jupiter, but I was indeed of Haitian stock, and they knew it. I felt as though my life could end at this moment, and it would be complete.

But of course this was not the end. I had one final thing to accomplish, and that was to unify the System behind the Triton Project and enable man to colonize the galaxy.

I had another dialysis treatment, and Dorian Gray, who was in this reality of Earth a Cuban, joined me again. "Do you want to visit Cuba?" I inquired.

She shrugged, and I realized that she couldn't really answer. The original Dorian Gray was Cuban, but Forta Foundling was not; what point in visiting a homeland that in no sense had been hers?

"Visitor," Spirit said.

"Here?" I asked. I was at low ebb after the dialysis, but I knew we were being protected from random intrusions. What person would the authorities allow through?

"From Jupiter," she said.

"Jupiter isn't speaking to me," I reminded her. "Make sure it isn't an assassin."

"No assassin," she said with a smile. Then, to the screen: "Send him in."

"Now?" I asked, appalled. I was in pajamas, ready for bed, and Dorian Gray was in a flimsy nightie. She jumped up, about to scurry into her room to change clothing and identities.

"As you were," Spirit said. "Robert won't tell."

"Who the hell is Robert?" I demanded querously.

There was a knock. Spirit went to the door—here on Earth they used actual, literal doors, not ports or locks—

and opened it. "My, how you've grown!" she said, stepping out to embrace the visitor.

I exchanged a glance with Dorian Gray. What was my sister up to?

Spirit brought him in. He was a solid, muscular youth in his teens, Hispanic, smiling somewhat foolishly. "Hi, Dad," he said.

I performed a double take. "Robertico!" I exclaimed.

Dorian Gray dissolved into astonishment and dismay. She sought again to leave, but I grabbed her wrist. Suddenly I was enjoying this, though surely my postdialysis depression distorted my judgment.

Robertico had grown monstrously in the four years since I had last seen him. He had been eleven; now he was fifteen, and that seemed to have added most of a foot to his height and fifty pounds to his mass. I had never formally adopted him, but he had become part of my family. My daughter Hopie had been first his baby-sitter, then his older sister, taking excellent care of him. Of course he was a welcome visitor!

"I come with a message," Robertico said. Then he faltered, staring at Dorian Gray.

I smiled. "Dorian Gray, meet my ward Robertico. Robertico, meet your mother."

For he had been the infant son of that woman. A promise is a promise, and the death of one of the parties does not abate the commitment. After I am dead, my commitments must be maintained. Now Dorian Gray had returned to me, in the only way she could, and so I was bringing her son to her.

Of course she was young, in this incarnation, only a few years older than Robertico himself. But that seemed not to matter. She stared at him, knowing what this meant, and he stared at her, seeing his mother for the first time. Then he stepped forward, and she stood, and they flung themselves into each other's arms and wept together.

Perhaps others would see this as a ludicrous scene. I did not. Dorian Gray was as close to the original as it was possible to be, and Robertico was of her flesh. If ever a man could go back in time and meet his mother as a young woman, this was the occasion. This was the only way this man *could* meet his mother. If this scene was wrong, then the universe is wrong.

In due course we got to Robertico's message. "It is this," he said. " 'Stay clear of Jupiter.' They do not want you there, and they will execute you if you violate your exile."

I had to laugh. I was feeling better, regardless of the dialysis. Dorian Gray was sitting beside Robertico, holding his hand, and I had no jealousy of this. "Jupiter needs no messenger to inform me of this!" I exclaimed. "I'm surprised they let you out to come to me!"

"Hopie sent me," he said. "And they let me go, because they knew you would see me. It isn't the same there, now. They mean it; you can't go there."

I remembered what the Prime Minister of Earth had said. Robertico of course would not know who was running the new political machine of Jupiter, which was another reason they had let him come here. Hopie would know, so she was kept there, surely as hostage. They knew I would do nothing to bring harm to my daughter.

"But the Triton Project needs the support of Jupiter," I said. "It is for the benefit of all mankind."

"They don't care about that," he said. "They just don't want you back."

"I wonder why?" I asked, as if ignorant.

"My sister told me," he said. "It's because the people would support you. Things were better when you were Tyrant."

"Things always seem better in the past," I said.

"No, Dad, it's true!" he insisted. "There are shortages all the time now, and a lot of police, and anybody who criticizes the government gets arrested and maybe disappears. It's bad!"

"Freedoms are being denied?" I asked. "What does the press have to say about this?"

"The news media are being shut down. They don't dare say anything."

"What about Thorley? Nobody could shut him up."

"He was arrested last year."

"What?" This time I was shocked.

"Well, first it was just house arrest, but when he

wouldn't shut up, they came and took him away last month. My sister said you'd want to know about that, even if he did criticize you a lot."

"Right," I said grimly. Thorley had been my most eloquent critic throughout, but despite the public impression we had close ties. At this moment I knew I had to do something about Jupiter. I didn't even need to catch Spirit's eye to know she concurred. This had been my daughter's real message: that the situation was serious. The first thing a truly repressive regime does is muzzle free speech, particularly as represented by the press. As Tyrant, I had never done this, though often excoriated by the media. That had been my promise to Thorley, when he saved my wife's life, and, as I said, I keep my promises.

We kept it polite, as though I hadn't really reacted to the message. Robertico was here on a limited visa, and had to return promptly. "Tell them I got the message," I said as he left.

"Yeah," he agreed darkly. "I'm sorry you can't stop by there. Hopie really wanted to see you."

"Tell her I'll do what I have to do, as I always have."

"And take care of yourself, dear," Dorian Gray said to him, exactly like a mother.

He left. Dorian Gray retired immediately to her room. What effect this had had on her I could not be sure. I had thrown her unexpectedly into a completely different aspect of her role, and I knew it had shaken her. She had, for a time, been a mother, and that was no light thing.

I turned to Spirit. "You know what to do," I said.

She nodded grimly. "You prepare Forta." Then she went to her own room.

Within the hour Spirit emerged, ready to go. Her appearance had changed; she was now in male clothing, and looked like a man. "Give me ten minutes," she said.

I summoned the hotel staff. When the servitor came, I told him that we were having trouble with a bathroom fixture. This was true; I had loosened it myself. He accompanied me to the bathroom, verified the problem, and brought out a tool. Soon enough he had tightened it, and the fixture worked.

"Thank you," I said. "Here is a tip." I urged a coin on him.

"No, sir," he demurred. "We do not charge for service."

"But I was once a workingman myself," I said. "You have done me a service, and I must repay you."

"It is a privilege to serve the Tyrant," he said. "Please, sir, I would lose my job if—"

"Oh." I pondered briefly. "Perhaps a commendation to the office, then?"

"There is no need—" he said, pleased.

By the time he got away, ten minutes had passed. Spirit was gone. She had departed in the guise of a hotel servitor, escaping undetected. If anyone was to be challenged, it would be the true servitor, emerging ten minutes after he had supposedly left. But in that case I would come quickly to his rescue; he was blameless. The report of the prior servitor would be dismissed as an error.

Spirit was on her way, and no one would know she was gone. Satisfied, I retired to my own repose—which I now sorely needed. I settled on the bed, touched Smilo's furry back, and sank into slumber.

In the morning I explained to Forta: Spirit was on a private mission, and she, Forta, would have to help cover for her. "You can do her?" I asked, knowing she could.

"Of course," she agreed, still surprised by this development. "But I can't be two people simultaneously. We are supposed to be a party of three—"

"You can do quick changes?"

She sighed. "You may have to help me, though. When we are guaranteed privacy, I can cope, but in any public or semipublic situation—"

"I will cover for you," I agreed.

"But where did Spirit have to go, so suddenly?"

"To Jupiter," I said.

She stared at me. "Is this something I should know about—or not know about?"

"After we finish with the inner planets, we are going to Jupiter," I said.

"But they will kill you there!" she protested. "And they hold your daughter hostage!"

"They hold the planet Jupiter hostage," I said. "I shall have to recover it."

"Tyrant, you frighten me! I am not inexperienced in the matter of repressive governments, and I know the record of such as Tocsin. They hate you, and they are completely unscrupulous. You are no longer in power there; you would be helpless. And your daughter—"

Indeed, she was not inexperienced! She came from Amnesty Interplanetary, specializing in the brutality of man toward man, and had been a victim of that in infancy, as her scarred face showed. "That is why my sister is preparing the way," I said. "She has always been the competent one."

She was unconvinced. "Oh, Tyrant, I am afraid for you!" She took my hand, moving into my embrace—then froze. I realized why: she was out of character, being herself at this moment.

I seized the moment, bringing her into the completion of the embrace. "I know I could have no better person with me at this time than you," I told her.

But she drew away, upset. "I must change!" she said.

I let her go. If I reacted to her differently, depending on the aspect she represented to me, so also did she react differently to me. She could not become physical with me unless she was in a role. But she was a good woman—one of the very best, in whatever way that could be taken.

She returned in a few minutes in the guise of Spirit. She was perfect in that role; there was nothing I could tell her to improve her performance. "You've got it," I agreed. "But maybe you should rehearse for quick changes. We can cover by using voices, too; when I call to Spirit offscreen, you can answer for her even when in your own format."

"True," she agreed.

We completed the Earth tour, rehearsing those role switches, and it worked well enough. I spoke at South

America, and then at Africa, and Spirit was normally at my side in the holo representations, with occasional shots of my secretary. We accomplished the mission; the government was deluged with volunteers from all races and cultures. And in the evenings Dorian Gray slept with me, seeming to need my comfort as much as I needed hers.

Chapter 15

VENUS

The first problem was in making the trip to Venus. We had our own Triton Project ship, and I could pilot it alone—but boarding it was another matter. There would be fanfare and a farewell party, and it would be obvious that our party consisted of one tiger and two human beings, not one and three.

I decided to call on the Prime Minister for help. I asked for a concluding meeting with her, a private one, and when this was granted I explained: "You advised me of conditions on Jupiter. My sister has gone to investigate. Will you lend us one woman of her likeness to join our party, so that we can depart without my sister's absence being known?"

She smiled. "I am glad you took my remarks to heart, Tyrant. For how long would you require this double?"

"Just to the ship. She can debark before we take off."

"And what of your arrival at Venus? Won't your sister be missed then?"

"My secretary is adept at impersonation. She can play the part of my sister."

"And who plays the part of your secretary as their car conveys your party in style to your lodging?"

Was I getting confused in my age and infirmity? I hadn't thought of that, and of course she was right. We could no more handle the arrival at Venus than we could the departure at Earth.

She put her hand on mine. "I can see how quickly you are lost without a woman to supervise your itinerary, Tyrant," she said. "I will lend you one for the duration."

"I wasn't asking that," I protested.

"When I said that Earth supports you, that is what I

meant. She will be competent and discreet, and will not interfere with your private affairs. You may park her at our embassies at Venus and Mercury during your stays there, and pick her up when you travel. She will find her way home when you have no further need of her."

I smiled. "You are very understanding."

"I want the Triton Project to succeed, Tyrant. You are the only one who can bring that about."

So it was that the woman I call Doppelganger, Doppie for short, joined our party. A doppelganger is a double, a person exactly like another, often in the supernatural sense. I knew her name at the time, but have forgotten it; I always thought of her as Doppie. It seemed that on a planet with five billion persons, one who resembled my sister should exist, and indeed it was so. Doppie was of a similar age and configuration, and I would have mistaken her for Spirit had I judged by sight alone. Her signals were wrong, of course, but most people were unable to read these, so for this purpose it didn't matter.

We boarded the shuttle with the expected fanfare, and rode to Luna to board our own ship. Doppie played her part perfectly. The Prime Minister had done me a real favor, and I would not forget.

Again we used the projection tube to cover the distance between planets, so there was no long journey. Forta remained as herself, as we did not care to advertise her other relationship to me.

We were assigned a parking orbit about Venus, and an experienced local pilot picked us up and took us down into the cloud layer. We certainly required this assistance; not only were the clouds seemingly impenetrable, the winds were about a hundred meters a second at the top, and circled the planet in four Earth-days, though the rotation of the solid part of the planet was virtually nil. In addition, the atmosphere was much thicker than anything we had had experience with, being about ninety times the pressure of Earth's at the surface. Of course there are much higher pressures in the giant planets, but Venus is smaller than Earth. We never descended to the ninety-bar region of Jupiter or Saturn; our bubbles weren't braced for it. Here we did.

So we came down to the surprisingly dark and quiet landscape of Venus, where the wind was only one meter a second. The vehicle that awaited us was a squat thing with wheels, braced to withstand the horrendous pressure, as was the shuttle. Our ship would have been crushed before it reached the ground. I began to experience the claustrophobia of pressure again. The vacuum outside a spaceship I could handle without significant qualm, as long as I had a good suit, but the horrendous planetary pressures unmanned me.

Doppie, evidently coached on this, did what Spirit would have done: she put her hand quietly on mine, reassuringly. I wasn't reassured, but I appreciated the gesture. For one thing, it lent verisimilitude; the driver would not suspect she was not my sister.

The terrain, as we saw it through the phenomenally thick porthole, was rough and rocky. Venus had been settled by northern Africa, and indeed the barren desert seemed to be equivalent. Here below the clouds it was possible to see some distance; I saw that there were mountains to the side. Our vehicle traveled a road that had been cleared of boulders, and was making good time; too good, for I feared its swiftness. If anything went wrong, and we crashed . . .

The dome was a dark mass, marked only by a locater beam on the top. It was formed of bubblene, of course, but of a thickness not seen elsewhere in the System. Only beneath the liquid oceans of Earth were residences placed under similar pressure, and there were few of those on Earth because it was so much easier to utilize the land surfaces and the shallow waters. Here on Venus there was no choice.

We entered the ponderous lock, and my claustrophobia abated somewhat. It was possible to imagine that this was a normal city, spinning in the atmosphere of Jupiter or Saturn or Uranus, beset by less than ten bars pressure. But I remained somewhat dazed, and really was not alert. My clearest memory of that approach is our arrival at the compact suite provided, where Forta dialyzed me. It seemed that every second event in my life had become the dialysis!

Forta arranged to drop Doppie off at the Earth embassy, as she was now off duty until we departed for Mercury. I'm not sure how they managed the transfer; I was out of it, sleeping, being baby-sat by Smilo. When I woke, Doppie was gone—and so was Forta. Instead, a new woman was with me: Coral.

Coral had been my bodyguard. She was oriental—that is, of Saturn derivation—and expert in personal defense. I had always felt secure when she was with me, though of course there were threats she had not been able to protect me from. She had been young and most attractive when she came to me, and when I separated from my wife she had been among those who had taken me as lover. She was healthy and athletic, and versed in the sexual lore of the East, and her liaisons had been a delight. When I saw her, I was gratified, for I knew that there would be marvelous times coming.

Of course it was Forta in another emulation. But she was so good at it that I simply accepted this manifestation as reality, maintaining only a technical reservation in my mind. The real Coral was now in her fifties, still attractive but not of the caliber she had been in her youth. This one was closer to thirty, and she virtually shone with health and vigor.

I watched as she removed her clothing, marveling yet again at the perfection of the emulation. Height, mass, skin color and tone, mannerisms—I doubt that anyone but me could have told her from the original, and I was half unsure. The body was compact and full, not at all like Forta's. How *did* she manage that? By the signals, of course; she was projecting Coral, and so I received Coral, and my mind filled in the details that I knew were there. We seldom truly see others; we see our images of them, which do not necessarily correspond closely to the realities. Never before Forta had I appreciated how thoroughly this imaging process operates. Perhaps this is what makes helmet love so realistic: it activates the images we already possess, or the capacity to accept images in lieu of realities. Sometimes we much prefer those images.

Naked, she smiled at me. Then she came to me, and

undressed me in the way Coral had, efficiently yet erotically.

Smilo yawned and retreated to his nest. The games that human beings played bored him. Now, if there had been another healthy tigress available, such as the one he had courted on Earth . . .

Some of the oriental sexual positions are heroic in the performance, but in deference to my weakness Coral did not lead into any of these. She merely put me supine on the bed and straddled me, so that I could see and touch her fine breasts and the rest of her without impediment while she made love to me. I really did not have to do anything, just relax and enjoy it, but I felt as if I were participating positively. At my age, there was no swift climax, but this had the advantage of giving me greater time to appreciate the act. Age does not necessarily diminish sexual pleasure; not if a person's partner is understanding. Intimately connected, I was enjoying this to the full.

Then the phone rang.

"Ignore it!" I rapped, afraid she would jump up and leave me stranded in mid-act.

But it was persistent. "It may be important," she said.

"Then I'll answer it," I snapped. "You stay put."

She did, but she abated her stimulation, merely containing my member in a state of stasis. I spoke to the phone. "Orient on me, head only," I told it.

The holo pickup swung across to hover above my head. I knew that it would project only what I had defined; phones were reasonably sophisticated appliances. There would be no evidence of my other activity, or even of my nakedness. "Tyrant here," I said. "I am resting at the moment."

The pickup disappeared into its projected image. It was the President of Atalanta, one of the more important planetary figures. Venus did mine iron, and was one of the more important System sources of it, though not in a class with Mars. However, there were a number of other strategic metals here, too, and the project needed them. I was here to deal; it behooved me to be polite, despite my predicament of the moment. "I apologize for disturbing you, Tyrant," the President said diffidently. There was a small pause in the words; he was speaking Egyptian, and there was an ongoing machine translation.

"Quite all right," I said graciously. "I expected to encounter you more formally at a later hour. I would have prepared." For my hair was mussed, and of course it was evident that I was horizontal, not vertical; the pillow framed my head.

"Indeed, you shall," he said quickly. "I should not have bothered you at this time. Perhaps if you transfer me to your secretary, we can make the arrangements."

Everything had to be scripted just so! We couldn't just talk. I understood that—but this request was distinctly awkward at the moment. "I think she is on another mission now," I said cautiously, trying to see through his image to Forta's face, but unable. "I regret—"

"Then your sister," he said quickly. "I do not mean to inconvenience you."

In the process of his politeness, he was doing just that! But what excuse could I make for Spirit? Naturally if my secretary were out, my sister would be here; it was known that the women of my staff never left me alone. To demur again would be to arouse suspicion, and that we could not afford. We wanted there to be absolutely no doubt about Spirit's presence here.

Forta tapped me on the thigh, in a signal for affirmative. I felt her body twisting, though she did not lift herself from my torso. She was changing masks! Apparently she had anticipated the possibility of interruption, so had kept her kit handy. "Let me alert her," I said. But I stalled for time, because I did not know how fast Forta could work in a situation like this. "I certainly appreciate your consideration, Mr. President."

Of course he had to be gracious again. He was, and we exchanged further meaningless pleasantries before Forta tapped me again as the signal she was ready.

"Switch to Spirit," I directed the phone. "Headshot only."

The unit switched, rotating to orient on Forta's head. Now I was able to see her as the holo image faded. She had indeed made the change, and now was Spirit from head to shoulders. She had even donned a blouse that was typical of my sister's taste, in case the pickup should stray slightly. "Yes, Mr. President," she said in Spirit's voice.

Now the President's head re-formed, facing her on the horizontal plane. It had been on the vertical plane for me, the holo aligning with what it took to be my proper orientation, so that he had seemed to hover right above me. I was treated to the view of a cross section of his neck and shoulders, where the image cut off, as though his top had been neatly separated and suspended above my bed. Above that I saw the back of his head, for of course the holo showed the complete object. At least, it did in this case; our pickup was of a simpler nature, so it only showed him the front portions of our faces. As the humor has it: How does a holo work? With mirrors. Anyway, he was facing Spirit, who saw the front of his face. "Welcome to Venus, Iron Maiden!" he exclaimed.

Forta was startled, and I felt it in that part of her body that didn't show on the holo: the part embracing me. The term Iron Maiden had been applied to my sister from time to time, notably by the caustic columnist Thorley, because of her toughness in organizing the Tyrancy and in dealing with problems. She had been the backbone of the Tyrancy, while I was mostly its figurehead; the average man did not realize that, but Thorley of course had known. Though Thorley had resolutely opposed our exercise of power, the appellation had not been intended maliciously, and I rather liked it. But it was a surprise to me to hear it used in this context, and it was evidently more of a surprise to Forta.

But she had a role to play, and she rallied; only I knew her momentary confusion. "Thank you, Mr. President," she replied, sending out Spirit-signals that he would receive unconsciously. That was the way her emulations worked; the average person came to accept them on the unconscious level, and so was completely convinced. All people read signals; I just happen to read them consciously, to my considerable advantage.

They went about the arrangements, and I was left to my own devices. I was struck by the oddity of the situation, not merely the matter of receiving a phone call while engaged in the act of love, but of being erotically connected to the nether aspect of a woman whose superior aspect was now that of my sister. To see her face, and hear her talk as Spirit, and then to trace my gaze down her body until the blouse ended and her bare flesh commenced, and on the site at which my own flesh penetrated hers—it was as though I were making love to my sister.

That shocked me on two levels. Of course I knew that it was not my sister, yet it summoned a long-buried memory of the time when I may indeed have made love to Spirit. I had been fifteen, and she twelve, and I had dreamed of love with my fiancée Helse; but when I woke I had known that Helse was dead, and there had been only Spirit. I had never since been quite certain of the truth of that situation, and had not dared to inquire. Certainly there had been nothing of that nature between us since, and I hadn't thought about it—until this moment, when the question of it resumed with sudden force. But the other shock was perhaps more fundamental. One would expect that the appearance of making love to my sister would appall me, and send my body into an emotional retreat in disarray. Instead my body responded with greater urgency, throbbing with eagerness for the culmination. This dismayed me, but I could neither doubt its reality nor escape the situation I was in. I could not disengage while the President was on the phone.

I lay there, steeped in my shame, realizing that there was an aspect to my passion that I had long suppressed. As a youth of that same age I had seen my beautiful older sister raped, and though I was appalled, I had also suffered an erection. Did that mean that I secretly wanted to rape her too? Surely not! I had recoiled against sex, and against the male reaction, ashamed of my heritage, until Helse had taken me in hand and shown me what natural, unforced sex could be. Now I was back at that early pass, caught as it were between my sisters: the one for whom I may have illicitly lusted, and the one with whom I may have completed that lust. Where was my true desire?

Now I remembered what Roulette, my Navy wife, had said to Hopie, my adopted daughter: that the one woman

I had truly loved in my life had been Hopie's mother. I had always believed that I had loved two: Helse early and Megan late. But love has many facets, and in the total picture there was indeed one I loved more. That one was my sister Spirit.

But that had been familial love, not sexual love! Love and sex are not synonymous, though oft confused. One may have sex without love, as in the Navy, and love without sex, as in the family. Where the two overlap, ideally, is in marriage. How could anyone accuse me of the wrong type of love for my sister? I would do anything for her, and she likewise for me, but sex was not an aspect of that relationship.

Yet here I was, throbbing within the body of the emulation of my sister. My mind exonerated me, but my body condemned me.

Then their conversation concluded. The holo clicked off, and the unit swung out of range. Forta smiled at me apologetically, then pried at the edges of her mask and wedged it off, revealing her natural face, gummed with the adhesive for the mask. Then she applied the Coral mask, and rearranged her hair; since she had black hair, as did both my sister and Coral, she had not used a wig this time. She drew off the blouse, her breasts popping out from under it, and changed the signals. Coral was back.

It was the first time I had actually watched a complete change, with clothing and mask. I was fascinated. And my erection remained almost painfully firm within her throughout. It was as though I were having intercourse with three women in succession, without withdrawing my member. I had lived a long time, and had experienced many things, but I think this was unique!

"Where were we?" Coral asked. She looked down at our connection. "Oh, yes, now I remember."

I had to laugh, and it was good for me to laugh now, for it dissolved much of my tension and doubt. She could not know what had been running through my head, and I hoped she would never know.

She leaned down to kiss me, and her fine breasts lengthened toward me as if drawn by my proximity. I reached up and hugged her with my arms, pulling her fiercely in to me, and as our lips met I detonated in her with a seeming force that I thought I was no longer capable of. And she joined me, her body convulsing, legs and abdomen and mouth, climaxing with that abandon that supposedly exists only in legend. We threw our essence each into the other, each drawing from the other, in a union the like of which the description "sex" seems hardly to do justice.

In due course I held the formal meeting with the President. This was by holo, as was customary, with translations, but now our dialogue was official. It went, approximately, like this:

"What is your business with us, Tyrant?" the President inquired.

"I wish to enlist the participation of Venus in the Triton Project," I replied. "We have need of the resources of Venus."

"I can speak only for my own nation. We have many nations here, and we do not speak with a unified thrust. Atalanta would feel privileged to join you, but we are not a rich nation."

"Our needs are in more than materials," I said. "We plan to project ships of colonists to many other planets, elsewhere in the galaxy. We have little way of knowing what conditions they will face there, but there is a fair statistical probability that some will be like Venus. We wish to develop a residence that can be adapted readily to any of a number of high-pressure situations, without requiring sophisticated procedures or highly trained personnel. Perhaps a technique for building such a residence from natural materials found on such a planet."

"But nothing is better than bubblene," the President protested.

"Some systems may not possess gas giant planets," I reminded him. "That would make bubblene impractical to cultivate—unless it could be done in the atmosphere of smaller planets, such as this one."

This caught him by surprise. "Bubblene—grown here?"

"We believe that the proper formula for seeding, and null-gee laboratories floating at the critical levels, could make this possible," I said. "If Atalanta and the other nations of Venus were to cooperate in such a project, none bearing the entire expense alone, the Triton Project would be prepared to supply expert personnel. I realize that this is a great deal to ask of you—"

"If such a thing should come to pass," he said, hardly bothering to conceal his eagerness, "to whom would the rights to that process belong?"

"To Venus, of course," I said. "With the Triton Project guaranteed the first licensing rights for other systems. Those of the Solar System would be entirely yours."

It was as if a calculator were clicking in his head. Bubblene, the stuff of city-bubbles, was the most precious stuff in the System. The giant planets had had a monopoly on it, because it could be grown only in their massive atmospheres. To break that monopoly, to make it possible for a small planet to produce it—that was the stuff of dreams. If successful in this, Venus would become a major economic power in the System.

"And the Triton Project would expect to pay for its right to license this technology in other systems by granting Venus appropriate colonization rights in the galaxy," I continued after a pause.

The President licked his lips. "Tyrant, I cannot speak for other nations, but I am sure that if you approach them similarly—"

"I shall be happy to," I said.

"But who will supervise the research? We of the planet of love tend to have certain territorial jealousies . . ."

"I will supervise it, through duly appointed intermediaries," I said.

"So it will be an aspect of the Tyrancy."

"Of the Triton Project," I said. "Which is under the joint auspices of Saturn, Uranus, Neptune, and their client bodies. I merely represent their interests."

"The Tyrancy," he repeated as if he hadn't heard. But our meeting was being recorded; my qualification was on the record. I was the Tyrant, but I claimed no power in my own right; I was working for others, and it was important that I maintain that distinction.

* * *

I traveled, bringing my tiger and my message to each of the leading nations of Venus. I never got used to the inordinate pressure of the atmosphere, and Forta had to sedate me for the longer trips across the surface. Thus my memory is hazy about the details, but I believe we traveled mostly by high-velocity rail, the train zooming along its set track with all the authority of singlemindedness. We covered the lowlands, or Planitia, of Niobe, Leda, Aino, Lavinia, Guinevere, and Sedna. We covered the highlands, or Terra, such as Ishtar, Aphrodite, and Rhea. We covered the regions between, stopping at the major city-domes. All this took time, for the land surface of Venus, being free of water, is much greater than that of Earth or Mars or any other solid planet; Venus is in fact huge when seen from the ground. Each nation required its own presentation and its own acquiescence. But in due course they did agree, and Venus, under the loose authority of the Tyrant, joined the Triton Project.

I need not relate further the problems we had concealing Spirit's absence from our party, or my own diminished condition of health. We never had quite as close a call as that first one, but many times we had to do fancy footwork. Sometimes Forta emulated Spirit, and on occasion she even emulated me, so that I could appear healthy and vigorous when in fact I was in the middle of dialysis. She was a wonder! I was bemused to see myself as others saw me, signals and all, and not totally pleased; still, the truth is the truth. I was no longer young, or even middle-aged, and it showed unconscionably.

But privately I was in a kind of a state of shock for some time. The experience of being *in* a woman who looked and sounded exactly like my sister preyed upon my mind, of course. But the worst part of it was my own reaction of the time, which had been positive rather than negative. I should have become instantly impotent, easy enough physically in my weakened state, and I had not. I condemned myself for that. All these years, these decades—had I secretly lusted for Spirit?

Forta became Coral, and tempted me, but my ardor was less than it should have been. This, too, bothered me. The real Coral had been a wonderful person and a terrific

lover, and no doubt remained so today, for she was alive
on Jupiter, as many of my women were. The emulation-
Coral was in all ways equivalent; I could fault no part of
Forta's impersonation. Why had I been potent for my sister, and not for my lover?

Actually, I reminded myself, I had been potent with
Coral—but that had been in the same sequence as the
manifestation of Spirit. That climax could have been a
mere surrogate for the temptation just past. Who can say
what is in a man's mind as he embraces a woman, thinking of another? Was Spirit the one I truly desired? If so,
how could I ever face my sister again, in reality?

Over and over I rehearsed it in my mind, trying to avoid
the conclusion that threatened. I had been making love
to Coral, and was already deep within her when the call
had interrupted. Then Forta had changed masks, appear-
ing as Spirit, then momentarily in her own guise, and
finally, at the end, as Coral. And we had had the most
emphatic culmination of all.

Then, on perhaps the tenth or the hundredth rendering
of that sequence in my troubled mind, it dawned. Like
sunlight striking through the impenetrable cloud cover of
Venus to illuminate the surface, understanding came to
me.

"It's all right!" I exclaimed joyfully.

Forta jumped. "I should hope so," she said, quickly re-
checking the tubing. For it happened that I was amidst
dialysis at the time; it is as good a time as any for reflec-
tion.

"I mean me!" I cried. "I'm not perverted!"

"Tyrant, I never suggested that you were," she said,
still troubled by my inexplicable activity. Normally I lay
on the bed during dialysis, reading or thinking or sleeping.

"Come and make love to me," I said.

Again she was taken aback. "Now?"

"This instant!"

"But you are in—"

"Woman, I know exactly where I am! Just strap down
the tubing and be careful not to jog it; it won't interfere.

Get your clothes off." Meanwhile, I was struggling with my own as my member swelled imperatively.

"I'll change," she said. She meant her personality, becoming Coral.

"No! As you are!"

She gazed at me, perplexed. "Tyrant—"

"Just do it, woman! I'll explain after!"

Hesitantly, she obliged, evidently ready at any moment for me to change my mind. Her lanky body came into view, well formed but by no means spectacular; she only became impressive when she used her supports and makeup and posture and signals to complete an emulation. Now she was doing none of this, and it showed. She was herself, and none too sure of herself.

I gestured her in. She got on the bed cautiously, on hands and knees, straddling me. I reached up and grabbed her hanging breasts in my two hands, hauling them down to my face, while her body followed to accommodate my urgency. I pressed her breasts into my cheeks on either side, and kissed the deep hollow between. Then my hands slid down and around to cup her buttocks, which were somewhat spare in this position.

Obeying my desire, she straightened out her legs and got into position to take in my member. It was the position Helse had used, when I was fifteen, but this was not Helse. Her weight settled down on me, her legs outside mine, her breasts against my chest, her face above mine, perplexed.

I stared at that deeply scarred visage. Then I took her head in my hands and brought her face down to meet mine. I kissed her savagely, my tongue forcing its way into her reluctant mouth. I bucked against her, but neither my position nor my strength was sufficient to enable me to gain the action I needed to complete the act.

Taking her cue from me, Forta began to move her torso, bringing her abdomen forward, then back, up and then down. It was the reverse of the thrusting done by a man; her downstroke was the one that gave me the deepest penetration. Working that way, she brought me to the highest pitch, and then to the culmination, our mouths still joined.

Gasping with the fulfillment, I broke the kiss but not the embrace. Her head rested lightly against my shoulder as I stroked my hands along her back. "Forta, it's you, it's you!" I whispered beside her right ear.

Now she lifted her head. "Me?"

I gazed at her face again. "You are beautiful, Forta," I said.

"Tyrant, I—"

"Call me Hope, Forta. You are my lover now. Not Coral, not Shelia, not Emerald or Juana. Not Spirit! You, Forta, you!"

"But I am not—"

"Not ugly," I finished firmly. "I see your scars; they are as the craters on the planet of love, affecting the surface in immaterial ways, not changing the reality. Your facial structure, your bones—you have a lovely face, Forta, and for the first time I am seeing it truly. It is like a work of art, that must be viewed from a distance lest the roughness of the palette knife distort the vision. Viewed with understanding. Your face is beautiful—but even if it were not, and I not privileged to see the physical reality of it under the mask of scars, I would know you to be a beautiful woman. I am chagrined that it took me so long to perceive the obvious! You were there all the time, concealing your splendor behind a mask that should not have deceived me for a moment. But now I see, and I don't need any of those masks anymore; you are my mistress now."

She looked at me, still not quite accepting it.

"When we were interrupted by that call from the President of Atalanta, and you changed masks—I thought I was attracted to the simulation of my sister," I continued. "But that wasn't it. It was you, in your versatility, all women in one. For the first time I saw it happening, and I saw you in the middle, between masks, and my ardor was undiminished. *That* was what tuned me on: the realization that you in reality were more than any of the emulations. Coral was not a surrogate for Spirit; they both were surrogates for you, Forta. Now the scales have fallen from my eyes, and I see you as you are." And I hauled her face down for another kiss.

She resisted. "Hope, this is too quick," she protested.

"You are not in the best condition. You must take time to decide whether—"

"It's late for that," I said. "We have already made love in the natural state." Indeed, we were still connected, though the sexual fervor was past.

She had to laugh ruefully, and I felt that laugh all the way down. "If you are sure, Hope—"

"Just lie with me," I said.

She put her head down again, and we lay embraced while the dialysis proceeded. It was as though this time it had cleaned not only my body but my mind.

Next day she looked askance at me, for no given reason. I kissed her. "I may be slow, but I'm sure," I said. "Once I learn something, I don't soon forget it. You need no more masks for me."

She turned away, but I would not let her go. "You are crying," I said. "Is my acceptance so hard to accept?"

"Megan told me it would be this way, but I did not let myself believe," she said.

"That it might take me years, but that eventually I would perceive your true beauty?"

"Yes. But I am happy to use the masks. It is my specialty."

"Use the masks, do the emulations when you wish," I said. "I like variety, and you have given me the most. But now you are the main object, not the emulations. You may love me as yourself." For she loved me, of course; I had long since read the signals. All my women did.

Her face turned back to me, all teary, and I kissed her again. Megan had been right: though I was partial to physical beauty, I was not entirely opaque to inner quality, and now that I had seen Forta as she was, she would never appear ugly to me again. Actually, Megan herself had been a precedent; she had been beautiful when I met her, but not young, and I had loved her in large measure for her inner qualities. Megan had proved, once again, just how well she knew me.

So, as we completed our circuit of the planet of love,

returning to pick Doppie up from the Earth embassy in Atalanta so that we could proceed to Mercury, we had discovered our own kind of love, and that was worth the journey quite apart from the technical or economic mission.

Chapter 16

MERCURY

For the first time since I had known her, I saw Forta apprehensive. It required no great exercise of insight to know why. We were coming to Mercury, her planet of origin, where she had been a foundling. Mercury had been colonized by the nations of the southern part of Africa, and the one we would be primarily dealing with regarded her as a mixed-breed creature of inferior status. Strict segregation laws would have prevented my keeping company with her here, were I not protected by diplomatic immunity, and were I not the Tyrant. Nonetheless, it would have to be made clear that Forta was my servant, under my authority and protection, and Spirit would have to handle all communications with officials.

I talked with Doppie. "I realize that you are on loan to us only to facilitate our travels between planets," I said. "But in this case, I would appreciate it if you would do me a greater favor."

She looked at me uncertainly. Like all woman of any age with whom I associate closely, she was somewhat taken with me; it is a power I have. Part of it may be the sheer notoriety inherent in my identity as Tyrant, and part my ability to read and relate to people. I disliked having to use her in this manner, but I saw no expedient alternative.

"You see, my secretary is what is known on Mercury as a mulattress: a female of mixed ancestry. The government will not accord her any status. It is true that she can emulate my sister—but if she is caught, there will be ugly complications. It will be better if she remains herself, and if you remain my sister, instead of going to the embassy. I would be most appreciative if—"

"Certainly, Tyrant," she said immediately. She wanted my gratitude. She was not aware that Forta was more than my secretary and nurse, though she did know about her ability to emulate others. Who could tell where the gratitude of the Tyrant might lead?

"Thank you, Doppie," I said, laying my hand on hers. As I said, I was using her, and I regretted it, but I would see that she was rewarded. I went on to explain that we might have to leave her with Smilo, but that he represented no menace to her. I had introduced her to him at the outset, and he had accepted her. In fact, he would protect her from any molestation by others.

The sun seemed monstrous here, more than twice the diameter as seen from Earth, and its radiation was ferocious. Our ship was suitably shielded, of course, but even the muted image on the screen was daunting. I felt hot, though the temperature within the ship was standard. I was afraid that some errant flame would lick out from that massive sphere and fry us without noticing. It was another kind of phobia; I seemed to be more subject to these in my infirmity.

Mercury was about the diameter of my home world, Callisto, but its density was triple, so it was a far more massive body. It had very little atmosphere, and took almost two months to rotate. Its surface was cratered like that of any barren body. In short, it seemed basically familiar to me. That helped, because I wanted to get onto land and out of the ambience of the huge sun.

We needed Mercury in the project because it was one of the richest sources of rare metals and crystals in the System. Gold, platinum, chromium, uranium, copper, manganese, diamonds, and of course iron—it was potentially as rich as Mars, but the difficulties of sunside mining inhibited operations. We had secured our iron requirements, but still had need of the others, and this planet could represent an enormous boost in our supply of raw materials. But the government of the Republic of South Mercury was notoriously tough, and I knew that negotiations would be difficult. As Tyrant of Jupiter I had not gotten along with Mercury well, for it exploited its majorities shamefully for the benefit of the minority, and there was chronic hunger and even starvation in many of its nations. There was little reason to suppose relations would be better now that I was out of power.

Of course I had power now; it just happened to be less direct. I suspected I would have to invoke it all too soon. I sent a coded message to Khukov, back on Saturn, alerting him; he could still pull the plug on this one if he chose. But he let it ride.

We put our ship in the assigned parking orbit, and a Mercury shuttle took the four of us down to the surface. We landed near the South Pole, at Cape Dome, one of the capitals. The advantage of this site was that the polar regions suffered neither the intensity of the month-long day nor the appalling cold of the month-long night; here it was always compromise. Not that the natives chose to gaze out upon the barren surface; the savings were mostly in terms of maintenance and access.

Inside, the city was much like any other, and I felt better immediately. But my tension about the physical environment was replaced by psychological tension. Though there was no direct allusion, it was evident by the signals that the authorities here resented the presence of Forta, and would gladly have relegated her to one of the segregated subsidiary domes.

But I was a foreign dignitary, and she was my secretary, and they could not impose their sanctions on her without suffering an interplanetary incident.

We reached our accommodations and proceeded promptly to my dialysis; this preliminary settling-in period was the best time for it, so that I could not be caught short later. While I rested I wondered what form Forta would assume this time. For I knew she felt more comfortable in a guise, despite my assurance that I now accepted her for herself. She was a mimic, a mime, and she was astonishingly good at it, and I would not deny her the pleasure of proving it as often as she chose.

But I fell asleep, and slept the night, so missed whatever it might have been, to my retrospective regret. For in the morning I had the first official meeting with the representative of South Mercury, which it seemed had to be personal, not holo. How the old ways linger, even in this modern age!

Doppie, as Spirit, accompanied me, leaving Forta to keep Smilo company. Doppie kept silent, letting me do all the negotiation. Though the Mercurians knew that my sister was the power behind my throne, they were happy to have her assume a subservient role for this official function.

After due formalities, we got down to business. "The Triton Project needs the resources of Mercury," I said. "We are uncertain of the structural stresses entailed in materialization and travel elsewhere in the galaxy. We intend to construct the first colonization ships to the most rigid specifications. For this we require diamonds, chrome, platinum—in fact, almost the full spectrum of the products you export. We are prepared to pay in System monetary units and in a favorable allotment for your own colonization of other stars. I am here to make the offer and an agreement."

"South Mercury should be interested in your proposal," the man said carefully. "However, there are certain considerations."

Oh-oh. I had thought I was past the worst when I left Mars; now, as I read his body, I realized that there was trouble here. "Considerations?" I asked guardedly, hoping that he was not going to raise the issue I feared.

"Your project, as we understand it, is sponsored jointly by Saturn and Uranus."

"True, with Rising Sun and Titania as major cosponsors."

"Some of these planets are known for a certain position on social integration."

He had raised the issue. How much easier it would have been had his government elected to yield to economic benefit and set aside its racial policy! "You refer to their objection to apartheid," I said, reading the confirmation as I spoke.

"In past times, such planets have attempted to base economic decisions on social criteria," he said grimly. "We regard this as improper. We do not attempt to dictate to Saturn how it handles its Phobos question." He meant

Saturn's oppression of those of Jewish background, preventing them from emigrating to Phobos. He had a point. "Or to Uranus how it handles its Mars question." Nations of Uranus, notably Prussia, had imported many workers from Mars, and then expelled them when their economies weakened. Another point. "We fail to appreciate why these planets should be concerned with our internal affairs."

"I am from Jupiter," I said cautiously. "I have no part of the social problems of other planets, and do not seek to meddle in them. I seek only to establish mutually beneficial trade relations."

"The society of Jupiter became remarkably egalitarian during the Tyrancy," he said. "It is so no more. Perhaps you should return to that planet."

I was getting news from all over about the deteriorating state of Jupiter society! "Perhaps I should," I agreed. "But first I must complete my mission here. The Triton Project will be in a superior bargaining position for negotiations with Jupiter if the resources of Mercury are available to it."

"Mercury will be happy to join the worthy effort of galactic colonization," he said. "Provided it is arranged on a businesslike basis, without irrelevant issues."

I had to concede the merit of his case. I had no brief for this nation's treatment of its citizens of mixed blood, who were given no part in their government, but it was true that my mission related to trade, not morality. But two things interfered. First, I knew that neither Saturn nor Uranus would reverse its prior objections to the social system of South Mercury. Second, I realized, through my continued reading of this man, that he was lying. *Mercury did not want to join the Triton Project.* This stunned me, leaving me at a loss for words.

South Mercury was in fact using the apartheid issue as a pretext for its denial of an agreement it had no intention of making. But why? The deal I proffered would be of enormous economic benefit to this planet, which was chronically starving for cash, and many of whose residents were literally starving too. The sanctions established by other planets had damaged the economy of South

Mercury severely. This offer of mine could at one stroke restore this planet's economic health. The amelioration of apartheid, just enough to make it acceptable to Saturn and Uranus, who did want the stone and metal riches of this planet, would be a tiny price to pay for the benefit received. I knew that the government understood this. Why, then, was it uninterested?

"You baffle me," I said frankly. "Why don't you want to join?"

"I did not say that."

"You're talking to the Tyrant!" I snapped. "I know when you are lying. Your government doesn't want to make any deal; the social issue is merely a pretext."

He nodded. "So it is true; you do read people."

"It is true. Now answer my question."

He glanced to the side, evidently seeking advice. In a holo encounter this would have been easy, but this personal meeting meant that there were no advisers to the side. "I regret I am not authorized to—"

"And why did you insist on a personal meeting, instead of a holo, when you had no intention of dealing?" I demanded.

He just looked at me, unable to respond because he was not authorized to tell the truth, knowing that I would immediately recognize a lie.

"What the hell are you up to?" I demanded.

He did not reply, but I read him anyway: They were indeed up to something.

"The Tyrant is not accustomed to treatment like this!" I said, some genuine anger developing.

"Perhaps it would be better if you departed the planet promptly," he said. Now he was telling the truth.

But the Triton Project really did need the resources of Mercury, if the colonization effort were not to be severely restricted. Most of the System's reserves of chromium were on Mercury, for example, and this was vital for high-grade steel. I had hoped to deal amicably, but if that proved to be impossible, I still had to deal. "Not without an understanding," I said.

He did not answer. In a huff, I departed, virtually towing Spirit behind me. I was angry, but more than that I was afraid. Something was wrong here, and I could not fathom what it was, and knew that I had better do so promptly.

We made our way back to our suite—and found disaster. Smilo was unconscious, and Forta was gone. Evidently the suite had been flooded with some kind of gas and my secretary abducted during my absence.

Now part of it became clear: why they had insisted on a personal interview. They had wanted to get me away from the suite. That was what their representative had not been permitted to tell me. His job had been simply to occupy me long enough to enable them to do their dirty work. He had succeeded.

Were age and frailty causing me to lose my grip on the realities of politics? I had never suspected the trap! That bothered me almost as much as the trap itself.

But almost immediately the more sober aspects of my situation claimed my attention. Without Forta, I could not dialyze; only she knew the procedures. If I tried it alone, I could botch it, and that could be fatal. Doppie had no expertise here; I could explain the essentials to her, but it would be awkward and chancy business. Dialysis is not a casual thing. My effective time here was now limited to two or three days; thereafter I would be on a descending spiral of oblivion as I was poisoned by my own internal wastes. Had Mercury planned on this?

No, the dialysis unit was untouched; it was unlikely that the intruders had even recognized its nature. They had struck with surgical expertise, taking only the thing they had come for: Forta. The predicament this put me in was coincidental.

Forta. Why had they wanted her? Because they were so angry that one of mixed blood should be housed in a Saxon residence? But it would have made no sense to aggravate the Tyrant that way, especially when completion of the deal would have brought departure anyway.

Forta was from this planet. Amnesty Interplanetary had rescued her from torture and probably death at the hands of this repressive regime. Had they bided their time, waiting for her to return so they could revenge themselves on her for her crime of surviving? Because one look at her face betrayed the nature of this government more explicitly than any words could have? Again, this seemed unlikely; I doubted they had even kept a record of her. Probably hundreds of babies had been tortured, and one more made no difference. Once she was gone, they would have ignored her, or perhaps even been satisfied to have her represent a lesson for others of mixed blood who might think of coming to this planet.

What, then? I had discovered that South Mercury did not want to deal. Could this be related?

There it was! They knew I would be hard to dissuade, so they had added this fillip of persuasion. If I departed the planet promptly, mission incomplete, I could have my secretary back. She was hostage to my decision.

Black rage overcame me. I may have faded out for a moment, for I found Doppie sponging off my face. "Are you all right, sir?" she asked. "I think you fainted."

"Yes, thank you, Spirit," I agreed, reminding her that she had a role to play. The suite was surely bugged. "You see to Smilo; I have a call to make."

She went to tend to the tiger, and I made my call. It was to the official government number.

"Have you killed her?" I rasped as the bland face appeared in the air before me.

Evidently my call had been expected. "By no means, Tyrant," the man said. "She is merely being detained for clarification of her status. It seems that she went out without the proper identification, and was picked up—"

Forta had not gone out; I hardly needed to read the man to know that lie. She had been abducted from the suite. They knew I knew that; that was not the point.

"Show me that she is safe," I said.

"Why, certainly, sir," he agreed. "This is merely a formality."

The formality of forcing me to depart the planet in a hurry. They either knew or suspected that Forta was my lover. That was surely another sore point with them: fraternization between races. In a moment the picture of Forta formed. She was in a prison cell, alone, seeming dazed but unhurt.

"Forta," I said.

She glanced up. "Sir," she said. She never got a role confused; she was my secretary now.

"Where are you?" I asked.

"Temporary detention center," she said. "I—it seems I should not have gone out—"

"An understandable error," I said. Obviously she understood what must not be said.

"I'm sure it will be cleared up soon," she said. "But, sir—if you would do me the kindness of bringing me my purse?"

"I shall," I said.

Her image faded, to be replaced by that of the official. "Visiting is permitted?" I inquired curtly.

"Naturally, Tyrant. We are a civilized planet. It will only take a day or so for her papers to be corrected. You will have time to arrange for your transportation out, and should be able to pick her up at the time you depart."

Uh-huh. "But I will bring her her purse now. Please provide me with the address."

"Tyrant, we shall be happy to transport you there." Oh, they were the soul of overt courtesy, knowing that they had me by the private hairs.

I nodded curtly. "In five minutes," I said.

Then I checked for Forta's purse, which rested beside her bed. I knew it had her special makeup in it, and two masks, and two wigs. She was able to emulate either Spirit or myself on short notice. The equipment was nonmetallic and would not alert the detection beams of the prison. I took the purse and rejoined Doppie.

"Spirit, I hope Smilo can survive without our company for a while longer," I said. "We must visit my secretary, and deliver her purse to her. I realize you are upset, but please say nothing until we return."

Doppie nodded, having no idea what I was up to, but ready to play her part. She was, as I have said, a good woman.

I took her arm, and we exited the suite. An escort was awaiting us. He conducted us to a vehicle, and we rode to the detention center. It was an imposing structure of stone; this was one resource Mercury had in quantity.

We were permitted to enter the cell with Forta, and to

talk with her privately. The government of South Mercury was making a show of accommodation, but the point was clear: my secretary would remain a prisoner until I left the planet. They had cobbled together a legal rationale for this that I could not disprove with the resources at my disposal. They would let Spirit and me out, but not Forta; I could not change that. This was the convention of this sort of thing; the reality was that my secretary was as much captive as if chained naked to a rock in a deep tomb.

But I was not exactly helpless. I had formulated my plan on the way, and knew that Forta understood. She had, after all, been my secretary for three years, and knew how to study people so as to emulate them; she was familiar with the way my mind worked. I hoped she grasped enough to follow all the way through.

I took her in my arms and kissed her. I knew there would be a camera on us, and we had to get out of its coverage. The authorities might assume that I was simply trying to aggravate them by this gesture. "Where?" I whispered in her ear as we embraced.

She made a tiny indication with her head toward a rear upper corner. I saw no lens, but of course it was concealed. Now I could judge the manner of its coverage. It would have a gap in the corner immediately below it. Of course it was intended mainly to detect escape attempts, and it would cover the entire front region of the cell.

"Your purse," I said, handing it to her. Then I turned my head and addressed Doppie, who was standing somewhat awkwardly behind us. "I have private business with my secretary; will you watch for intrusions?"

Doppie, obviously embarrassed, turned to face the front of the cell, her body partially shielding us from observation from the front. Of course that was not where the real spying occurred, so the authorities did not intervene; whoever was on the camera figured that I wanted to do some intimate handling, and that did not matter. The more intimate my relation with Forta, the better hostage she made; if I wanted her enough to make love to her right in the cell with my sister present, I would never let her be stranded on Mercury. So they were happy to allow me to proceed; no one would bother us from the front.

We stood in the corner, our heads near the pickup lens. The ceiling of the cell was not high, for though space in planetary domes was not at the premium it was in city-bubbles, neither was it plentiful. I positioned myself so that my head blocked virtually the entire field of its vision, and Forta positioned herself so that Doppie's body cut off most of the view from the front. Then, silently, quickly, efficiently, we stripped our clothing. Because I could not bend down, lest my head move clear of the lens, Forta helped me. Without hesitation she put her clothing on me, and mine on herself. I was taller than she, but not by a great amount, and her clothing was highly adjustable; she made it fit me handily. In a very short time the exchange was complete.

Then, facing me and standing close, she donned the Hope mask and the Hope wig, fitting them together with her special expertise. She took her makeup stick and worked on my face, drawing scar tissue. She gave me back the purse. Last, she drew down my head, below the level of the lens, and set a wig on my head; then we turned about and straightened up so that now the back of her head, which resembled mine, was blocking the lens. This maneuver would be taken for some sort of body kiss occurring just out of camera range. Even such evidence of our dishabille as showed peripherally would be taken for our desperate love scene.

We separated. Forta seemed to have inserted wedges in my shoes, for now she stood almost as tall as I, and of course I hunched down to lessen my height. "We'll clear this up soon enough," Forta said in my voice. It was like seeing a holo recording of myself; her emulation was perfect.

She led the way to the gate, and Doppie followed, seeming relieved that our sordid tryst was done. Doppie herself did not know what we had accomplished; she would find out in due course. That was part of the beauty of this maneuver: If Doppie didn't suspect the exchange, no one else would.

I watched them go. Then I sat on the prison bunk, staring disconsolately at the floor. All I had to do was maintain the ruse long enough to let them get back to the suite. Then, God willing, hell would break loose.

After a time I got up and went to the toilet cubicle of the cell. I didn't think anything could be seen here, but I played it safe, sitting down to urinate, hiding my penis, using tissue to wipe myself though I didn't need it. If the prisoner had just made love standing up in the cell, she would need to clean up now, so I took the time required.

Time—that was all we needed. Time and nerve. I hoped that Forta had the savvy to play it correctly. She would have to assume the role of Spirit for this, which would put Doppie in an awkward position; Doppie would have to become Forta, and she might not like that. But, correctly played, this would win all the marbles.

I returned to the bunk, lay down, and slept. Evidently my appearance had passed inspection; there had been no commotion. I would need my rest for the scene to come; meanwhile I wanted to be as much like Forta as I could. I found it intriguing to be playing the role of the role-player instead of watching her or having sex with her.

When I deemed the time to be propitious, I retired to the sanitary cubicle and methodically stripped my costume. I washed the scars off my face, tore up my wig, and flushed it down the toilet. Then I did the same for my dress and underwear. The shoes were harder, but I finally managed to separate them into components and flush them also. How fortunate that Mercury, being a planet, insisted on showing off by using water facilities, even though it had to be expensive mining the extra water. Naked and masculine, I sat on the pot and waited.

I was right: the process of hell breaking loose was audible in the distance, and then in close. Men charged into my cell. I stepped out to meet them, naked. "Are you going to beat me now?" I inquired. "That's the next stage, isn't it?"

The men gaped. I fancied I could almost see the officials on the other end of the lens pickup doing the same. They had thought they had a woman hostage, and suddenly here was the Tyrant! There was no news crew, for the press was controlled here, but it would be next to impossible for them to suppress *this* news!

Indeed, Forta gave them no chance to do that. In a moment a holo formed, Spirit's face in it. "Oh, Hope!" she exclaimed for what I knew were cameras. "I knew it! They've humiliated you! They've stripped you naked!"

The man in charge managed to stifle his gasp. "Get the prisoner some clothes," he said, and an underling took off. At least I think that's what he said; he spoke in Afrikaans, and there was no translator handy.

"And they've tortured you!" Forta cried with horror, still in the role of my distraught sister. "Your legs—all scarred and bandaged!"

The scars were from prior loop-sites, and the bandage concealed the present loop. But who would believe that at this moment, when my kidney ailment was not even known? "Just get me out of here, Spirit," I said urgently.

The face of a higher government official appeared, evidently overriding the prior transmissions. "We are being framed!" he exclaimed in English. "We never touched the Tyrant!"

Spirit's visage reappeared. "Then how is my brother locked in your cell, naked and scarred?" she demanded half hysterically. And without giving him a chance to formulate a reply, she continued: "You meant to force him to do your will, didn't you! To endorse apartheid! But he resisted your torture, and now I've found him, and I demand you free him instantly!"

"But we never—" the official protested, obviously at a loss in this abrupt and astonishing turn of events.

"So you refuse!" she said indignantly. "Well, my brother is here as the representative of the Union of Saturnine Republics, and we consider this to be an act of war." Her head turned as she addressed an offscreen party. "Saturn Commander, what is your authority?"

Now the head of a Saturn Navy marshal appeared. "My fleet is at the disposal of the Tyrant, Hope Hubris." He faced me, and I read in him a certain grim humor. Evidently he had been properly briefed, and knew the nature of this ploy, and enjoyed it. Saturn never had had much liking for Mercury, and navies of any stripe enjoy the flexing of muscle. "Sir, what are your orders?"

"All I want is a pair of trousers and a fair-trade agreement," I said innocently. "I never thought I'd find myself like this!" Indeed, not until Forta had been abducted.

"We never—" the Mercury official cried, but was unable to continue, being overwhelmed by the preposterous situation.

I had intended only to reverse the ploy on Mercury, giving this planet a taste of the Tyrant's medicine in response to its attempt to coerce me. Now it occurred to me that I had opportunity to do more than that. The government would never accede to the trade agreement after this embarrassment, even if it had been willing before, which it had not been. Suddenly I realized why it had balked: It was not merely the problem of apartheid, it was power itself. If Mercury participated in the Triton Project, there would be plenty of room and resources for everyone, whites and blacks and all the shades between. There would be no way for the present regime to control those others. So it preferred to remain restricted, and in charge. It would never yield power voluntarily, or allow a situation to develop that forced the eventual yielding of that power. This government was a loss to me; it would never deal.

Accepting that, I had two choices: use my leverage to free myself and Forta and depart the planet, mission failed—or draw on the power of the Saturn Navy to overthrow the present government and install one that would participate. It would be a major move, of questionable ethics—but Mercury had started this quarrel. It was evident that Forta and the Saturn authorities had analyzed this similarly. That was why the marshal was placing himself under my command; that would make it a takeover by the Tyrant, not Saturn, and that would be far more palatable politically to the remainder of the System.

"Sir?" the marshal inquired, prompting me. I remembered how my onetime wife Emerald had done that, when the Jupiter Navy backed my takeover of the government of the United States of North Jupiter.

"I seem to have no choice," I said with staged regret.

"I must assume power in South Mercury. Orient on the major cities, and destroy them if I die."

"Understood, Tyrant," the marshal said with ill-concealed relish.

In this manner I came to be the Tyrant of Mercury. It was no bluff; several Saturn battleships had been projected to this region, so that this military presence had developed virtually without warning, giving Mercury no chance to maneuver. The force was overwhelming; Saturn was, after all, a major planet, and Mercury a minor one. There was some resistance, and a military complex was destroyed, but once the nature of this trap was clear, the officials of the former government of South Mercury pleaded for sanctuary under the auspices of the Tyrant. Otherwise the huge nonwhite majority would have risen up and slaughtered them all. Only my benign presence maintained order.

We had to bring in executives from other planets to establish the new government, as the people did not trust the former officials, and this was complicated and time-consuming. But in a few months we had a viable administration that extended around the entire planet; it was amazing how cooperative the other nations of Mercury became when they appreciated the reforms we were instituting at the south, and the eagerness of the Saturn warships to test their formidable weapons. I don't want to pretend that this was not a military conquest, but it was as bloodless a takeover as was feasible. We now had access to the mineral resources of the planet, and the majority of the people were better off than they had been. In due course I was able to appoint a President of Mercury to run the government; he was a popular Black native we had freed from prison, educated but unversed in government. That didn't matter; we equipped him with a competent staff of advisers and administrators, so that he could operate as I did: being a popular figurehead who nevertheless got the job done. Programs were instituted to eliminate the hunger and homelessness that were rampant across much of the planet, and to improve the lot of the common workers. Human rights had come to Mercury.

Meanwhile, I had Forta. She had played the role of Spirit beautifully, while Doppie had stayed out of sight. Without Forta's ability to emulate not only the aspect of my sister but her mode of operation, we could never have brought this off. My respect for her was enhanced, and when I made love to her now it was never with a mask. Beauty is as beauty does, and she was beautiful. A significant part of my motivation to help the ordinary folk of the planet was that I knew how much that would please her.

Chapter 17

RUE

I think I was sixty-five years old when we went to Jupiter. I dislike supposing that my powers of memory are fading with my age and health, but perhaps it is true. When I review the events of my recent life, there seem to be gaps of days or weeks that I cannot account for. Probably they were spent in routine travel, dialyses, and pauses between significant events, and my mind has simply telescoped the material to leave only the salient matters.

Yes, now I remember one important matter I was about to overlook. While we were consolidating Mercury, fresh news came from the Triton Project: One of our bright young engineers had worked out a way to make the projection self-receiving. That is, to fashion a receiving tube into a ship, which of course it was, and to project that ship in the normal manner. But instead of requiring an established receiving tube for its arrival, this one could retranslate itself, and solidify at the destination. The mechanics of it were complicated, really beyond my understanding, but the essence as I understand it is that this modified tube projects its receiver field outward rather than inward, so affects itself rather than whatever passes through its interior. The fact that it is made of light at the time of operation doesn't seem to matter; it applies the rematerialization field to itself, and converts instantly, exactly as it would if it encountered that field in the tube of a physical receiver. I am sure I am overlooking some critical stages, but I hope this suffices. The point is, it meant that we no longer faced the prospect of having to send tubes out to the stars at tedious sublight velocity to establish receiving stations; we could do it at light speed. This would accelerate our program immeasurably.

But of course this was still in the prototype stage; years of testing would be required before we were sure of it. It would also require new facilities to develop, as the present ones were already operating at capacity. So one unit was all there was. It worked, but it wasn't enough.

I pondered briefly, and realized that I could facilitate a couple of things if I had the nerve. Since my time was limited, I decided to take the plunge. "Ship it here immediately," I told them.

Of course it wasn't immediately, but they did expedite it. They shipped it via the regular tube, so that its self-manifestation would not arouse curiosity, and it appeared as a regular ship. We inspected it and outfitted it for occupancy and travel, for of course it had a regular drive. This was not so much for space travel as to provide the considerable power required for translation.

At any rate, this was one of the things that took my attention and time during this period. Odd that it should have slipped my mind until I looked for it, for it was certainly significant.

One thing was coming clear: Though my powers may have been failing, and my status was that of an exile dependent on the largess of an alien planet, the larger situation made my political power greater than ever before. I was now known as a statesman, an envoy of goodwill, laboring to secure a project that would benefit mankind as a whole. But in the name of statesmanship I had come into considerable executive influence. The Triton Project was conducted in my name; the treaties with Mars, Earth, and Venus were in the name of the Tyrant, and Mercury was entirely under my control. Saturn backed me absolutely, and Uranus to a considerable extent. They had a great deal invested in the Triton Project, and I was the unifying symbol of it. Now that power was to have its major challenge.

Jupiter did not intend to join the Triton Project. The case was similar to that of Mercury; illicit elements had recovered power, and knew that this would be eroded if the planet became a contributory to the effort to colonize the galaxy. Jupiter had warned me not to attempt to return, and Jupiter held my daughter Hopie hostage. Former President Tocsin had taken over again, covertly, and I knew that he was absolutely unscrupulous. That was why Spirit had gone ahead to prepare the way; this was to be our greatest challenge.

For the Tyrant was going to have to take over Jupiter again. I had been exiled, but I honored that only as long as my wife Megan required it; now she was out of power and her worst enemy was in charge. If Megan still barred me, I might stay clear—but when Tocsin had seen fit to make our daughter a hostage, I knew he had alienated Megan. She would not help me, but neither would she hinder me.

Spirit had gone to reconnoiter the situation in detail, and to reestablish connections with the Jupiter Navy. Of course Tocsin had by now replaced my top personnel with his own henchmen, so I could not simply march in and have the support of my old units. But I had had forty-five years of association with the Jupiter Navy, and had known it intimately, and my personnel existed within it from top to bottom. It would have taken more than five years to remake it even had Tocsin had full power all that time and spent his full effort there. He had not. So I knew that the Jupiter Navy was a fine organization whose superficial loyalty had changed, but not its nature. Spirit, of course, was even more conversant with it than I was, and in the months she had had, I knew she had done what needed to be done. Perhaps Tocsin had some notion of repelling my incursion by force; I doubted it would occur if the Jupiter Navy were involved.

As it turned out, Tocsin did indeed have his sinister eye on me. Our scouts reported that Jupiter subs were intercepting ships from Mercury, inspecting them nominally for contraband or drugs, but actually checking the identities of all travelers carefully. I hardly needed to guess whom they were looking for.

We set up a diversion. We arranged for our small ship to set off for Jupiter on a diplomatic mission: Mercury wished to have its new government recognized by Jupiter. Of course this was a futile mission; if Jupiter had been cold to Mercury before, it was frigid now. But we sent our ship on an easy voyage, scheduled to arrive in two weeks.

Sure enough, our ship was intercepted. It submitted to inspection readily enough, and of course I was not aboard. Instead, while Jupiter attention was on my ship, I boarded the new vessel with Doppie and Forta. We set course for Ganymede, whose primary loyalty remained to Saturn despite its heavy sugar trade with Jupiter. Despite that sugar, relations between Gany and Jup had soured after my departure. But I now represented Saturn, and the Premier of Gany was glad to have me visit.

I will not say that I made this trip without concern. This was, after all, new technology, not yet properly tested; I was well aware of the prospects for oblivion in transit. I did not require Forta to accompany me on this venture, but she insisted. To my surprise, so did Doppie: she pointed out that until I rejoined forces with my sister, I needed someone to stand in for her, and Forta could not always do that. I do inspire such loyalty in women, but still it touches me.

As it happened, the jump was successful. It required something like thirty minutes, perhaps forty, objective time, even at light speed, but to us it seemed like an instant. We had made such trips before, but this was the first without an established receiver. The alignment was not quite perfect; we overshot our target a smidgeon and found ourselves within the mine field surrounding the planet. So we had to wait for a Gany tug to come haul us out, for only the locals could navigate the mine field with certainty. But we had arrived intact. That, after all, was what counted. We breathed some shuddering sighs of relief; I think we had been more nervous about this than we had admitted, prior to the jump.

Had Jupiter's spies observed us? It really didn't matter if they had; Jupiter could do nothing now. What would a technician think if his instruments indicated that something the size of a ship had appeared near Ganymede, seeming to come from nowhere? He probably would assume there was a glitch in the record.

So we came to the surface of Ganymede: Forta, Doppie, and I. The Premier was an old friend, if that is the proper term; we had understood each other for over twenty years.

He was waiting to greet me personally as the tug brought us in to port.

I was tired, more from the nervous energy of the chancy trip than from any heavy duty, but I did not stand on ceremony. I felt safe here, both as an acquaintance and as the representative of Saturn. The Premier knew that I had come to tackle Jupiter, and that could only be to his advantage. The last time there had been such business afoot, Jupiter had been invading Gany; this was a reversal. He ushered us into a private office.

He looked at Doppie. "And here I thought your sister was elsewhere," he said in Spanish.

I was alarmed. "Who has news she is not with me?" I replied in the same language. If Doppie had ever had to speak in that language, she would have been lost!

He smiled. "There was no leak, Tyrant! She came to me herself."

I relaxed. "So long as Jupiter doesn't know."

"Only those she chose to advise. Your sister is circumspect. But if I may inquire now: Why was this subterfuge required?"

"To nullify the Jupiter Navy," I said.

He nodded wisely. "So it is true: you mean to recover power."

"In the name of the Triton Project," I said. "I serve at the will of Chairman Khukov of Saturn, whom I will not betray."

"The same for me," he agreed.

We returned to English and exchanged pleasantries. Then my party was ushered to decent accommodations so we could relax.

In a few days two visitors arrived: one male, one female. I recognized both the moment I saw them, and embraced both in turn. The male was actually my sister Spirit, who had her own talent of emulation; no one suspected her identity this way. The female was my former Navy wife, Roulette. She was also in disguise, as an enlisted person, serving as an aide. Now fifty-four, she remained a stunning woman, having retained her outline and her bright red hair. Oh, perhaps her figure was no longer classically hourglass, for she was more solid in the waist than in her youth, but what woman exists who can retain the contours of eighteen into her fifties? My memory clothed her with the firm flesh of her youth, and she remained beautiful to me.

We settled down to business. Spirit updated me on her activities for the past months while Roulette took Forta aside and acquainted her with relevant details. Forta was an excellent secretary, and had a firm grasp of the essentials; I was glad I had prepared her as I had, when she emulated my sister and rescued me at Mercury. She might have to do something similar again one day, so whatever she learned from Rue was good.

The details would be tedious, and my patience has eroded with my years; I will simply say that Spirit had contacted all the key officers and enlisted personnel of the Jupiter Navy, and ascertained the exact status of every relevant chain of command. My sister had always been good at organization, and despite the passage of thirty years she had kept in touch.

Tocsin had started his machinations the moment I left Jupiter, but it had taken him a couple of years to gain a foothold, and another two to lever himself into a position of real power. There had been those, even within his own party, who were not eager to have him return politically; their elimination had occupied his attention at first. But for the past year he had been the power behind the scenes at Jupiter, steadily replacing the appointed officials with his own personnel. He had done the same with the Navy, engineering the retirement of those who had been in change during the Tyrancy, notably my former wife Emerald, and installing officers on the basis of loyalty to him rather than military competence. It was his determination to see that in the next confrontation between himself and the Tyrant, the Jupiter Navy backed him.

But as yet the change was superficial. Top officers had changed, but the massive bureaucracy of the Navy depended on many lines of command, and the middle echelons remained solidly pro-Tyrant. There was a considerable pool of competence here, for my officers had been well trained, and their promotions had been balked by the changes at the top. Spirit had noted which ones

were most competent to assume higher commands, and
had planned for key changes that could be implemented
as opportunity arose.

But mainly, she had arranged a network of interference points, so that when the confrontation came, no significant action could be taken without suffering confusing
delays and misconnections. That was what I had known
she would do. The Navy would manifest as monstrously
inefficient—until the proper officers were elevated to command.

And the powers that existed now on Jupiter didn't even
suspect, for Spirit had nominally been with me on Earth,
Venus, and Jupiter for this entire period. I have seen subsequent reports that remarked on the sheer luck of my
situation, the incredible foul-ups that occurred to my advantage at key points. Chance may have played its part,
but the essence of it was Spirit's quiet and careful preparations. The Navy had been nullified by an expert, before it even saw action.

Now I had the names to name for elevation, when that
time came. More important, I had the assurance that the
job had been properly done. A smart commander always
makes sure he knows the elements of the terrain and the
military forces available to each side, before he provokes
the action. The stupid one trusts to conventional assess-
ments and assumptions. Tocsin had assumed that he had
done what was necessary to rebuff my possible return. He
had not.

Of course it took time for me to familiarize myself with
the necessary data, both of the Navy and of planetside
operations. I was not as quick a study as I had once been,
and my need for dialysis, and consequent loss of a day's
working time, reduced my efficiency further. Spirit and
Roulette could not stay long enough to prepare me completely, they explained, so after a few days they departed
as they had come, as a male Jupiter Navy officer and his
aide. All of us were becoming adept at emulations!

Forta had the data—piles of it. Actually—well, let me
just present this as I saw it at the time, because not everything was as it seemed.

You see, when I woke from my sleep following dialysis,

Roulette was with me. "I thought you had gone!" I said, pleased. The truth was, she had always been the ultimate sexual object to me, and if she was now a bit beyond her prime, well, so was I. She had retained the habit of showing intriguing portions of herself, seemingly innocently, that stirred my passions. I wished I could possess her again, just one more time, but of course I could not.

"Yes and no, Hope," she said. "I thought it was time for something you liked."

"Oh—Forta!" I exclaimed, realizing. I shook my head ruefully, no pun. "You had me fooled!"

She touched the side of her face where the mask merged seamlessly with her natural flesh, concealed by the flowing tresses of the wig. "I always had you fooled, Hope," she said.

I gazed at her, fascinated. Of course Forta had perceived my half-buried passion for Rue, and studied her well, so as to make this emulation perfect. Had I realized the obvious, I would not have been fooled. The truth was, she had overdone it a trifle. The hair was too bright, the eyes too gray, the bosom too full; this was more like Rue ten years younger than like her present aspect. I liked it, of course; I suppose I would have liked an emulation of Rue at age eighteen even better. But not immediately after encountering the reality; that would have destroyed the illusion. So she had taken some off the present age, adding to the appeal without voiding my suspension of disbelief. A nice compromise; she still was amazingly realistic.

"So now I can have you, in my fashion," I said.

"You could always have had me in your fashion," she said. Which was just about what the real Rue would have said.

"No. You're married." I was falling willingly into acceptance of the role, treating her as I would have treated the original.

"Gerald died three years ago," she said. "I am free now."

I had really been out of touch! "Your husband died? He was a good man!"

"He was the best man," she agreed. "I didn't love him, but I respected him, and I was true to him while he lived."

Three years ago—yet it struck me like a fresh event. "I'm not sure I want to—to—"

"To score with his wife? You know he always felt guilty for taking me, knowing that I loved you."

How much talking had Forta done with Rue? This was getting uncomfortable! "It was the Navy way," I said. "He had to take you, to preserve the unit. He did it as duty."

"So did I," she reminded me.

Indeed she had. I had won her fiery love, then turned her over to another man. We all had understood, but it had not been easy. "The Navy way," I repeated softly.

"Now we are unattached," she said. "We return to the Navy way."

Which, again, was what the real Rue would have said. The Navy did not acknowledge such gentle emotions as married love; it acknowledged the biologic need for sex.

I did not require any great amount of persuasion. "The Navy way," I said once more. I reached for her.

She moved away, giving me the slip. "My way, Tyrant," she said.

I stared at her. One other thing had distinguished Roulette from other women: her penchant for violence. She had been a pirate lass, and among the pirates violence and rape had been the rule. She had been incapable of passion without violence: that of her lover against her. That had been the hardest thing for me to accept. I had been required, literally, to attack her and rape her on our wedding night. I had done it, but it was an experience I had had no desire to repeat.

Yet, even as I had slowly educated her to the ways of gentle love, she had educated me to her style. I had found myself brutalizing her, at her demand, and at our last encounter in space I had struck her on the chin so that she bit her tongue and blood had flowed: a vicious act, but an act of love. I had never done that to any other woman, and had never thought the occasion for such a thing would arise again.

Now Rue, in emulation, was assuming the role so completely that she wanted violence. I understood, but could not accept it. "I can't do that," I said, and turned away.

"You can do it," she said tersely.

I turned back, embarrassed. "Even if I wanted to, if I were that type of man, I couldn't. I'm old now, and weak. You could overpower me. It would be a damned charade."

"When you conquered me, Hope," she said huskily, "I forsook all defense against you. I became yours to ravish at will. Now I have returned to you. Ravish me."

Had this been the real Rue, this would have rung true. But Forta was not a masochist, and I could not see myself mistreating her just because she had assumed the likeness of that kind of woman. But neither could I say that now; it would prejudice the emulation. This left me in an awkward position. "Sex, yes," I said. "Violence, no."

"You're not playing the game, Hope," she said.

"There are limits to my game-playing abilities."

"You sniveler!" she snapped, so exactly like the original that I jumped. "When in the Belt, do as the pirates do!"

And damn it, she was tempting me! I have never been a man to practice violence on women, but Rue had never been an ordinary woman, and this was indeed her way. She would settle for a token, I knew; if I struck her only hard enough to sting, she would turn on to me as if I had savaged her. But I also knew that those tokens would inevitably escalate as she bent me to her perverse will, and I would find myself hitting her harder, drawing blood. I had been that route when I married her; I could not go it again at this late date.

I turned away again. "Change," I said. "I need to complete the briefing."

"Change, hell!" she flared. "You don't just turn *me* off, Worry!" She came up behind me and put her arms around me, and her breasts pressed into my back with a firmness that electrified me, and her thighs touched mine. "I have waited decades for this chance, and I shall not let it pass." She put her mouth to my neck and nipped me lightly.

I could hardly believe the accuracy of this emulation! The original had to have cooperated, telling and showing Forta every nuance of her way with a man. My member hardened, striving to break free of my clothing. And then the bitch reached down and stroked me there.

Angered at the facility with which she pushed my buttons, I turned abruptly, rotating within her embrace. "I will not be toyed with!" I exclaimed.

But as I completed my half-turn her lips came up to intercept mine, and she kissed me and tongued me, holding me close. The years peeled away like so many layers of paper, and it was as though I were twenty-nine and she eighteen. My hunger for her overwhelmed me, and I kissed her fiercely.

And she broke again. "Hit me, Tyrant," she breathed.

I shoved her away. "No!"

"Yes!" She bent toward me, and of course her blouse fell open, as it was crafted to do, showing the formidable curve of a breast or two.

"You whore!" I exclaimed. "I don't want it that way!"

"Yes, revile me!" she whispered.

She was making me brutalize her verbally! That was part of it. I stalked to my room, frustrated. I had forgotten how maddening Rue could be; it was part of her phenomenal appeal.

She followed me. "I'll behave, Hope," she said. "We have to get through the briefing."

I sat on the bed. Smilo was snoozing under it, of course; he hardly paid attention to what went on above, having long since written off human relations as too perplexing for feline comprehension.

She joined me there. "Emerald's husband is dead, too," she said. "They forced her to retire; she's your age, Hope, and they rigged the regs. But we know exactly who supports the Tyrant, and we control every task force, every key unit. Spirit and I worked it out methodically."

"Spirit and you," I repeated.

She punched me lightly on the shoulder. "You know what I mean, Hope. Just accept me as I seem to be; I'm into this role and I mean to do it right."

Why indeed was I balking? I had always enjoyed Forta's emulations, and I could not condemn her for excelling in her art. If she wanted to handle everything as Roulette, it behooved me to go along. "Sorry," I muttered, my gaze straying to her cleavage.

She twitched a shoulder, causing that cleavage to flex, exactly as was her way. Rue always knew when she had captured the gaze of a man, and could never resist teasing him. She had at times driven me half crazy with desire during my time as the Tyrant of Jupiter, and she had reveled in it.

But Forta, though possessed of all the necessary attributes, lacked the sheer mass of bosomic flesh that Rue sported. The signals of emulation could do a lot, but they could not make mountains of mounds. My gaze lingered, compelled by this additional intrigue. She must have used some kind of foundation, some support, some added substance, to achieve this grandeur. Yet I could see no seam, no attachment. That breast looked real, even as I peered down inside her hefty halter. How had she done it?

She touched her blouse, and it parted down the front, falling entirely away from her breasts. "If something grabs you . . ." she invited.

"You promised to behave," I muttered, sorely tempted to grab back at what grabbed me.

"*I'm* behaving; your eyes aren't. You act as if you've never seen mammaries before. Here, let me get this halter off." She reached behind her.

Perhaps she was expecting me to tell her no. But my resentment of her taunting had faded, because it really was an accurate emulation, and my curiosity about the mechanism of the added flesh had increased. I let her proceed.

The strap parted in back, and the halter came loose. She drew it off, and those twin marvels were entirely exposed to my view. They still looked real.

I simply could not resist. I touched. The right breast was soft and warm, and it hefted exactly like the real thing. She was if anything more solidly endowed than she had been in youth; the truth was that without the halter she sagged somewhat, whereas in youth she could have taken a breath and held her breasts erect. Age did that to a woman.

I touched the nipple, and it responded properly. If flesh

had been added, it wasn't at that site. I passed my fingers
around and down—and felt a tiny seam. It really didn't
show to my gaze, but my sensitive fingers could trace it.
Apparently she had been able to apply pseudoflesh along
the natural contours, filling out the breast, and the heat
of her body had suffused it, making the whole seem genuine. This must have taken her some time to prepare; no
wonder she wasn't eager to change back. Whatever adhesive kept the added flesh in place without support had
to be strong, not readily nullified. Forta had gone to a lot
of trouble to set up this emulation, physically as well as
in character.

So I was stuck with this for an extended period. I could
live with it. Naturally I did not make any fuss about the
seam. She knew I had found it; her body indicated a kind
of relief. She had known that the emulation could not
withstand this close an inspection, and since I evidently
had not been turned off by the discovery, there was no
further concern. Well, that was not entirely true; some
tension remained in her.

If I turned away from her now, it would seem to be
because of this discovery. I did not care to do that; she
had done a truly superlative job of this emulation. In fact,
the discovery of the seam reassured me; a genuine bosom
of this magnitude simply could not belong to Forta, and
that had bothered me. Now I knew the mechanism, and
could play the game. To a limited extent.

I bent to bring my mouth to her nipple. I kissed it, then
took it in, sucking. Then I bit it, not hard, but firmly
enough to bring some token pain to her.

Rue reacted as I had known she would. She clasped my
head with her hands and pressed it in to her breast, for
the moment smothering me. She fell back on the bed,
bringing me with her, my face mashing her breast, or vice
versa. "Oh, Hope, you hurt me!" she breathed.

I hoisted myself up and ripped at her remaining clothing. "I've got to have you, you bitch!" I said.

"Rape!" she squealed, moving to facilitate my attack.

I slapped her across the face. "Shut up!"

She turned on further. "Brute!"

Suddenly we were together, her naked, me clothed, but

my trousers were open; she had somehow done it while I worked on her. I rammed into her, spurting almost immediately as her hips bucked against me. She nipped at my ear, and her nails pressed sharply into my back, and the pain intensified my climax. Whether she was truly climaxing with me I was uncertain, but she chose to make it seem so, and I chose not to debate it. It was just like old times.

I collapsed on her, panting, her bosom providing me a soft landing. I had, indeed, done it her way. I suppose that had been inevitable. The odd thing was that instead of letting me relax, as she normally did once I had expended my energy, she got hold of my head once more and kissed me savagely, again and again, as if our lovemaking were just commencing.

"I can't do it again," I reminded her regretfully.

"Once was enough," she replied, but continued to kiss me and hug me, belying her words.

Which meant that she had not climaxed with me, but had gotten far enough to desire the completion. I felt guilty; I should have taken more time. I simply could not repeat; my member was diminishing. "I'm sorry," I said, abashed.

"Hit me!" she whispered fiercely.

Oh. I lifted myself, formed a fist with my right hand, and cracked her on the chin. I was not strong, and the angle was wrong, but it caused her to bite her lip so that blood welled out. Déjà vu!

She hauled me in again, for a bloody kiss, and her body convulsed. *Now* she was climaxing, and it was a formidable thing. I held as firmly as I could, realizing that my cooperation was as important for her pleasure as hers had been for mine. How I wished I had a fully hard member for her!

But it was not the member but the violence that activated her. Her blood smeared our faces as she throbbed against me and around me and came to her conclusion.

Then at last we could relax. "Oh, Worry, it's been so long!" she whispered in my ear, kissing it.

I marveled; this emulation was complete indeed. Except for one thing: There was now a coating of whitish powder on my fingers, and perhaps also on my face. That would be the makeup employed to convert olive-skinned Forta to thoroughly Saxon Rue. But I was now quite tired, and I slept.

I expected her to be back as Forta when I woke again, for it could not be comfortable for her to carry all that pseudoflesh around on bosom, hips, and posterior. But I have to confess that that I was not disappointed to find Rue still with me, though I would not have been disappointed with Forta either.

She ran through the briefing material with me, drilling me on the key names and situations, so that I could use them with confidence when the time came. Her command of the subject was impressively thorough; she seemed to have committed it all to memory. Despite our recent tempestuous lovemaking, she kept flashing flesh at me as was her wont, and I kept appreciating it. Apart from the violent aspect, I had thoroughly enjoyed Rue's body when we had been married, and had desired it in retrospect thereafter. Now it was mine again, however re-created, and it was as though I were finishing what had been interrupted thirty-five years before. So she was older now; so was I. There can be much joy of a woman of any age. So, inevitably, we lapsed into lovemaking, though I was required to do it her way, which I think pained me as much as it did her. Perhaps I am saying that it did not pain either of us much. The second time we did it I was not actually able to climax, but there was great joy in the trying, and she seemed satisfied. The woman was eager for me, despite her insistence on roughness, and that was a most conducive thing.

When it was time for my dialysis, we had a call from the Premier. In him I had confided, for it might be necessary for him to cover for me in the crisis. "Señor Tyrant, we have excellent facilities here, and I insist that you allow us to do this favor for you and give your lovely secretary a rest," he said, his gaze passing me to fix on Rue behind me. She flexed her cleavage at him, smiling. "No one shall know, I assure you."

I tried to demur, but he was serious, and to avoid bad feeling I agreed to try his proffered unit. Young and esthetic Hispanic nurses escorted me to the chamber, leaving Rue and Doppie to keep Smilo company and handle any incoming calls. I had to confess that these people knew their business; I was well taken care of. Indeed, I reflected, it was fitting to give Forta a break; she had been doing very well for me, but should not always be yoked like this.

Thus the days passed, and, indeed, weeks. Once I was caught up on the background detail, I prepared for my major move. This was to be quite simple in outline, but perhaps not simple in execution. I was to use the Gany broadcast system to make an address to Jupiter, saturating all major channels, declaring that because of malfeasance on the part of the present government, I was returning to resume control, restoring the Tyrancy. We knew that the majority of the people of the planet, fed up with the iniquities and mismanagement of the recent government, would support this; the problem, as with the Jupiter Navy, was the top personnel, who would never yield their power gracefully. Those were the ones who had to be neatly and cleanly neutralized. That was what Spirit was doing now, and was why she was unable to contact me. She was operating in complete secrecy on the planet. At this point I was merely waiting for her signal.

Meanwhile, Doppie answered calls, showing that my sister was with me, and Rue continued to entertain me, making of me a woman-beater but rewarding me in the fashion only she could manage. Despite the tension of the approaching crisis, it was one of the more pleasant periods of my life.

Chapter 18

HOPIE

The crisis came upon us at a time not of our choosing. President Tocsin had of course discovered that I was on Ganymede—indeed, we had taken no great precautions to conceal that—and elected not to sit and wait for my action. He ordered the Jupiter Navy to quarantine Ganymede, and demanded that my sister and I be extradited to Jupiter for justice. Of course the justice he had in mind was execution for our violation of the exile. Naturally the Premier of Ganymede refused.

Accordingly, the ships of the Jupiter Navy moved into place about Ganymede—and warships of Saturn appeared in Jupiter space. Abruptly there was a planetary crisis, for both these maneuvers were technically acts of war. It was time for me to act, even if my sister had not completed her preparations.

When I received the news of the deployments I was—well, let me describe it as it happened.

"Hope," Doppie called, in her guise as Spirit.

I lifted my head from Rue's architecture. "Can it wait?"

"No," she said firmly.

Fortunately, I was clothed. I got up and went to the holo unit. There was Tocsin's head, talking. ". . . for the duration of the crisis," he was saying.

"Is that—?" I asked.

"Has to be," Rue said behind me.

Tocsin's visage was replaced by that of the Premier of Ganymede. "Tyrant, Jupiter is striking," he said without preamble. Then he paused, looking past me, as he tended to do when Rue was present.

I glanced about. She hadn't bothered to don her halter

or blouse. "Go change," I told her, then faced the Premier. "What's the situation?"

He recovered his attention. "Blockade," he said. "Ships orienting on our planet. The poison demands your head."

"The poison" was the Saturnist name for Tocsin. "Then it is time for countercheck," I said, experiencing the excitement of the burgeoning crisis.

"Done," he said. It was not immediately apparent on our holo, but at that point the Saturn ships began to manifest.

"I'll give my address now," I said. I regretted having to jump the laser on Spirit, but we had known this could happen.

"Connected, Tyrant," he said grimly.

"I've got the phone," Rue said, and took Doppie's place. This was of course no business for Doppie, who was able only to emulate Spirit in appearance, not action.

"Good enough," I said, glancing across at her as I took my seat by the holo broadcast unit. And saw that she was still bare-topped. That was the sort of stunt only Roulette would pull! Well, she could set the pickup for head only, and no one would know. Of course it would seem strange when Rue answered incoming calls instead of my secretary Forta, but that could not be helped; it was the penalty for being caught unexpectedly.

My holo showed the great planet of Jupiter as seen from Ganymede, its clouds clear in their bands and convolutions. That was my signal that the override broadcast was operating. Virtually every functioning holo receiver on Jupiter would receive my broadcast, not the program it was tuned to. It would not take long for the Jupiter technicians to void this, perhaps only ten minutes, but that should be enough.

"Hello, people of Jupiter," I said in English. "I am Hope Hubris, your former Tyrant. I was exiled five years ago, but now I have returned to resume the government of Jupiter." I paused, glancing at Rue.

It took a few seconds for the reaction from Jupiter to start, because Ganymede is about three light-seconds out, and of course this broadcast was coming as a complete surprise to the planet. Many holo sets had a feedback mechanism, whereby the recipient could send a positive or a negative reaction to what he received. The positive would manifest as a musical note at my end, while the negative would be a somewhat sour bleep.

Of course I was concerned about the nature of the sound I would hear. I believed the people would support me, but could not be sure; politics is a treacherous business, and the public can be fickle. I had to have the mass of the people with me, or this would not work.

The sounds started. First a few bleeps, dismaying me, then some mixed notes. Then, as if suddenly finding the range, the music came on loudly: hundreds, then thousands, then tens of thousands of notes, drowning out the scattered bleeps.

I smiled. "I see you remember me," I said, letting the music play as a background to my voice. "You also know that your current government has descended rapidly into corruption and incompetence. The good officials I installed have been replaced by creatures of the ancient sort, who are more interested in the public trough than in the public good." As I spoke, the music swelled steadily. I was reaching my audience, in the fashion I had, moving them though I could not see them.

"Industrial efficiency has declined," I continued, following the script we had prepared. "The planetary debt is rising. Freedom of the press has been curtailed. In fact, the leading critic of my day, Thorley, *is now in prison.*" This time I paused for a full ten seconds to let the reaction manifest. It came like a crashing chord; I had indeed scored.

Rue was watching me instead of her holo, rapt. She was sending out signals of wonder and joy, delighting in the way I was moving the people of Jupiter. The monitor of the number of sets tuned in was rising rapidly; I had started on a preemptive basis, but now they were seeking me.

However, I knew that Tocsin would be barking orders between curses. I had only a few more minutes before I got cut off; I had to make them count.

"I was deposed by my wife, Megan," I said. "She believed I was abusing the power that I had, and that madness was distorting my judgment. She believed in the democratic process, and I was not honoring that. I have known many women, and some have been beautiful." I glanced across at Rue. The monitor of the holo indicated that she was now being picked up, nude torso and all. In six seconds the sound would go crazy! "But the one I most truly respect is my wife, and she is the one I still heed." I peered into the holo as if searching for a particular person, while the sound did indeed go crazy, on its delayed response to Roulette. "Megan! Are you on?"

The seconds passed, and abruptly the sound abated, as if every watcher were holding his breath. Then my wife did indeed appear, hardly even seeming surprised. She was older than I remembered her—but of course I had not been with her for fifteen years, and she was now past seventy. "Megan," I said to her. "Do you still oppose—"

But now Tocsin cut in. The delay meant that he had started earlier, but this was where I heard him. "Mrs. Hubris," he said. "You cannot allow this dictator to return!"

Now I was silent too, along with Jupiter, awaiting her reaction.

Megan turned her gaze on Tocsin, her ancient enemy. She said no word. Then she turned her back on him.

The holo cut off. Tocsin's technicians had established their intercept, and my broadcast could no longer get through. But it had been enough. Megan would not oppose me—and the people of Jupiter knew it.

I relaxed, for the moment. I felt my age after brief periods of effort like this. I had swayed the common folk of Jupiter to my support, in the way that I had, but it had required energy, and I was abruptly tired.

"It may take a day to restore communication and prepare for the next stage," I said. "Maybe you had better dialyze me now, so that I can be fresh tomorrow."

"I'll call the Gany unit," Rue said.

"No, Gany has problems enough getting the Saturn ships routed through," I said. "They have to come in via the tube, and then pass through the mine field; it's a tricky job of organization. They have to be in place when Tocsin threatens military action against Ganymede."

"Still—" she began.

"Damn it, enough of this ruse!" I snapped, my fatigue making me grouchy. "Roulette is great, but now I need Forta." I crossed to her and put my hand to her face, my nails catching at the edge of the mask to pull it off.

She stood frozen. My nails raked across her cheek, scratching it. First the marks were white, then red.

Irritated by this intransigence, I attacked the other side of her face, determined to get the mask off. She did not resist me. Instead she began to sing, softly, with imperfect pitch but clearly enough. "Come all ye fair and tender maids / Who flourish in your prime, prime."

My fingers dug in to the side of her head, unable to find the seam. Where was it?

"Beware, beware, make your garden fair; / Let no man steal your thyme, thyme; / Let no man steal your thyme." The herb thyme was pronounced "time," and the double meaning was clear. It was Rue's song, the one we had given her in the Navy when I married her.

Impatiently I gave up on the mask and descended to her heaving bosom, seeking the seam there.

"For when your thyme is past and gone, / He'll care no more for you, you." Women were of course apprehensive about the onset of age, the loss of the flower of youth, and with it the loss of the interest of the men.

I found the seam, caught it with my nails, and ripped forward. The seam came loose, a strand of pseudoflesh, leaving the main portion still attached to her body. Her breast rolled back and forth under my attention, flaking off powder, still seeming totally real. So I attacked the other—and that seam, too, ripped away in a strand.

"And every day that your garden is waste," she continued blithely, "Will spread all o'er with rue, rue, / Will spread all o'er with rue."

"Damn it!" I hissed through my teeth. I took hold of her right breast with both my hands and pulled, trying to dislodge the pseudoflesh. But the thing would not yield; it drew her body along after it, causing her to fall into me.

"A woman is a branching tree, / A man a singing wynd,

wynd; / And from her branches, carelessly, / He will take
what he can find, find; / He'll take what he can find."

I became conscious of our situation. I was standing
there, her breast in my hands, holding it against me, as
if it were some large fruit from her tree, while she sang
her song despite the discomfort she was in. This aging
but still beautiful and desirable woman who loved to be
brutalized. The welts on her cheek were now burning
brightly.

What kind of mask did that?

I stared at her, the realization coming at last. "There
is no mask," I said, aghast. "No pseudoflesh."

"Abuse me some more, Worry," she invited me, her
eyes shining.

"You put on those strips to fool me," I continued. "And
the makeup powder. To make me think—"

She brought her head to mine and kissed me. No wonder the emulation had been so apt! It had been Roulette
all the time, playing herself!

I jerked my face away. "Why should you do such a
thing? I demanded angrily. "Making a fool of me like
that?" I took hold of her shoulders and shook her. She let
her head rock back and forth, as if being violently thrown
about.

"Ravish me, Tyrant!" she whispered. "I've always loved
you since you mastered me!"

And so she had arranged to switch places with Forta.
Forta had emulated Roulette and departed with my sister, while the real Rue had remained to seduce me. Because, even after thirty-five years, she still loved me and
desired me. Spirit and Forta had understood, so had facilitated the ruse.

Would I have acceded if I had known? I wasn't sure. I
had desired Rue thoughout our separation, but once she
had married another man, I had known she was no longer
for me. That man was dead now, but still I saw her as
his. But the emulation of her had been all right; I could
take any woman in emulation, knowing she was really
Forta. That had been a most intriguing game.

Now I knew Roulette for what she was: a woman in her
fifties who had used cosmetics not to change her identity

but to make herself seem more youthful, both to please
me and to resemble a younger woman emulating an older
one. And I had indeed been pleased; Rue had given me
an excellent time. Until I demanded what she could not
provide: the dialysis. She was not trained for that, so had
evidently elicited the Premier's aid to finesse it. That had
been her undoing.

"Ravish me!" she repeated, and now her eyes were
overflowing. She had submitted to my scratching and
pulling without reaction, but now she was crying—and I
was the only man she ever cried for. She had given her
tears to me, during our marriage, and that had been as
significant a submission for her as when I had raped her,
for she valued her heart more than her body. Now she
stood exposed, her desire for me manifest. Was I to reject
her?

Hardly! What I would have done had I known at the
outset I did not know, but that had become academic. I
had had much joy of this woman in emulation; now I could
have the same joy of her in reality. It was, I thought,
similar to my affair with Amber, the teenaged girl whom
I had known intimately first in the helmet-feelies, then
in the flesh. Rue was a masochist, but it was sexual
expression it led to, not rejection.

"You deceived me!" I said, slapping her face, not hard.
"Do you know the penalty for that?"

"My maidenhood!" she exclaimed, kissing me again.

She dropped her skirt, and I dropped my trousers, and
suddenly we were doing it where we stood. This position
can be difficult and uncomfortable, and even impossible if
the woman resists, but it can work if she cooperates and
knows what she is doing. Rue knew. She leaned back
against a wall so as not to have to be concerned with
balance, and supported me as I thrust into her, and this
time she was as ready as I. We kissed deeply, and just
before I climaxed I nipped her on the tongue, and I felt
her react below. She went crazy against me, and her body
convulsed about my member, bringing me off within her.
I cannot claim it was the best climax I have had, for the
awkwardness of the position did detract, but it was highly
satisfactory, and not only on the physical plane.

"Oh, lover, thank you!" she said, kissing me a final time. "I did so much want to have you, as *me.*" Then she broke, for the vertical position does not allow a woman much time to clean up. She retreated to the bathroom while I got back into my trousers.

Then I became aware of Doppie. The calls had continued to come in during our intermission, for it was only the planetary broadcast that had been jammed, not the phone service. She had taken over the phone, fielding those calls as Spirit. I had made love to Rue in Doppie's presence.

That had been unkind, for Doppie was smitten by me too. She was as old as she seemed to be, and hardly foolish, but I did not need to read her to know that she would have traded places with Rue if she could. It is a mistake to assume that older women have no desires; they are merely more careful about showing them. In fact, the desire in age can be greater than that in youth, in women and perhaps in men, too.

I had never intended to take advantage of Doppie. Now I realized that I had done her wrong. "Doppie, I owe you," I said to the back of her head.

She did not turn, but I knew she heard and understood. Her hurt turned to joy. Then she contacted the local dialysis unit, and I went for my treatment.

The appearance of the Saturn ships had nullified Tocsin's siege of Ganymede; the Jupiter Navy was now outgunned in this region of space. Ploy and counterploy; it was not the first time this had occurred here. But now the Saturn ships were spreading out to menace Jupiter itself. That was the muscle behind my takeover of the planet: my words were merely the declaration of intent, while Saturn was the mechanism. I had of course cleared this with Khukov. He had hesitated to make an attempt on Jupiter, lest it provoke mutually destructive war, but Spirit and I had believed that the Tyrant could do it without that dread result, and that we had to do it. The Triton Project needed the resources of Jupiter, and Tocsin had made it plain that the present government would never join.

How had the Saturn ships been able to spread without molestation? That was where Spirit's advance work came in. Naturally Tocsin had ordered action, heedless of the consequence—but somehow the task forces ordered into action had gone astray. Orders had been confused, and foul-ups had occurred. Not one Jupiter ship had fired on a Saturn ship. That was part of what had kept Tocsin occupied during the interim; he had realized that the Jupiter Navy had been partially subverted.

Of course it could not be as simple as using projection to bring Saturn vessels of war within Jupiter's defensive perimeter. The true balance of terror lay not with the ships but with the subs. Largely invisible, the subs of each planet surrounded the other, ready to fire their missiles and lasers and blast the enemy cities out of atmosphere or space. The System had lived for centuries under that threat, and no one liked it, but there had been no way to escape it.

Until now. That was another reason that the Triton Project was so important. It was why this terrible risk was necessary.

My first broadcast had preempted the holo sets of Jupiter and Jupiter-space. Tocsin's forces had in due course zeroed in on it and jammed it out. But within a day we were ready for the next move: we had located the sources of the jamming, and could nullify it, temporarily. I was ready for my second broadcast.

I made it. "This is the Tyrant, again," I said. "As I explained yesterday, the government of Jupiter has been corrupted, with the same bloodsuckers feeding on public resources as were there before the Tyrancy existed. I do not blame my wife for this; she did what was right. I blame the corrupt leader who sidled back into place the moment he was able. That is Tocsin, who has twice brought to ruin the good that my wife has tried to do. I charge him with treason against the planet of Jupiter, and I require him to step down and turn himself in for justice. How say you, Tocsin?"

Of course the man was listening. This second broadcast had caught him as flat-footed as the first, because he thought he had nullified this sort of thing. He had reck-

oned without my sister's thorough preparation, and had
not yet realized that it was the technical staff of the Jupiter Navy that was nullifying the jamming signals.

Tocsin, thus challenged, came on. But he seemed neither astonished nor dismayed. It was not an act; I read
him, and found that he believed he had the upper hand.
Why was that so?

"Tyrant, you think you have won," he rasped. "But
you've lost. You think your friend on Saturn supports you,
but he doesn't."

"He supports me," I asserted before Tocsin's words concluded, so as to minimize the delay. "At such time as he
does not, he will let me know first. But I am merely borrowing the Saturn fleet for this purpose; I am acting as
the representative of the Triton Project, and will govern
Jupiter as a supporting planet, not as a conquest of Saturn. On this we have agreed; there will be no Saturnist
interference in the affairs of Jupiter."

But before I was done, he was speaking again. "You
fool, he doesn't support you because he *can't* support you!"
he shouted. "Do you want to know why? Because he is
dead!"

Now I was shaken. "What?"

"Check with your staff," he said gloatingly. "Chairman
Khukov was assassinated this morning. The news is leaking out."

Rue switched her phone to the Premier of Ganymede.
He looked drawn. "It is true, señor," he said. "We learned
of it an hour ago, but did not wish to undercut your effort."

But Tocsin had known. How was that? I read the answer in his bearing: he had known because he had arranged it. While I was setting up for my second address,
he had not been idle; he had implemented an assassination plot he must have had ready for some time. I realized
too late: all he would have had to do was make a deal
with the nomenklatura of Saturn, and they would have
done the job for him. The deal would not have any benefits for the people of Jupiter or Saturn, just for the henchmen. Even threatened as they were with extinction as a
class, the nomenklatura would not have dared do such a

thing on their own; but with Tocsin ready to take the credit, they had surely been happy to act. They had known that they could not get rid of me while Khukov remained in power.

Khukov had sent me out to organize the Triton Project and establish System support for it, because my safety could not be guaranteed on Saturn. What a fool I had been not to realize that he himself remained as vulnerable! Suddenly, at one foul stroke, Tocsin had nullified everything. For without Khukov, my position lacked the support of Saturn; the nomenklatura would resume power there exactly as Tocsin and his minions had done on Jupiter, and they were not my friends. The Triton Project would be scuttled or perverted, and the riches of the galaxy would go, not to solve the problems of the System, but to enrich the illicit powerholders of the major planets.

Tocsin watched me in silence, a cruel smile playing about his homely face. He was savoring this moment of victory over the man who had deposed him once and threatened to do so again. All Jupiter was watching.

What could I do? It was true that without Khukov I could not direct the Saturn fleet, and without that fleet I could not take over Jupiter. The Jupiter fleet had been neutralized, not converted; now its admirals would reassert themselves, rallying to Tocsin.

"Damn it, sir, you know what to do!" Roulette snapped.

I turned to her. Today she was more decorously garbed, with only some deep cleavage, her trademark, showing in front. "I do?" For I was genuinely at a loss. I wished my sister were here; she would have had some course of emergency action.

"Take over!" she said.

"But without the Saturn fleet—"

Tocsin, listening in, smirked. The time-delay seemed not to register; it was as though he were responding to my last words, instead of to my prior stunned silence. "I will accept your surrender," he said. "For the justice of Jupiter."

"Not Jupiter," Rue said, *"Saturn!"*

I don't claim to be fast on the uptake when caught by

surprise; I'm sure I was better in my youth. "But I have no—"

"Saturn is without a true leader," she said. "Their people will trust you before they trust Tocsin. Strike now! It's yours to take! Like a willing woman!"

That last analogy may have seemed unkind or irrelevant, but it scored with me. Perhaps it was my recent discovery of Rue herself, unveiled after her masquerade. The people of Saturn did generally support the Tyrant, whose policies had revolutionized their agriculture and industry, and whose Triton Project promised them the Dream. Suddenly I understood.

"Saturn fleet!" I rapped. "Chairman Khukov is dead. He supported me; I still support him. I am doing what he wanted to be done. I am assuming direct command of the fleet. You will answer to me exactly as you have been doing." I did not ask the commanders of that fleet, I simply told them, not giving them the chance to think about it. That was the way it had to be done: swiftly, before contrary orders could arrive from Saturn.

"Jupiter Navy," I said next. "I am similarly assuming command over you. I hereby depose your present admirals, and elevate those of my choosing. Specifically, Admiral Lundgren is retired as of this instant, and Admiral Emerald Mondy restored to that command."

"You can't do that!" Tocsin protested. "You have no base! No authority!"

I ignored him. I continued to name particular admirals for retirement and restoration, drawing on the names we had reviewed. When I had covered them, I said: "You will cooperate with the Saturn Navy to safeguard the planet of Jupiter from attack. My aide, Roulette Phist, will provide the details of the transition and assignment." For Rue was conversant in a way Forta would not have been with the protocols of the military; she had been a ranking Navy wife for thirty years, and part of the Tyrancy as well.

"Countermand!" Tocsin exclaimed, realizing what I was doing. "There is no legal basis for this action!"

He was correct, technically. But too late. "I am not basing this on legality, but on power," I said. "The officers of the Jupiter Navy know what is best for the Navy, and the people of Jupiter know what is best for Jupiter. Participation in the Triton Project is best."

Then I launched into the major aspect of my presentation. "As many of you already know, Chairman Khukov of Saturn had a Dream," I said. "He shared it with me, and I am sharing it with you. It is the Dream of peace and prosperity for all men. It is the abolition of oppression, restriction, and hunger. One thing has prevented all men from possessing most of the things they desire, and that thing now threatens to eradicate man entirely. That thing is war. We squander our resources in the effort to make weapons with which to destroy each other. If those resources and that effort had gone to secure the good things for mankind instead of for war, we would all be better off than we are. Except for those who profit from the misery of others." I glanced at Tocsin. He was no longer on the holo, but my audience would understand.

"Earth was on the verge of self-destruction back in the twentieth century," I continued. "Only the onset of the gravity-shield, that enabled man to expand from Earth to the Solar System, enabled us to avoid that fate. The gee-shield made it possible to lift objects of any mass from the surface of any planet, and to approach the giant planets without being trapped or crushed by gravity, and to enhance the gee on moons locally to match Earth-norm. All else followed from that single breakthrough. The System was apportioned to the several nations of Earth according to their natures and the nature of the available territories, and the expansion of several centuries commenced. In that time the threat of war abated; the resources of each nation went to the development of its major colony. Only in the past century has our past returned to haunt us, as our cultures reenact the conflicts that threatened to destroy us before. We have filled the Solar System, and the pressures of increasing population and diminishing resources, coupled with the absolute folly of warfare, are threatening again to destroy us. We have to have a new direction for our energy, to avert forever the negative consequences of our nature. We have to look outward, not inward; to reach for new riches beyond our current knowledge, instead of competing and eventually warring for larger shares of a shrinking pie. When that very competition destroys the resources we seek."

I gazed into the holo of the planet of Jupiter, knowing that my eyes were fixing on every person watching. "This is the Dream that Chairman Khukov had, and that I share, and that the entire System must share. It is the Dream of the colonization of the galaxy itself. We have made the technological breakthrough; we can travel to the stars. By means of the light drive we can reach any other point in space at the speed of light—and no matter how far that is, how long it takes, we shall not age in the process. I have used this drive a number of times; it is like stepping directly planet to planet. I am confident that if we use this method to travel to the stars, and to the planets of those stars, it will be no different; it will be in effect instantaneous. Any one of us could board a ship today, and be in Sirius tomorrow, and return the day after, no older. Or anywhere else in the galaxy. The risk is minimal, because now we do not even need a receiver; our ships are to be self-receiving. This is how I came to Ganymede, despite the defenses of Jupiter. Our ships will set out fully equipped for colonization, as they did when they left Earth for Jupiter; they will expend virtually no fuel in transit, only some for the process of rematerializing at the destination. If no suitable bodies for colonization are found, new projection stations will be set up, and the ships will travel as readily elsewhere. It is true there will be challenges, and losses—but perhaps no more than there were in the colonization of the Solar System. The rewards are potentially much greater. War will be a thing of the past, for each nation can have an entire system to colonize, or a complex of systems. There will be no need for competition for resources or living space. Only for peaceful trade between systems. This is the Dream, and this is what I bring to Jupiter. The rest of the Solar System has embraced it; only Jupiter remains excluded—because of the selfish desire for continued power of a few leaders. I am here to remove those leaders and bring the Dream to Jupiter. Are you with me, people of Jupiter?"

Now we turned on the response feedback circuit. It

hardly seemed to take six seconds; a roar of music came forth. There was no question: the people were with me. They wanted the Dream.

"It's a lie!" Tocsin shouted. "He's just making it up so as to seize power for himself!"

He was the one who was lying. But I was ready to counter this, regardless. "I need no further power for myself," I said. "My time is limited. I seek this power only as the means to the end of the salvation of the future of humanity. Before I die, I want to establish the Dream for everyone." Then, forestalling Tocsin's objection, I undid my belt and dropped my trousers, remaining on holo broadcast. "You see, I am no longer healthy," I said as I undressed. "I have lost my kidneys, and am sustained only by hemodialysis, because my system rejects all other mechanisms. Here are the scars on my legs where my blood has been tapped; here is the bandage that secures the loop that taps into my blood at present." I undid the bandage and showed the blood-filled tube. "The doctors will be able to verify the validity of this condition," I said, lifting my leg so that the tube showed clearly. "I have only a few years to live, because my sites are running out; when I can no longer be dialyzed, I shall die. I have no further use for power, other than to forward the Dream."

I had won my point; the feedback reaction showed that. The people of Jupiter were with me, and, perceiving that, the officers of the Jupiter Navy were stepping down and stepping up according to my listing. My bloodless coup was proceeding. I had been out of power here for five years, but I had been in power for ten years before that, and active elsewhere in the System in the interim, so the people knew me. They knew what kind of government I stood for, and it was clear that it was superior to what they had now. They also knew they could trust me to tell them the truth, and the truth I was telling them was the Dream. The victory was not yet complete, but it was clearly going to be mine. Rue had done what was needed when she told me to seize the initiative despite Khukov's death.

But Tocsin would not yield gracefully, if at all. He knew

the people did not support him, and that the Jupiter Navy was no longer his instrument. But he had a ploy yet to make. "Tyrant, you know that the balance of terror is not in the conventional planetary navies, but in the fleets of subs," he said. "Jupiter subs surround Saturn, and Saturn subs surround Jupiter. Either fleet can destroy either planet. The Jupiter subs answer only to me—and the Saturn subs do not answer to you. I can destroy Saturn, and you cannot prevent it."

"Saturn subs," I said into the holo. "I know you are receiving me but will not answer. The man you answer to is dead, assassinated by parties as yet unknown. But I swear to you that I, as the representative of the Dream that Chairman Khukov made, will in due course root out the assassins and destroy them. To do this I must govern Saturn for a time, and this I will do, until a successor can be named who is guiltless in the assassination. Support me, and I will do this. The blood of the guilty will course through the streets of your cities. No other person can make this promise and keep it; you know that the nomenklatura are even now scrambling for new power, and if they did not engineer this crime, they surely support it. The same is true of President Tocsin here. In any event, you have heard him threaten to strike directly at Saturn. Accept my authority, and accept my order now: If any signal travels from the White Bubble toward Saturn, destroy the White Bubble instantly.

I returned to Tocsin, whose face was turning ashen as he assimilated this news. He knew that at least one of the hidden Saturn subs would accept my directive, because it made sense: destroy the man who ordered the destruction of their home planet. He could send the order, and they could not prevent it, but he would be dead an hour before the order reached the vicinity of Saturn. That was not the way Tocsin liked to operate.

Now I spoke to Saturn, knowing there could be no response within hours, but knowing what that response would be. "People of Saturn, I, Hope Hubris, the Tyrant, am assuming the office vacated by my friend Khukov, who is dead. My purpose is to stabilize the government of North Saturn and bring the assassins to justice. The fleets of Jupiter and Saturn support me, and I am preventing the Jupiter subs from attacking the planet. In the interim I appoint Khukov's most trusted deputy to maintain the present government on a standby basis, until my return to Saturn." I named the deputy; he was a competent and loyal man who did not aspire to power for himself.

My power over these planets was being constructed largely on bluff and imagination, but it seemed to be working. In this moment of crisis, they had no better figure to turn to. It was the special magic I had with any audience. They knew they could trust me to do as I promised, and I promised justice and the Dream. It was an easy compromise to make.

But Tocsin was not yet finished. Indeed, he seemed to have recovered his bravado. "I have a little ace in the hole here, Hubris," he said nastily. "You don't dare order this dome destroyed." Technically, it would be the Saturn subs that destroyed it, needing no further order from me, but they would not act unless he did. If he did not send the order to Saturn, only my direct action could put him away. "Bring out the prisoner," he called, turning his head to the side.

In a moment a woman was brought forward. I sagged with dismay: it was my daughter Hopie! She was now a woman of thirty, pretty enough, with her dark hair flowing about her face. I had adopted her as a baby, and she favored me in a number of physical and mental ways. She had always been the delight of my later life. Tocsin evidently believed that this hostage would protect him.

Unfortunately, he was right. I simply could not knowingly order the destruction of my daughter, though the fate of worlds hung on it. Hopie was the closest thing I knew to posterity, and that carried increasing weight as the end of my own life span approached. Apart from that, I loved her. Tocsin had, with his unscrupulous cunning, fixed on the one thing that would balk me completely.

"Don't do it, Daddy," Hopie said. "Don't let him have his way. I can die if I have to."

But I couldn't order it. Tocsin, gloating to the side, knew it. "Now back off, Tyrant," he said. "I won't give the order to destroy Saturn; I don't have to. I just need to put you under arrest."

How could I deal with this? Tocsin would never yield his hold on Hopie; he would squeeze her for all she was worth. I knew this, yet I could not let her be harmed. It was ridiculous to be caught by this elementary ploy, but I was. I remembered Hopie as a baby in my arms, and as a child sharing visions with me, and as a teenager trying to manage the Department of Education. I remembered her blazing anger when I took as mistress a girl who was younger than she. She was my daughter, in every sense that counted, and I could not sacrifice her.

"You don't respond, Tyrant?" Tocsin inquired. "Then I will encourage you. I will have your agreement, now, to surrender yourself for arrest, or I will have this woman dispatched before your eyes. Guard!"

And at that a female guard stepped up, carrying a laser pistol. There were of course other guards in the White Bubble, who could fire at anyone anytime, but this was being presented for effect. Slowly the woman raised her pistol, until it pointed at Hopie's head.

And I think I would have wet my pants, had I had any urine in me. I did not, of course; that was why I required dialysis. My shock was not from the direct threat to Hopie; it was because that guard was familiar.

"Go ahead, shoot me," Hopie said, though she was shaking with reaction; her bravado was evident for what it was. "Then you'll have no hostage, and you'll be finished." Which was true, but not the whole truth; I could not let her be shot at all.

But I would not need to. Suddenly I knew why this elaborate hoax on me had been perpetrated: the substitution of Roulette for Forta. I had thought it was at Rue's behest, because she wanted to make love to me once more. Certainly that much was true, but Spirit had had other reasons to do it. She had known that my face-off with Tocsin could come to this, so she had, in her meticulous way, prepared for it. She had fashioned what in chess was known as a discovered check.

"Your time's up, Tyrant," Tocsin said. "Make your commitment now, or I will give the order."

"Give your order, hemorrhoid," I said.

It took those six seconds for his double take to manifest, but it was worth it. Tocsin could not believe that I had said what I had said. But I had.

Meanwhile, I was already speaking again. "And that order will be your last, because that laser is not pointed at my daughter, but at you. I doubt that you can order your other security guards to take out either my daughter or my secretary before you die."

Tocsin actually gaped when this news reached him. "Your what?"

Now the guard put her free hand to her face and drew off her mask, her laser never wavering from its target, which was Tocsin. The scarred features of Forta Foundling came into view, never more beautiful than at this instant. Only she, with her superlative powers of emulation, could have infiltrated this bastion, but she had done it.

I was of course to receive credit for a strategy bordering on genius, because of this ploy. But I had not known it was in the making. My women tend to do that to me; it is a type of conspiracy that seems inherent in their nature. I don't suppose I have cause to object.

Tocsin stared at her. Now he knew he had lost. He was not the suicidal type; he always made the best deal he could, in whatever circumstances existed. "Exile," he said.

So he would back down, in exchange for exile, which meant no trial, no direct punishment. He didn't deserve it—but if his guards obeyed him, he could still exchange his life for that of Forta and Hopie. Two for one. It wasn't worth it to me. "Granted," I said.

"We await your ship," Tocsin said simply. He knew I would keep my word, however much it galled me. He had lost the planet but preserved his freedom. I would arrange for him to be sent to the planet of his choice, and that would be that. Meanwhile, I would soon be reunited with my secretary and my daughter. That seemed as important to me, at this moment, as the conquest of worlds.

Chapter 19

MIDDLE KINGDOM

It was hours, but it seemed like a moment, and Forta and Spirit and Hopie were with me. I hugged each in turn, then reverted to immediacies. "Why didn't you tell me about Roulette?" I demanded.

"You were asleep," Spirit said simply.

I looked at Rue. "They thought you would tell me," I accused her.

"Well, I meant to," she confessed. "But then I thought it would be more fun the other way."

Forta raised a scarred brow. "He thought you were me?"

"For a time," Rue agreed.

"But the figure—"

"She connived," I said.

Hopie caught on. "Forta emulates your former wives?"

"Something like that," I admitted, embarrassed.

"Only the crisis came before I could return," Spirit said. "And evidently as a surprise to you."

Because of Rue's bare bosom. "I didn't want anyone disconnecting early," Rue said.

"Nobody on the planet disconnected!" Spirit agreed. Then she got on to business. "I'll have to remain here and organize for the production of self-receiver units; only Jupiter can do the job in time to match the production already in progress elsewhere." She turned to me. "You'll have to go get Saturn settled."

"There shouldn't be any problem," I said. "They know I'm doing what's right."

"That was an act of genius, taking over Saturn too," my daughter said. "Now there can't be war between the major planets."

I glanced at Rue. "Well, actually it wasn't—"

"Of course it was," Rue said quickly. "It showed that the Tyrant is still the leader he used to be."

So she wanted me to take credit for her idea. Well, maybe that was best, politically. But I couldn't help wondering whether I would have done it if Forta had been with me instead of Roulette. This impersonation could have benefited me far more than just romantically. Rue had worked me over, her way, but she had paid her way.

"I'll join you when I can," Spirit said.

She did. The consolidation of Jupiter and North Saturn took about a year, and the production of the self-receiving units another two years. I went to Saturn with Forta, but first we dropped Doppie off at Earth. Freed from her need to impersonate my sister, Doppie became herself, and then she really didn't resemble Spirit much; her hair, clothing, and attitude differed. Before we parted, I took her out for a social evening on Earth, and made it publicly clear that it was the Tyrant who was escorting her. Actually it wasn't sex she wanted, just appreciation, so I kissed her and let it be understood that she was my woman of the moment, providing her a notoriety that would carry through the rest of her life. I felt I owed it to her, and it really was no chore. I was grateful to her for the service she had done us, and I respected her as a person, and that really was enough. Partial as I have always been to youth and beauty in women, I nevertheless respect personality more. Doppie understood that, and was satisfied.

We ran down the assassination plot. As suspected, it was a collaboration between Tocsin and the nomenklatura of Saturn. Tocsin we could not touch; he was in South Saturn, where they still respected him. But the nomenklatura we routed out and tried and executed. It was the justice of the Tyrant, reminiscent of the destruction of Big Iron on Jupiter some years before, and the people of the USR reveled in it. There were indeed hangings and beheadings, done not because of any madness of mine but because it was politically necessary for the Tyrant to keep his word, and to make an example. I suspect the judgment of historians will not be kind to me on this score, but historians do not face the realities of the moment, when blood is a sacrifice required for legitimacy. I, as Tyrant, assumed responsibility for the savage justice the people required.

But there was some vengeance in it, because Khukov had played straight with me, and had given me power and the Dream. I had really done what he would have done, had he been in charge.

I had thought to turn over the reins to native officials, but discovered again that power can be as difficult to yield as to achieve. I was of course a figurehead, freely delegating the governing duties to those who were competent and trustworthy, but it seemed that they valued that figurehead. I was the symbol about which the governments supporting the Triton Project rallied, and as long as I did not interfere unduly with the details of administration, that was the way they liked it. The people supported me, and assumed that executive orders were mine; that made them more palatable. Since I had arranged to have top-quality personnel throughout, the administration tended to be excellent.

It was similar elsewhere in the System. Thus, while my actual power was nominal, my reputed power was greater than ever before. I was hailed as the Tyrant of Space, governing the entire System. Illusion, of course, but if that's the way the histories choose to record it, I suppose I won't be in a position to object.

In this period, conscious of the slow approach of my own demise, I wrote this record of my activities, and sent it to QYV of Jupiter. I will of course be updating these notes as convenient, keeping them current, as I cannot be certain when the final entry will come. My daughter will inherit all my records at my death, though she does not, at this writing, know it. I trust they will prove to be interesting reading. Hopie does not necessarily approve of all my activities, but she is of my blood and surely understands. Sometimes I think I can share her mind, seeing through her eyes, though she is on another planet. I get the feeling that I could communicate directly with her, without even any lapse of time for the traveling of the mind-waves, if I really tried; that in a sense I *am* her, our identities merging. Then I laugh and tell myself, "Not in *this* life!" Sometimes it becomes difficult to separate the sense from the nonsense, as I undergo dialysis and let my thoughts wander. But it is comforting to feel my daughter's presence on such occasions, in whatever manner that may be.

I should mention also the manner in which my relationship with Forta matured. After the excitement of the rescue of my daughter and the incorporation of Jupiter subsided, and I found myself alone with Forta, I felt awkward. You see, despite the number of women I have known, it is not my practice to relate to them promiscuously. After I had come to terms with Forta on Venus, I had had no intention of dallying with any other, apart from the single episode with Doppie. Roulette had been out of turn, and now it bothered me.

Forta quickly enough fathomed my concern. "But you thought she was me," she said.

"I should have realized," I mumbled, the guilt intensifying.

"My emulations are that transparent?"

I smiled, for the ploy was obvious. "I delight in your emulations, but it is important to me now to know that that is what they are. Then I can enjoy the forms of others without separating from you. That is the best of worlds."

"Would it help if I confessed that I knew she would attempt to carry through the masquerade?"

It was phrased as a question, but it was a statement; I read her clearly enough. "But did you know it would deceive me?"

"Only if you wanted to be deceived."

I pounded one fist into my other hand. "There's the key! I should have known, *would* have known, had I not desired Rue herself! And in that I wronged you."

"Did you, Hope?"

"I should have recognized her, and kept my hands off her. And would have, had I not deceived myself. I did desire her, and I yielded to that desire, and that is the apology I must make to you."

"Give me a moment," she said. She went to her bedroom, while I returned to the writing of this manuscript, as mentioned.

In due course she emerged. I looked up—and there was Roulette, exactly as she had been so recently. Her body, her signals—

I got up. "May I?" I asked.

She spread her hands, accepting. I opened her blouse, unfastened her halter, and ran my fingers around her heavy breasts. This was a clinical examination, but my body reacted as I touched those wonders. There was the powder, coming off on my fingers. There were the tiny ridges, marking the juncture of real and pseudoflesh. I caught at a ridge and pulled—and the ridge came off, leaving the breast, as before.

"Damn it!" I swore. "I'm not going this route again!"

She lifted her hands and removed her mask. "But it *is* me, Hope," she said.

Indeed, it was Forta. I embraced her and kissed her ardently. "You could have fooled me," I said after a moment, realizing that the cement that held on the pseudoflesh adhered to her entire breast, and needed no ridges; those had been, as it were, decorations. Probably that flesh would not come off unless a neutralizer was applied and allowed to work its way through. Forta had played a little trick on me.

"And she *did* fool you," she agreed. "You might have fathomed it, had you any further reason to suspect. You were guilty of carelessness, not ill intent." She restored the mask. "And what are you going to do about it, Tyrant?" she said in Rue's voice.

I did not reply in words. I took her into my bedroom, where Smilo snoozed, and stripped her clothing but not her emulation, and I made love to her in the guise of Roulette, and it was as good as it had been with the real Roulette.

"Which do you prefer," she asked as we relaxed, "her emulating me, or me emulating her?"

I considered, and remembered how the real Rue had insisted on violence. Forta had not. "You emulating her," I said.

"Then make no apology," she said.

And I realized that I had indeed paid her the ultimate compliment. Roulette had been the most striking (forget

the pun!) woman I had known, and I really did prefer
Forta now. I also appreciated the compliment Roulette
had paid me, seeking me so ardently after all these years.

I lifted myself and removed her mask. "You are the
first ugly woman I have loved," I said. Then I kissed her
on her scarred cheek, and ran my tongue across it, savoring her as she was.

"And you are the first philandering man I have loved,"
she said.

We started laughing, together, and it was some time
before we stopped. We understood each other, and that is
a joy of its own type.

Of course she knew that when I used the word "love"
I did not mean exactly what she did by it. What I felt for
my various women might better be described as crushes.
But it was also true that I had developed as solid a respect
for Forta as for any woman, and not merely for her ability
to emulate others.

Forta had never attempted to proselytize; she had accepted me as I was, and cooperated with me in all things.
She had also saved the life of my daughter, a debt I could
never adequately repay. But as I came to respect her, I
sought to do that which I knew would please her. She
wanted no jewelry or clothing or even compliments, so I
did not offer these. She wanted to alleviate suffering
wherever it existed. As a member and beneficiary of Amnesty Interplanetary she was concerned with man's in-
humanity to man, and she knew a great deal about this,
and answered when I queried about it. Thus, as the Tyrant came to have power over various planets, a persistent investigation and alleviation of human-rights abuses
of those planets followed. Wherever we went, the life of
the common man improved, and the abusers suffered. Because of Forta. In fact, the only period of real strain between us was during the bloodletting of the liquidation of
the nomenklatura; she elected to visit Jupiter at that
time, and did not return until the killing was done. She
never spoke to me about the matter, but I got the message.

"Is this why you came to me?" I asked her once. "Be-

cause you knew that through me you could do more good
for your cause than you could otherwise?"

"Yes." She made no attempt to avoid the issue. She
was not the type.

"And my wife sent you for the same reason?" I always
meant Megan when I referred to my wife, though I had
been married several times.

"Yes."

"May I never disappoint either of you."

"You have not so far."

"But you expect me to in the future?"

"When you die."

Oh. And of course my end was approaching, for the
exhaustion of my access sites for dialysis was accelerating
as I had increasing trouble with clotting. We had moved
from my legs to my arms, no longer needing to conceal
the scars. I was at this point sixty-eight years old, and
considering it realistically I judged that two more years
was all I could expect of mobile, functional existence.
Thereafter I would be bedridden, and deprived of the various pleasures of independent existence, sex among them.

I think it was at that point that I decided to die in my
own fashion, not waiting for the inevitable degradation
to have its way with me. I did not fear death; I feared a
helpless, meaningless life.

"What unfinished business do I have?" I asked her.

She ticked items off on her fingers. "Completion of the
Triton Project. Incorporation of the Middle Kingdom. Designation of a successor to the Tyrancy."

"And only a year to do it," I muttered.

"Pardon?"

"Let's get on it." But of course she had heard me the
first time.

We took the tube to Triton. By this time there were
many projection tubes, serving all the planets, and the
self-receiving projection units were coming off the Jupiter
lines. These actually amounted to the preset conversion
of light beams in photon computers, the beams calibrated
so accurately that the mergence of the key beams did not
occur until the set distance had been traveled. The far-

ther the distance, the more precise the settings had to be. We had used a very crude version to travel from Mercury to Jupiter; the difference between a span of a light-hour or so and that of a thousand light-years or so is manifest. But with the perfection of that technology, we were ready to send colony ships virtually any distance into the galaxy. It was time to officially inaugurate that program, and Forta was right: it had to be done by the Tyrant, the unifying figure for this effort. If I didn't see it started in my lifetime, it might very well dissolve thereafter into factional fragmentation, and the chance to do it peacefully would be lost.

For though the Triton Project represented the gateway to man's future, a channel for man's aggressive energies in lieu of internecine warfare, it also represented danger. In the wrong hands, that technology could be turned to the projection of bombs, and against these there was no reasonable prospect for defense. Mankind had to colonize—or risk destruction. Once the colony ships reached their locations, there would be no incentive for war. The challenges of the local systems would be enough to absorb the full attentions of the expeditions, and what point would there be in projecting a bomb to another system, that would not arrive for many years or decades even at light velocity? In fact, since the colonists would be traveling to widely differing regions of space, one colony would be setting up at a nearby system while others were still on their way, perhaps not materializing for another twenty years. Though transit would seem instant for those aboard each ship, it was not. Never again would man be cramped within a single system, able to attack his neighbors within a span of hours. As I saw it, interplanetary warfare would be over—and that was the Dream. Chairman Khukov had conceived it, and not lived to see its completion, but I was seeing it through.

That reminded me of Lieutenant Commander Repro, the officer of the Jupiter Navy who had conceived the dream of the perfect unit, and had implemented it through me. He had died when it seemed that unit was finished, but it had survived, and with its assistance I had become the Tyrant. Now I was doing the same for Khukov's

Dream. Khukov himself had been a tough, unscrupulous man, who had used his talent, which was similar to mine, to win his way to his planet's highest office and position of power, but his Dream had been a great one. Perhaps there is good in the most evil of men, and while Khukov had not been truly evil, his Dream was truly good. Forta was right: I had to see it through while I lived. The fate of my species might well depend on it.

Of course I was nominally in charge of the Triton Project. But once I got it organized, I had hardly been there. So this was an inspection trip. Spirit joined us for it; she was more conversant with the details.

As our ship approached Triton I was amazed. The project had started as a single dome on the planet. Now it was a monstrous complex spreading from crater to crater. Projection tubes orbited it, not one or two, but hundreds. As we drew near, I discovered the size of them: each greater in diameter than any ship I had known in the Navy. What monstrous vessels were they designed to accommodate?

Then, in closer orbit, we spied those vessels: colony ships of a scale hardly imagined before. Even after allowing for necessary supplies for a decade or so, including construction equipment for planetary sites, each ship looked big enough to handle tens of thousands of colonists. Yet these, I knew, were not the major vessels; the big ones were bubbles, to be projected entire, with up to a million residents each. Those were being outfitted in the atmosphere of Neptune. No wonder this project was expensive!

It had been happening all along, and I knew that Spirit had been running it and Forta had been receiving bulletins on progress throughout; I simply had not been paying attention. I plead age and illness; I had been more interested in dialysis and distaff anatomy than in the business of the Solar System. Though my physical powers were waning, my interest in performance had not; consequently my romantic life had taken more attention, not less. Perhaps this would not have been the case, had Forta been less versatile. She had provided me, in her fashion, with every type of woman from Helen of Troy to the

barely nubile. She had given me another affair with my
teenage lover Amber, who in real life was now in her late
twenties. But I really should have kept up on what was
happening around Triton!

I had already decided to complete my business in life
expeditiously, but this was a forceful reminder. The project I was nominally running had outstripped my awareness while I dallied; I was allowing age to narrow my
compass, and I regretted it. Yet I also felt pride, for, however circuitously, I had wrought this thing. I had only to
see the first great colony ship projected, and then I would
know that even if I died that instant, mankind was on its
way to the stars at the velocity of light, and my work in
life was done.

Spirit squeezed my scarred arm, signaling her understanding. Her life, too, was merged in this project. She
had done the actual organizational work to make it come
to pass. It was really hers more than mine.

I glanced at her. She had been apart from me much of
the time in recent years, traveling to Jupiter and the inner planets, handling the myriad executive details of the
organization of man's effort of colonization. She was sixty-
five now, and looked it. She had not bothered with the
treatments and cosmetics that retarded the semblance of
aging, and the faint pattern of scars on her face had become more pronounced. The scars of the burns received
when she handled a drive-rocket with her bare hands,
saving our lives. She had been twelve then. Now her face
changed, in my view, and I saw again that sweet, tough
child who had supported me so well. From that time until
this, Spirit had been my true strength.

I found myself kissing her. I had not known I was going
to do it, or that I was doing it; it was as if my consciousness formed in the middle. She was kissing back. Then I
drew away, and looked away, and she neither moved nor
spoke. On the one side I wondered why a man should feel
apologetic for kissing his sister; on the other, I knew why.
But this could not be spoken.

Forta was gazing ahead, looking at Triton and the massive complex of the project on its surface. "You left your
kidneys here," she murmured.

And there was another thing to ponder. The beginning of the ending of my life had been here, too, as well as the beginning of the completion of it. Coincidence or design of fate—which was the more accurate description? I wasn't sure I cared to know.

We landed and were ushered into the complex. The personnel were ready to answer any questions and had enormous stores of ready data, but I was tired already, and very soon Forta put me to bed and held my hand while I drifted like a disabled ship into the orbit of slumber.

I dreamed of flying, only I was not the flier, I was being carried, borne by a great fantasy creature, an ifrit. He brought me to a castle, and into a high tower of that castle, and laid me on a bed beside a truly lovely young woman. She was garbed in the robe of a princess, and a circlet of precious stones bound down her flowing hair. Then the ifrit changed into a bedbug and bit me on the rear, and I woke, startled, for the first time becoming aware of the damsel. In my dream this made sense, as it would not have in life; I had more than one level of awareness.

I gazed upon the damsel, and lo, she was the fairest creature I had ever seen, the image of my first love Helse, and I said to myself "Oh, if this be the princess my father wishes me to marry, I have been a fool to resist his wish!" Then I put my hand on the girl's shoulder and tried to awaken her, but she slumbered on soundly. I stroked her body, moved to desire by the perfect rondure of her breast and the firmness of her thigh, but she would not wake and I would not rape her. So I lay back down beside, resolved to tell my father in the morning that I agreed after all to marry the one he had selected.

When I slept, the ifrit spoke to the ifritah, the female of his species. "Now do you wake your charge, and we shall see how she reacts to him." And she became another bedbug and bit the princess on her plush behind, and she woke, slapping at the place, then spied me sleeping beside her. "Oh, what a charming prince!" she murmured, and it was true; I was as young and attractive for a male as she was for a female, and set onto my head was a thin crown of gold, and my robe too was encrusted with gems. But I remained asleep.

She put her hand on me, and shook me by the shoulder, as I had with her. "Oh, wake, Prince!" she whispered, but I did not.

"If this be the man my father wishes to betroth me to, surely I have been willful to deny him!" she exclaimed. Then she stroked my handsome face, and when I still did not wake, my arms and chest. She opened my robe and ran her hands down inside, and caressed my belly and my thighs and my member, but I slept on. She lay across me and kissed me, and finally returned to sleep, embracing me.

Then I woke—but the princess was gone, and I was myself again, old and frail and unhandsome. Ever has it been thus, in reality! I pondered the dream, and recognized it: It was from the depths of my childhood memory, a tale of sorcery, in which ifrits had had a beauty contest, each believing that the person he or she had discovered was the most beautiful in all the world. So they had brought the two together, and awakened them by turns, letting the young folk judge by their reactions which of them was the most attractive. The ifrit favoring the man had because the woman reacted more to the man than the man had to the woman. Then the ifrits had returned the two human folk, sleeping, to their own residences and thought no more of the matter, leaving each longing with futility for the unknown other. A good, and frustrating, story.

Why had I remembered it now? Why had I dreamed it, as if I were a figure in it? I did not know.

"Forta," I said.

She was there immediately. "Yes, Hope?"

And what did I want of her? That she be young and beautiful, like a princess, and I like a prince? Ludicrous! She would do it, I knew, if I asked her—but why should I put her to this trouble, just because of a foolish dream?

"Tell me, Hope," she said.

So I told her. She nodded. "Be right back."

But by the time she returned, I had fallen asleep again, and her emulation was wasted. Well, perhaps not entirely, for in the morning I found her sleeping beside me, garbed as a princess and resembling Helse. I kissed her on the mask, appreciating her effort; she tried so hard to please me, and I hardly felt worthy of it.

In the day we talked with the officials of the project, and ascertained that they could ship the first colony vessel at any time; it was not necessary to have facilities for the entire System before starting, as the complete process would take years or decades. The logistics of handling five billion living human beings guaranteed that.

But almost a third of the living people of the System were not yet committed to the project. That was because South Saturn—the Middle Kingdom—had not joined. I had invited that huge nation to participate, but a mistake I had made before haunted me. I had allowed my old enemy Tocsin to be exiled there, and, true to his nature, he had poisoned the people against my works. Short of conquest, which would have been ruinously expensive and risky, there had been no way to obtain their commitment, so I had let it go. Now I realized that I had to do something; we could not leave the Middle Kingdom behind. Those many hundreds of millions of people would overrun the remainder of the System unless they had their own quadrant of the galaxy to colonize.

So it was we traveled next to South Saturn. We were treated cordially there; it seemed that the officers had been watching the development of the Triton Project, and had increasingly desired to participate in the conquest of the galaxy, because the need of their nation was greater than that of any other except populous Earth. But it was difficult for them to reverse themselves; there was a matter of face.

Of course they did not state this directly; I read it in their reactions as they spoke, while Forta translated their words for me. They were ready to cast off the malign influence of Tocsin, who it seemed was wearing out his welcome, but they needed a suitable pretext to do so. Well, I was a statesman, which is a polite term for an executive who is out of power; surely I could devise such a pretext.

"How goes it with the rings?" I inquired.

There was a scowl. "The rings are rightly part of Saturn," the Premier said. "But we lack the navy to do what should be done."

"The rings are a far better place from which to launch colony ships than the surface of Saturn itself," I reminded him. "If it were possible for you to join forces with Wan—" For that was the name of the Nation of the Rings. The former government of the Middle Kingdom had retreated to the rings when defeated on the planetary surface, and only the presence of the Jupiter Navy had prevented further action there.

"We should be glad to join forces—by reuniting that territory with the planet, as is fitting," he said grimly.

"Yet you hardly need the rings, other than as a station for departure," I pointed out. "What use will they be to Saturn—after Saturn has colonized a major segment of the galaxy?"

He nodded. "You are clever, Tyrant," he said via the translation. "We might settle for conquest in name only, provided there is no public denial, and the shipping facilities of the rings were made available to us."

"Let me talk to Wan," I said.

We traveled to the rings. I speak as though this happened in hours; actually I have greatly abridged these proceedings in this narrative. They took months, because we had to talk also with the several major provinces of the Middle Kingdom, a time-consuming process. But this was the essence.

I had never before been actually *in* the rings of Saturn, because they were proprietary territory; our ships had gone around them, and I had admired them in passing. Now that changed. For the first time I saw them at truly close range.

From a distance, as we know, the rings are beautiful, a gigantic halo around Saturn, perhaps the most dramatic sight in our System. Up close, it fuzzes somewhat, because it is composed of small separate stones or balls of ice, and they are not artistic individually. We nudged inside, seeking the capital-bubble of Pei, and now the fragments seemed to float all about us. It was like being in a magnified fog, with each droplet of water expanded. It reminded me of a vision I had had, decades before, when

I had been with Roulette, using poles to push away float-ing rocks so our ship could get through. That had been a dream; this was real. Why does so much of my present experience remind me of my past?

We pushed on, moving slowly through the pebbles and rocks and scattered boulders of the ring, noting how the system was not rigid, but liquid on the larger scale, the inner fragments orbiting faster than the outer ones. Per-haps this was not directly visible, but in my fancy it was; I saw the channeled soup of it, this living substance of the ring. I remembered also the time I had emptied the refuse containers of our little space bubble, as we drifted toward Jupiter; the stuff had gone into orbit, and surely remains there now. These rings of Saturn—could they be the refuse of some ancient alien spaceship, whose crea-tures needed to unload before departing for home? How ironic, that such beauty should come from such an origin! True, scientists had long since sampled and analyzed the substance of the rings, and pronounced it natural—but who can say what alien refuse might resemble?

Thus my experience in passing through the rings was not the average, but it was worthwhile for me. Now I felt I understood the rings. Perhaps this would help me ne-gotiate with the authorities of Wan.

The Generalissimo of Wan was courteous but firm: his nation would join forces with the Middle Kingdom only by conquering it, as it was his firm intention to do. Of course it has been his intention for thirty years, and his chances of success, should the Jupiter Navy even allow him to try, were practically nonexistent, but that was his attitude. It was a matter of face.

I broached the same argument I had made to the Pre-mier of the Middle Kingdom: Suppose the conquest were in name only, since the rings would need no use of the mainland once they had their own entire system else-where in the galaxy. He, too, appreciated the logic. "But," he pointed out, "the usurper of the Middle Kingdom would never accede to that."

All too true. But then my genius of insanity, or vice versa, struck. I remembered my dream, and applied it to reality. "If it is only the name that is in question, not the cooperation for mutual advantage—like a marriage for convenience, not for love or procreation—would it not be fair to put it to the decision of fate?" I inquired. Fate would not be precisely the term used here, but I trusted Forta to render it suitably.

"How do you mean?" he inquired.

"Suppose each nation chose a champion," I said. "A representative, who would meet the champion of the other nation, and the decision of that encounter would bind the nations, without shame or loss of face?" I did not discuss the source of my notion, which was the dream of the ifrits' beauty contest, because I did not believe that was relevant. The point was that the decision could be made vicariously, relieving the leaders of the onus of loss of face.

It took a while to persuade him, but persuasion is a thing I am talented at, and in due course he agreed. We then returned to the mainland of Saturn, and I broached the notion there. More time elapsed, but in due course we succeeded in hammering out the agreement. Each nation was to choose a champion; the two champions would then be memory-washed, so that neither knew anything of the broader situation, and placed together in a prison with limited supplies. It would be possible for only one to escape, and whichever nation that one represented would win the right to the name of the joint effort and symbolic conquest of the other. Holo cameras would be built into the prison, so that all that occurred within it would be a matter of continuous public record; there could be no cheating. Of course the two champions, their memories lost, would not know this. It promised to be a considerable vicarious adventure. All of the Middle Kingdom and Wan would be tuning in, surely.

The Middle Kingdom selected a champion martial artist: a husky man in his twenties who could kill swiftly in a hundred different ways, and kill slowly in a thousand more. Of course he would not remember this—but even mem-wash could not entirely eliminate the ingrained routines. In any event, he was extremely strong and agile and strong-willed, and it seemed unlikely that Wan could field a champion his equal.

But Wan was smarter than that. It selected a young

woman, the fairest flower of her age, stunningly beautiful, skilled in the creative and performing arts and of an
endearing disposition. Any man would welcome her as his
bride, and probably would do anything for the mere favor
of her smile.

"Foul!" cried the Premier, approximately, in Chinese;
Forta would not translate the term he actually used.
"There can be no fair combat!"

"Fair," replied the Generalissimo. "Gender was not
specified, only that we select a representative. Let your
warrior smash her and take the victory; it is surely within
his power to do so."

The Premier wanted to abort the contest. But his ministers advised him that face could be lost if their side reneged, especially if it seemed that they were afraid to risk
their champion against a mere girl. Also, news leaked to
the public, together with a holo photo of the girl, and
suddenly the imagination of the nation was caught up in
the notion of their virile hero having total access to such
a creature while they watched. Let him use her, *then* win
the contest by escaping.

So it was set up. They used a honeymoon bubble: an
enclosure with supplies for two for one week, rather lux-
uriously appointed, and a single jet-powered space suit.
The two were placed within it unconscious; then the watch
began.

It was stupid, I knew, but I found myself riveted to the
holo broadcast. Perhaps it was because I knew that my
own time was limited, the only question being whether I
would accomplish the Dream before I died. It was easy to
identify with the situation of the contest. There had to be
a decision, and no one could know what it would be. Would
the man use his strength to take the suit and escape, or
would he defer to the woman and sacrifice himself for her?
Would he love her, and would he die for that love? It was
his decision to make; he had the power, just as the Middle
Kingdom had the power. The question was one of will.

The two woke together, as the equipment of the bubble
bathed them in radiation that neutralized the sleep medication. I identified with the man, as I am sure other men
did, while the women identified with the woman. I could

almost fathom his thoughts, hardly needing my talent to read him.

They had names, and remembered these, though little else. He knew he was from the Middle Kingdom, and she knew she was from Wan, and they knew that these nations were not on friendly terms, but the rest had been taken by the wash. So I will call him King and her Wan, for this narration.

King found himself on a mat on the floor of a tiny bubble. He knew it was a bubble, because he could feel the change in gee as he stood; his head was lighter than his feet. But he could not remember how he had come there.

Quickly he explored. In the next chamber he encountered a beautiful young woman, garbed like a princess, with a jeweled diadem binding back her hair. She looked like Helse. Of course he did not know that; only I knew that. My image of early love is always Helse, just as my image of late love is always Megan. Bear with me; I'm an old man. She stared back at him, startled. "Do I know you?" she asked nervously.

"I don't remember," he replied. Her dialect differed from his, but they could understand each other.

"You don't remember?" She glanced about. "I don't remember—anything. How did I come here?"

King did a swift appraisal. "I suspect I have been memwashed. I don't remember anything since—since my fifth birthday. Is it the same with you?"

She considered. "Yes." She was evidently uncertain whether she could trust him.

"You are of the rings," he said.

"Yes. And you are of South Saturn. I can tell by your accent."

"Our nations are not friends," he said.

"I have no concern with politics," she replied. "At least, not that I can remember."

King looked at her again, already smitten by her beauty. "There is no need for us to be enemies," he said. "It seems that we have both been washed and left here. Perhaps there is a way out."

She got lithely to her feet. "Then let us be companions, and see what we can learn of our situation." She remained somewhat in awe of his evident physical power, deciding that it was the safest course to be polite.

"Perhaps," he agreed.

They explored their confinement. It turned out to be a beautifully appointed bubble, with the very best in food and beverage and appointments. King surveyed the supplies with a practiced eye, though he could not remember the practice. "One week," he said. "For two."

"How much air?" she asked.

He checked the indicators on the bubble's master control. "One week. And one week for power."

"That means that even if we economize on the food and air, we will perish when the power dies," she said. "We cannot survive in a sealed bubble without heat."

"True," he agreed grimly. "It seems we are prisoners, and our execution date has been set."

"What could we have done to deserve this?" she asked plaintively.

"Treason?"

"We are of two different nations," Wan protested. "Surely what would be treason for one would be patriotism for the other."

"Not if we had a treasonous liaison."

She turned on him a gaze of innocence and surmise. "Could we have been lovers?"

"I see you are fair," King said carefully. "Had you been willing, we could have been."

She lowered her gaze modestly. With the colonization of the System, many of the old ways had passed, but it was still considered a virtue for a woman to be chaste until marriage.

King busied himself with further checking. He discovered that the lock was operative, but that there was only one general-purpose space suit. It would fit either of them, being adjustable in the limbs and torso, and had a competent locomotion jet; with it, a person could travel a fair distance through space. It also had a locator, which meant that it would tune in on the nearest general-access port. The chances were that a person could reach an inhabited bubble, using this suit.

He explained this to Wan. "I'm sure they would not

have provided us with this suit if safety were not within range of it," he said.

"But there is only one," she reminded him.

"That I do not understand," he said.

"It means that only one of us can go," she said.

"It doesn't matter. That one can fetch help to free the other."

"Not if we have been condemned for treason."

"Yet why leave even one suit, then?" he asked.

"To add to the punishment," she said. "If we were— were lovers, it would hurt either one to leave the other. How would we choose who was to live, and who to die?"

"This is a kind of torture known to my culture," he said gravely.

"And to mine," she agreed with a shudder.

"Yet if this is so, why would they allow even one of us to survive?" he asked. "Perhaps there is no refuge within range of the suit."

"Oh, King, I am afraid!" she said.

He put his arm about her shoulders. "Perhaps we misjudge the situation," he said reassuringly.

"Then we were not lovers," she said.

He removed his arm, self-consciously. "Perhaps not."

She retreated to the sanitary facility. This, at least, was shielded from the holo camera. In due course she emerged. "We were not lovers," she said.

King paused, assessing her meaning. Obviously she had checked, and discovered herself to be still a virgin. Embarrassed, he turned away.

"I meant no affront," Wan said quickly. "Only that there must be some other reason for our confinement."

They completed their exploration of the premises. King was pleased to discover a small but nice collection of weapons on one wall: a long sword, short sword, assorted daggers, and two laser pistols. Wan gazed at these and shuddered; she had no use for such things. However, there was also a nice collection of cloths and threads, and a modern sewing machine. This delighted Wan, who found that she knew exactly how to use it.

Then Wan prepared a very nice meal from the available supplies, and they ate. Then, discovering no holo news input or entertainment features, they retired to their separate chambers and slept.

Which gave the rest of us a chance to return to mundane matters. So far there had been no sign of rivalry or hostility between the contest participants, just the mutual confusion and search for the reality of their situation. Very little, really, had happened. But how riveting the course of that happening! As long as no decision was forthcoming, no one could rest. All in all, it was a very satisfactory contest, though proceeding along a course that had not been anticipated.

In the morning the two woke and performed their toilets and had breakfast, and discussed their situation. "Obviously we were put here, and if we were not lovers, perhaps we are being tested," King said. "It is our challenge to obtain our freedom within our deadline."

"Then there must be a way," Wan said.

"There must be a way," he repeated.

But though they quested all day, they found no way for both to go. They explored every possible avenue, and all came to nothing. Only one could be sure of escape.

They filled in empty hours in their own fashions, staving off the boredom and the fear of their fate. King practiced with the weapons, finding himself marvelously fluent with them, and Wan did dances, her body discovering familiar patterns of motion. King paused in his activity to watch her, making no comment, but his interest was manifest. He was a warrior, true; but it seemed that he also subscribed to a code of honor that prevented him from taking advantage of one who was definitely not a warrior.

It was Wan who, on the third day, caught on. "This is the test!" she exclaimed with dismay. "To see which one of us escapes!"

"To decide some issue between our nations," he agreed, seeing it.

She lowered her gaze. "I could not prevent you, King."

He paced the chamber, reflecting. "May I speak with candor, Wan?"

She laughed, but did not look at him. "I cannot prevent you," she repeated.

"You are fair, and I am smitten with you."

"That is not the way a man of the Middle Kingdom addresses a woman," she replied, her color intensifying.

"I do not know the appropriate manner to say what I wish, so I will say it outright. Give me your favor, and I will let you take the suit."

"And perhaps betray your planet?" she asked. "I would not sell my favor thus."

"Then take the suit anyway. I cannot let you perish here."

"You are generous," she murmured.

"You are fair," he repeated.

"Then I suppose it is decided," she said. "Help me get into the suit."

He went to the lock and fetched the suit. He helped her don it, and he adjusted its limbs to fit her properly, and cautioned her about wasting the drive. "We do not know how far you must go," he said. "If there were any way to avoid this risk, I would not have you take it."

"But you could take it," she reminded him.

"I think the worse risk is remaining here." He meant it; I was reading him.

She donned the helmet and entered the lock. Sealed within it, she touched the air-evacuation control. Then she touched it again, and the dropping pressure rose again.

She returned to the interior of the bubble, and lifted the helmet.

"Something is wrong?" King inquired anxiously.

"Yes," she said quietly.

"Then we shall fix it! I thought that suit was in good order!"

"I apologize," she said.

"What?"

"For doubting you. I did not think you would actually let me go."

"I told you: If I may not have your favor, I can at least save your life."

She lowered her gaze in the way she had. "You have my favor now."

He paused, then slowly nodded.

She got out of the suit, and there followed a scene that one seldom has opportunity to witness on holo broadcast. Wan's favor, once won, was a spectacular thing.

"We are lovers *now*," she murmured before they slept.

And Forta came to me in the guise of Wan, a lovely make-believe princess. But I hesitated. "She was never one of my women." Actually, my hesitation was because of that Helse image; I enjoyed making love to the replicas of my other women, but Helse and Megan were sacred.

"At your age," she said, "you have to learn to live vicariously." She brought out a mask and her makeup kit, and she put the mask on my face and secured it, and she worked on my body with pseudoflesh. I let her proceed, for I liked the touch of her hands on my body, and I liked what she was doing.

In due course she brought me before a full-length mirror. I was amazed: my scarred arms and legs had become smooth and powerfully muscled, and my face was that of King. I was the make-believe prince, and she the princess, and we made as fetching a couple as the one we had watched.

"You have my favor now," she said.

I fear that if it could be objectively viewed, our subsequent performance would hardly have approached that of the originals. But in my fond memory, it was identical. I felt young and strong, and she was ravishingly delicious, and we made love that should not have shamed the model on which it was based.

Ah, Forta! What a joy she was to me in the late stage of my life! She was correct about the joys of vicarious existence, and she rehearsed the loves of all my life, except the major ones. Perhaps it was inappropriate of me to deny her those; if it was right for my lesser loves, how could it be wrong for the major ones?

I had to have my dialysis, and though I tried to watch the ongoing holo, and thought I followed it perfectly, my memory fogs out, and I realize that I must have lost concentration and slept through goodly portions. This I regret, but it is another sign of my advancing weakness. That love scene with Forta's Wan emulation evidently took much out of me, though it was worth all it cost.

My next clear memory is of crisis: King and Wan had seen themselves coming up on their week's deadline, and their extraordinary efforts to lose themselves in loveplay had not blinded them to their reality. They had concluded that there was only one satisfactory way out: They would die together. They planned their suicide carefully. He would use the largest sword to decapitate her cleanly, then stab himself through the heart. Their blood would mingle, and they would travel together to the afterlife. "And don't go without me!" he cautioned her with mock severity. "I will join you in fifteen seconds."

"My spirit will wait at least that long for you, my love," she said seriously.

They set it for the final day, when the food ran out and the power had only one hour to go. That was only two days away. In the interim they proposed to love each other to the maximum possible extent.

There was of course a storm of reaction and protest outside. Not only did this totally unanticipated conclusion threaten to bring no victory to either side, the people of both Wan and the Middle Kingdom had in the course of these few days become enraptured by the romance of their representatives, and could not bear to see them die. Delegations marched on the capitals, and the media were filled with a single coalescing sentiment: It hardly mattered by what name the mission operated. What mattered was that the lives of these two noble lovers be saved.

An accord was achieved in record time: The project would proceed under the title King/Wan, and the two of them would be placed in charge of the project, each to represent the interest of his/her nation and that of all its people. The two would be informed of this on the planetary holo, and all other officials would defer absolutely to their decisions. They were, in truth, to be Prince and Princess.

Chapter 20

LAYA

Only one step remained, on the day before the suicide deadline: The provinces of the Middle Kingdom had to ratify the decision. These provinces had a good deal of autonomy, and the terms of the hasty accord were that any province could cast a veto. None was expected—but the unexpected occurred.

My old nemesis Tocsin naturally opposed the accord, and he had retreated to the Province of Laya, in the "mountainous" ragged-wind band of South Saturn. Tocsin had lost favor elsewhere in the Middle Kingdom, but Laya was his final stronghold, and Laya it was that cast the lone veto.

Thus the challenge was abruptly on us. There was just one day to get Laya to reverse its veto, and I knew it would never do so while Tocsin had influence. The Premier of the Middle Kingdom, having finally achieved an accord with the rings that would give his nation access to the galaxy, was furious; he threatened to invade the errant province and execute its leadership. Certainly it was in his power to do so—but such a mission would have required months to organize properly, and at least a week as an emergency spot measure. Meanwhile, the lovers would die; no one doubted that.

I knew it was up to me. Only the Tyrant of Space could hope to achieve a reversal in a single day. I had no idea how I would do it, but I intended to do it. I would go to Laya.

"I'll have to take Spirit," I said. "She can organize—"

"She's on a private mission to Triton," Forta advised me. "It would take several hours just to reach her with a message, and several more for her to get here. I don't think you can afford to wait."

With time already critical, I knew she was right. "But I'll bungle it alone," I said. "I'm a figurehead; I need her to set me up for a score."

"But if Laya sees you coming with her, their officials will know you will score," Forta said. "The psychological aspect is half the battle."

"But—"

Already she was changing. "By the time more is needed, she will be able to join us—as me."

Now I understood. Already she was donning the mask, and resembled my sister. Certainly she could fool the Layas.

We sent a private message to Spirit, with no answer required; I knew she would join us as rapidly as possible.

"But you cannot go to Laya alone!" the Premier protested when we notified him. "They will kill you, Tyrant!"

"And bring the wrath of the planet on their heads?" I asked. "Even rulers who hate me are not that crazy."

"Just the same, I will provide an armed escort."

"That will just lead to violence," I said. "Just let me go in alone, no threat to anyone. I am sure I can persuade the Panchen to reverse the veto." The Panchen was the ranking religious official of Laya, and therefore in that framework the political leader too. He had been installed some years back by the Middle Kingdom, over the protest of the people of Laya, whose prior ruler, the Dalai, had fled to Earth.

"He will not see you," the Premier said. "I know him; he is intractable. Tyrant, this is dangerous!"

"I have faced danger before. I know the people of Laya support me. After all, I tried to get the Dalai restored—" I broke off, realizing what I had said. Naturally the Panchen hated me! But still, there was no time for complex maneuvering; I had to brave the enemy in his den and win his cooperation. It was a fitting challenge for the Tyrant. "Anyway, I'll have Smilo along; he's the perfect bodyguard." The truth was that Smilo was now getting old, and he spent most of his time sleeping. But he was my mascot, and his worth was considerable.

"I will send a fleet after you," the Premier said, acceding to my seeming folly. He knew the stakes as well as I did. So we took a plane directly to Laya, just the three of us, making the dramatic play.

We passed the region of the Great Wall as we traveled to the far province. This was an enormous net set up to balk intruders, theoretically the nomads near the equator, but actually the Union of Saturnine Republics. The People's Republic of the Middle Kingdom was somewhat paranoid about potential invasion from the north. The net was girt with bubbles and checkpoints, and of course it was mined, so that intruding ships would have trouble penetrating it. But of course today any such invasion would be by missiles, so the Wall had become a historic artifact.

The winds at thirty degrees South Saturn were not nearly as strong as those of the equator; they were equivalent to those of the Jupiter equator. But the band of greatest velocity was very narrow, and the shear on either side was ferocious. There was a similar zone at forty-five degrees North Saturn, called Beria, where political prisoners were exiled. Such regions of shear were called mountains, because it was dangerous to cross them; an airplane could be thrown out of control. Our pilot was experienced and careful as we approached Hasa; even so, we experienced considerable buffeting as we navigated the eddy-swirls. This region was thinly populated, and it was easy to appreciate why.

We arrived at Hasa, the so-called Forbidden City. I really had not expected a rousing welcome, and I received none. A lowly functionary met us at the lock and informed us that the Panchen was not accepting visitors this day.

Forta, emulating Spirit, drew herself up impressively. "He will see the Tyrant," she said.

"No one," the functionary repeated stonily.

Spirit had never been one to take no for an answer. She marched out of the terminal and commandeered a vehicle large enough to accommodate Smilo. The driver seemed reluctant, but Smilo growled mildly, and the man decided to cooperate. In moments Spirit had called up a local map on the car's screen and was zeroing in on the Panchen's residence. Forta, as a secretary, was versed in this sort of thing, but it was impressive enough even so.

We caught brief glimpses of the city of Hasa as our car moved through the narrow streets. Ancient-style buildings were interspersed with completely modern ones, but overall the city appeared to be poor rather than rich. There were many temples and lamaseries, evidence of a devout people. Near the center was a large shrine, with a statue of Buddha as a young prince. I remembered that he had renounced the royal life in favor of piety and asceticism. "Stop!" I cried.

"What?"

"I must pay homage to Buddha."

Spirit had the driver stop, and we got out. "Buddha was a great man," I said. "And Asoka was a great leader who honored his principles. I always wanted to be like Asoka, but never came close."

"But you tried," she said.

"I tried," I agreed. "Now here is Buddha, and I wish I could be one with him."

I stood for a time, just gazing at the statue, and the tears flowed down my face. They were not tears of sadness, but of appreciation for greatness. "He spoke the four great truths," I said.

"Existence is suffering," Spirit said, only perhaps I should say Forta, because she it was who truly understood these principles.

"The origin of suffering is desire," I said, remembering the next truth.

"But suffering ceases when desire ceases," she continued.

"And the way to reach the end of desire is by following the Eightfold Path," I concluded. "Oh, how I wish I could have done so!"

We returned to the car, passing by the people who had gathered. They were common folk, and I knew they knew me and were with me. But none spoke. They simply stood and gazed at Smilo with awe. We resumed our drive.

"There," Spirit said. "There in the park."

"The leader of the province lives in a park?" I asked.

"It is his retreat at the height," the driver explained.

"Then drive us there," she said. I am rendering this dialogue approximately; the fact is the driver spoke only Chinese, and Forta was using her linguistic ability and equipment to communicate, and translating in snatches for me. Spirit could not have done that; in this sense I was better off with Forta.

"I cannot," the driver protested.

"Why not?"

"There is no road, only a footpath up the mountain."

Indeed it was so. The driver dropped us off at the edge of the park and took his pay and buzzed away.

The park was impressive. At the low fringe it was planted with native trees, but the interior was a massive mountain slope, covered with snow. Apparently this was a bubble large enough to support as many as a million people, but only a hundred thousand actually occupied it. The remainder of its capacity was devoted to this monumental internal park, that cut across many levels and dominated the interior.

No one came to help us; indeed, the entire city seemed hostile, except for the few common folk we had encountered at the statue. When I looked back, I saw a crowd gathering, but now the local police were herding them away. The common man might be with me, but the authorities were not, and the authorities had the power. We were not in physical danger; the extermination of the nomenklatura of North Saturn had spread a message throughout the System that the Tyrant was not to be molested. But these people did not want us here; that was clear enough.

The route was plain: a winding footpath to the summit, where the Panchen's palatial retreat perched. This was the Potala, taken from the Dalai. He was surely aware of our arrival and approach, but gave no signal; he preferred to pretend that he knew nothing of the visit of the messenger. He played a dangerous game; if this were in deference to the antipathy of Tocsin, it would in due course become apparent where the power ultimately lay.

But now was now, and we had a deadline, and only the Panchen could reverse the veto Laya had cast. If he did it now, the agreement would take effect, and the Prince and Princess would be freed and promoted, and more than a billion people would reap the joy thereof today, and to-morrow the Dream would be realized as mankind commenced its colonization of the stars. If the Panchen did not reverse the veto, it would cost the lives of King and Wan, and sow dissension that could torpedo South Saturn's participation in the Triton Project, and throw the very Dream into doubt. Oh, Tocsin's mischief was manifest!

However, I knew I retained enough of my ability to read and influence a man to enable me to persuade the Panchen of the error of his way. Once we reached his house, I would of course speak directly to the point. He had to recognize that the interest of his people would not be served by the foiling of the Dream. For one thing, the colonization of the galaxy represented Laya's best opportunity to escape the dominance of the Middle Kingdom. That was a thing that Laya most wanted to do, for it had always regarded itself as an independent nation. I knew I could make this clear to him, once I talked to him personally; it was only his isolation that had set him up for the deceit spread by Tocsin. Tocsin could be very convincing, when a person lacked access to the facts.

So we wended our way along the path toward the mountain. "This must be the Eightfold Path," I said, but the humor seemed weak.

Soon another hurdle manifested: It was cold here, and we were not dressed for it. We would never make it to the top of the mountain afoot without winter clothing. Surely the local authorities had known this, so had not interfered with our progress.

Spirit tackled the problem in her typical fashion. "We'll get gear," she said, and led the way off the path toward a park supply building.

I told Smilo to wait outside the building, and he settled down for a catnap by the door. Inside the building we offered to buy the clothing we required, but the surly proprietor claimed there was none in our sizes. Snowsuits in a full range of sizes hung on racks along the wall, plainly intended for rental to the tourists, but he stuck by his statement. It was evident that we would get no help here.

Again, Spirit reacted typically; Forta really understood my sister! Her laser appeared in her hand, bearing on the proprietor's nose. "Hope, put the money on the counter," she said. "Then select suits for us."

I did as directed. The proprietor made as if to reach for a holophone, but a laser beam scorched the table just beside his hand, and he snatched it back. Spirit never bluffed, and never missed her target. The warning sufficed.

I made the selections, and got dressed; then I held the laser while Spirit dressed. Fully outfitted, we left the building, after lasering through the holophone's connecting line. By the time the proprietor was able to alert the hostile authorities, we would be at the Panchen's retreat. Isolation is a sword that cuts both ways.

Outside, I roused Smilo. But I was beginning to regret bringing him along, not because of any bad manners on his part, but because he was a warm-weather creature, and old, and this was cold. I decided that he should be safe enough in the park for a couple of hours. "Smilo, stay," I said, gesturing to the warmer region behind us. "We'll come back this way."

The tiger didn't understand all that, of course, but he was familiar with "Stay." He walked back down toward a pleasant copse and found himself a place to make a nest. He would snooze until we returned. In past years he would have insisted on coming along, protecting me every step, but now he was satisfied to accept the easy course I urged on him. Age can do that to some of us.

We resumed our trek. The path ascended, and the cold quickly intensified; we really needed our protective clothing. But the scenery was beautiful. As we gained height the mountain also opened out below, showing a deep snowy gorge; the entire interior of the park, high and low, was evidently maintained at subfreezing level.

The path became little more than a niche in the steepening slope, and ice crackled under our boots. Though gee lessened as we climbed, because we were drawing away from the high-gee rim, this was not enough to compensate for my weakness, and I was soon tired. The mountain had seemed impressive but not huge at the outset; now it seemed that we had just as far to go as we had at the bottom, after an hour's climb.

Spirit took my arm, helping me walk. "I should have anticipated this," she muttered. "Minimal research—"

My sister surely would have done that. But I could hardly blame Forta. "We came on spot notice," I reminded her. "No time for research. Had I paused to reflect, I would have brought along a powered snowsled."

Her strength buoyed me, and we managed the steep path and closed on the summit. It was apparent that soon we would beard the Panchen in his den. I was sure that by this time he knew that he would have to face me, even if he hated me; there would be no further way to avoid it. He would not be able to deny the Tyrant his interview.

The path opened onto a sloping plain leading up to the retreat. We were almost there.

There was a roar. Startled, we looked—and saw a huge white creature charging down the slope toward us. It most resembled an ape, but it was about three meters tall, with massive furry arms and legs, and a horrendous snout.

"Bigfoot!" Spirit exclaimed.

"Impossible," I said. "That creature never existed, even back on Earth."

But the thing bore down upon us. I tried to scramble out of its path, but my foot slipped and I fell. Spirit caught my arm and hauled, but too late; the monster bent to sweep at us with its giant paws, and sent us tumbling down the slope of the mountain.

Spirit managed to catch at an outcropping of ice, and braked her slide, and hung on to me and brought me to a halt also. But the white monster was not finished; it pounced on me and swiped at my suit, its sharp claws slicing the cloth apart and gashing my flesh beneath. In a moment it stripped me of the better part of my protection, evidently preparing to consume me.

Spirit drew her laser and fired at the monster's furry ear. The burn evidently stung but did not really damage; the monster whirled around, caught her suit with the claws, and shredded it, too. It brought its toothed snout to bear. She lasered it in the mouth, but still it did not stop, though steam boiled out. It took another bite of her clothing, evidently mistaking it for flesh.

I scrambled across and caught at its leg. I hauled. The monster turned on me again. It seemed that it oriented on whatever attracted its attention at the moment.

Spirit leaped at it, her hands scraping at its back. I knew that this was futile; the thing would only throw her off. But abruptly there was a snap, and the monster reacted as if stabbed through the heart. It convulsed, then straightened, falling to the snow.

But we were near the brink of the falloff of the mountain. The monster slid over, carrying Spirit along with it. I grabbed for her, but was only hauled over myself.

The slope sharpened. I could not find leverage to halt my slide, and Spirit was no better off. Neither, it seemed, was the monster, if it still lived; the three of us were sliding down into the deep crevasse.

For a moment I thought that this was the end of my life. Then I caught a better glimpse of what lay ahead, and I was sure of it. Helpless, I fell into my doom.

But as it turned out, the end was not quite yet. The slope eased at the base, and we tumbled to a bruising halt at the bottom of the chasm.

I became aware of the cold. I had lost much of my outfit, and the temperature here was well below freezing. Spirit was no better off—and in addition, I saw with horror, the fall had broken one of her legs.

But her concern was only for me. "Hope, your loop!" she cried.

I looked—and saw that my loop had been ripped out of my arm. My blood was flowing out, staining the snow. I clapped my other hand on it, but knew that such a crude measure could not properly stanch the flow. I had to have prompt medical attention—and there was no certainty I would get that, here.

Spirit pulled herself over to me, her leg dragging. "I'll help, Hope!" she said.

But she could not help. Already the cold was numbing my limbs, and the loss of blood was weakening my consciousness. "Just hold me, my sister," I told her.

She put her arms around me, and I rested my head

against her bare breast while our lives seeped into the snow. Now it didn't seem cold.

"That monster," she said, her voice sounding deeper because my ear was against her chest. "It was a robot. I realized when the laser didn't hurt it. I found the switch in its back and turned it off, but—"

"You did well," I said.

"We'll be rescued," she said.

"It doesn't matter," I said.

"Of course it matters!"

"I did not have very much left to do anyway," I explained. "Not very much longer to live. Perhaps I intended it to be this way."

"Intended?" she asked, perplexed.

"It must have seemed pretty stupid, marching into enemy territory unprotected. I could so readily have come prepared."

"I should have thought of what we needed."

"No. It was my decision. I knew that it would take too long to reverse the veto, going through channels. I had to force their hand." As I spoke I believed it: that at a nether layer, my competence was manifesting, that I had not acted in idiotic, old-man, has-been fashion, that it was really genius. Yet who can say, now, that it was not?

"But we never made it to the Panchen!"

"He knew we were coming. That was his error."

"Hope, I don't understand!"

"Yes, you do, Spirit. You have always understood. We have won."

"We have won," she echoed faintly, humoring me.

I nuzzled her breast, the only part of her that remained warm. I was bleeding, she freezing; soon we would both sink into shock, and thence into oblivion. "You were always my true love, Spirit," I said. "Now I understand what Rue said: I thought I loved two, but only truly loved one."

"Only one," she agreed.

"Only you, my sister. I remember when you were twelve, when you lay with me, to ease my pain. You would do anything for me, and I so undeserving."

"No . . ."

"And when you had the baby—"

"What?" She sounded genuinely confused.

"And gave it to me, because I was sterile from space—"

"My baby?" she asked, amazed.

I laughed, weakly. "How could you forget, Spirit? But I made her mine."

"Yes, of course," she agreed.

"We must sing our songs," I said.

"Songs?"

I sang the song that had been given me by the members of my migrant labor group, the song that had identified me ever since. I sang not well but with feeling:

> It takes a worried man to sing a worried song
> It takes a worried man to sing a worried song
> It takes a worried man to sing a worried song
> I'm worried now, but I won't be worried long.

Then Spirit, remembering, sang her song, that had been bestowed on her by the members of our Navy unit:

> I know where I'm going, and I know who's going
> with me
> I know who I love, but the dear knows who I'll marry.

Those Navy folk had had a rare perception! They had known that my sister could never marry the one she truly loved. So they had nicknamed her "The Dear," and she had ever since allowed others to assume that it was "The Deer" in token of her grace and speed in achieving her objectives. Spirit, the mainstay of my life, throughout her life. The Tyrant never knew a better woman than the Iron Maiden.

I pressed into her breast. "Oh, my sister, I am dying."

"No, Hope!"

"And so are you." For the frost was forming on us, or so it seemed, as our skin chilled toward death. We were rasping rather than speaking clearly, but we understood the words.

She capitulated. "So am I. But we can still be rescued."

"Perhaps. But to what point? Existence is suffering."

"And the origin of suffering is desire," she agreed weakly, repeating the Buddhist truth.

"But we can end that suffering by following the Eightfold Path," I continued. "Right belief, right resolve—"

"Right speech, right conduct," she agreed.

"Right living, right effort—"

"Right-mindedness," she said.

"And right ecstasy," I concluded. "Oh, Spirit, it is not too late for that!"

"Oh, please, Hope, it must not end here!" she exclaimed.

"But we are about to escape to nirvana, to the blissful annihilation, to nonexistence and the end of suffering."

"No, we must be rescued!" she insisted. "The common people are with you, Tyrant! They will not let the evil authorities do this! We will survive!"

I saw a figure from the corner of my eye. I twisted my head to look. My vision was blurring as the cold closed on my eyeballs, but I hardly needed much for this. "I think not. Helse has come for me."

"Helse," she repeated.

Helse was in her patchwork wedding dress, exactly as she had been when she died. She was sixteen and beautiful. She held out her arms to me.

"Now at last I join you!" I cried, trying to rise. But I was too weak and cold, and could not.

Then Helse merged with Spirit, and it was Helse's breast I lay against. "Now at last," she agreed.

I kissed her, what I could reach of her, and sighed. I had waited for this moment for over fifty years: to join my love in heaven. Or nirvana. Wherever it was that she awaited me.

Now time seemed to slow, or perhaps my thought accelerated. My understanding expanded to embrace the entire city, planet, System, and galaxy. I knew everything I cared to know, everything there *was* to know; in fact I was the essence of information. I was able not only to perceive my body and that of the woman with me, but to grasp the complete significance of our being. I grasped the meaning of all my life and all life itself. This brought to me a mighty peace of mind; the brilliance of my unity with the cosmos suffused me. I perceived the universe in its totality, and the local events simultaneously. It was as though I were tuning in on everything that was happening everywhere, and that had happened, and that would happen; all time was one in me. I was the Tyrant, and now at last I had become one with the people I served. Death had no meaning for me; I had transcended it. Thus it became easy for me to summarize the events surrounding my death.

Meanwhile, my daughter Hopie had projected to Saturn at the first sign of the trouble with Laya. She had understood the threat instinctively. She brought picked men and picked equipment. She met Spirit, and the two joined forces with a contingent of the Middle Kingdom.

The common folk of Laya were rising, too, knowing that there was no welcome for the Tyrant in the hostile capital city. The common folk within the city had spread the news of my presence, and of my devotion at the shrine of Buddha, but the police held them back. They lacked the power to help.

It was hours before a party came to us, and it was no rescue operation. Our bodies were still locked together, my face against her breast. They dumped us unceremoniously in a sled and brought it to a holo unit. "The Tyrant and his evil sister are dead!" they exclaimed for the camera, and broadcast the picture to the System. "They fell down the mountain, and we could not reach them in time."

"Daddy!" my daughter cried in anguish.

But my sister was of sterner stuff. "Here is the first lie," she said on the planetary holo. "I am not dead. It is the Tyrant's secretary who died with him, garbed as me."

Astonished, the men of the city of Hasa went to Forta. Her mask came away. Their chagrin was manifest. They had thought to abolish the power of the Tyrant at one stroke, but they had eliminated only the figurehead. I think they knew at that moment that they were lost. Had Spirit died, the effort to complete the Dream could have fallen apart, but now it would be pursued.

"And the second lie," Spirit continued resolutely. "It was no accident. The Panchen sent his robot snow monster to throw them down. See, there is the wreckage of the machine in the background." And, indeed, the guilty robot was there.

"And the third lie," Spirit said. "The rescue party did not try to come promptly. The Panchen knew what had happened the moment his robot crashed. They waited four hours, until they were quite sure the Tyrant was dead, before sending out the party. They could have reached any point in that park in minutes, had they wanted to. Instead they prevented the common folk of the city from coming."

Now her face set into hard lines. "Hasa murdered my brother," she said. "What does Laya say to that?"

Laya's answer was grim.

Hopie came to claim my body. But her ship was barred by police bubbles of Laya. "First there is business we must do," they informed her.

And while they barred her entry, the people of Laya rose up as one, their car-bubbles massing against the city of Hasa. They covered it with the cannon of a cruiser, forcing entry even as the common folk of the city charged the locks and opened them. Then, armed, the people stormed in, making prisoners of the authorities and all who had supported them. There was little love for the Panchen beyond the city, and now he had given the people the pretext to rebel.

"Now watch what we do," the rebel leader announced on the holo.

Then an automatic lock was set up, and the first prisoner was fired out into the atmosphere of Saturn. He had no suit. He had been alive. Now his body was pulped inward by the tremendous pressure of the atmosphere, as it fell toward even greater pressure.

It was followed immediately by the second prisoner, and then a stream of them, at one-second intervals.

Appalled, Hopie watched the holo. "But this is barbaric!" she protested. A line of bodies was forming, streaming steadily down from Hasa: the Panchen's supporters.

"Then come and stop it," the leader said grimly. "We

will admit you to the city after the same delay that occurred for the rescue of the Tyrant."

And, indeed, it was four hours before she got into the city. "Stop it! Stop it!" she cried.

The leader turned to the man about to be fired out. "Your life is spared by the intercession of the daughter of the Tyrant," he said. "To whom is your loyalty now?"

But he got no answer, for the man had fainted.

So the carnage was stopped—but almost fifteen thousand had been executed in this fashion. The people of Laya had made known their sentiment and saved face for their province. Face does not come cheap, in the Middle Kingdom.

Hopie hurried to locate Smilo, whom she had never known personally but wanted to rescue. But he was dead. He had passed away naturally at about the time I did unnaturally, as though he retained his rapport to the end. Hopie stroked the beautiful fur and wept, and it was for more than the tiger she cried.

And, in this manner, the veto of Laya was reversed, and the lives of the Prince and Princess were saved. An order was sent for the Dalai to return from Earth, his long exile over. The Middle Kingdom had installed the Panchen, but now the Premier made no objection to the restoration of the Dalai.

I had a fancy funeral, of course, but this is not a subject of interest to me. I will only say that everyone of note came: Megan, Thorley, Hopie, General D of Gaul, all the ranking leaders of the System, all welcomed to the Middle Kingdom for the honor paid the Tyrant of Space. What was important was that my death had accomplished expeditiously what my life might not have: the salvage of the Dream. I was spared the humiliation of a bedridden decline. My only regret is that Forta had to die with me; she deserved better, but it was the way she wanted it. She was a good woman, my final one in life.

And mankind was headed for the stars.

Editorial Epilog

Within weeks of my father's death, the woman named Reba delivered to me the diaries he had kept throughout his life. This was a surprise to me; I had not known that he was writing them, or that I was to be the beneficiary of this information. But I had to read only a few pages of the first manuscript to realize that these should be published, because it was manifest that a major aspect of the Tyrant's existence was unknown to the public that his life benefited so greatly. It is true that there is now an impressive monument to the Tyrant of Space, the conservator of the Dream and architect of man's diaspora to the galaxy; he turned man's vision outward to space instead of inward to self-destruction. But the intensely personal and human side of him was known only to his close associates, a number of whom predeceased him. He was known as a ruthless killer and insatiable womanizer, but these diaries show that he was neither, once his nature is understood. I myself have on occasion condemned him for his "women" without understanding that it was indeed a reciprocal relation, and that sex was only one component of relationships that were anything but casual. If I, his daughter, misunderstood him, how much worse must it be for those who knew him only by reputation? So now I knew I owed it to him to present this side of him.

I edited these five manuscripts, covering the five major periods of Hope Hubris' life, in chronological order, not getting into the next until the prior was complete. I did this because I did not want to introduce any distortions, conscious or unconscious, into the manuscripts. This policy led me into surprises and perhaps traps, but I maintained it to the end.

Thus it was that I came to the conclusion of my father's life story, and received a shock. It didn't stop at his death; it carried a short distance beyond it, as has been seen. I hesitate to call this impossible, but it does lead to some interesting speculation. How can we account for this?

Could the Tyrant have written it himself, before traveling to Laya, somehow anticipating the details of his demise? This seems extremely doubtful, if only because the finale was so bizarre he could not have anticipated it in such detail. All the facts presented in it are accurate, as far as I have been able to ascertain. The manner I was met at the Laya border and delayed until they had completed what they deemed to be a suitable retribution for the murder of the Tyrant, even the words I spoke at the end—I simply do not believe that he could have anticipated this. If he had, certainly he would have acted to save Forta, even if, as he claims, he sought his own death to force the issue of the veto.

Could someone else have written it? No; the manuscript was locked in a safe whose mechanism recognized only his own touch and mine, and it was undisturbed when I recovered it. No other person had access to it, not even his sister.

I examined the handwriting. Only at this point did I recognize the change in it. The major portion of the manuscript is written in his own hand; the final portion is written in my hand. *I* wrote the conclusion—and yet I did not. I had no intention of doing such a thing, and no memory of it; it is not the way I work. I could not have done it—yet my hand gives me the lie.

I can offer only one explanation: My hand wrote it, but I did not. The spirit of my father must have visited me and used my body to complete his narrative. I realize that this sounds preposterous, but it was the way he worked. He was visited throughout his life by others he had known, living and dead; perhaps it should not be surprising that subsequently he visited his daughter. He did say, in the course of the manuscript, that he believed he could do something very like this, and I must confess that at times I was aware of his presence, even when we were geographically separated by the planets. I was surprised and pleased to read the confirmation of such contact; as nearly as I can ascertain, our experiences did coincide. At any rate, whatever the explanation, I accept the manuscript as written, and leave its mystery for others to ponder.

I received another shock when I realized what my father had written about his sister Spirit. He said she had a baby. Forta, then emulating Spirit, was naturally astonished; she had known nothing of this. So was I, for he made it clear that that baby was me.

All my life I have assumed that I was the illegitimate offspring of Hope Hubris, adopted because he felt a tie of blood he could not otherwise acknowledge. Certainly a blood affinity was evident; many physical tests have indicated a closeness that can hardly be ascribed to chance. But here he says he was rendered sterile in space, and it is true that sterility in men varies in direct proportion to their time in space, and he had logged much time. Sterility? Surely he would have known, and if he said it, it was true. But that means that he could not have been my father.

Now, abruptly, the obvious was apparent: Hope was not my father, Spirit was my mother. She had logged similar time in space, but women are not similarly affected, and remain fertile. Suddenly many things fell into place: why Hope had seemed so unconcerned about the charges against him. "Show me the mother of this child," he had announced publicly—knowing that as long as the search was for a Saxon mother, it could not be successful. For I am, as he puts it, a Saxon/Hispanic crossbreed; the evidence of my genetic heritage is clear.

Why should Hope Hubris have suffered a lifetime of suspicion about this matter, when he could readily have demonstrated its falsity? And why had his wife Megan so firmly supported him? Now it was clear: both were protecting Spirit. It has always been known that Spirit would do anything for her brother, literally, even to having sex with him or to letting him die in his own fashion; her loyalty knew no bounds. Now it is clear that that loyalty was returned. Hope truly loved his sister, and never was it more apparent than in the manner he protected her from scandal by taking it on himself. Only when he was dying, and losing his judgment near the end, did he let slip that secret, thinking that the conversation would never be known. Only in his private account is it revealed—an account that could only be made public by the hand of the very person concerned. His daughter—*Spirit*'s daughter—me.

And so I went to Spirit, and now I recount, as aptly as I am able, the conversation that we had.

"You are my mother," I said.

Spirit is a hard woman, generally known by others as the Iron Maiden, but now she opened her arms to me, and I fell into them, and we cried for some time. Then she said: "So he finally told you, Hopie."

"He wrote it in his manuscript," I said. "I never suspected, before."

"Because you are so like him," she said. "You inherited so many of his ways."

I laughed. "I can't read people!"

"Have you ever tried?"

That silenced me on that subject; indeed, I had never thought to try. But I had another subject: "Then who is my biologic father?"

"When Hope debated Thorley, in Ybor, at the outset of their respective careers, a man tried to assassinate my brother. It was so fast, we were unprepared. Hope avoided him, of course, and so did I, but then he turned his weapon on Megan, and she stood frozen, being unused to violence. He fired—and Thorley leaped out of his chair and intercepted the beam. He saved Megan's life. But he sustained a grievous injury himself. 'Take care of this man!' my brother told me, and I knew that nothing we could do for Thorley could repay the favor he had done us, for had Megan died then, so would Hope have died. I took Thorley to his home, for he was no better off financially than we were then, and I took care of him. I used a disguise so that there would be no suspicion; it was a trick I had learned from Helse, Hope's first love and a truly nice girl. I became a Hispanic boy, Sancho, and obtained groceries and performed chores in that guise, sustaining him while his wife was absent.

"But he knew my identity, of course. He asked me to be open with him, when we were in private, and so I was. It was in my own guise that I dressed his wound and helped him get around and bathe. I did it because of what we owed him, but the better I came to know him, the more I respected his qualities. He was a handsome man, and an intelligent one, and an honest one, and though we existed at opposite political and social poles, I found myself attracted to him. And he—his wound, taken in our service, was in the groin, deep and serious, and though the medication healed the flesh, he was fearful for his potency.

"Thus it was that what happened happened. He recovered his potency, and I had his baby. But we could never let it be known, because he was married and I was Hispanic; news of it would have destroyed his career, and that of my brother. But I could not give up the baby. So I brought it to Megan, and she—she was, is a great woman." Here she could not continue, for she was crying again. But I already knew the rest. I held her, as she had held me in my infancy, and now the secret between us was gone.

I knew too that Megan had not been entirely unselfish in her adoption of Spirit's baby. She had done it to please Hope, of course; but more than that, for herself. She had perhaps not realized that she wanted a baby, until she had been offered one. Possibly she had not wanted just any baby, but this particular one overrode her reluctance. Because she had been the one Thorley's act of heroism had saved. Megan had always been one to pay her debts, of whatever nature, and she owed Thorley her life, and had no way to repay it. Spirit had done what Megan could not; Spirit had brought a life to Thorley. That love child could not be acknowledged, but it required loving care. Megan took that baby, and in that manner she repaid Thorley and Spirit for her life, using her life to raise their child. It was also the closest she could come to having Hope's child, and so she would have wanted it even if there had not been the debt.

I was that child. I could not have had a better mother than Megan, or a better father than Hope Hubris, and I do not deny them now. But how much my new knowledge of my natural parentage adds to my life!

"Must this remain secret?" I asked.

"That is for you to decide."

"But people could be hurt—"

"Thorley's wife is dead. My brother is dead. Times have changed. I may marry Thorley. We can no longer be hurt by your origin. Do what is right for you."

I was stunned. "You—Thorley—still?"

"I am the mirror of my brother. Apart from him, I have loved two men, and dallied with others. The first is dead; the second is not. What would you have me do?"

"I . . . I meant no judgment of you! I only—" Now I remembered the times Thorley had been with us, as when he joined Hope's first expedition to Saturn, when Hope was Governor of Sunshine. That had been, nominally, for the news—but also for the secret love between Hope's leading critic and his sister. And, perhaps, to be with me, the child who had not known. So many events to be reinterpreted!

And who was to interpret them? "Aunt Spirit—" I faltered, embarrassed, but she only smiled. The habit of a lifetime is not readily erased by a single revelation. "Spirit, your story must be told!"

She shook her head. "Hopie, I have never written personal things down; only my brother did that. Now I am the Tyrant, carrying on in his stead; I have no time for such a narrative."

"Then tell me, and I shall write it for you!" I said. "There is so much that you alone know, that will otherwise be lost with you."

"But the time, even for that—"

"In snatches," I pleaded. "At odd moments, when you are free. Tell me, or dictate briefly for a tape that I can later transcribe. Any way possible, so that I may have your story, for now I realize that it is not finished with my father—with Hope Hubris. All the details he omitted, because you took care of them—"

She shook her head in negation. "Hopie, it just isn't feasible! You have no idea how busy I—"

"It cannot end here, my sister, my love!"

Spirit stared at me, though I had not spoken. At least, I don't think I—it must have been the presence who wrote the final chapter of the Bio of a Space Tyrant. I do not know; I cannot explain it. I only know that for a moment I felt the presence of my father, the Tyrant. I had, it seemed, inherited a number of his traits; I hoped I had not also inherited his madness.

Then Spirit bowed her head. "As you wish, as ever, my brother, my love," she whispered.

And so it was that I commenced the editing of another volume after I had thought the task complete. The narrative of the Iron Maiden, my natural mother. The current Tyrant, as she guided mankind on toward the stars.

SOLAR GEOGRAPHY

Planet	*Earthly parallel*
Mercury	South Africa
Venus	North Africa
Earth	India
Luna	Ceylon
Mars	Asia Minor (Moslem)
Phobos	Israel
Deimos	West Bank of Jordan
Asteroid Belt	Pacific Islands
Hidalgo	Hawaii
Chiron	Cyprus
Jupiter North	North America
South	South America
RedSpot	Mexico
Amalthea	Bahamas
Io	Puerto Rico
Europa	Jamaica
Ganymede	Cuba
Callisto	Hispaniola
outer moons	Lesser Antilles
Saturn North	Russia
South	China
inner satellites	Philippines
outer satellites	Indonesia
rings	Taiwan
Titan	Japan

Uranus	Europe
Miranda	Crete
Ariel	Sardinia
Umbriel	Ireland
Titania	England
Oberon	Iceland
Neptune	Australia
Triton	New Zealand
Nereid	Tasmania
Pluto	Antarctica
Charon	Falklands